RECKLESS DESIRE

Was I imagining it all? Was this real: his low voice, his strong arms, his hard slender form so disturbingly close to mine? I was intensely aware of his touch, of his hands at my back, of the whisper-soft movement of his mouth on my cheek. His mouth was warm as I'd imagined it would be, but his words were lost to me as I sank deep under the spell of his mesmerizing voice.

I was dimly aware that *his* passion too had been aroused, but for Mark, of course, it was not the first time. How many other women had he kissed like this, expecting a response that I, thank God, was too numb to reveal? I wanted him to kiss me. I wanted him to do more than kiss me. If that placed me among the ranks of his countless conquests, it mattered not. I wanted Mark, I wanted him with a hot, reckless yearning that took my breath away . . .

FOREVER, MY LOVE

JEAN NASH

AVON
PUBLISHERS OF BARD, CAMELOT, DISCUS AND FLARE BOOKS

FOREVER, MY LOVE is an original publication of Avon Books. This work has never before appeared in book form.

AVON BOOKS
A division of
The Hearst Corporation
1790 Broadway
New York, New York 10019

Copyright © 1983 by Jean Nash
Published by arrangement with the author
Library of Congress Catalog Card Number: 83-91038
ISBN: 0-380-84780-9

First Avon Printing, September, 1983

AVON TRADEMARK REG. U. S. PAT. OFF. AND IN
OTHER COUNTRIES, MARCA REGISTRADA, HECHO EN
U. S. A.

Printed in the U. S. A.

WFH 10 9 8 7 6 5 4 3 2 1

For my husband
with love and gratitude

PART ONE
Joanna

Hypocrisy, the gift of lengthen'd years,
Matured by age, the garb of prudence wears.

GEORGE GORDON, LORD BYRON
Childish Recollections

I

I HAD NOT expected to like Mark Van Holden. For one thing he was quite indecently wealthy, he *owned* so much, and I have always disliked acquisitiveness for its own sake. And then there was the matter of his reputation. It was whispered among the ladies of my set that no married woman had ever refused him, which is of course ridiculous, because in so saying, those same gossiping cats implicated themselves in the very scandal over which they tittered. There was no denying Mark's appeal. I had seen his likeness in all the New York City newspapers, for his many interests, business and social, brought him into constant contact with legislators and entertainers, monarchs and sports figures (his interests were extremely diverse); but when I met him at last, my first thought was how startlingly different he was in the flesh from those clumsy, colorless sketches which previously I had thought so attractive.

The man was a Florentine portrait. He had a narrow dark face from which shone the most brilliantly dark eyes I had ever seen. His hair was a lustrous cap of coffee brown curls, not in the least effeminate when crowning that hard, relentless, uncompromising face, and his mouth, smiling as he was presented to me, suggested a hint of sardonic amusement and more than a hint of the most disturbing sensuality.

I saw at once how he had gained his reputation. It would be tremendously easy to fall under the spell of a man so devastatingly vital and so extraordinarily without scruples where women were concerned. When I gave him my hand in greeting, his own was warm and dry, and as my flesh touched his, I felt a sudden curious weakness in my limbs and withdrew my hand with an alacrity so patently fearful that I felt myself blushing for the first time since I was ten years old.

His smile changed, warmed. His eyes, so dark as to appear black, held mine. I gazed at him in paralyzed fascination as the crowded ballroom around us seemed to disappear, leaving us alone, two solitary figures, frozen in time, in space, till a light hand at my elbow quite broke the spell. I turned with a start and saw my husband's face, a welcome reality after that mystifying moment of submersion in the illusory depths of Mark Van Holden's gaze.

"Edward!" I exclaimed. "There you are! Have you met Mark Van Holden? Mr. Van Holden, this is my husband, Edward Sinclair."

I was mortified to discover that my voice was quavering. The two men shook hands and to my profound relief immediately found they had many friends in common, and so they began to speak at length, thereby saving me the embarrassment of speaking further myself. As they chatted amiably I studied them both: Mark, slim and dark; my husband, older, heavier, his brown hair sprinkled liberally with gray, though he was still quite attractive at fifty-three. People were always a bit shocked to learn Edward was my husband. We had been married four years earlier, in 1881; he had been forty-nine, I had just turned eighteen. My mother had recently died. There had been just the two of us for as long as I could remember. My father had been killed at Gettysburg when I was an infant, and my mother had never remarried. She had had, however, a great many suitors, and Edward had been one of them. Thus, when she died, leaving me alone in the world, a child still in the eyes of Edward Sinclair, I suppose he took pity on me, and out of a sense of duty or of obligation to my mother, he offered to marry me. He was very kind, very understanding.

"My dear Joanna," he said when he proposed, "I don't expect you to love me. And if you have any reservations about the physical side of marriage, I am more than prepared to wait until you feel you are ready to enter into such a relationship. I'm very fond of you; I believe you've always liked me. You would do me a great honor by becoming my wife, and for my part, I shall try in every way to make you a good husband."

"But, Edward," I said, after recovering from the impact of so unexpected a proposal, "why ever would you want to marry me? I'm so . . ."

"Young?" he supplied. "Was that what you were going to say?"

"Well, yes," I blurted. And then, knowing that he had misunderstood me, I said rapidly, "What I mean is you're so sophisticated, so experienced, and I . . ." I faltered again. Oh, surely he knew what I was trying to say. Why would a man of his principles, his class, want me, the daughter of Monica Trent?

My mother, though of impeccable family, was not highly respected in her circle. Although her background was of the highest order, she had married my father, an army officer with an impressive military record, but unfortunately a man of rather humble family from the backwoods of Pennsylvania. To make matters worse, after he died . . . Well, she was lonely, and a woman of ardent nature, and she wanted to be true to my father's memory—in her fashion. That is to say, she never wanted to marry again. But she liked the company of men—our house was always filled with them—and I think her friends begrudged her that comfort. They would sooner have seen her wither and die, which eventually she did. But not from lack of men. No, never from lack of men.

It was a month or so following her funeral when Edward asked me to marry him. If I had been older, wiser, I might have recognized his proposal for what it was: an expiation for the wrong he thought he had done my mother by seducing her. But the poor man had done nothing of the kind. No man, to my memory or knowledge, ever had had to go to the bother of seducing my mother.

In any case, I was only seventeen. At that stripling stage of life, I imagined that a man such as Edward might fancy a young wife, a malleable being whom he could mold into whatever image pleased him. And, too, I was frightened

and terribly uncertain of my future. At my mother's funeral, my grandmother, a formidable lady in her eighties,
suffered my greeting and my shy kiss as one might endure
an attack of *la grippe*. I had felt her shudder of distaste as
my lips grazed her withered cheek, and before I could
speak she had rapped her cane on the floor as if calling a
meeting to order. In a harsh voice she had announced that
under no circumstances was I to expect a copper in assistance from her, as my mother had all of her life made it a
point to shame and degrade the Bennington name, and
that I, the daughter of that shame, would find no welcome
from any Bennington, now or hereafter, as long as my
grandmother lived. Thus, my uncles, my mother's four
brothers, were duly informed before a roomful of witnesses
and in the presence of my mother's remains that my name
was anathema, and that anyone who was so foolish as to
give me succor would find himself disinherited posthaste
by my grandmother.

My future was bleak. I was bred to a wealth I could
never claim, and alone in the world though blessed with a
family I could not call mine. I should have snapped at Edward's proposal; he was offering me his modest fortune, his
fine name, shelter, and freedom from the fear of further os-
tracism. As his wife, my position would be unquestionable.
I hesitated. Incredible as it may seem, I, who had nothing,
wanted more.

"Edward," I said when he proposed. "I had hoped—"

"My dear girl," he said, smiling. Edward had the nicest
smile. "My dear Joanna, I daresay you had hoped to be loved.
May I say, that there is an excellent chance I might love you,
given time. You're very lovely, you know, and despite your
youth you have an inherent dignity, a natural grace which,
fully developed, will be quite irresistible when added to your
more apparent attributes."

"Why, Edward," I stammered. I was deeply moved. In
his own stilted way, he was telling me I was attractive.
And I suppose I was at that age, in an eager, coltish sort of
way. But I was nothing like my mother. My mother had
been a true beauty, raven-haired and creamy-skinned, and
no man had ever been able to resist her. How I wished I

were more like her. And how I wished Edward were proposing because he was so dazzled by my charms that he had been utterly unable to control himself. But I realized glumly that no such thing had motivated his proposal.

"Mrs. Sinclair?"

The ballroom came sharply back into focus with these words, and I looked up at Mark Van Holden in much the same manner as might a startled doe. He was smiling that sensuous smile, and he had obviously asked me a question, for he waited patiently while I cast about desperately in my mind, trying to recall his words.

"Joanna," Edward suggested, "why don't you consult your card, my dear? I'm sure you'll find that this dance is free."

A dance? Is that what Mark had wanted? Somehow I felt, as he regarded me quietly with those languid dark eyes, that he had wanted something far more significant than a dance.

I went into his arms, and for a time he was silent, dancing so skillfully, so smoothly, that it seemed we'd been partners for years.

"Have you been married long?"

I had been expecting that question. People were invariably curious about my marriage, or rather about the thirty-year age difference between my husband and me.

"Yes," I replied. "We've been married four years."

"That long?" he laughed softly, and I had the distinct impression he was laughing at me.

"You find that amusing?" I said in my haughtiest voice.

"On the contrary," he said. "I find your conception of time most intriguing."

"Indeed?" I bristled. "In what way?"

"Four years," he said, smiling, "is but a grain of sand in the vast desert of infinity."

"How poetic," I muttered disdainfully, then I wondered with a start why I was suddenly behaving like an ill-bred child. Surely he had not offended me, surely there was no reason to raise my defenses.

Incongruously, I then thought of my mother, of her grace and beauty and charm, none of which had I inherited.

Had she been dancing with Mark Van Holden, and he made some remark which unaccountably irritated her, she would have gazed up at him through her lashes and pursed her pretty mouth in a pretty pout. He then would have apologized profusely, begging her forgiveness in a voice fraught with shame. He would have sworn his contrition. He would have been putty in her hands. He would have loved her.

"My husband and I are very much in love!" I burst out, then cringed in embarrassment as Mark's smile faded.

"I've no doubt of it," he said politely, then stepped back and released me as the dance, to my utter gratitude, ended.

"Thank you," he said as he escorted me back to my husband, "for the dance and for taking me into your confidence." And when I gave him a puzzled look, he said softly, "So few married couples are happy these days. It's gratifying to know that you and your husband enjoy that rare pleasure."

And with a courteous bow and a polite word to Edward, he was gone.

When we returned home that evening, I found myself still thinking of Mark Van Holden. I wondered how old he was—he appeared to be thirty-five or thereabouts; and I wondered, too, how a man that attractive could have managed to remain unmarried all those years.

"Edward," I said as my husband extinguished the light and joined me in bed, "Mr. Van Holden is a bachelor, is he not?"

"He is a widower, my dear. Why do you ask?"

A *widower? How very interesting,* I thought as Edward's arm went comfortably around me. "How long was he married? How did his wife die? What was she like? Did they have children?"

"Joanna," he laughed, "how inquisitive you are tonight."

For the second time that evening I felt myself blush, and was thankful that in the darkness Edward was unable to see my face.

"I was merely curious," I said lamely.

"Yes, I noticed." And again he laughed that soft, indulgent, fatherly laugh.

"Really, Edward," I snapped as a puzzling sense of guilt assailed me, "there's no need to treat me like a half-wit simply because I'm younger than you." His arm under my neck tensed suddenly, but confused by that strange stab of guilt and a quite inexplicable feeling of rage, I drove on: "I know I'm not like my mother; I don't expect ever to be like her. She was beautiful and witty and intelligent, and you probably married me thinking I'd become like her in time. But I won't, Edward! I'm just myself, and I'm sorry if you feel cheated—"

I broke off, and to my own further confusion, burst into tears. At first, Edward said nothing. I daresay he was more shocked than I, for in all the years I had known him I had never once shed a tear in his presence. My mother had often said that people who wept were despicable, weak-kneed creatures. "Tears are for children and fools," she had been fond of saying, and so all of my previous crying had been done in secret. Not that I'd ever had much reason to weep. Edward was the kindest and most considerate of husbands, and except for my mother's death I had never experienced any profound unhappiness in my life.

"My dear girl," Edward finally said, "I don't feel cheated in the least. Why, I've never been happier than these years with you. Joanna . . ." He drew me close, kissed my cheeks, my mouth. "Joanna, my darling, I make no comparisons between you and your mother. My God, child, don't you know how much I care for you?"

"Do you?" I sobbed, knowing full well how much he cared yet needing to hear it for no reason I could imagine. I felt lost, alone. In my husband's arms, as he kissed away my tears and murmured endearments in my ear, I felt a devastating loneliness such as I had never felt in all my twenty-two years. I kept thinking of my mother, of her silky dark curls framing the fairest of faces, of her china blue eyes and her perfect pink mouth. She had only to crook her little finger and men would stumble over themselves to do her bidding. With a glance she could captivate, with a smile she could charm; she had been everything I was not, and somehow that had never bothered me. Until tonight.

"Joanna, please, my dear, you must stop crying. If I've said anything—if ever I've led you to believe . . ." He groped for words and fell silent. His arms tightened round me as if trying to communicate the concern and affection he was suddenly unable to express. Clearly I had distressed him by my most unexpected behavior, and as my tears abated at last, he began to murmur reassurances while soothingly stroking my back. "My dear child," he said, "I had thought my feelings for you needed no verbal expression, but I can see now that I was sorely mistaken."

"Please, Edward," I whispered, "there's no need. . . . You don't have to. . . . "

Now I was the one who groped for words. My husband was not a demonstrative man. Our marriage was a happy one, I thought, based on mutual respect and admiration, but declarations of love or displays of passion were unknown to either of us. The first time Edward made love to me, he explained very carefully and very tactfully what I should expect. I suppose he didn't want to frighten me—I was so very young, and I think perhaps he was rather frightened himself, of hurting me or of offending me in some way. As a result I found my first encounter with the physical side of marriage rather disappointing despite an uncommon gentleness and consideration on my husband's part. In time, matters improved somewhat, but I always had the feeling when he made love to me that he considered the act as embarrassing and as uncomfortable as I did. Here again my youth put me at a disadvantage. I realized only years later that Edward's restraint stemmed from a profound desire to protect my sensibilities, and had I been a bit more perceptive, I would have seen that his seeming lack of emotion concealed the deepest and most loving regard.

"Please forgive me," I said as I strove to regain my composure. His arms about me were trembling; I was both ashamed and afraid of the unfamiliar emotions I had aroused in him. "Edward, I can't imagine what's got into me. It has nothing to do with you, I assure you. I'm just tired I think. We've been to so many parties this season. . . ."

I raised my head and saw him watching me. In the darkness I was unable to read his expression, but I knew he was distressed, for he held me tighter and pressed my head to his shoulder as if protecting me against some unknown terror.

"I want you to know," I heard him say, "that I love you very deeply."

His voice was low, hesitant. So stunned was I by his words that I could not respond. He loved me? Edward loved me? That couldn't possibly be true. He was fond of me, yes, as an uncle is of a favorite niece. But love? Good Lord, no. Why, I was nothing at all like my mother. I hadn't her eyes, mine were brown; nor her smile, mine was grave. I was twilight, cool and dim; she was dawn, the radiant sun. She had shimmered, she had blazed. She was earth, wind, and fire. Men had worshiped her, fought over her, loved her. Edward had loved her. He could not possibly love me.

He made love to me afterwards with a fierce, almost possessive, passion. For the first time in our marriage I felt a faint stirring of desire, but before I could explore this new sensation his body tensed, his mouth closed hotly on mine, and I knew that in a few moments he would ease away from me, lace his fingers through mine, and drift quietly off to sleep. But this night, he did not.

He lay down beside me, and when at last he was able to speak he said gently, "I do love you, Joanna. I want you to believe me."

I felt his eyes on me, but I stared at the ceiling in silence. I couldn't speak; my mind was spinning, a dozen different images dancing dizzily on my brain. I saw my mother surrounded by suitors, myself in a corner like some stealthy spectator; I saw Mark Van Holden gazing down at me, those languid dark eyes in that Medici face. I pictured myself as I must have appeared to him: prim, plain, uninteresting, ordinary.

"Joanna." Edward's soft voice intruded on my thoughts. "Are you all right?"

"Yes," I murmured at length. "I'm all right. Please don't worry about me, Edward."

But as my husband embraced me and settled down to sleep, I lay quietly in his hold, stared dully at the ceiling, and thought all the night long of another man's arms.

II

SALLY MONROE was my closest friend. She was married to Edward's nephew, and although she was ten years my senior we had taken to one another immediately the first time we'd met. Stephen, her husband, was a great deal like Edward: taciturn and grave, observant of codes, conscious of class; but Sally was different. Sally was cheerful, a rascal, a scamp. She was an outrageous gossip, an inveterate tease. She was pert, poised, and pretty; she loved everyone and everyone loved her. I loved her too. She was very much like my mother.

It was from Sally that I learned more about Mark Van Holden, although why I should wish to know anything at all about him I did not consider. As was our custom on the first Monday of the month, Edward and I had dined with the Monroes, and while the gentlemen remained at the table with their port and cigars, Sally and I went to the drawing room where she graciously complimented my new gown while tactfully refraining from commenting on its color. Mauve did not become me but in dress, as in all things, I was guided by Edward, whose tastes ran to subdued shades. And that was curious, I would sometimes think when gazing glumly at my assortment of violet and gray and cocoa brown frocks, for my mother, with her raven hair and ivory skin, had worn only the most radiant and jewel-bright of colors, and Edward had always greatly admired my mother's attire.

"I missed you at the Carlsons'," I said to Sally. "It was a lovely crush. So many people."

"I wanted to go," she sighed, smoothing the folds of her

peacock blue silk which enhanced the luminous blue of her
eyes. "But Caroline was feverish and Mary had been
grumpy all day. I knew it was only a matter of time before
she'd be ill too, and indeed she was, before the night was
over. Who was there? Tell me all. I love the Carlson
parties!"

"The usual crowd," I said casually. "A few new addi-
tions though. Mark Van Holden for one. Do you know
him?"

I put down my coffee cup, which all of a sudden had become a heavy weight in my hand. Sally's eyes had brightened with interest at the mention of Mark's name, and I
looked away as that strange feeling of guilt engulfed me
once more.

"Yes, I know him," she said in an oddly breathless voice.
"Stephen is his broker. Mark has been to the house several
times on matters of business, and once, at Stephen's insis-
tence, he stayed to dinner. Isn't he fascinating?" she declared. "And such a beautiful man!"

"Beautiful?" I laughed. "Why, Sally, what an inappro-
priate way to describe a gentleman. Mr. Van Holden is
attractive, I'll grant you, but I would hardly call him beautiful."

"Oh, but, Joanna, he *is* beautiful! When he dined with
us I could barely keep my eyes off him. Thank goodness he
and Stephen talked of business throughout the meal, for I
know I couldn't have said a lucid word if my life depended
on it. And he's so charming!" she gushed as a new and
most disturbing emotion began to replace my guilt. "After
dinner he told me of his family—his wife was still living at
the time—and he spoke of his son—"

"His son?" I broke in. Somehow I hadn't thought Mark
would have a son. I had pictured him with daughters, surrounded with daughters, all of them pretty and graceful
and fair.

"Yes, Alan must be fifteen or sixteen by now. Stephen
tells me Mark is devoted to him."

"How long has he been a widower?" I heard myself say,
and was thankful that Sally's enthusiasm prevented her
from commenting on my uncharacteristic curiosity. Nor-

mally I displayed only the mildest interest in her gossipy prattle, but tonight my attention was riveted on her every breathless word.

"She died five years ago," Sally told me. "So sad, so untimely. She died giving birth to a stillborn son. Mark was devastated. I didn't know her myself but Grace Simpson told me she was the loveliest woman. A Van Rensselaer, I believe Grace said. She and Mark were the most devoted of couples. I doubt if he'll ever remarry. He loved her so completely. They were inseparable, totally committed to one another. Her name was Lenore."

Lenore. The name conjured a vision of cornsilk hair crowning a fair face, of gilt lashes framing silvery gray eyes, of a slim, graceful form clad elegantly in silk, a shadowy figure more real than reality, yet shrouded in the imagery of a twenty-two-year-old's fanciful dreams. What manner of woman must she have been to intrigue the most intriguing of men? What had she been that Mark Van Holden, five years after her death, still remained unmarried, devoted to the son she had given him in love? No wonder he had spoken to me so wistfully of happiness. Having had it and lost it, he prized it all the more. I perceived the full measure of his grief and was deeply moved.

Sally's voice droned on, but her words were lost to me as I pondered my own life and its emptiness. Mark's marriage was the kind I had always envisioned for myself: an ardent relationship, a profound spiritual communion between two vital and caring people. How Lenore must have loved him, and how full her marriage must have been. Unlike mine, I had no doubt; unlike the loveless empty marriage that was mine. When the gentlemen joined us several moments later, Sally was still chattering while I, lost in my traitorous thoughts, gazed broodingly at the fire.

"My dear," said Edward gently, "is something wrong?"

For the past few days he had been uncommonly solicitous and, to my inexplicable irritation, watchful of my every move. He had not reiterated his declaration of love, and I suspected that he regretted his words and wished that I make no further reference to the episode. He needn't have worried; I hadn't the least intention of speaking out on a subject which was evidently as embarrassing to him as it was to me.

"No, Edward, nothing's wrong," I said quietly, and I avoided his gaze as I'd been doing since the day following the Carlsons' ball. I was angry with him, angry for no reason I could imagine. I wished he would let me be; I wished he wouldn't speak to me, look at me, touch me. I needed to think, I wanted to be alone. If only he would go away, if only he would let me alone.

"I'm afraid I've depressed her, Uncle Edward," said Sally, who somehow managed to overhear any conversation no matter how quietly it was conducted. "I was just telling Joanna of Mark Van Holden's misfortune."

"Misfortune?" Edward repeated.

"Yes," Sally told him. "He lost his wife, poor man, and he's so lonely without her."

"Sally," said Stephen, his careful, measured tone so like his uncle's, "Mark Van Holden is one of the least lonely men I know. He's far too—"

"If you're going to mention his numerous affairs," she interrupted crisply, "don't bother. A man such as Mark would naturally seek—"

"I most certainly was not going to mention his affairs. Not, at any rate, his *affaires de coeur*. Those," Stephen reminded her pointedly, "are none of your concern and should be absent from your conversation as well as from your thoughts. I was referring to his interests, Sally, to his oil and real estate and other holdings which keep him far too busy to indulge in a five-year-old grief. Moreover, he has his son, a difficult boy, I am told, who—"

Stephen stopped suddenly, as if realizing he had inadvertently tossed his wife a new bone with which to toy. He paused momentarily, then collecting himself, said in his sternest voice, "In future, Sally, I would appreciate it if you would refrain from discussing Mark Van Holden. As my client, anything he has said to either of us should be regarded as highly confidential."

"Humbug!" she said with a toss of her head. "Mark's activities, professional and otherwise, are common knowledge. And if you think—"

"Sally!" he commanded. "The subject is closed."

"Oh, very well," she said crossly. "What a stick you are, Stephen."

"Sally," said Edward with his usual smooth tact, "how are the children? Have they recovered? Stephen told me last week that they were both indisposed."

"Yes, Uncle," she pouted, aware of how fetching she looked when she frowned. "They are up and about and rowdier than ever. Stephen spoils them so," she remarked with a sigh, thus flinging the final stone in a battle she had already lost.

"They're delightful children," Edward said pensively, and I knew he was thinking of his own lack of same. It was only natural that he should want children, although why he had waited forty-nine years to marry was beyond my comprehension. If he had wanted a family so much, he should have married earlier. And if he had, I thought with a sudden revival of guilt and rage, he would not have married me. He could not have married me.

I stared at him fiercely, and my thoughts must have somehow been reflected in my face, for when he turned and caught my expression, his gentle brown eyes grew puzzled and hurt. I looked quickly away; I sensed he had guessed my feelings and I was ashamed. Rising abruptly, I went to the piano and ran my fingers nervously over the keys.

"Play for us, Sally," I said. "Play something gay."

My voice was tremulous, and again I felt the treacherous tears which had plagued me for days. What was happening to me? What were these new and violent emotions over which I had no control? Why did I feel resentful, frustrated, stifled, and trapped? And why was I so angry with Edward?

"Joanna," I heard him say, "perhaps we'd best be getting home. I think you're tired, my dear. You look—"

"I don't want to go home!" I snapped, then instantly regretted my inexcusable burst of temper, for Sally was gaping at me, her eyes wide as saucers, and Stephen had paused in mid-motion, his coffee cup inches away from his mouth. "Must I cater to your every whim?" I cried as my being seemed to split in two, the saner part of myself watching the other in absolute horror. "I don't want to go home! It's not past my bedtime! I'm not a child and I'm not an old woman. I won't go home at nine o'clock and trundle off to bed at ten—"

"Joanna!"

I fell silent at once and looked about the room in a dazed, fevered fog. I was going to be ill. My stomach churned, my ears rang. I clapped my hand to my mouth, the room began to spin, and as my vision dimmed and my consciousness failed, I felt my husband's arms go swiftly around me, and then I felt nothing at all.

When I awoke some time later, I was in Sally's bed and Edward's physician was bent over me, his stethoscope moving coldly on my half-exposed breast.

"Hello," he said, and smiled as he listened intently to the mysterious rumblings of my heart. "Welcome back."

"Dr. Shelley," I murmured, "what happened?"

"Quiet, please," he said, his genial young face sobering with concentration.

He was such a nice man. His father had died some years ago and left his thriving practice to his son. At first Edward had considered seeking the services of another, older physician, but he had liked young Shelley and had decided to commit our care into his capable, if comparably inexperienced, hands. Edward had, from childhood, suffered a chest complaint, a condition no doubt aggravated by the cigars he smoked interminably against the repeated warnings of both of the doctors Shelley.

"You, sir," the elder had told him, "are digging yourself an early grave. If you persist in filling your lungs with killer smoke, you alone will be accountable for the consequences."

"I repeat my father's admonition," the younger had warned when the old man died. "Mr. Sinclair, you do yourself a disservice by continuing a habit which is at best harmful and at worst fatal."

But Edward would not listen. Smoking was his only vice, and every man, he would rationalize, is entitled to at least one vice in his life. As a result he took cold easily and often, and invariably Dr. Shelley would scold him and Edward would vow to abandon his habit, but as soon he was well again he would smoke "just one, my dear, after dinner," and before I knew it the one became five, ten, fifteen, till I would lose count and all patience with this otherwise reasonable man.

"Mrs. Sinclair, I'm afraid you've contracted influenza," Dr. Shelley announced as he abandoned his stethoscope and reached into his bag and withdrew a vial of pills. "Take one of these four times a day, remain in bed for at least one week, and keep to a simple diet. I shall stop in on you in a few days. Will you be staying here, madam? I advise that you do. I prefer not to have you outdoors even though it's but a short journey to your home."

"Oh, but I want to go home," I said faintly. "I shouldn't want to impose on the Monroes. I must go home. I want to go home."

I felt so ill. It was an effort to speak, even to move my lips. How swift the onslaught of this malady; I'd felt perfectly well all day, but now I felt weak as a kitten. "Please," I said with effort, "I want to go home. I want my husband." And I did want him. I wanted him so badly, so desperately that I began to cry, and Dr. Shelley took my hand sympathetically in his.

"Mrs. Sinclair," he soothed, "you may go home if you wish, but you must avoid all contact with your husband. Influenza is highly contagious and you must remember your husband's susceptibility to infection. We don't want him ill too, do we?"

I shook my head weakly. No, I didn't want him ill, but I did so want him to hold me. Surely if he held me he would not be endangering his health. "I want to go home," I said again. I only wanted to go home. I forgot that earlier I had expressed quite a different desire. I forgot that for days I hadn't once looked directly into my husband's eyes. What I wanted now was my own bed, the comfort of Edward's arms, his gentle voice murmuring softly near my ear. I wanted my husband, his strength, and the only security I had ever known.

I cannot recall the carriage ride home. I remember only strong arms lifting me, holding me close to a rapidly beating heart. I remember a rush of cold air and a blanket drawn up to my chin, and then nothing, nothing, till I opened my eyes in my own room, in my bed, and found my-self cradled in the warmth of my husband's embrace. It was the dead of night. I had thought Edward was asleep, but when I stirred, his arms tightened around me, and I felt the soft movement of his lips against my cheek.

"Are you all right?"

I reached up to embrace him but found myself too weak to move. "Edward," I whispered. "Edward."

He drew me closer, brushed my mouth with his. "I'm right here, my darling."

Dimly I recalled a warning, something Dr. Shelley had said. The words were unclear in my mind, but the essence of the warning alerted me, frightened me. "Mustn't," I murmured, moving feebly in my husband's arms. "Mustn't, Edward."

"My dear child," he said, stung, "I am not going to make love to you if that's what you're thinking."

"No," I whispered, wanting to explain, attempting to set right his misconception, but the effort was beyond me. I remembered now what Dr. Shelley had said. *Highly contagious. Avoid all contact. Avoid all contact.*

"Edward," I tried as I felt my consciousness slipping, "don't touch me. You mustn't touch me."

Had I spoken aloud? I couldn't be sure, for I think I fell asleep, and when I awakened the following morning, Edward was gone.

He avoided me thereafter, and I, thinking he had discussed the risk of contagion with Dr. Shelley, breathed easier knowing that now he must realize that my seeming rejection was only a profound desire to protect his health.

But he hadn't spoken with Dr. Shelley. I learned much later that he had never spoken with him at all.

III

I WAS ILL for only three days. Edward was ill for a month. And then he died.

"Complications," said Dr. Shelley. "His chest, you know. I warned him about his smoking; my father had warned him for years. And now that filthy weed has finally killed him."

Poor Dr. Shelley. I felt so sorry for him. I knew he blamed himself for Edward's death. He was very upset and kept talking about Edward, of how long he had known him and of how much he had always admired him. "He gave me my start," he said shakily. "When he accepted me after my father's death, all of his friends did too. My practice might have failed if it hadn't been for him." He grew pale as he spoke and his eyes became moist and rimmed with red. "I knew those damned cigars would eventually kill him."

But that wasn't true. I alone knew what had really caused my husband's death.

So many people came to pay their last respects. Sally told me afterwards that Mark Van Holden had been at the funeral, but I hadn't seen him. I hadn't seen anyone really. I kept looking at the coffin, and as morbid as it may sound, I kept trying, without success, to picture Edward lying inside. He's not in there, I kept thinking. He can't be in there. When I go home he'll be waiting for me. But of course he wasn't.

When I returned home, I excused myself from the crush of mourners who crowded the drawing room, and went up to his room. The curtains were drawn, a small lamp was lit. I went to his dresser and picked up his brushes, turned

21

them over in my hand, then laid them down. I wanted to
cry, but I couldn't. Somehow I felt it would have been a des-
ecration to cry, a blasphemy. It was I after all who had
killed him.

Numbly, I crossed the room and opened the wardrobe
door. His clothes, dark and subdued, hung neatly in rows.
A pomander ball hidden on the shelf did not fully dispel
the faint aroma of cigar smoke which clung to the clothing.
I closed the door swiftly and turned toward the bed.

The coverlet was new, green in color: I had chosen it myself a short time earlier when I noticed the shabbiness of
the old one. It was customary, Edward had told me when
we were first married, that husband and wife should oc-
cupy separate bedrooms; I made it a point, thereafter,
never to enter his room unless invited. But I had run out of
stationery one day, and I knew Edward always kept some
in his desk. It was then I saw the coverlet. I was appalled
by its condition. The lace had torn loose in several places
and signs of wear were evident throughout.

"Edward," I scolded that evening, "you must tell me
when an item in your room needs to be replaced. Your bed-
cover has gone quite to ruin. I shall order a new one for you
this week."

He smiled at me then as if my simple domestic gesture
had pleased him immensely. Edward never asked anything of me. The house was run efficiently by Mrs. Porter;
Edward's personal needs were seen to by his man; and this
left me free to devote all my time to the leisurely pursuits
of reading, sketching, and needlework, suitable pursuits,
Edward told me, for a young lady of my station, although I
would sometimes wonder what precisely was my station. I
felt more his daughter than his wife. It wasn't merely the
age difference; it was that Edward was so unbelievably indulgent with me. Our relationship was totally one-sided:
Edward gave, I took. It never occurred to me to question
this arrangement; I had been very young when we married, and since my mother had not had a husband with
whom I could compare Edward's behavior, it had always
seemed, to my uninitiated mind, perfectly natural. But as
the years passed and I came to know his friends, I discov-

ered that it wasn't at all natural for a man to be so kind, so undemanding, so inordinately devoted to his wife. Our marriage had been unique, Edward had been unique. And I had killed him.

"For heaven's sake, Joanna, what are you doing up here?"

I hadn't heard Sally come in. I was sitting on Edward's bed, running my hand over the smooth silk fabric of the new coverlet. How pleased he had been when he saw it. "My dear," he had said, "it's magnificent. Did you choose the fabric yourself? You did? In that case I shall treasure it all the more."

I was so proud of myself that day. After all Edward had done for me, I had finally done something for him. I remembered thinking that in future I would do more, give more to the man who had given always to me. But time had run out.

"Joanna, come downstairs. Some of the guests have already left and the others are asking for you. Come along now."

I felt Sally's arm go around my shoulder. I stiffened and turned away. I didn't want to go downstairs. I didn't want to leave Edward's room.

"Come, dear," she urged. "You mustn't stay up here and brood. I know how you feel but, Joanna, Edward would be the first one to tell you that personal feelings should always be put aside for duty. Your guests are waiting for you, Edward's friends, all the people who loved him as you did."

"Don't," I said wretchedly. "Don't speak of him, I can't bear it." Love, did she say? I hadn't loved him. I hadn't loved that dear, gentle man who had spent the last years of his life ensuring my happiness. Oh, I had been fond enough of him, in that brutal, careless way of the very young, but I hadn't loved him. "Please make my excuses," I begged, my voice shaking with shame. "Please, Sally, I can't face anyone now."

"Don't be a child," she said brusquely. "Joanna, you must come down. You must speak to his friends. It's what he would have wanted."

"Oh, please . . ."

"I don't please," she insisted, her pretty face set adamantly, her hands planted firmly on her hips. "Get up at once and go wash your face. Joanna, do as I tell you!"

And I did. I was still enough of a child that the commands of my elders must be obeyed. In the drawing room, I received my husband's friends, with Sally on one side of me and Stephen on the other. With their help I survived the afternoon, though its memory has completely vanished from my mind. I was told later that I conducted myself admirably, that Edward would have been proud. But all I could think of for months afterward was that I had been responsible for his death.

I never told anyone of my guilt. I never mentioned to Dr. Shelley that Edward had shared my bed, that his illness had been contracted as a result of my own. I kept all my shame to myself. I was alone again as I had been four years earlier. My mother was dead, my husband was dead but, ironically, my grandmother, who was almost ninety years old, still lived. She did not attend the funeral nor did my uncles. I hadn't really expected that they would. Marrying Edward Sinclair had not changed my status. To their minds I was still "Monica's daughter" and would remain so till the day I died.

It was difficult being alone, more difficult still since my memories of Edward were tainted with guilt. If only I'd loved him, if only I'd been kinder to him, more giving. If only he hadn't stayed with me that night and contracted my illness. If only . . . if only . . . if only . . . My remorse was driving me mad. Added to remorse was the painful regret that I had darkened Edward's last days with my inexplicable behavior. In the midst of my grief I still thought of Mark Van Holden and of how meeting him had affected me in a way I did not fully comprehend. It was surely meeting Mark that had motivated my shrewish conduct toward Edward at Sally's house; it was thoughts of Mark and of the exquisite woman he had married which had turned me so violently against the good and gentle man whose wife I had been for four serene years.

So I sequestered myself in the house, cut off by my own

choosing from all human contact. I received no one for months. Blandford, the butler, would come to my room, sundry calling cards on a silver tray, but I would see no one. I wasn't fit to be seen; I felt I hadn't the right to seek solace from the friends of the man I had killed. The Monroes had gone to Paris; Stephen had been so devastated by his uncle's death that Sally had whisked him abroad. She apologized for leaving me alone, but I understood. Stephen came first with Sally; he always had. I wasn't surprised. Sally loved her husband. I wished with every fiber of my being that I had loved mine.

Mark Van Holden paid me a visit on the last day of May. Coincidentally it was my twenty-third birthday, but under the circumstances the occasion would pass unobserved. It was rather late in the evening when he called; I was in the library searching for my copy of Shakespeare. A passage had been running through my mind for weeks: "Farewell the tranquil mind! farewell content!" I suspected the source of the quote was to be found in one of the Bard's plays but I wasn't positive. I had just pulled the book from the shelf when Blandford came into the room.

"A gentleman to see you, madam," he announced and presented Mark's card on a tray.

I picked up the vellum card. "Mark Van Holden?" I said, staring at the letters as if they were Sanskrit.

"Yes, madam," said Blandford, a study in dignified indifference. "Shall I tell him you're indisposed?"

For months Blandford had been telling callers I was indisposed, but suddenly I felt differently. "Please show him in," I said, then flew to the Hepplewhite mirror as Blandford left the room.

I looked dreadful. I had no color at all and the unrelieved black of my dress only enhanced my pallor till my eyes seemed the only feature in a dead-white face. My hair was simply fashioned, coiled low at the nape of my neck, with a few errant strands that had sprung loose curling untidily at my cheeks and on my brow. But before I could smooth them in place Mark had entered the room, and as I turned slowly to meet his gaze, I felt the fugitive color rise and splash wildly across my face.

He was beautiful; his shining hair curled charmingly over his brow, his eyes were clear and dark and fringed with lashes so thick that his lids seemed lowered slumbrously with their weight. His mouth was straight yet seductive in its strength, and as he regarded me quietly with those dark all-seeing eyes, my guilt and my loneliness strangely and suddenly vanished.

"Mrs. Sinclair," he said. "Good evening."

I had forgotten the peculiar hypnotic quality of his voice. It was thoroughly masculine yet oddly musical with clean, pure, accentless speech that fell easily and most pleasantly on the ears.

"It was good of you to see me at such a late hour. My schedule regrettably does not permit earlier calls."

"Yes," I said stupidly, and then remembering my manners I murmured, "Won't you sit down, Mr. Van Holden?"

He chose Edward's chair near the fireplace, a deep, leather chair that had seen better days, and automatically I took my own seat opposite, the book of Shakespeare's plays closed and forgotten on my lap.

"May I offer you something?" I said. "Some coffee? Whiskey?"

"Thank you, no," he replied, leaning courteously toward me as he spoke. "I should not like to inconvenience your servants. I daresay they're unused to callers at this hour. Your butler, in fact, would not let me past the door until I had presented my card. Such admirable caution," he added with a smile.

"Blandford is a cautious man," I said, and found myself smiling in return. "No member of the Praetorian Guard was ever more vigilant than he. It is one of the reasons my husband engaged him—" I stopped, the smile fading from my lips. I had almost forgotten about Edward, I had almost forgotten he was dead. "Forgive me," I murmured after a moment. "I did not mean to—"

"Mrs. Sinclair," Mark said softly, "if you wish to speak of your husband, by all means do so. Repressing your grief now will only cause it to present itself at a later time, a time perhaps when you'll be less capable of dealing with it. You will find as the years pass that there is a measure of comfort to be found in one's memories. I speak, as you may know, from experience."

"Oh," I could only say as I gazed helplessly at his compassionate face.

"You may be wondering," he went on, "why I haven't paid my respects long before now. It is also from experience that I postponed my call until such time as your initial grief might have been spent. Directly after my wife died, the house was filled with people, all well intentioned to be sure, but I had no desire to share with any of them so intimate and personal an emotion. I take the liberty of assuming that your feelings parallel mine in this regard. There is nothing so frustrating as entertaining guests, no matter how sympathetic they may be, when what one really wants to do is to weep without intrusion in the privacy of his own room. In my opinion, Mrs. Sinclair, it is also a period which should be reserved for the exorcism of all the illogical guilt which unfortunately abounds in such a situation. I'm sure you blame yourself in some way for your loss, just as I felt solely responsible at the time for my wife's death. How sanity deserts us when most we need it!"

Was this man a sorcerer? He had come to my home at the precise moment when I was desperate for social contact, and further, he had opened the book of my innermost self and had read the pages as easily as he would a child's primer.

"What's that you're reading?" he asked, changing the topic of conversation as if sensing my confusion.

I did not answer at once. For one thing, my mind was spinning with the improbable accuracy of his insight, and for another, I had totally forgotten the book on my lap. I stared at him blankly till he gestured with a smile toward my skirt.

"It's Shakespeare," I said at last. "But I wasn't reading. I was searching for a line that keeps running through my mind."

"Which line is that?" he asked, and when I quoted it for him he said quietly, "Ah, yes, *Othello.* Are you familiar with the plot?"

"No, not really," I confessed. "I'm afraid I prefer somewhat happier themes."

"*Othello,*" he said, his clear dark eyes suddenly shadowing, "is not one of Shakespeare's happier themes. It's a tale of love and jealousy, of brutal betrayal. It reflects all of man's wickedness and nothing of his virtue. It's a biased, discriminate, intolerant piece of trash. I have always despised that play."

I was not prepared for so emotionally charged a critique; I was likewise unprepared for the alacrity with which Mark rose and prepared to take his leave. He seemed sorry he had come, avoiding my gaze as I walked with him to the door. But just before he left, he turned to me and said rapidly, "I should like you to meet my son. I realize it's only been a few months since your husband died, but if you dined with my son and me I doubt you'd be breaking any rules of etiquette. I think you'll like him. He's a quiet, sensitive boy, and I know he'll like you. Please think about it, won't you? With your permission I'll stop by at the end of the week for your answer."

And then as if fearing a hasty refusal, he left without saying good night.

I returned to the library in a daze. The book of plays was still in my hand and, unconsciously, I flipped through the pages until I came to *Othello.* I was vaguely familiar with the plot: Othello had been tricked by the treacherous Iago into believing that his wife Desdemona had been unfaithful to him. If I remembered the outcome correctly, Othello murdered his innocent wife and then took his own life when he learned he'd been duped by his friend.

I shuddered and closed the book. No wonder Mark hated the play. What a ghastly theme. I was glad I had never read it; I decided then and there that I never would.

I replaced the book on the shelf and went upstairs to my room. With my maid's assistance I disrobed, unpinned my hair and gave it the customary one hundred strokes. We talked for a while—Myrna was my age and we'd always got on well together—then I climbed into bed and fell instantly to sleep. It was the first night since Edward had died that I didn't dream of him.

IV

AT THE END of the week I said yes to Mark's invitation. When he came to call for me on the evening of our dinner engagement I was waiting for him in the foyer, already cloaked and gloved, so it was not until we were in the great hall of his magnificent house that I removed my wrap and he saw my gown for the first time.

It was black of course, as I was still in mourning, but the shimmering satin skirt, cut in wide panels over black lace, and the shockingly deep décolletage suggested anything but bereavement. My dressmaker had been scandalized when I presented to her the sketch I had clipped from *Harper's Bazaar*. But my mind was made up, and she could not dissuade me. I had made my choice, my very first personal choice regarding my own attire, and I was not to be denied. When Mark took my wrap from my shoulders, however, and I turned, affording him full view of my gown, I wondered frantically if I had made a dreadful mistake.

His eyes swept over me in the most disturbingly astonished manner. He hated the dress, I just knew it. Very possibly he also hated the new Grecian fashion in which Myrna had styled my hair. She had turned the long masses into a smooth chignon at the back, and she had cut and arranged the strands near my face so that springy curls bounced buoyantly on my cheeks and brow. As it was freshly washed, my hair gleamed dark as sable, and my face shone with color as it had never done before. The cut of the gown was extremely flattering, showing to advantage a waist more slender than even my mother's had been. When I had inspected myself in the long mirror in my bed-

29

room, I had thought the whole effect charming, and had even dared to think that Mark might be pleased with my new image. I imagined that when he saw me looking so smart and *soignée*, he would compliment me at length as men had always complimented my mother. His eyes passed over me and came to rest on the necklace of jet at my half-exposed breast. And he said nothing at all.

I was so ashamed. I stared at the floor in an agony of embarrassment, and after a moment I felt Mark's hand at my elbow. "Shall we go into the dining room, Mrs. Sinclair?" he said neutrally. "I have told my son all about you, and I know he is anxious to meet you."

I moved sheepishly down the long hall, ignoring the portraits on the walls and the bronze and marble statuary elegantly displayed on eighteenth-century tables. We came at last to an immense room with tall, silk-hung windows and a dazzling table set grandly with lustrous china and a profusion of fragrant flowers. A young man stood near the cavernous fireplace. His back was to us, and when we entered he turned slowly and looked steadily, unsmiling, at Mark.

"Mrs. Sinclair," said Mark, "may I present my son, Alan."

I hadn't expected him to look as he did. Except for his slender height he was nothing at all like his father. His hair was light, the color of wheat, and his eyes were pure gray with not a trace of blue or green. He had a fair, almost delicate, face with finely molded features and a jaw as sweetly curved as a young girl's. I learned later he was only sixteen, but he comported himself like an adult, a grave, solemn, self-confident adult. Although I was seven years older than he, I felt very much his junior as he took my hand and said in a fine, clear voice, "How do you do, Mrs. Sinclair. My father has told me much about you. I'm delighted to meet you at last."

Without further ado we sat down to dine, Mark at the head of the table, myself at his right and his son at his left. The boy was very quiet throughout the meal; he ate little and he seemed uninterested in anything his father had to say. Since I too had fallen into a painfully self-conscious silence, Mark dominated the conversation and spoke easily about the horse races at Jerome Park, Alderman Duffy's arrest in connection with the Thirty-fourth Street railroad franchise, Congress's difficulties with the fisheries question and the Land Grant tax, and lastly about President Cleveland's recent marriage to the fetching Miss Folsom, and the ceremony which Mark had attended.

"The table was splendidly decorated," he said, turning his full attention to me while his son stirred restively in his chair. "A great floral ship rested on a mirror which gave the most convincing appearance of water. The illusion was carried further by scarlet blossoms and pieces of coral suggesting shoals and rocks, and the banks were cunningly fashioned of Jacqueminots. Roses, smilax, garlands and festoons also adorned the table, and masses of greenery and bay and plants were banked high against the walls. It was an elaborate yet tasteful scene, and all the ladies seemed duly impressed. I think, Mrs. Sinclair, that you would have enjoyed seeing it."

"Yes," I murmured inadequately.

"Shall we have our coffee in the drawing room?" Mark said, and I looked up to see that both he and his son had risen and that a footman stood behind me waiting patiently to pull out my chair. I rose clumsily, upsetting my wineglass and sending a stain of red halfway across the white tablecloth.

"Oh, I'm sorry!" I cried and began to dab at the stain with a napkin until a discreet servant deftly took the linen from my hand.

"Come along, Mrs. Sinclair," said Mark with a puzzled smile. "There's no need to fret about the cloth. A soapy soak will banish the stain. Alan, would you escort our guest, please?"

The boy presented his arm and I took it blindly, not noticing that his cool gray eyes had turned warm with an emotion that, had I seen it, would still have defied definition. In the drawing room I sat miserably in a lyre-back chair while Mark and his son glanced first at each other, then at me, and then at the Georgian coffee service that stood untouched on a table at my side.

"Mrs. Sinclair," said the boy after a moment, "my father tells me you are an artist of some accomplishment. I have always envied the creative mind. I myself have no talent in that direction but prefer the Pythagorean art of mathematics which is precise and predictable."

I looked up with a start into his sweet, fair, childish face. He was not smiling, but his features had changed in a subtle, indescribable way. He regarded me courteously, awaiting my comments with a serene self-assurance I would have given my soul to possess, while Mark watched him with a curious mixture of pride and surprise. I remembered suddenly that Stephen Monroe had mentioned Mark's having a difficult boy, and I wondered dimly if the relationship between father and son was all as it should be.

"I like my coffee sweet, don't you?" said Alan, reminding me tactfully that the coffee was cooling in the pot.

"Why, yes," I said, finding my tongue at last and picking up the elegantly wrought pot. "I have a terrible sweet tooth. My husband often scolded me for indulging it."

"Your husband scolded you?" the boy exclaimed, and his gray eyes widened and his mouth curved into an astonished smile. "Mrs. Sinclair, you're joking!"

"Not at all," I assured him. "My husband was a good deal older than I, and he often—" I stopped suddenly, the last cup poured, and replaced the coffeepot on the tray. I didn't want to speak of Edward. I could hardly think of him without experiencing the most devastating torment of guilt.

Alan's eyes had sharpened with interest, and he was waiting, I supposed, for me to go on. It must have seemed strange indeed to a boy of sixteen that a woman so many years his senior should have been scolded like some callow girl. But that's what I was in truth: a callow, self-conscious, and hopelessly inadequate girl.

I glanced miserably about the room, raking through my mind for a brilliant remark to offset my childish gaffe. It was then I saw the painting of Lenore. It hung over the mantel, and only my earlier distress had kept me from noticing so arresting a portrait. The background was stark, midnight blue in color, and the subject was all fair hair and ivory skin, with eyes so intensely alive they seemed a mirrored reflection rather than a painted likeness. I rose from my chair as if compelled by some unknown force and moved toward the fireplace, toward the mesmerizing magnetism of those wonderful golden-lashed eyes.

"How lovely she is," I murmured in awe. "How incredibly lovely."

"That's my mother," said Alan, moving close behind me, and as my gaze turned from the portrait to his perfect face, I saw in him the very soul of Lenore. No wonder Mark was devoted to him; he was the living image of his dearest love.

"You're so like her," I told the boy. "How proud she must have been of you."

"I like to think she was," he said softly. His eyes met mine for a moment, searchingly, imploringly, but then he turned quickly away. I had caught a glimpse of his face before he turned. His cool composure had slipped; he was struggling desperately against a sudden surge of emotion too deeply intense to control. In a shaking voice he said to Mark, "If you don't mind, sir, I should like to retire now."

"Very well." Mark's voice was low, his tone even, but somehow I knew he was displeased. Perhaps he thought it unseemly that his son should parade his sorrow, for it was obvious that Alan still grieved for his mother. Mark was watching him, his dark eyes unreadable in a likewise unreadable face. "Good night, Alan. Sleep well."

"Good night, Father." Alan paused a moment, glanced in my direction, and murmured another good night. He looked again to his father, but Mark was examining his watch, and so the boy turned, rather dispiritedly it seemed to me, and trudged glumly from the room.

For a time Mark said nothing. He picked up his cup, found the coffee cold, and returned it to the tray. He seemed restless. He wandered about the room, straightening a chair, touching a lamp, then he went to the window, slipped his hands into his pockets and gazed out on the summer night.

"He has called me 'Father,' " he said moodily, "almost

since the moment he first spoke. I called my own father 'Papa' until the day he died at the age of sixty-five. I have always considered it a term of the most affectionate regard. I had hoped that any children I might have would address me in the same manner."

I did not answer. There seemed no appropriate reply. I could not in good conscience assure Mark that Alan loved him; I was not certain myself that he did. There was no logical basis for my doubt. Perhaps Stephen's words, added to a perceptible coolness on Alan's part toward his father, had formed my opinion. Whatever the reason, I kept silent, feeling that any remark I might make would be easily detected by Mark as insincere.

At length he turned from the window, and seeing that I was still on my feet, he bade me sit down.

"Do you like him?" he asked as I settled again in the lyre-back chair. "He's a handsome boy, isn't he?"

"He is the picture of his mother," I replied. "I have never seen such a remarkable resemblance."

"Yes." Mark's gaze turned and rested pensively on the portrait. "He resembles my wife."

How odd those words sounded. Mark had always seemed to me a bachelor. I knew of his reputation with women, and even if the rumors were only half true, it was an image not in keeping with a married man. Of course, his wife was dead and there was no reason he should lead a celibate life, but he was not like any married man I had ever known. He was especially not like Edward.

"You look very lovely this evening."

He had turned rather abruptly from the portrait, and his dark eyes now rested on my startled face. Was he serious or was he just being kind? His gaze told me nothing. He regarded me steadily, with no discernible emotion, until flustered and confused, I looked down at my lap and began nervously to pick at the lace on my skirt.

"I should like to see you again," I heard him say, but his words only added to my distress, and dumb with bewilderment I continued to stare at my lap. My hands were shaking. I heard him sigh. "Of course, if you'd rather not . . ."

I looked up at him then. The oddest expression was on

his face. He seemed hurt, which amazed me, for I had thought where women were concerned, nothing but his wife's death had ever deeply hurt him. He seemed angry too, but more with himself than with me, as if he regretted his words, wished he could retract them, as if he hadn't really meant what he'd said at all.

"I am in mourning," I said stiffly.

The full impact of my appearance suddenly struck me—as it must have struck Mark—a wren disguised as a peacock. What a fool I had been to think a few yards of satin might transform me. I knew who I was. And Mark knew it. He need not have said what he did. He need not have lied.

"Will you take me home?"

I rose from my chair, bristling with the same murderous rage which had plagued me months ago. I was as angry now with Mark as I had been with Edward those strange, confused weeks before he died. All men are liars, I thought irrationally as I glared at Mark with scorching contempt.

"Take me home!" I demanded, and I felt suddenly like Alan: young, alone, ensnared in the throes of an anguished bereavement from which there was no escape. But it wasn't Edward I mourned, it was something else. Something I had perhaps never had. Nor ever would.

V

I DID NOT see Mark Van Holden again for a year, but during that time his name was so much in the newspapers that I couldn't, even had I wanted to, forget him. Mark was principal stockholder and chairman of the board of the Eastern Seaboard Oil Company whose refineries stretched from New York to Pennsylvania to the oil-rich fields of Ohio. Over the past several years he and a group of supporters had formed a cartel with various railroad men which fixed rates of transport so that smaller independent oil companies found it virtually impossible to ship their product profitably or indeed even to remain in business. Mark would then step in, offer the unfortunate owners shares of Eastern stock in exchange for their foundering firms, and although most owners accepted eagerly, the staunch few who held out soon found themselves bankrupt and their companies embraced by the all-powerful, far-reaching tentacles of Eastern Seaboard Oil. By 1887 Mark had cornered the market, and his company refined ninety percent of all the oil produced in the United States. The outcry raised by the few remaining independent refiners came to naught, for it was rumored that while Mark was buying almost every refinery in sight, he had bought the entire legislatures of three states as well.

Stephen Monroe was jubilant. As Mark's broker, his own fortune was growing proportionately. He eventually decided, at Mark's suggestion, to dispense with his other clients and to service the Van Holden account exclusively. Sally, too, was thrilled at the propitious turn of events.

"He comes to the house so often now," she told me one

day in the spring while I was visiting at her house, "and he
stays to dinner more times than not. We've dined at his
house too, of course, and he has even invited us to his son's
seventeenth birthday celebration next month."

I murmured an appropriate reply, but Sally was far too
exhilarated to hear me. She pulled dresses from her wardrobe in a fever of excitement, a cherry-colored satin, an embroidered surah, a stunning brocaded tulle.

"I haven't a thing to wear!" she cried. "Look at these
rags! I've worn them all a dozen times."

"Sally," I reminded her, "you wore the satin only once,
to Mavis Greer's coming-out party. I haven't seen the
other two. They are new, are they not?"

"Yes, they're new," she pouted. "But they're awful! Hid-
eous! I wouldn't be caught dead in either of them."

"Then why," I asked dryly, "did you have them made
up?"

"Joanna, really! You're as bad as Stephen. I've changed
my mind, is that so terrible? I liked them at the time, but
now— Oh, they're just too boring!"

"Sally," I laughed, "you're incorrigible. All of your
gowns are lovely and very suitable for a young man's
birthday fete. Come now," I coaxed. "Try the surah. I'll
wager you'll like it once you see it on."

"No," she said petulantly. "I hate it. . . . Joanna"—she
turned her blue gaze on me, a devious smile curving the
corners of her mouth—"why don't *you* wear it to the party?
Mark asked me to invite you, you know."

"He did what?"

"When he was here last week he asked about you, mentioned in fact that he'd had you to dinner last year while
Stephen and I were in Europe. You sly puss, you never saying a word! Why didn't you tell me?"

"I—I—"

"Oh, it doesn't matter," she said impatiently. "You've
always been such a secretive little soul. Honestly, dear, if I
didn't know you better I'd think you had something to
hide." She regarded me thoughtfully, an almost unpleasant expression on her camellia-fair face. "In any case," she
went on with a shrug, "Mark asks about you constantly.

I've told him how devastated you were by Edward's death. You *are* still devastated aren't you, Joanna? I told him further not to expect you to attend his son's or any other party, as you've become a virtual recluse since Edward died. Of course, I didn't know you had dined at Mark's until he mentioned it to me, and I didn't let on that you hadn't told me. It would probably have embarrassed him if he thought he'd betrayed your little secret."

"It wasn't a secret," I said hotly. "You were away at the time, and when you returned home I— Well, I'd forgotten about it by then."

Forgotten? No, I hadn't forgotten that disaster of an evening. How could I ever forget Mark's face, puzzled at first and then turning courteously remote as I demanded to be taken home? He had fetched my wrap and summoned the carriage at once. We rode to my house in silence, and only when we were on my doorstep, and then only once, did Mark speak. "I meant no disrespect earlier," he had said softly, and in the dim light cast by the flickering streetlamp his eyes were darker than the starless sky above us. "I think perhaps you misinterpreted my meaning, but if I've offended you in any way, I apologize sincerely."

I tried to respond but could not. I wanted to tell him that I was the one who should apologize, that I was the one who had ruined the evening, but the words would not come. I stared at him, my pale, stony face concealing my anguish, until finally, miserably, I opened the front door and stumbled blindly inside. It was the last time I saw him, but it was far from the last time I would think of him.

"Well, you needn't get yourself in a lather," Sally said tartly. "It merely seemed odd that you would forget to mention the one time in over a year you'd been out of the house."

"Don't be a fool!" I snapped. "I've been out—"

"To church!" she interrupted harshly. "To the cemetery! I would hardly compare those jaunts to a dinner engagement with Mark Van Holden. I was wondering how long it would be before you'd get around to telling me. I can see

now that if Mark hadn't mentioned it, I would still be unaware of your . . . tryst."

I rose from my chair and took a deep breath. Never in my
life had I ever wanted to strike anyone, but I very much
wanted to do so at that moment. Sally eyed me narrowly,
her face contorted with— Good Lord, could it possibly be
jealousy? "Sally, please," I tried. "It wasn't a tryst. Let's
not quarrel over something so trifling as a dinner. Mr. Van
Holden wanted me to meet his son, that's all, and I saw no
harm in doing so. The evening amounted to nothing, as
you can see, for he did not call on me again."

"He had called on you?"

"Yes," I explained. "To offer his condolences. It was
shortly after you sailed for Europe. It was, as a matter of
fact, the night he asked me to dine with him."

"And you accepted?" she said, her voice rising shrilly.
"Knowing his reputation with women, you accepted?"

"His reputation," I said, my own voice growing suddenly cold, "does not seem to bother you, Sally."

Her eyes narrowed even more, and her pert pretty
mouth became a thin rigid line in a hard rigid face. "And
what exactly do you mean by that, Joanna?"

I could not meet her gaze; my own faltered and came to
rest on the pale pink gown of brocaded tulle which lay on
the bed. How lovely it was with its gracefully draped
sleeves and daintily scalloped hem. How startlingly different from the dull black frocks which it seemed I'd been
wearing for years. "I meant nothing," I mumbled dully. "I
meant nothing, Sally, I assure you."

Why, I thought as I continued to stare at the pattern of
the gown, was Sally so angry? She had called my meeting
with Mark a tryst, and that was strange, for she was forever teasing me about my lack of romanticism. In fact, for
the past few months she had been urging me to go out
more, to meet people—specifically gentlemen—and yet
now she was white-lipped with rage because I had dined
one evening, almost a full year ago, with Mark Van
Holden.

"Please," I said again, "let's not quarrel." I raised my
eyes imploringly to hers. Sally was my dearest friend. Now

that Edward was gone, she and Stephen were the only family I could call my own. I loved Sally and needed her. I didn't want to lose her.

Her eyes, hard and cold, met mine, and for one horrible moment as I returned her icy gaze I thought our friendship had come to an end. But then her expression changed, as if she too realized the absurdity of the quarrel, and she came toward me with open arms and embraced me with a fierce burst of emotion which thoroughly embarrassed me.

"My dear Joanna," she exclaimed, "you must forgive me! What a meddlesome witch you must think me, but I am only concerned for your welfare, I assure you." She drew me to the chaise and when I sat down beside her, her arm went about my waist and she stroked my hand much in the way one would stroke an old pet. "You're all alone now," she continued, her voice sad and full of worry, "and you're so young, my dear. Now that Edward is gone, I feel responsible for you, Joanna, and I feel that I must guide and protect you as Edward did when he was alive."

"Yes, Sally," I mumbled.

"You must admit," she said sternly, "that you should have told me of your dinner with Mark if only to avoid a misunderstanding such as just occurred."

"Yes, of course, you're right."

"He does have a reputation you know, and although Stephen and I must, of necessity, entertain him socially, I never for a moment forget that reputation." She paused significantly, squeezed my hand until I felt the cold hard metal of her rings press into my flesh. "Nor should *you* ever forget it, my dear."

"I won't, I promise you."

"Good!" She rose triumphantly and gave me an exultant smile. "Then I shall tell Mark definitely that you won't be attending the party."

"If that's what you think best, Sally."

"That *is* what I think best, Joanna."

And so we were reconciled. That is to say, Sally was reconciled to a decision which she alone had made. Once again I was placed in the position of a mindless subordinate. Once again I no longer controlled my own destiny. In

a way I was relieved. It was so much simpler really to be
guided by someone older and infinitely wiser than myself.
I doubt that I'd ever made a decision on my own except for
the catastrophe of choosing a gown for Mark's dinner, and
that particular experience was sufficient to prove that despite my almost twenty-four years of life, I was no more
mature than an infant.

Then, two weeks before the party, Alan Van Holden
called on me.

I received him in the garden; it was a lovely spring day
and I had been basking in the sun on a cushioned wicker
chair while listlessly thumbing through a book of poetry. I
stared when I saw him. He had grown so in a year. He
looked almost a man, and yet the sweet curve of youth lingered in his jaw and in his smooth, fair cheek.

"Mrs. Sinclair, I hope I'm not intruding," he greeted me.
"And I hope you won't think me presumptuous when I tell
you the reason for my call."

"Sit down, Alan," I bade him, then instructed the hov-
ering Blandford to bring us some refreshment. "No, you're
not intruding. And do tell me," I continued, smiling
warmly, "the reason for your visit."

I liked Alan. I barely knew him, but during that one
brief evening we'd spent together, he'd seemed such a
lonely boy despite his cool self-composure, so much a prisoner of his lonely reserve, so painfully like myself, that I
couldn't help but feel a special kinship with him.

"First off," he said hesitantly as he sat opposite me,
"will you promise me something?" He looked more a boy
now, leaning forward in his chair, his gray eyes hopeful,
expectant.

"Yes, anything," I said at once.

"Don't tell my father I was here."

His voice had changed; whether it was fear or dislike of
the man of whom he spoke I could not tell. His eyes had
changed too. Where only a moment before they had been
open and trusting, they were now hard, guarded, and startlingly adult in that angel-pure, childish face.

"As you wish, Alan," I agreed, not wanting, however, to

enter into a conspiracy, no matter how innocent it might prove to be, with Mark Van Holden's son.

He leaned back in his chair, relaxed now and obviously at ease with my complicity, while a sudden uneasiness of my own awoke like a sleeping serpent in my breast.

"Your tea, madame."

Blandford stood over me, a tray in his hands, his vigilant eyes appraising my guest and deliberating on the nature of his visit. Why *was* Alan here? I too was curious, and as Blandford relinquished his burden and silently withdrew, I asked the boy again why he had come.

His young face colored; I feared my tone of voice had been sharper than I'd intended. He straightened in his chair, flicked a nonexistent speck of lint from his immaculate trousers and cleared his throat. "I want you to come to my party."

I must have smiled then, for his face brightened and he was all eager youth, the sweet trusting boy once again.

"Mrs. Monroe told my father you wouldn't come," he said rapidly before I could reply. "She said you never go anywhere, that you mourn your husband still, and believe me, Mrs. Sinclair, I fully understand your feelings. But if you will allow me the impertinence of suggesting that an evening's entertainment now and then would benefit you immensely . . . Oh, please don't be angry with me!" he cried abruptly, but I was far too astonished to be anything of the sort.

I was a stranger to this boy; we had met only once, had barely spoken to one another, and now a year after that exceedingly brief encounter, he had come to my home to personally request my presence at his party. Why?

"Alan . . ." I began, but then stopped. He was watching me hopefully, his entire young soul reflected in the luminous depths of his silver-gray eyes. *How young he is,* I thought as I gazed silently at his perfect face. *How utterly dear.* I wished suddenly, with a violent surge of unaccustomed passion, that he were my son. I wished suddenly, with every fiber of my being, that he were mine.

"Mrs. Sinclair, please," he said earnestly, his voice a whispered plea. It seemed his very future hinged on my reply. It would be wrong, wicked, to disappoint him. I forgot about Sally, I forgot about Mark's "reputation." Only Alan mattered now, dear, sweet, beautiful Alan.

In silent response I held out my hand. He took it at once in his and raised it reverently to his lips.

VI

I WAS TOO much of a coward to tell Sally I was going to attend Alan's party. I traveled to the Van Holden house in my own carriage and I arrived early, knowing that when Sally saw me amidst a crowd of people she couldn't possible register her disapproval. What would happen afterward was another matter, but I didn't care. Alan was of the prime importance here, a young boy's wishes which I'd decided, on my own, to fulfill. He wanted me at the party. Mark did too. Mark had asked Sally to invite me, he had spoken of me, inquired after me. *Why,* I wondered as the Van Holden butler showed me into the gaily decorated ballroom. *Why?*

I was the first guest, but for once my shyness was forgotten as Alan, tall and handsome in evening clothes, came forward to greet me. My own attire was most assiduously correct. After much deliberation and a good many meetings with Mme Renaud, I had chosen a lemon yellow silk with charmingly embroidered bodice and embroidered short sleeves. The gown was very smart, a variation of a Worth design I had seen in the pages of *Bazaar,* and it was far more in keeping with my taste and with my nature than that disaster of a dress I had worn on my first visit to Mark's home.

"Mrs. Sinclair, good evening!" Alan's face was lit with a radiant smile, his eyes shone through the pure gilt shadow of his lashes. "You look lovely, absolutely splendid! Come, let me get you some wine."

"Not yet, Alan," I laughed. "I don't want to be tipsy

45

when your other guests arrive. I'm sorry I'm so early, but—"

"I'm not," he declared, taking my arm and drawing me toward the long buffet. "I'm delighted you're early. I was afraid you wouldn't come at all. Please, just one glass now—with me—before my father comes down."

He motioned to a servant who filled two crystal glasses from a frosty champagne bottle, and as I drank the bubbling wine Alan smiled, raised his glass to me, then emptied it in one swift draught.

"Alan," I cautioned, "you'll be ill if you drink that way all evening."

"I don't plan to," he said in a confidential tone. "My father prefers that I abstain from wine and spirits until I'm twenty-one, and I shan't be drinking once he comes down. He doesn't forbid it, you understand. My father wouldn't presume to dictate a code of behavior to me." His voice had gone hard and bitter. He signaled the servant to refill his glass, then drained it as quickly as he had done the first. It startled me a little, that swift, practiced movement, and it startled me more when he gestured peremptorily with a slim hand for still another glass of champagne.

"Alan," I ventured, "do you really think you should?"

"It's my last, Mrs. Sinclair," he assured me, and fortunately it was, for as soon as he had replaced his empty glass on the table, Mark entered the ballroom, and at his side was one of the most beautiful women I had ever seen.

She wore a Paris gown of blue *peau-de-soie*, and in her ears and at her throat diamonds and sapphires glimmered and shone. Her face was a perfect oval, her complexion cameo-pure, its fairness accentuated by the black silken hair which she wore parted simply and drawn back to a smooth Psyche knot at the base of her long, graceful neck.

"That's Mrs. Winslow," Alan muttered as I gaped openly at that vision of perfection. "Her husband manages my father's refinery in Bayonne. Mr. Winslow was unable to be here tonight," he added pointedly, "but Mrs. Winslow, as you can see, was free."

They came toward us arm-in-arm, and as they drew

near, Mark said with a pleasant smile, "Mrs. Sinclair, this is an unexpected pleasure."

"Mr. Van Holden," I murmured.

"You've come alone?" he asked, surprised. "I wish you had let me know. I would have escorted you here myself."

"I should not have liked inconveniencing you in that way," I said formally, and I realized at once from the look in his eyes that I had, without meaning to, amused him.

He turned to Mrs. Winslow, whose arm was still linked with his, and said, "Lavinia, I'd like you to meet Joanna Sinclair. Mrs. Sinclair honors us by her presence tonight."

"Really, Mark?" the woman drawled. "And why is that?"

"This, I believe, is her first social engagement in almost two years. Is it not, Mrs. Sinclair?"

He turned back to me, his eyes clear and dark, yet I sensed that behind his smooth, courteous, impeccable behavior there lurked that curious source of amusement known only to himself.

"It is," I said primly.

"Mrs. Sinclair," Mark explained to his companion, "lost her husband in the winter of eighty-five."

"How dreadful," the woman remarked, but since her eyes were scanning the heavily laden buffet, I sensed that she was more interested in the *haute cuisine* than she was in my husband's demise.

"Mark!" she exclaimed, catching sight of a platterful of prawns. "You remembered my favorite! Darling, would you think me terribly bad-mannered if I had just a teensy plate now?"

"Not at all, Lavinia. Jenkins, will you fill a dish for Mrs. Winslow? Mrs. Sinclair, may I tempt you with something?"

Mark had turned once again to me, his courteous smile concealing, I was sure, the highest degree of hilarity. Could he tempt me, indeed! What a fool he must think me, what a dull-witted, colorless fool.

"I very much doubt that," I said tartly, and slipping my hand through Alan's arm, I said, "Do show me the rest of

your house, won't you, Alan? The newspapers say it is
quite the palatial mansion and I never did get to see it all
the last time I was here."

As we walked away, I heard the murmur of Mark's voice
and then a soft, contemptuous laugh from Mrs. Winslow.
My hand clenched on Alan's arm, and he turned to me, his
beautiful gray eyes sharp with discernment. "Don't mind
her," he said tersely. "She's a whore." And covering my
hand with his, he escorted me briskly from the room.

I had no chance to ponder his astonishing pronounce-
ment, for he began to show me through room after room of
gilded and mosaic ceilings, Circassian paneling and Adam
mantelpieces, Greek friezes and seventeenth-century tapestries, commenting all the while on the history and
sources of the furnishings. It was magnificent! I could not
contain my awe.

"How you must love this house," I said breathlessly as
we came to rest in a charming room which was filled with
family memorabilia, and was furnished less grandly
though no less tastefully than the rest.

"I loathe it," he said, his voice low and cold. "I wish it
would burn to the ground."

"Alan!" I gasped.

"It's a bloody museum!" he cried. "It's his way of im-
pressing people. He has raped and pillaged every villa and
château in Europe to impress his bloody friends. My
mother hated this house. She always hated it!"

He broke off suddenly as if horrified by his startling
breach of decorum. "I'm so sorry," he said desperately, his
face white with anguish. "Mrs. Sinclair, I'm truly sorry.
You won't tell him what I said, will you?"

"Alan, of course not." I took his hands in mine and gave
them a reassuring squeeze. What a strange boy he was,
but I supposed it was that disconcerting time of life, that
painful emergence from the warm cocoon of childhood into
the cold and perilous depths of adult independence. "I
would never betray your confidence," I told him firmly.
"But, Alan, don't you think you're being a little unfair?
Your father hasn't pillaged anything. He has only pre-
served what might otherwise have been lost to posterity.

So many fine families abroad have become impoverished and have been forced to sell heirlooms and treasures."

"Ha!" he said and wrenched his hands from mine. "*Forced* is precisely the right term in my father's case. That's how he gets what he wants. Coercion is his hallmark. He never asks, he demands. He thinks his money can buy anything in the world, but it can't, you know. It couldn't save my mother. He got her the finest doctors, the best possible care, but she died anyway. What a blow that must have been to his monumental ego!"

"Alan, please! Don't say any more." I was numb with embarrassment. I had no right to hear these things, I couldn't bear to hear them. Is that why he hated Mark? Did he blame him for his mother's death despite the fact that Mark had done everything possible to save her?

"I'm sorry," he said again, and I saw in his tormented eyes the fledgling man struggling for dominance over the resident child. "I didn't mean to upset you. I'll speak of him no more, I give you my word."

"I'm not upset," I said quickly. "It's only that . . ." I paused, searched frantically for words. "It's just that when one suffers a great loss, one seeks to place blame, thinking somehow that this will mitigate the grief and the guilt which accompany such a loss. You blame your father, Alan, yet think what he must be feeling with no one to blame but himself."

"He feels nothing," the boy said bitterly. "He accepts no blame. He didn't love her. He never did. He was glad when she died, glad I tell you!"

His eyes blazed brilliantly, his slim frame shook with a passionate rage, and as I stared, dumb with shock, at his bloodless face, a figure appeared at the tall open doors of the tension-charged room. The boy turned, sensing an intrusive presence, and gazed with open loathing at his father's tranquil face.

"Alan," said Mark, his voice low, his tone neutral, "your other guests have arrived and are asking for you. If you'll go down to greet them, I shall be happy to show Mrs. Sinclair the remainder of the house."

I braced myself for a scene. Alan's face was murderous;

he opened his mouth as if to refuse, but there was a look in Mark's eyes that stopped him. They regarded each other, father and son, in a bone-chilling silence. It was Alan at last, the younger, the undisciplined, who slowly lowered his gaze. "Very well," he said sullenly. "Mrs. Sinclair, will you excuse me?"

I nodded automatically, then sank with a sigh onto a chair. Alan left the room; Mark closed the heavy double doors, and after a moment he drew up a chair by my side.

"I see he has unburdened himself to you."

"What do you mean?" I asked faintly. I was limp with emotion. Never in my life had I encountered such hatred. I could scarcely credit its existence, and that it should exist between father and son was simply more than I could grasp.

"My son," Mark said quietly, "cannot accept the loss of his mother. It has been many years now, as you know, and yet he mourns her as though it were only yesterday. Added to this insupportable burden is the fact that he holds me responsible for her death. I have never attempted to investigate his reasons; determining the origin of one's convictions does not, unfortunately, change them."

"Oh, please," I said wretchedly, "don't tell me any more."

"Forgive me," Mark persisted, "but I must tell you these things. You see, Mrs. Sinclair, my son has taken a fancy to you."

"A fancy?" I whispered.

"He sees in you, I think, an innocence, a vulnerability"—Mark paused, his eyes growing dark—"and other such qualities which were possessed by his mother. I see them too. I saw them the first night I met you. I was struck at the time by this remarkable resemblance of character, for my wife was, in my estimation, unique. When I saw you again after your husband died, I was struck further by the indefinable yet unmistakable similarity of nature. It was then I decided that you should meet Alan, that you could perhaps help to fill the void in his life."

"What?" I cried, rousing at last from my lassitude. "Are you suggesting that I should marry a mere boy?"

"Marry? Oh, good Lord!" He burst into laughter, and I felt myself color in mortification. Once again I had exhibited that maddening naiveté which seemed to amuse him so.

"Mrs. Sinclair, you're delightful!" The laughter shone still in his eyes, but he became aware all at once of my painful silence. "Please," he said, his tone sobering, "don't be offended. Everything I say seems to offend you. I'm afraid I am too much in the company of women far different from yourself and my behavior, unhappily, reflects that fact. But let me assure you that, like my son, I have only the highest regard for you, and it is our combined wish that we might count you among our friends. Will you permit that, Mrs. Sinclair? Will you be Alan's friend? And mine?"

How dark his eyes were and how thick the lashes which half veiled them. His voice was low, almost sensual in timbre; I imagined it would sound much the same if he were proposing something far more intimate than friendship. For just a moment I envisioned such a scene: Were he planning to seduce me he would lean toward me and his mouth would graze my cheek and then it would trail to my ear where, in the most erotic of terms, he would describe the relationship he sought. I would of course recoil in shock, but his arms would go round me, and lifting me to my feet, he would crush me to him and cut off all protests with a mouth closing firmly on mine. So vividly did I feel that hard, warm, sensuous mouth that I gave a small start, and a soft, helpless cry escaped my lips.

"Christ!" he said suddenly, and pushed himself out of his chair.

I stared at him in bewildered panic. He towered over me like some dark avenging angel.

"Mrs. Sinclair," he said angrily, "I suspect you've been listening to gossip. Whenever you're in my presence you all but swish aside your skirts in repulsion. I begin to think you've discussed me with your friends."

"No, never!" I gasped.

"I think further that you give credence to tales of feats

which astound even me, the purported performer of those feats."

"Mr. Van Holden—"

"I had thought a lady like yourself would discredit such scurrilous reports."

"Mr. Van Holden!" I was crimson with embarrassment. He was angry and rightly so, for I realized that those same scurrilous reports had been in the back of my mind since the night I'd first seen him. "Please," I stammered. "I didn't—I don't—"

"You didn't? You don't? Then why when we first met did you hasten to tell me how much you loved your husband? Why, when you dined at my house, were you so tense, so unresponsive? Why did you refuse my repeated invitations to this party and then accept my son the very first time he asked?"

"But how—?" I stammered in confusion.

"How did I know?" he said harshly. "I make it my business to know all that concerns me personally. And my son, Mrs. Sinclair, is my chief personal concern."

I couldn't speak, couldn't think. Never in my life had I suffered such a fierce verbal attack. Harsh words were unknown to me; tempestuous emotion was unknown to me and I was simply unable to deal with it. Mutely I gazed at Mark's eyes, blacker than night in that turbulent Moorish-dark Medici face. My heart pounded, my throat was parchment dry. I wanted desperately to bolt from the room, but my limbs would not obey my frantic commands. Trembling from head to toe, I remained in my chair, a frightened captive of his most frightening gaze.

And then it was gone. As swiftly as it had flamed, his anger died, and in his eyes was the same wretched look I feared was in mine. "God, I'm sorry," he uttered. "Mrs. Sinclair, I'm so sorry."

Only moments ago—or was it years?—his son had spoken the same words. Man and boy, they were alike. Alan might resemble his mother, the serene and lovely Lenore, but his emotions were his father's: quick, volatile, and relentlessly brutal.

Mark's apology did little to quell my fears. I stared at

him still, and to my further distress I began suddenly and helplessly to cry. I had never in my life wept before a stranger, and to be doing so now in Mark Van Holden's presence was a humiliation I could barely endure. Like the child that I was, I covered my face with my hands and succumbed to a misery which had been born on the night we'd first met. On that night too I had wept, but then it had been in my husband's arms. And as I thought of Edward, of his gentle voice and his wonderful smile, my misery increased and I sobbed as though my heart were breaking. How alone I was and how utterly vulnerable. No man protected me, no man called me his. Had I the love and affection of family, my desolation might not have been so great. But there was no one in life who would shelter me now, no one.

I felt Mark's hands on me then, and he lifted me from my chair just as I'd envisioned a few moments ago. His arms went round me, his mouth grazed my cheek, and as I lay sobbing against him I heard him murmur sweetly, gently near my ear.

"Don't cry," he said softly. "I'm sorry I frightened you. Don't cry."

Was I imagining it all? Was this real?—his low voice, his strong arms, his hard slender form so disturbingly close to mine. I was intensely aware of his touch, of his hands at my back, of the whisper-soft movement of his mouth on my cheek. His mouth was warm as I'd imagined it would be, but his words were lost to me as I sank deep under the spell of his mesmerizing voice.

At last my sobs ebbed and ceased. The room was very quiet; Mark had long since fallen silent, and I raised my head as one last sob caught painfully in my throat. His eyes, dark and still, met mine. My face was wet with tears, my mouth trembled. He watched me for the longest time and then his arms tightened, he drew me closer, and when his mouth touched mine it seemed the most natural thing in the world. His kiss was slow, tentative, as if he weren't quite sure how I'd react. He needn't have worried; I was far too drained emotionally to register even the slightest protest. When he encountered no resistance his lips parted mine, his kiss deepened, and for the first time in my life I knew passion, and I knew as well that I wanted Mark Van Holden as I had never wanted anything before.

What a strange emotion is passion, and how curious that it saps the will while at the same time deliciously stimulating the senses. I felt weak, nerveless, unable to move or think, yet my heart was beating wildly, and a wellspring of warmth was diffusing a fever through every fiber of my being. I was dimly aware that Mark's passion too had been aroused, but for Mark, of course, it was not the first time. How many other women had he kissed like this, I suddenly thought. With a supreme effort of will I tore my mouth from his. "No," I said faintly and thought, *Yes, yes, I'm yours, yes.* I wanted him to kiss me, I wanted him to do more than kiss me. If that placed me among the ranks of his countless conquests, it mattered not. I wanted Mark, I wanted him with a hot, reckless yearning that took my breath away. But again I said, "No."

He did not release me but his arms slackened and he held me loosely, his dark eyes fixed questioningly on mine. Why did he stare so, what was he thinking? Had he guessed my true feelings? Did he know I was his for the asking?

"Let me go," I whispered helplessly. "How dare you treat me like that? I am not one of your—"

"One of my what, Mrs. Sinclair?" His arms fell to his sides, he stepped back and watched me still, his midnight-dark gaze holding mine. He seemed curiously pleased by my anger, as if he expected it, welcomed it, though I couldn't for the life of me think why.

"You know what I mean," I said miserably. "What gave you the idea you could—that I would—? You have no right to think—"

I broke off in confusion. Mark waited for me to go on, but when it became evident that I had nothing further to say, he said calmly, "Mrs. Sinclair, I'll spare you the hypocrisy of an apology because quite frankly I should very much like to kiss you again. Nevertheless, I understand your feelings; you're shocked and offended by my actions, but let me assure you that by no stretch of the imagination do I class you with the women whom you earlier mentioned. I believe that except for tonight I have shown you all due deference and have given you no personal cause to avoid me. If, however, my alleged reputation with women distresses you, by all means tell me straight out and I shall then discontinue my efforts to court you."

"To court me?" I repeated dully, like a half-wit.

"To court you, Mrs. Sinclair. Ultimately to marry you. Did you think," he asked with a sardonic smile, "that I had something else in mind?"

VII

WHEN I WAS very young I lived with my mother in a small house on the north side of Washington Square. At that time it was considered fashionable to live on the square, and I remember how charming it was with its small park and graceful trees, but I remember most of all that despite the proximity of the houses and the friendliness of the neighbors, my mother was friendly with no one. Her days, I recall, were spent in her small boudoir, peering into the mirror in search of blemishes, wrinkles, or gray hair which fortunately never appeared. My mother was obsessed with her looks, and, in all fairness, were I half as beautiful as she I think I too might have feared the grim prospect of encroaching old age.

She did, however, have friends who lived elsewhere, ladies almost but not quite as lovely as she, married ladies whose husbands, strangely, were never in evidence. Sometimes in the afternoons my mother would take me with her when she went to tea at the Fifth Avenue or Madison Avenue home of one of these ladies. I was never permitted to speak at those functions, only to say "Yes, please" or "No, thank you," and I was cautioned to sit properly with knees close together, both feet on the floor, and hands folded neatly in my lap.

I detested those visits. The conversations invariably bored me, and I would amuse myself by counting the buttons on our hostess's tea frock while she chattered at length about Commodore Vanderbilt's disgusting alliance with Tennessee Claflin and Victoria Woodhull, or about the shocking murder of Jim Fisk by Ned Stokes. Mr. Fisk,

it seemed, had appropriated Mr. Stokes's mistress, the cur-
vaceous Josie Mansfield, and in a fit of jealous rage, Mr.
Stokes cold-bloodedly shot the passionate purloiner on the
steps of the Grand Central Hotel. These lurid tales fascinated my mother, who would wring every last bit of information from her happily compliant source. But upon our
return home, my mother would tell me sternly that under
no circumstances was I to repeat a word of the day's conversation. "Irresponsible gossip," she would proclaim,
"has ruined many a fine name, mine among them. If ever I
learn that you've indulged in such talk, I shall take a
switch to you, as God is my witness!"

My mother was a consummate hypocrite. She protested
most strongly that which she religiously practiced. Another of her favorite admonitions was: "Keep yourself
pure, Joanna. Above all things, a man prizes chastity in a
woman." Her popularity tended to refute that statement;
in my mother's case it was my reasoned opinion that above
all things, a man prized exactly the opposite.

I wondered sometimes what forces had shaped my destiny. I was nothing at all like my mother, but perhaps her
sanctimonious adjurations had somehow left their mark
on me, for I *was* chaste, in thought as well as in deed, and I
abhorred gossip, and despite the fact that my mother rep-
resented everything in life I repudiated, I loved her very
deeply.

When she died of pneumonia at the age of thirty-five, I
wondered in childlike awe if God had punished her for her
wicked ways. I remember asking Edward, in the most ob-
scurely phrased manner, if such a thing were possible, and
he told me in his kind way that God was not in the habit of
striking people dead as he had considerably more important matters to attend to.

"However," Edward added, never once suspecting that I
was aware of his relationship with my mother, "God does
expect us to adhere to his commandments lest we suffer
the loss of our immortal souls. That, Joanna, is a fate
worse than death, as I'm sure your dear mother taught
you."

In a sense, Edward was correct. My mother *had* taught

me the meaning of morality—through her own bad example. She had taught me the difference between right and wrong, between good and evil; she had directed my spiritual steps on the pathway to heaven, while she herself had brazenly trod the other. I think that was one of the reasons Edward married me. Despite his illicit alliance with my mother, he was basically a moral man, and I believe he would have married her had she lived. But when she died he was so stricken with guilt by the wrong he thought he had done her, that in expiation for his sin, he made me his wife, thereby ensuring that no man would ever seduce me, as dear, sweet, misguided Edward thought he had seduced my mother. It was ironic then that my second proposal of marriage should come from the most notorious seducer of women in all of the state of New York.

Fortunately, when Mark made his astonishing proposal, he refused to hear an answer then and there. "Give it some thought," he suggested. "Don't reject me out of hand. Consider Alan; think of the boy." And tucking my hand through his arm, he escorted me back to the elegant ballroom, which was now overflowing with guests.

Mark knew so many people. I recognized Louise and Frederick Vanderbilt, Tessie and Hermann Oelrichs, Pierpont Morgan, who had come without his wife, and Mr. Henry Abbey, the famed impresario, escorting Christine Nilson, who would later favor us with an aria from *Tristan und Isolde.* I did not see Mrs. Winslow, but Mark, it seemed, was not in the least concerned as to her whereabouts.

The orchestra was playing a Viennese waltz, and as we entered the ballroom Mark took me in his arms and whirled me out onto the floor as though we'd been dancing together a dozen years. I'd forgotten how divinely he danced. He guided me gracefully through the throng of guests, his movements minimal, effortless, assured. I looked up shyly at his strong, dark face, and feeling my scrutiny, he glanced down, drew me slightly closer in his arms, and smiled.

"Joanna," he said. "Such a pretty name for a pretty girl. May I call you Joanna?"

I blushed like a schoolgirl. "If you like," I murmured and self-consciously lowered my eyes.

"And you must call me Mark," he said. When I didn't answer, he released my hand for a moment and lifted my chin, compelling obedience with the silent command of his sultry dark eyes. "Joanna?"

"Yes, Mark," I whispered and once again, as I'd been doing all my life, I surrendered my will to the will of another.

Mark's wife. What would it mean to be his wife, his second wife, and mother to his son? Surely Alan was the reason Mark wished to marry me. Alan had taken a fancy to me, Alan was Mark's chief concern; hence his proposal of marriage. Or, I thought suddenly, was it to be only a marriage of convenience? Was I to be the dutiful wife, a surrogate mother, while Mark remained free to pursue less familial endeavors?

"Mark," I said abruptly, "if we should marry . . ."

"Yes?" he said, his eyes alert with interest.

I paused, hesitant to explore so intimate and distressing a subject. And yet if I were to consider marriage with this man, I had to know his intentions.

"If we should marry," I tried again, steeling myself to meet his gaze, "you *will* be faithful?"

His expression changed ever so subtly, his lids lowering lazily as he gave me a slow smile. "What at extraordinary question. Why do you ask it?"

"Please," I persisted, astonished by my own audacity. "I have to ask. I must know."

He regarded me quietly, his smile replaced by a sudden sober curiosity. It appeared for a moment that I was as great a puzzle to him as he was to me. I returned his gaze with a bold forthrightness I had not thought I possessed, and at last he said simply, "Yes, Joanna. I intend to be faithful."

I sighed audibly and closed my eyes. As Mark escorted me from the floor, I wished tiredly that this night, which had only just begun, would end. I needed desperately to be alone, to think, to sort out my feelings. I was certainly attracted to Mark, that much I knew, but did I want to marry him? Did I want the burden of a full-grown and possibly difficult son? I liked Alan and I knew he was fond of me, but would he accept me as his father's wife?

"Joanna! What are you doing here? My dear Mark, how did you ever persuade her to come?"

Sally Monroe, pink and pretty in a new violet gown, descended like a pall on my already gloomy thoughts. She clung to Stephen's arm like an enraptured bride, yet the look she gave Mark held the same dormant excitement that had glimmered darkly in Lavinia Winslow's eyes.

"Joanna, you sly puss! You changed your mind, didn't you? Really, Mark, Joanna is so unpredictable. She told me in no uncertain terms that she was not yet ready to re-enter the social whirl, and here she is. And looking so radiant! Joanna, that's a new dress, isn't it? Confidentially, my dear, you're showing a wee bit too much bosom. Stephen, I really think you should scold her. After all, dear Uncle Edward isn't here to guide—"

"Do be quiet, Sally," Stephen said wearily. "Her dress is fine. You look lovely, Joanna. I'm glad you decided to come after all."

I gave him a grateful smile. Stephen was so kind, so very much like Edward.

"Mark," he asked, "where is Alan? We haven't seen him yet."

"You haven't?" said Mark. "That's odd." He looked about the crowded room, and failing to spot his son, he said with apparent annoyance, "Will you excuse me for a moment? I'll see if I can locate him."

He strode away without waiting for an answer, and I wondered uneasily if they would quarrel. Father and son, they were so alike, so strikingly, dangerously alike.

"Well, my dear," I heard Sally say, "it appears your period of mourning has officially ended."

"Did you think," Stephen said, "that she would mourn indefinitely? Joanna is young, Sally. She has a long life ahead of her, and I for one do not expect her to spend it alone."

"Nor do I, dearest," she said at once. "But, Stephen, honestly! Mark Van Holden? Of all men with whom to ally herself!"

"Ally herself? My dear Sally, attending a gentleman's party does not constitute an alliance."

"Quite so," Sally agreed. Then turning to me she said pointedly, "But from the look on your face, Joanna, I believe this particular evening has become far more significant than a simple birthday celebration."

"I'm sure I don't know what you mean, Sally."

My cool voice belied the emotions which warred within me. I wanted to tell her everything, I longed to announce that Mark had asked me to marry him, and yet at the same time, some profound self-protective instinct warned me to keep silent. Sally's honeyed tone, so at variance with the hard, cold glitter of her eyes, frightened me. She had looked much the same on the day we'd quarreled over Mark. It occurred to me now that that was the first time, the only time, Sally and I had ever had words. How curious, I thought as I returned her hostile gaze, that she should object so strenuously to Mark when she herself seemed inordinately taken with him.

I could no longer bear her venomous stare. My nerves were stretched to snapping and if I stayed a moment longer I knew we would quarrel. Mumbling an excuse, I dragged myself away, stumbling blindly past the chattering guests and whirling dancers. In the great hall, groups of people were clustered here and there, and in an effort to escape them I climbed the marble staircase in search of the small, charming room where Mark had proposed. There I could be alone; in that lovely havenlike room I could gather about me the tattered ruins of my composure. But my wits had deserted me, and the house was so large that after trying several doors with no success I realized I was lost.

Glumly I trudged down the wide corridor, my destination the grand staircase which, incredibly, was nowhere in sight. And then I heard a voice, Mark's voice, from a room near the end of the hall. With a sigh of relief I approached the room, but stopped just short of the door when I heard him say quietly, "If you thought to embarrass me, Alan,

I'm afraid you've failed. It is your own dignity which has suffered here. You see, I am fully aware of Mrs. Winslow's character, and for you to have lain with her here, now, does you more discredit than it does her. Mrs. Winslow has several outstanding attributes, as I'm sure you've just learned, but intelligence, unfortunately, is not one of them. By the same token, despite what differences may exist between us, I have never questioned *your* intelligence . . . until now. The fact that your conduct was shoddy, base, and execrable needs no further articulation, but I will say this one thing. If you insist on acting like a man, you should first learn to think like one. And now, Alan, I would appreciate it if you would finish dressing and come downstairs at once. Several of our guests have already commented on your absence, and I think you'll agree that you've behaved badly enough for one evening.''

I froze. I tried to turn, to flee, but again my traitorous limbs refused to obey. Petrified, I watched Mark step into the hall and quietly close the door. When he looked up and saw me standing there, his face registered first bewilderment, then shock, and finally a swift devastating rage that set me trembling.

"What the devil are you doing here?"

"I—I—"

He strode toward me, and taking my arm in a painful grip he literally dragged me down the hall and into the very room I'd been trying to find. He closed the door firmly behind us.

"Sit down, Joanna," he said stiffly. "How much," he then said, as he led me gently to the sofa, "did you hear?" He sat so close beside me that I could feel his warm breath on my cheek, yet he did not touch me. I could feel his eyes on me, and dimly I wondered why Mark's anger had changed to this tender concern. In the corridor, when he'd spotted me, his face had been murderous, terrifying, but now as I sat listlessly beside him he seemed anxious only that my sensibilities had not been offended by his son's actions.

But had I heard correctly? Had Alan actually been intimate with that woman while a houseful of guests awaited

him downstairs? Perhaps I had been mistaken, perhaps I
had misunderstood Mark's reprimand, and in that desperate hope I replied, "I heard nothing." But Mark knew I
was lying, and I knew when I raised my gaze to his that I
had not been mistaken at all.

"Mark," I said faintly, "would you mind if I went home?
I have a dreadful headache. . . . In fact, that's the reason I
was roaming about. I thought if I could just sit for a while
in an empty room . . ." I trailed off feebly. Mark's face
showed clearly the pain and humiliation I had so clumsily
attempted to spare him. He knew I was lying, he knew I
had heard everything, and I realized, with my first insight
into his complex nature, that he would sooner I despised
him than ever think ill of his son.

"Must you go?" he asked quietly. "I should very much
like you to stay. You see, Joanna, if you don't face Alan tonight, I'm afraid you won't ever be able to face him again."

For a time I said nothing. Mark was right, of course. If I
delayed seeing Alan, I would very likely postpone it indefinitely. But did I want to see him again? Did I want to em-
broil myself in this distressing contention between father
and son? Mark loved Alan but Alan quite clearly hated
Mark, and he had gone to great lengths this evening to express that hatred. The thought of what he had done sick-
ened me. What dark pleasure had it given him to lie with
his father's mistress? For surely Lavinia Winslow was
Mark's mistress. One had only to see the possessive way
she touched him or the languid narrowing of her eyes
when she looked at him to know that theirs was a relationship of the flesh.

"Joanna." Mark's low voice gently penetrated my
thoughts. "Please try not to think too badly of him. By no
means do I excuse his actions, but Alan is . . ."

I didn't hear the rest. I had neither the maturity nor the
inclination to deal with such a situation. Perhaps such incidents were commonplace in the ultrasophisticated world
of Mark Van Holden, but I wanted no part of them. I
wanted a safe life, a predictable life, such as the decorous,
well-ordered existence I had shared with Edward.

I rose unsteadily. "I want to go home," I whispered, and

on shaking legs I moved toward the door. In an instant
Mark was on his feet and he deftly blocked my exit.

"Joanna, don't go. Not like this. If you leave now, I know
you won't come back."

"I don't want to come back. I don't want to marry you. In
fact, I don't want to see you ever again."

I opened the door and plunged dazedly down the corridor. Where was I going? Where were the stairs? Unwit-
tingly I had once again chosen the wrong route, and as I
stopped to get my bearings a door opened and Alan Van
Holden stepped out into the hall. He smiled when he saw
me, a wonderful radiant smile. His eyes were a pure, clear
gray, his face gleamed ivory beneath the lustrous crown of
his yellow-gold hair.

"Mrs. Sinclair!" he exclaimed. "Have you come looking
for me?"

He was obviously delighted to think I had sought him
out. He took my hand in both of his and gazed at me just as
he had gazed at the portrait of his mother. I tried to associate this boy with the odious deed he had earlier done, and
could not. Alan was too young, too sweet, too pure. His
father might consort indiscriminately with whores, but
not Alan, never Alan.

"Yes," I said faintly. "I've come looking for you."

With a jubilant smile he tucked my hand through his
arm and directed me toward the stairs while Mark, who
had been watching us from across the hall, returned to the
room where I had left him, and quietly closed the door.

VIII

MARK BEGAN TO call on me as if that ghastly evening had never taken place. We never discussed it. It was as if each of us for our own reasons preferred to obliterate it from our memories.

I was going to marry him. I realized it even while in my own befuddled mind I fought against it. I knew what Mark was and it repelled me. Yet at the same time I was not impervious to the glamour and magnetism which had won women far more worldly than I. His appearance alone was enough to set my heart thumping. He was always faultlessly groomed, impeccably attired, and he was so incredibly, irresistibly handsome. Everything about Mark was different, foreign to me; his was the treacherous allure of forbidden fruit.

His behavior at the beginning puzzled me. He did not again attempt to kiss me; indeed, he only touched me when handing me into a carriage or when we danced, and I found this disquieting, unnerving, as if a pacing tiger lurked just outside my door. It seemed the lull before a storm, his unlikely restraint, and I shuddered to think what would happen if ever the tempest should break.

In June, Sally Monroe confided to me that she was pregnant. I was delighted for her; it had been nine years since her last child and she had often expressed a desire for more. We were back on the friendliest terms, since I had not mentioned I was seeing Mark. I suppose I should have told her, but coward that I was, I did not.

"It's due in December," she informed me, and though

she was paler than usual and somewhat subdued I quite naturally ascribed it to her condition.

"How wonderful, Sally," I said with a hug. "Stephen must be elated."

She withdrew from my embrace and leaned back listlessly against the sofa. "He does not know."

"He doesn't know? But why?"

Her head was bent in a mournful way and her mouth curved sadly downward. She gazed apathetically at her skirt while folding and unfolding the lace-edged handkerchief in her hands. "I've been meaning to tell him," she said with a sigh, "but . . ."

"But what, Sally? Why should you keep it from him, for goodness' sake? It's his child too."

"Yes," she said grimly. "It's his child too."

She would say nothing else on the subject. Rising abruptly, she rang for tea, then gave me her sauciest smile.

"Tell what you've been doing, Joanna. What a stranger you've become of late. Stephen and I have missed you, and the children have too. You rarely call in the afternoons, and you haven't been to dinner in ages. I must say, though, you're looking positively grand. Have you changed dressmakers? No? But I've never seen you looking so smart. That frock you're wearing is a love. Who designed it? You? Why, Joanna, you surprise me, you really do. You've changed, my dear, do you know that? Is there a reason by any chance? Have you got yourself a beau? Joanna, good heavens, you're blushing! Then it is a man, isn't it? Tell me who, tell me all! Is it serious? Will you marry? Do I know him?"

I could have told her then. I should have told her then. But I chose not to. I cannot explain my reluctance; it was foolish as well as dangerous. Sooner or later, Sally was bound to learn I was seeing Mark Van Holden. And when she did . . .

I gave her a noncommittal reply. She was tingling with curiosity, but for once she did not press me. It appeared she had other thoughts on her mind, and I assumed they concerned her pregnancy. But why hadn't she told Stephen? He had a right to know.

I took my leave directly we had finished our tea. I was expecting Mark that evening, and as usual when he called, I took forever to prepare, choosing and discarding dress after dress until Myrna would throw up her hands and declare in frustration, "He's only a man, Mrs. Sinclair, like your dear late husband. I'll wager Mr. Van Holden neither notices nor cares which gown you wear."

But Mark always noticed. That night, for an evening at the opera, I wore a dove white gown of shimmering silk with a simple slim skirt and a bodice of hand-fashioned lace. The dress was the most elegant I had ever worn, but I especially wanted to shine that night, for it was my first time at the Met and of course—since Mark was on the board of directors—we would be sitting in his box in the fabled Diamond Horseshoe.

Mark called for me promptly at seven, but before we left he took a slim case from his coat and placed it in my hands.

"I have taken the liberty"—he smiled—"of buying you a gift. It is merely a gesture of my utmost regard. Do not, I implore you, misinterpret my intentions."

I understood what he meant as soon as I opened the box. On a background of velvet lay the most exquisite necklace I had ever seen. It was a circlet of diamonds in graduating measure, culminating in the center with a stone quite nearly the size of a twenty-five-cent piece.

"I couldn't possibly!" I protested.

"I had a feeling you would say that."

"Mark, I simply cannot . . ."

"Joanna, please. My motives, I assure you, are the purest. If you were my wife you wouldn't think twice about accepting such a gift."

"But I'm not your wife."

"But you will be."

I could hardly refuse in light of such logic. And, moreover, I had never in my life owned a piece of jewelry as magnificent as the necklace Mark clasped about my neck.

"Do you like it?" he asked, directing me toward the mirror where he stood just behind, almost but not quite touching me.

"It's exquisite," I whispered, stricken with awe by my own mirror image. I looked truly beautiful. My eyes blazed darkly in a flushed face, my lips were pink with a color of their own. Could this be me, I wondered dizzily, this dazzling creature in diamonds and silk?

I turned excitedly to Mark. "Oh, thank you!" I exclaimed. "It's the most wonderful gift I have ever received."

"Is it?" He smiled. "I'm happy it pleases you."

The opera was Mozart's *Così fan Tutte*, and between the diamonds and the Met and the music, I don't know when I'd felt so alive.

The next night we were to dine at the home of his friends, John and Constance Chandler. I had met them before and I liked them. John was president of the Connecticut Central Railroad, a member of the cartel which had been responsible for Mark's cornering the refinery market. He was very much like Mark: attractive, polished, but beneath his veneer of smooth urbanity lay the same savage brutality which had brought an entire industry to its knees. Perhaps I should have shunned such people, men who strove only toward their own selfish ends with little regard for the countless unfortunates whose lives they either ruined or exploited. But in my mind I could not connect the grand concept of villainy and corruption with the sleek, cultured gentlemen who lived in grand houses in New York and Newport and Bar Harbor, and who reveled in their collections of medieval manuscripts and ancient Etruscan artifacts. And so I accepted them, Mark's ruthless, unscrupulous friends, as my own.

As we rode in the carriage to the Chandler house, Mark sat near the door, a considerable expanse of elegant upholstery between us. He was talking about Alan, who was summering in Saratoga with his grandparents, the Van Rensselaers. I had not seen Alan since the night of his birthday celebration, and until tonight Mark had not spoken of him at all. In truth, I would have preferred not to speak of him. I was still undecided as to the actual events which had taken place at the party. Had Alan been intimate with that woman or had he not? It was easier to believe that he hadn't; I wanted to believe that he hadn't. But yet . . .

"He'll be entering the university in the fall," Mark said as he watched the passing scene outside the carriage window. "I had hoped he would attend Harvard as I did, but he has chosen Yale instead."

"Perhaps," I ventured timidly, "he feels more deference will be shown him at Harvard because he is your son. It might be that he wishes to gain merit on his own and so has chosen a school where he will be judged solely on his own performance."

"Whether at Yale or at Harvard," Mark replied, "his name remains Van Holden. There are those who will judge him on that basis alone, and Alan is well aware of that fact. No, Joanna, his decision is based on other reasons."

I said nothing. Mark had opened a perilous avenue of speculation I would sooner not travel. That enmity existed between father and son was evident, and I chose, with my usual lack of courage, not to pursue the cause.

In an attempt to distract Mark from his thoughts, I said brightly, "I learned today that Sally Monroe is expecting. I'm so happy for her. She has wanted more children for years."

Mark turned from the window, and in the dim light of the fast-gathering dusk his eyes seemed a cryptic black glow. "Really?" he said. "When is the child due?"

"In December," I told him, and wondered why he watched me so deliberately as if seeking a hidden meaning behind my words. Unnerved by his strange gaze, I gabbled stupidly, "She hasn't told her husband. I can't imagine why. It's not as if he doesn't want more children. Of course, she'll have to tell him eventually. Her condition is not one that can be concealed indefinitely."

I trailed off in a horror of embarrassment. Why had I said that? I never gossiped. I never divulged information entrusted to me in confidence. Why had I done so now? And why was Mark looking at me as if he waited for me, expected me, to say more?

At length he turned away, back toward the street. He appeared deep in thought, as though he had forgotten I was there. Attuned to his mood, compliant with his frame of mind, I neither spoke nor stirred for the remainder of our journey.

When we arrived at the Chandler house, John and Constance greeted us at the door, and Constance said mysteriously, "We've planned a surprise for you, Mark, but unfortunately we must wait until after dinner to present it."

"A surprise?" Mark laughed. "I think, Constance, that I have outgrown surprises."

"Not this one," John assured him as the butler took my wrap.

"Joanna," said Constance, "how lovely you look, as always. Come upstairs with me, my dear. I haven't said good night to Deirdre, and I know she'll want to see you."

We left the gentlemen to enjoy their aperitif, and went upstairs to the nursery. As it happened, the child was already asleep, but before we went down again I asked Constance about Mark's surprise.

"Oh, I know he'll be delighted," she said cheerily. "We've invited an old friend, Spencer Halston, who's been out of the country for years. He and Mark are the dearest friends; in fact, he's Alan's godfather. Hasn't Mark ever mentioned him?" And when I shook my head, she went on. "Spencer arrived in New York only this morning. John was at the pier when his ship docked, he was meeting Freddy Brentwood— You know Freddy, don't you, Joanna? Well, that's when John spotted Spencer, and he asked him to dinner at once, knowing how pleased Mark would be to see him. Spencer declined dinner but told John he would stop by later in the evening, which is just as well, I suppose, for otherwise I'd have had to produce a young lady on indecently short notice, and Spencer is so frightfully particular about his dinner partners. Actually," Constance added as we started down the stairs, "it's to be a double surprise. John didn't mention to Spencer that Mark would be here tonight. Can you imagine the looks on their faces when they see each other?"

I smiled and said nothing. It struck me as rather peculiar that Mark had not mentioned the existence of such a dear friend. Mark had made it a point in the past several months to acquaint me with all of his friends, and we would spend long evenings together, either at his house or mine, while he discussed the many people he knew and explained in detail which aspect of his life they shared. I knew he was preparing me, in a tactfully oblique manner, to become a fitting and knowledgeable mistress of the Van Holden household. Mark's social life was extremely diverse: He entertained journalists and pugilists, actors and statesmen, clergymen and kings, and his guest lists were drawn up with care and precision. One did not, for example, invite Jay Gould to the same fete as Knights of Labor leader Powderly, nor did one seat the feuding Clay Frick and Andrew Carnegie within arm's length of each other. I was apprised of all friendships and all hatreds within Mark's circle. I learned, almost by rote, the likes and dislikes, the foibles and eccentricities of every member of his set. He did not, however, speak of his wife. And not once, I thought now as Constance and I joined the gentlemen for dinner, had he ever mentioned the name of Spencer Halston.

The meal was a feast! We began with cold vichyssoise followed by lamb exquisitely seasoned and glazed with *sauce menthe*, complemented deliciously by creamed asparagus and potato croquettes, scallops in aspic and rice amandine, and for dessert we had cherries jubilee so saturated with brandy that when Constance and I left the gentlemen to their port I could barely walk properly from the room.

In the drawing room I sank into a chair and applied my fan vigorously in a vain attempt to clear my head. I felt numb, besotted, and it took all of my willpower not to curl up in a ball, put my head in my arms, and drift peacefully off to sleep. Dimly I heard Constance's voice like the low drone of bees on a summer day, and then I heard nothing, felt nothing, till a light touch on my arm startled me into awareness and I looked up, chagrined, into Mark's lazy, laughing eyes.

"Joanna," he said gravely while those dark-lashed eyes danced with amusement. "Your coffee." He indicated a cup on the table by my side, then left me to pick up his own cup which he'd apparently left on the mantel.

I glanced sheepishly about the room. The Chandlers were nowhere in sight, and noting my bewilderment, Mark said casually, "I believe my 'surprise' has arrived. Constance and John took off like a shot when the doorbell sounded. I'm curious," he admitted, smiling, "to learn which ghost they have unearthed from my past. John would give no clue as to his identity. Did Constance, by any chance, tell you who it is?"

I was about to reply, but before I could, the Chandlers returned accompanied by a light-haired gentleman whose fair, boyish face froze in mid-smile as Mark turned, cup in hand, toward the door.

No one spoke, no one said a word. The gentleman stared intently at Mark while the Chandlers looked quizzically at each other. The room rang with an ominous silence. Spencer Halston's face, finely featured, very fair, grew pale. I looked at Mark. His expression was blank, his slender figure, tall and still, seemed carved of stone. I rose from my chair, drawn to Mark by a sudden protective instinct I could not explain. My movement seemed to break the spell; Mark turned, put down his cup, took my arm in a hurting grip and escorted me, without a word, from the room.

"Mark!" Constance's pursuing footsteps echoed loudly in the hall. "Mark, where are you going?"

He said nothing. His hand on my arm tightened painfully, and even when I cried out softly he did not let me go.

"Mark," Constance implored. "What is it? Why are you leaving?"

"Mark, for God's sake!" John had appeared, following closely on his wife's heels. "What the devil do you think you're doing?"

"Don't ever," Mark uttered, swinging round to face him, "don't ever—" He broke off, breathless with an emotion so fierce, so patently violent that my own breath caught fearfully in my throat. His face had gone ashen, his hand bruised my flesh. He dragged me to the door, swung it open, then closed it behind us with a great resounding crash.

"Mark," I said, trembling, "what is it? Who is that man? Why did you—?"

Ignoring my questions, he handed me into the waiting carriage, then sat stiffly upright as the horses took off with a jolt.

I was too frightened to speak. There emanated from Mark an almost tangible current of murderous rage. He was trembling. I could see, could feel, the tremors that shook him. Timidly, I put a hand on his, then started in alarm as he turned his hot, brutal, dark eyes on mine. He stared at me fiercely for a moment, an eternity. My heart pounded; I was more afraid than I had ever been in my life, but still I held on to his quivering hand.

I shall never know what calmed him. I shall never know why, with a slow and gentle movement, he took me in his arms and held me to his heart till his terrible tremors lessened and ceased. My brain, drenched in brandy, soaked with fear, refused to function. I lay against him like some limp rag doll, and all I could think as he held me in his arms was how long it had been since he'd touched me, how unbearably, infinitely long.

When the carriage drew up in front of my house, he did not release me. I could feel his heart beating against my cheek, I could smell the starch in his shirt and the faint aroma of Pear's soap on his skin. The night was cool; we had torn out of the house without my wrap, but I felt warm, warm as toast, in the strong supportive circle of Mark's embrace. I was drowsily content where only a moment before I had shuddered with fear. A soft sigh escaped my lips; I felt Mark stir. He drew back slightly, lifted my face, and rested his dark gaze on mine. I watched him quietly, his curling hair, his silky smooth brow, the fathomless depths of his midnight-dark eyes.

"Joanna." His voice was low as his sweet breath brushed my face.

"Yes?" I whispered. "Yes?"

"Did you know he would be there tonight?"

"What?" I said faintly.

"Did you know Spencer Halston would be at the Chandlers'? Had you met him previously? Had you talked with him?"

"No." I shook my head, as much to rid myself of the sensuous stupor I had been in as to respond to Mark's questions. "Constance first mentioned him to me just before dinner. I've never met him."

He held me a moment longer, his eyes searching mine. A multitude of thoughts crossed his face, and it seemed at one point he would speak. But he released me and said nothing.

"Who is he?" I asked.

"He was a friend."

"Was?" I pursued. "But Constance told me he's Alan's godfather, isn't he? She said you were the best of friends."

"That's right, we were."

"But . . ." I paused uncertainly, alerted by his tone and by an unmistakable warning in his eyes. He did not wish to speak of it, that much was evident. But why?

"Did you quarrel then?" I finished lamely, and realized at once the absurdity of the question. Of course they had quarreled. Any idiot might have guessed that. But incredibly, Mark said, "No, Joanna, we did not quarrel."

And on that baffling note, he handed me down from the carriage, escorted me to my door, and quietly bade me good night.

Much later that night, as I lay in bed unable to sleep, recreating in my mind the disturbing events at the Chandler house, my thoughts kept wandering to the carriage ride home, to Mark's arms around me, my cheek against his heart, the feel of his body, lean and strong, close to mine. It was not in my nature to dwell on such things, and yet it occurred to me that I had thought of little else since the first time Mark had kissed me. I thought always of his kiss and of the feelings he had aroused in me; I thought constantly, obsessively, of the touch of his body pressed full length against my own. Even now, when I should have been wondering at Mark's shocking reaction upon seeing Spencer Halston, all I could think of was the way Mark had held me, the wonderful warmth of him, the touch of his hands, the fragrance of his skin, and the hard seductive curve of his sensuous mouth.

IX

I SHOULD HAVE let matters lie, but I didn't. Several days later, driven by an impulse I could not control, I called on Constance Chandler. As fate would have it, Constance was entertaining another guest that day, and as the Chandler butler showed me into the morning room without first announcing me, I found myself face to face with the last man on earth I expected to see.

I saw at once that he recognized me; he rose to his feet with an exclamation of surprise, then looked questioningly to Constance, who said rather sharply, "Don't be a fool, Spencer. I did not invite her. Joanna, what are you doing here?"

My nerves tightened, my hands clenched. Coldly I answered, "I've come for my wrap."

Had it been a conspiracy, then? Had Constance purposely invited Spencer Halston that evening knowing in advance how Mark would react? But why would she want to do that? John and Mark were not only business associates, they were to my knowledge the dearest of friends. But then again, Constance had said Spencer Halston, too, was a "dear friend."

"I'm disappointed in you, Constance," I burst out. "I thought you were Mark's friend."

"You're disappointed in *me?*" she bristled. "I cannot begin to tell you how shocked and affronted I am by Mark's inexcusable behavior. How dare he leave my house like that? How dare he insult my husband and me in that manner?"

"Constance!" Mr. Halston's peremptory voice silenced

us both. "Sit down," he said sternly, and then turning to me: "Mrs. Sinclair, please be seated. I should like to explain, if I may, the reason for that unfortunate misunderstanding the other evening."

I subsided warily, as did Constance. I was not ready to trust this man whose mere presence had roused such passionate rage in Mark. Who was he, and what had he done to Mark? I was certain he had hurt him, hurt him badly, and for that reason alone, I disliked him.

"I was about to explain to Constance," he began, "that before I went abroad, Mark and I had a quarrel."

"A quarrel?" I said suspiciously. Mark had told me there was no quarrel. From the outset, this man was lying.

"Yes, Mrs. Sinclair, a rather bitter quarrel, the details of which I prefer not to discuss. Suffice it to say that the nature and intensity of our disagreement has irreparably damaged our friendship. The Chandlers were not aware of the quarrel; no one was. Hence their plan for a happy reunion which, regrettably, turned out to be quite the opposite. I couldn't have been more shocked to see Mark, and I daresay he felt the same. My behavior that evening proved little better than his; I too left immediately without an explanation, and I came here today to offer my apologies." He turned to Constance and nodded, then turned back to me. "And I apologize to you also, Mrs. Sinclair, for being the cause of your distress."

I didn't believe him. He was smoothly deferential, contrite and sincere, but I didn't believe him. Despite his facile tongue and a practiced charm, there was something slighting jarring about him; even his appearance disturbed me. His attire was fashionable and of the finest cloth, yet there was a vaguely disreputable look about him, as if he were not quite a gentleman. He was undeniably attractive with his cheerful blue eyes and his boyish, fair face, but it was the sort of attractiveness which would fade at an early age, for already his jawline was losing its distinctness and his eyes were faintly traced with red and smudged with the telltale shadows of excess and self-indulgence.

"Spencer, what nonsense!" said Constance crossly. "You

must make up your quarrel at once. Why, you and Mark were closer than brothers, and besides, you are godfather to his son."

"Yes," he said pensively. "I regret that part of it. I love Alan as though he were my own, but I doubt I shall ever see him again. No, Constance, there's no making up this quarrel. We're finished, Mark and I."

"Finished, my foot! Spencer, you cannot end a lifetime of friendship because of a silly disagreement. Why, if that were the case, no one in the world would have a friend left to call his own. Let me speak to Mark. Let me arrange—"

"No!" The word rang out like a pistol shot. "Don't speak to him." He looked suddenly embarrassed. He lowered his voice almost to a whisper. "Don't interfere, Constance, I implore you. We cannot be reconciled. We can never be friends again."

I stared at him openly, stunned by his distress which seemed as deep as it seemed genuine. He slumped into a chair and gazed morosely at the floor.

"I am totally at fault," he admitted, and I was stunned afresh by a candor I had little expected. "Mark is blameless; he is the wronged party. You see, Constance, it was more than a quarrel that separated us, and if you speak to him, you will only exhume ugly memories which are best left at rest."

"Spencer," she said, "surely you exaggerate."

He raised his head and smiled, a thin, sad smile, and said tiredly, "On the contrary, my dear. If anything, I've deliberately minimized the gravity of the situation. This is not a simple spat we're talking about. I've hurt Mark badly."

So I'd been right then, he *had* hurt Mark. And he had at last confirmed that a quarrel was not the cause of their rift.

He turned to me then and smiled that weary, sad smile. "Mrs. Sinclair, you've been very silent. I daresay you think me a scoundrel."

I didn't know what to think. I had disliked and distrusted him almost on sight, yet now my feelings were disturbingly unsettled.

"Mr. Halston," I ventured, "we've only just met. I've hardly had a chance to form an opinion of you."

"My dear lady," he said, his smile brightening, "what commendable tact."

"Not tact," I said softly, "merely truth." Self-consiously, I rose. "Constance, I must be going. I—I'm sorry about what I said to you earlier."

"Oh, my dear!" She rose from her own chair and embraced me warmly. "A misunderstanding, Joanna. A horrid misunderstanding. Come to dinner next week. Speak to Mark. I'm sure he thinks John and I are angry. Tell him—"

"May I suggest," Mr. Halston broke in quietly, "that you tell him nothing." He regarded us both from his chair, shoulders hunched tensely. "It might be better for all concerned," he added, directing his attention specifically to me, "if Mark never learns that we've talked."

I could feel myself pale, and my first thought was: *I want no part of deception and lies; I shall tell Mark the instant I see him.* But I never did. I simply couldn't. Years later, I would wish that I had.

Alan returned from Saratoga in late August, and several weeks later he departed for New Haven. I did not see him while he was home; Mark was extremely busy, and furthermore, I had told him I was involved in some charity work which left me too fatigued by the end of the day for socializing. He accepted my excuse without question. I think he knew I was lying; I think he knew I was not yet ready to face Alan, but he did not pursue it. In December, however, when Alan returned home for the holidays, my period of grace came to an end.

On Christmas Eve, Mark called for me at seven, and as we waited for Alan to join us in the family room before dinner, he said, "I told my son this morning that we're to be married."

He handed me a glass of sherry, then walked with his own to the fireplace. He seemed uneasy, disquieted. I guessed that the news had not been well received.

"What did he say?" I asked and clenched my glass so tightly that I feared it would shatter in my hand.

For a moment Mark was silent; it appeared he was uncertain of a reply. At length he said simply, "He wished us well."

He finished his wine, then went to the side table, where a crystal decanter gleamed brilliantly on a silver tray. His uneasiness was contagious; my hand on my glass was trembling. I set the sherry aside and rose nervously. "Mark, if there is a problem . . ."

"There is no problem," he said at once. "Alan was surprised, that's all, and I think . . ." He paused and looked up from his empty glass. "I think I will have more wine."

"Mark," I braved, "that's not what you were going to say. What do you think? About Alan, I mean." And when he didn't answer but only busied himself with refilling his glass, I dared further. "If he is against the idea, perhaps we shouldn't marry."

Mark raised his head. His eyes, dark and direct, met mine. "We will marry, Joanna. Unless you yourself wish otherwise.'

"Then he *does* object," I persisted.

"I did not say that."

"Mark, please be truthful with me. If Alan—"

"Mrs. Sinclair, good evening."

I turned toward the door. Alan had entered the room without my notice, and as I stared wordlessly at his perfect face he came toward me, his mouth curving into a delighted smile. He looked older, harder, but indescribably beautiful. His hair shone like spun gold, his eyes a silvery light beneath the gilt fan of his lashes. "How long it's been since I've seen you! Has my father been keeping you away from me? Not that I'd blame him; if you were mine I wouldn't want to share you either!"

"Alan!" The tone of Mark's voice startled the boy as much as it did me. "Fetch Mrs. Sinclair's sherry, if you please." He had lowered his voice but his dark face clearly reflected his displeasure. Obviously he had interpreted an insinuation behind his son's remark.

"Here's your wine, Mrs. Sinclair. I'm sorry I can't join

you, but as I told you before, I am a teetotaler . . . for another four years, at any rate. My father feels that at the age of twenty-one a boy becomes officially a man and may then indulge himself without limit in those areas earlier restricted to him."

"Alan," said Mark, "that's enough."

"Forgive me, Father, but it's not nearly enough. I am merely attempting to acquaint Mrs. Sinclair with your unique and somewhat unorthodox moral standards. As your wife, she has a right—"

"I shall acquaint Mrs. Sinclair with my standards, moral and otherwise. You, Alan, should reacquaint yourself with the basic standards of gentlemanly behavior."

The boy was humiliated. He glared at his father, his beautiful, sensitive face contorted with rage. I held my breath, fearing a scene. If they quarreled, I would die. "Mark, please," I implored. "I'm sure Alan only meant—"

"Excuse me, Joanna, but I know all too well what my son meant." He took the glass from my hand and set it down angrily on the tray. "Shall we go in to dinner? Alan, you may join us provided you keep in mind that this is your home and not a campus barroom. However, if you find it too difficult to comply with my wishes, I suggest you dine alone in your room."

Again I held my breath as Alan's eyes narrowed and his hands at his sides closed slowly into fists. I glanced swiftly at Mark: The look on his face chilled me.

"Alan," I said faintly, "will you escort me to the table?"

I left Mark's side and took Alan's arm, never realizing the implication of my action nor the impact it might have upon Mark. At the moment I was concerned only with Alan, the innocent and defenseless child. Alan needed my protection; Mark did not. Mark was a successful man; he needed nothing, least of all from me. "Please, Alan," I whispered, "take me in to dinner."

My hand tightened on his arm. He looked down at me at last, his young face struggling for control. He looked such a child now and yet not a child, for he towered over me and his arm under my hand was as hard and sinewy as a man's. *How beautiful he is,* I thought numbly. *How beautiful and clean and untouched.*

In my absorption I was unaware that his expression had changed. He returned my gaze with a sudden rapt intensity; his hand, warm and hard, covered mine. He watched me a moment longer, a message in his eyes I could not decipher. Then he raised his head, looked past me to his father, and gave him a victorious smile. It did not occur to me until much later the momentous significance of that smile.

Dinner was a nightmare. Alan teased and flattered me as though I were a young girl, while Mark, on the other hand, spoke not a word. Throughout the meal I glanced anxiously at his dark face; he never once raised his eyes though I knew without doubt he was aware of my scrutiny. In the drawing room over coffee it was the same: Alan complimented my gown, my coiffure, the diamond necklace that glittered about my throat, but Mark said nothing at all. And when I handed him his cup it seemed he took special care that our eyes should not meet and that his long slender fingers should not brush mine.

I was white with mortification. Why did he treat me this way? Why was he angry? Why had he proposed marriage when he went out of his way to avoid touching me? Why, indeed, had I consented to his proposal when he embodied all in a man which I thoroughly despised? He was a known seducer, totally without principle in both his social and professional life. He deceived, manipulated, exploited, and cheated, and that which he could not extort he simply stole outright. That I had even considered marriage with him was insanity of the first order. What had I been thinking? What had I expected to gain by becoming Mark Van Holden's wife?

When the clock struck eleven I rose like a shot from my chair. "It's late," I said curtly. "I should like to go home."

"But, Mrs. Sinclair," protested Alan, "won't you stay until midnight? I've bought you a present. . . ." He took a small box from his coat and pressed it into my hands, much in the manner of a small boy. "Open it now," he said, his sad tone echoing the disappointment in his eyes. "Please," he urged when he saw my reluctance. "It's a tradition. We . . . my mother always opened my gift at midnight."

I looked toward Mark; he had rung for our coats and was now watching me in silence. His gaze told me nothing. My own, I feared, spoke volumes.

"Please, Mrs. Sinclair." Alan's voice demanded my attention. I turned away from Mark and rested my uncertain gaze on the face of his son.

The boy was a chameleon. Gone was the insolence, the sullen defiance with which he had confronted his father. Gone was the hard look of maturity I had glimpsed earlier in his eyes. He was a child again, his mother's child, and it was Christmas Eve and he had chosen to cast me in the role which his mother before me had so lovingly and so indulgently performed.

I was deeply moved. I lowered my gaze lest he see the emotion in my eyes, and tore open the wrapping on the gift. The box was of blue leather and embossed with the name "Tiffany & Co." I raised the cover with a sudden and unwarranted foreboding. Inside, nestled on white silk, was a tiny gold heart suspended on the most delicate of gold chains. I lifted it from the box and saw, on close inspection, the initials J.S. minutely engraved on the heart. J.S. Joanna Sinclair. It was as if Alan himself had engraved the name indelibly so that it would ever remain the same.

"Thank you, Alan," I murmured. "It's a lovely gift and I shall treasure it always."

"Do you really like it?" he said eagerly. "It's ever more suitable than diamonds, don't you think? What I mean to say, Mrs. Sinclair, is that despite the attractiveness of your necklace, you're far too young to wear diamonds. Would you like to try it on? Shall I help you with the clasp?"

I looked helplessly toward Mark, whose attention had turned to the servant who had entered the room with our coats.

"I shall wear it tomorrow, Alan," I promised, then hastily made for the door. "Mark, isn't it lovely?" I said, presenting the heart for his inspection.

"Yes, it is," he agreed solemnly. "Are you ready, Joanna?"

He held my coat and—was I imagining it?—as he slipped it about my shoulders his hands lingered on my arms.

"Good night, son," he said, pulling on his own coat.

"Good night, Alan," I murmured. "Thank you again."

The boy merely nodded and turned glumly away. He was hurt, I could see it. He felt shut out, abandoned, feelings to which I myself was not a stranger. So many nights when I was a girl I had watched my mother leave the house on the arm of her newest suitor; so many nights I had been left on my own, a sad, lonely child in a sad, lonely house. How well I knew what Alan was feeling now, and I felt compelled, driven, to ease that feeling. I took a step toward him, but in the next instant Mark's hand closed firmly on my arm. "Come along, Joanna. The carriage is waiting." And before I could offer a protest, he escorted me briskly from the room.

In the carriage he was silent and I, plagued with a dozen conflicting thoughts, did not speak either. Now was the time I should tell him. Now, before I became too deeply entangled, was the appropriate moment for escape. I couldn't marry him, I simply could not. I had neither the courage nor the maturity to be his wife, let alone be mother to his son. As fond as I was of Alan I was not equal to the task of keeping his hostility in check, and obviously that was to be my function. Mark had told me almost straight out that his proposal of marriage was a direct result of Alan's affection for me; therefore it appeared that my chief service as Mark's wife would be simply to supervise his son. But I wanted none of it. I'd had one loveless marriage, I would not have another.

"Mark," I said faintly, "I want to tell you something."

He turned from the window, but as soon as his eyes met mine I looked away, unwilling, unable, to go on.

"Yes, Joanna?" His voice was calm, unperturbed. It appeared he had not guessed my thoughts, and that was odd because Mark always seemed to know what I was thinking.

"Mark," I tried again, "about our marriage . . ."

"Yes?"

"Don't you think we should . . . ?"

Once more I stopped, silenced by my cowardice and by the disturbingly dispassionate tone of Mark's voice. I stared out the window, struggling in vain for the transient courage which eluded me always when I needed it most.

"What I think," Mark said presently, "is that we should marry soon. After the first of the year, if you have no objection."

"But . . ." I turned from the window, helpless, confused. Why had he said that now, tonight? He had never before expressed the desire for a hasty wedding. It had only been months since his proposal, and in truth we were little more than strangers to one another, and I had thought . . . What exactly *had* I thought? I couldn't remember now.

"So soon?" I stammered at last.

"Yes, Joanna. I've waited long enough."

"Waited? Waited for what?"

"I have wanted you," he said easily, "from the first night we met. But I knew, after we talked, that marriage was the only means by which I would ever have you. And then your husband died, which seemed . . . providential. Forgive me, Joanna, but I think it important that you know the truth. When I called on you after the funeral it was plain that you still grieved, and my first thought was to let the matter rest until you had come to terms with your loss. I had not intended to ask to see you again so soon. I shouldn't have invited you to dinner when I did; as it turned out, you were not ready to accept me on any terms, be it friend, lover, or suitor. At any rate I felt it best after that night to give you a year. A year on your own, a year to adjust without undue pressure from me, a year, Joanna, added to the six months I've been seeing you, which is more than enough time for any man to wait for the woman he wants."

I stared at him in stupefied silence. Needless to say, whatever comment I might have made would only have proved superfluous in the wake of so astonishing a revelation. He wanted me. Mark Van Holden wanted *me*. Was I dreaming? Was he joking? Not once had he mentioned his son. At no time had he said, "It's for Alan's sake. It's the boy who needs you, who wants you." No, he had said, *"I want you,"* and *"I* have waited long enough." Waited. But a man does not "wait" for a woman unless . . .

"Mark," I whispered and swayed toward him, and as I did so his arms went round me and his mouth closed on mine, and every qualm, each vague doubt about marrying this man was dispelled by his kiss and by the warmth of his tender embrace. His arms held me close, as if he feared I might resist him, but resistance, at the moment, could not have been further from my mind. He had never thus wooed me, as lover woos lover; he had never breathed my name, against my lips, against my throat. And when he moved aside my coat and bent his head to my breast, it seemed natural and right that I should kiss the dark curls that lay tumbled and fragrant on the curve of his warm silken brow.

I should have been shocked by such ardor, both on his part and mine, but in truth I felt nothing but the most exquisite pleasure. His kiss, his very touch, had benumbed sense and logic; only passion remained, a slow heady passion, as he lifted his head, held my gaze for a moment, then covered my waiting mouth again with the sensuous persuasion of his.

X

SALLY MONROE'S BABY, due in December, was born the last day of the month. It was a son, her first son, and Stephen was ecstatic. When I called on her several days after the happy event she was still in bed, thin and wan and uncharacteristically quiescent. She lay against the pillows, plucking idly at the blanket, and when I offered my felicitations she only said listlessly, "I want no more children. This one is my last."

She was very pale. Stephen had told me earlier that the birth had not been an easy one, and for that reason I paid no mind to her apathetic remark. Sally loved children. She had told me often that she wanted six at the very least, but it had always been difficult for her to conceive. Caroline, her oldest, had been born two years after the marriage, and Mary five years after that. Another nine years had gone by until her latest pregnancy, an event I had thought would please her far more than it apparently had.

"Don't talk nonsense, Sally," I said brusquely. "You're just tired, worn out from the birth. As soon as you're up and about you'll forget this experience, and six months from now you'll be wondering frantically why you haven't conceived again."

"No," she said dully. "I won't."

Puzzled by her despondency but not dismayed, I tried another tack. "Sally, have you decided on a name? Will it be Stephen Junior?"

"Yes, I suppose so."

"Stephen is a good name, a strong name for a man."

"Yes."

91

"He's a beautiful baby. I can't decide whether he favors you or Stephen. His eyes are so dark, but he has your chin and the shape of your mouth."

"Has he?"

"Of course, babies change almost daily, and being that he's a boy he's bound to resemble Stephen when he grows older. And yet . . ." I paused, suddenly thinking of Alan. He was all his mother; no son had ever resembled his father less.

"And yet what, Joanna?" Sally sat up with difficulty. Her apathy had vanished and in its place was the most avidly attentive interest. "What were you going to say about family resemblances?"

"Oh, it's nothing," I said vaguely. "Mark's son . . ."

Sally's eyes widened, her face grew even paler. "Mark's son?"

"He looks," I explained, "the very picture of his mother. It's strange. . . ."

"What do you mean, Joanna?" Her voice had risen sharply, and she clutched the blanket with trembling hands. "What are you trying to say?"

"Sally, what's wrong?" I rose anxiously as I noted her peculiar agitation. "Are you in pain? Shall I ring for—?"

"No!" she cried. "I am not in pain. Nothing is wrong. Tell me what you mean. Why do you call him Mark's son?"

"What are you talking about? Sally, calm yourself. No, please, don't get up. Sally, don't!"

She swung her legs painfully over the side of the bed and was attempting, against my frantic restraint, to rise. "Please," I begged, "you mustn't get up."

She writhed like a wild thing in my hold, and as weak as she was it took all of my strength to subdue her. We grappled briefly, but when finally she realized her struggle was useless she fell back against the pillows. Panting for breath, she uttered fiercely, "He is not Mark's son!"

"What?" I said, shaking. "Sally, what's come over you? Of course he's Mark's son. I know they're not on the best of terms, but Alan is young, confused. He blames Mark for—" I broke off with a short strangled sound. What had she said? Not Mark's son? I sank into a chair while the enormity of her words sank like a stone to the innermost chamber of my soul.

Alan Van Holden was not Mark's son.

Why hadn't I guessed it? Apart from the obvious, why hadn't I seen that no natural son could possibly detest his father as Alan did Mark? Oh dear God, did Alan know? Yes, of course he knew. Why else did he hate Mark so? And Mark? But Mark loved Alan, cherished him. Why? Because he was Lenore's child? Lenore. The lovely, the perfect, the adulterous Lenore.

"How do you know?" I asked hoarsely. "Who told you, Sally? Who told you such a ghastly thing?"

She looked suddenly ill, wretchedly, dreadfully ill. And older than her years. She swallowed convulsively; beads of perspiration dotted her brow. I thought for a moment she might faint, but at length she said, "You misunderstand me, Joanna."

"No," I contradicted, my voice a harsh whisper. "I understand you perfectly, Sally, for the first time since I've known you. You know about Mark and me, don't you? You know I'm going to marry him, and for some twisted reason you thought to prevent it by—"

"Marry?" she choked as a new sickly color splotched hotly in her cheeks. "You're going to marry Mark? You fool, you can't marry him!"

"Why?" I cried. "Because of Alan? I don't care about that. It's not Mark's fault. He is blameless; *he* is the wronged party."

I stopped, my words ringing loudly in my ears. But they were not my words, I had heard them before.

"Joanna," said Sally, her eyes frigid blue, "you cannot marry Mark Van Holden. He is a lecher, a debaucher. He filthies everything he touches. He will drag you down to his own sordid level, and when he's had his fill he will toss you aside like the trash he has made of you."

"Be quiet!" I shouted and leaped to my feet. "How dare you say such things, you who with a cruel tongue have branded his son a bastard? *You* have dragged me down to *your* sordid level by revealing a truth I would sooner not know. How many other people have you told? No, don't bother answering. I'll wager the whole of New York is privy to your vicious tale.

"Shut up!" I cried when she opened her mouth to speak. "Don't say another word or I shall strike you, I swear it!"

She lay corpse-still on the bed. Her eyes, wide with fear, implored mine. She was terrified and I knew it and I was glad. She deserved to be terrified, she deserved a sound thrashing.

I do not recall leaving the room, nor do I recall leaving the house nor the carriage ride home nor climbing the stairs to my room. I remember later lying on my bed fully clothed, feeling cold, perhaps because the fire was low and not as effective as it should be. I had escaped the turmoil of my thoughts in a fitful doze, and when I awoke I felt disoriented, confused.

What was I doing lying on my bed in the middle of the day when I had so much to do? I got up and went to the long mirror to smooth my dress and to rearrange my disheveled hair. How very pale I looked, and how hard the dark glimmer of my eyes. I studied my reflection with a curious detachment. I had changed in the past year, changed drastically. It was more than my new wardrobe or the modish style of my hair. I was older, wiser, and this wisdom manifested itself in the very contours of my face. It was a woman's face now, an attractive face, and my figure was slim yet newly provocative in a subtle and appealing way. Is that why Mark wanted me? He *had* said "want," he had not said he loved me, he had only said "want."

How ironic, I thought with a grim, inward smile, that Mark should desire me as men had always desired my mother. I should have been insulted, outraged, but instead I was bitterly pleased. I wanted to be wanted in that way; I think I had always wanted it.

"Mrs. Sinclair. Mrs. Sinclair."

A tap on the door and Myrna's urgent voice interrupted my thoughts. I unlocked the door—had I locked it?—and let her in.

"Mrs. Sinclair, are you all right? I've been knocking all afternoon; I thought you might be asleep, but when six o'clock came and still you didn't answer—"

"Six o'clock?" I said and looked vaguely about me. The curtains were drawn and the fire was the only light in the room. Night had fallen without my noticing. How long had I been lying down? "What time is it, Myrna?"

"It's half past seven, madam. Mr. Van Holden is waiting downstairs."

"Mr. Van Holden? He's here?"

"Yes, Mrs. Sinclair. You told me this morning he was taking you to the theater. Have you forgotten?"

She was watching me anxiously; no doubt she was alarmed by my behavior. I felt dazed, unsettled, and my fumbling, mindless comments must have shown it.

"Myrna," I said, "tell Mr. Van Holden . . ."

I stopped and turned dizzily away. Tell him what? What message could I send him? Forgive me, Mark, but I can't go to the theater tonight. You see, I just learned that Alan is not your son and I—

"Oh, God," I moaned softly.

"Mrs. Sinclair!"

I felt Myrna's hand on my arm. I think I would have fallen if she hadn't touched me at that moment.

"Mrs. Sinclair, what is it? Are you ill? Shall I send for Dr. Shelley?"

"No!" I said sharply. And then, softer: "No, Myrna. I'm not ill. I'm still groggy, I think, from my nap." I gave her hand a reassuring squeeze and turned her gently toward the door. "Tell Mr. Van Holden I'll be down directly."

"But, madam, you'll be hours dressing."

"No," I said. "It's too late now for the theater. I'm just going to freshen up and change my dress. Show Mr. Van Holden into the library and ask Blandford to bring him some whiskey."

She left reluctantly, her young face furrowed with worry. I washed and changed rapidly, choosing a gown of willow green wool which buttoned from waist to throat. By the time Myrna returned I was already dressed and she had only to smooth my tumbled hair.

"Are you sure you're all right?" she asked anxiously as I started for the door. "Mrs. Sinclair, you've no color at all. Please let me call Dr. Shelley."

"No, Myrna," I said with a faint, grateful smile. "I'm fine, really I am." But as I descended the stairs to meet Mark I felt less fine than ever I had in my life.

He rose when I entered the room, and I saw at once that Myrna had confided her fears to him. His eyes were dark with concern; he took my hands in his and regarded me closely with an intensity I found both comforting and alarming. "What's happened?" he asked, and again I marveled at his amazing powers of perception. He knew I wasn't ill; he knew at a glance that the origin of my distress was other than physical.

I stared at him numbly from a maelstrom of emotion, my gaze imprisoned by those relentless dark eyes, and I was suddenly filled with so deep a compassion that I knew if I spoke I would weep. How he must have suffered. What a cruel burden of humiliation he had borne all these years.

"Mark," I said at last and leaned toward him, disengaging my hands so that I could reach up to embrace him. I held him tightly, protectively, as if my arms alone could shut out his pain. "Oh, Mark," I whispered passionately, "it doesn't matter. It really doesn't matter."

"Joanna, for God's sake!" He held me away from him, his hands pressing into my arms. "What's happened? Why are you like this?"

"I don't care, Mark, truly I don't. It's in the past, it's over with. It has nothing to do with us. You needn't be ashamed. I understand. I understand so much now. And I promise you I'll never speak of it again, but I want you to know—"

"Joanna, what the devil are you talking about?"

"Mark," I said weakly, "I know about . . . your son."

"My son?" His hands came away from my arms and he stepped back, frowning in bewilderment.

"Today I learned . . ." My voice was hoarse, shaking; I cleared my throat and clutched nervously at a fold of my skirt. "Today Sally told me about your son."

"What?" he said incredulously. "She told you what?"

"I don't care, Mark!" I cried. "It doesn't matter, I swear it."

I reached out for him again, wanting to assure him that

in no way did I hold him responsible for his wife's despicable treachery. But he drew back from my touch, his eyes, black with rage, scorched mine. "Why?" he demanded. "Why did she tell you?"

"She . . . she didn't want us to marry. She thought if she told me—"

"Christ!" he said fiercely.

"Mark, I swear I don't care about the past."

"By God, I'll kill her!"

"Oh, please don't say that! I shouldn't have told you. I shouldn't have said anything, but I wanted you to know that I don't blame you. . . ."

I was trembling now, and Mark saw it. I watched helplessly, fearfully, as he came toward me slowly. When he took me in his arms he held me as closely, as protectively as a moment ago I'd held him. "Joanna," he said in a voice low and strained. "Joanna."

"Mark," I implored him, "promise me you won't do anything. I should never have told you. I'm sorry I told you, but I was so shocked when she . . ."

He drew back slightly and gave me a long, puzzled look. Were I not so consumed with my own turbulent thoughts I might have questioned that look of half-surprise, half-bewilderment, but I didn't. My only concern was that Mark should know my feelings. I didn't blame him; I could never blame him for such a thing. Lenore was at fault in this matter; she and only she was worthy of censure. My blood boiled at the thought of her duplicity. That she should so betray her husband enraged me, infuriated me.

"She is to blame," I blazed, "not you. You mustn't feel guilty, Mark. Only she is to blame."

Again that strange look of stunned surprise. It appeared he didn't quite know what to make of my reaction, and that too was strange. How else did he think I'd react? How in the world could I possibly blame him for a wrong in which he'd taken no part?

"Mark," I said and reached up hesitantly to touch his face, "let's not talk of it ever again. I know you're shocked; I know it must hurt you to even think of it. But it's better this way, don't you see? Now there are no secrets between us. That's as it should be. That's the way a marriage should be."

My boldness astonished me, and I could see that it astonished Mark even more, for at length he said doubtfully, "Joanna, are you sure you understand the situation? Perhaps we *should* talk about it."

"No," I insisted. "I will not talk of it. It's over and done with. It's a dead issue, Mark. Talking will not change what's happened."

He watched me for the longest time. How odd, I thought as I calmly returned his inquisitive gaze, that he should think me such a mystery when I had made my position unequivocally clear. My newfound courage had served me well. I felt proud that I had handled a potentially unpleasant situation with the wisdom and tact of a diplomat. I had grown up at last. The thought cheered me, encouraged me to new heights of audacity.

"Mark," I said abruptly, "shall we marry soon? You said after the New Year; I don't want to wait any longer. Can you arrange something right away? I don't care about a big wedding or a reception afterward. I want to marry you as soon as possible. Next week if we can. . . . Mark?"

He appeared not to have heard me. He turned away and moved toward the fireplace, his face partially concealed from my view. I wondered in a panic if I had hurt him by letting him know that I knew. I simply couldn't go through life with a secret so vile in my heart. And I think in a way I was glad that I no longer had to compete with the memory of his first wife. I didn't realize this at the time, however. I didn't realize that my uncharacteristic outspokenness and my urge to marry immediately stemmed simply from a monumental relief due to the sudden removal of the single major obstacle to future happiness, namely Lenore. But then again, there were many things I didn't realize on that night. How different my life might have been if I had.

XI

ON TUESDAY EVENING, January the tenth, I became Mark Van Holden's second wife. I would always think of myself as his second wife; his first was not easily forgotten. Lenore had been, after all, Alan's mother. Therefore her portrait still hung in the drawing room, the paintings and furnishings and art objects she had chosen stood unreplaced throughout the house. In a chill, ghostly way it was as if she herself still roamed the stately rooms. It was as if she had never died.

Mark chose not to have Alan present at our wedding, and I concurred wholeheartedly with his decision. Only John and Constance Chandler were in attendance at the ceremony as our witnesses. After a delightfully festive dinner at Delmonico's we deposited them at their house on Forty-eighth Street, and Mark and I were alone for the first time that day. As we rode to his house on Fifth Avenue, he turned and glanced out the window. "We're almost home."

Home. Our home, Mark's and mine. It was not until that moment that I realized we were married. At Delmonico's we had laughed and eaten and drunk champagne as we had done so many other evenings with the Chandlers or with other couples we knew and liked. But tonight was different. Tonight Mark would not escort me home, waiting on my doorstep till I was safely in the house. Tonight he would share my bed.

A thrill of alarm went through me as the carriage came to a halt. "Come," Mark said when I hung back like a child. "Come along, Joanna, we're home."

He handed me down from the carriage, and as he escorted me to the house, a hand at my elbow, I felt a tension in his touch, a barely suppressed emotion that was all the more intense for its suppression. My own emotions were in a turmoil; I was acutely aware of his hand on my arm, of the closeness of his body, of the look in his eyes when he turned to me at the door.

"Come," he said again, his low intense voice a hypnotic caress.

"Mark," I whispered, and without conscious knowledge, I leaned toward him pliantly.

His hold on me tightened; his dark gaze held mine. For a long breathless moment I stared at him, mesmerized. In his eyes I saw reflected what he had never before revealed to me. In his Medici eyes I saw an ages-old question, and in mine I knew the answer was most volubly evident.

We entered the house, which shone and blazed with light. All the servants had gathered in the hall to await us, and each one in turn wished us well. Kelsey, Mark's butler, had set out canapés and champagne in the family room, and as I warmed my hands before the fire, Mark neatly popped the cork and poured two glasses of wine, then handed me one as he raised his own in a toast.

"To you, darling," he said, and the endearment, the first he had ever addressed to me, drove home to me the fact that in an hour, or sooner, this man, my second husband, would be sharing my bed. He was watching me quietly, his midnight-dark eyes oddly lucent. His lashes cast shadows on the curve of his cheeks; his mouth, straight and sober, masked the passion I knew he restrained. In an hour, or sooner, I would know that passion firsthand. At the thought, my face grew hot and my hands, about my glass, began to tremble.

"Mark," I said, too brightly, too gaily, "you've never mentioned your family. Have you anyone?"

"Yes," he replied after sampling his wine. "I have a younger sister."

"A sister? But why have you never told me? Does she live in New York? I should like to meet her."

"I have never told you," he said, "because you have

never before expressed an interest in any family I might have. My sister does live in the city. She is married to a banker and has two daughters. But we are not on friendly terms; I haven't seen her for several years."

"Oh," I said stupidly, and was immediately sorry I had broached the subject.

"We quarreled," Mark explained, "one Christmas."

"Please," I said as I stared in embarrassment at my glass, "you needn't tell me about it. I did not mean to pry."

"Joanna," I heard him say, and I looked up quickly at the change in his tone, "you seem singularly uninterested in anything at all that concerns me."

"That's not true, Mark!"

"Oh, but it is."

He put down his glass and moved away, stopping near the sofa where a gilt-framed photograph stood in solitary splendor on a rosewood table inlaid with ivory and mother-of-pearl. The photo was one of Lenore holding her infant son. Alan was wearing a christening robe of white silk and lace, and Lenore was clad in a timelessly elegant gown of almost medieval design. She appeared a madonna, her face a perfect oval, her fair hair drawn back and coiled intricately at the nape of her neck. Mark looked at the photograph as if recalling happier times, and then he looked at me.

"I think," he said carefully, "that we should discuss what Sally told you."

His words caught me unawares. I stared at him in a panic; I couldn't talk of it, I didn't want to talk of it.

"If we don't," he went on, "there's a possibility you may attach to the matter an importance it does not merit."

"Please, Mark," I whispered. "I don't want to."

"Joanna . . ." He sighed impatiently, slipped his hands into his pockets. "Joanna, if you recall, you are the one who raised the issue."

"Yes, but I—"

"And in all fairness to both of us, an open discussion can only serve to put the facts in their proper perspective."

"Please," I said desperately, my face growing hot, "it

doesn't concern me. . . . . *us*. It's not that I'm uninterested, Mark, it's just . . ."

I groped frantically for words. Mark was angry, I could see it, angry because he thought I cared nothing about his life, about him. But I did care for him; I realized at that moment that I cared very deeply, and the last thing in the world I wanted was to hurt him by opening old wounds, by having him speak on a subject that could only cause him pain.

"Mark," I implored, "please forgive me but I simply cannot talk of it."

"Very well," he said, and when he turned away, purposely averting his face from my view, I knew I had displeased him.

What an inauspicious way to start a marriage! We'd been wed less than six hours and already we had disagreed. I cringed inwardly and put aside my untasted wine. Mark moved to the door. He opened it, turned to me, and said distantly, "Shall we retire?"

I followed him in wretched silence, lagging slowly behind as an agony of guilt overcame me. I had hurt him; in attempting to spare him pain, I had in fact hurt him.

We stopped at a door near the end of the hall. "This is your room," he told me. "I hope the decoration suits you. If it does not, let me know and I shall arrange to have it altered according to your wishes." He opened the door, stepped aside so that I could enter, and said coolly, "I'll join you shortly." And with that he was gone.

Hot tears sprang to my eyes, but I brushed them away as Myrna, who had been dozing in a chair, leaped up to greet me. "Mrs. Sinclair—I mean Mrs. Van Holden. Congratulations, ma'am. I wish you much joy."

Much joy. That seemed highly unlikely in light of my abiding stupidity. Why, I thought, fighting tears, had Mark married me? I was not the sort of woman he was used to. I hadn't an original thought in my head; I was naive and unsophisticated. What did he want of me? What could I possibly offer him that women far prettier and smarter and more desirable than I could ever hope to be had offered him before me?

"Will you bathe, madam?" asked Myrna.

"Yes," I said glumly and submitted to her deft ministrations.

Thank goodness I had her. My other servants, Blandford included, were to stay on at my house—my former house—until such time as Mark found each one of them a new position. I would miss Blandford, my protector, but Mark had assured me that he would find him a worthy home. *"I* shall protect you now," he'd said wryly when I'd indicated a reluctance to let Blandford go. "And I shall be sure to place Blandford with a family who needs him and will appreciate him as much as you did."

He'd been laughing at me again, not unkindly, but laughing all the same. Why did he always laugh at me? I resented it. If he thought me so amusing, so empty-headed, then why had he married me?

I was lacing my peignoir when he joined me. He nodded at Myrna, who bobbed a curtsy, gathered up her mending, then left the room.

"Is everything to your liking?" he asked politely.

"Why, yes," I stammered, but in truth I had noticed nothing of my surroundings. I looked about me now. The room was perfection. On the ceiling was a painting of Aurora at dawn; at my feet a densely piled Savonnerie covered the floor. The gilded furnishings were authentic pieces of the Louis Seize period and were delicately upholstered in Beauvais tapestry. On the mantel of the marble fireplace a Sèvres clock ticked gently between two cloisonné urns. The bed, the most arresting feature of the room, looked wide enough to sleep four. The massive mattress was covered with a white satin quilt and the sheets and pillow slips were of hand-embroidered silk.

"It's a beautiful room," I murmured, gazing uneasily at the bed.

"I'm glad you like it."

He was standing near the door to his room. After a moment I looked up and he was watching me quietly. I was so terribly nervous. I knew he was going to make love to me, and it wasn't as if I were a virgin. But for some reason I felt like one. I felt, as Mark watched me, that no man before had ever touched me.

"Come here," he said, and at the sound of his voice I began to tremble.

I moved on leaden legs to where he stood. His gaze, dark and drowsy, held mine.

"You look very lovely with your hair down."

"Do I?" I whispered.

"Yes," he said, "you do."

My trembling increased. My gaze wavered and fell, and then gently, like a summer breeze, I felt his arms encircle my waist.

"Why are you frightened?" he murmured. "I only want to hold you."

"I'm not frightened," I said with a quiver.

"You're not? Then why are you trembling?"

I didn't answer, I couldn't answer. I felt weak, dizzy, faint. His mouth brushed my ear, trailed to my cheek, then closed on my mouth. For an instant I resisted, straining away from him, but his arms held me fast, and his kiss was insistent, hard and insistent, and deliciously, sensuously warm. His lips moved on mine with an ardent design; his hands, zephyr soft, stroked my skin. I felt nothing but him and his hands and his mouth and the heat of his body like a fire on mine.

He took me to bed, and with exquisite leisure he unlaced my peignoir and loosened my nightdress, pressing slow burning kisses on each part of my body he uncovered. I lay breathless beneath him, my heart racing and leaping as a flood of new sensation brought a flush to my cheek and a fever to the depths of my being.

His mouth brushed my breasts, then trailed lingeringly downward; his hands caressed the curve of my tremulous thighs. I wanted to speak, to protest this ardent intimacy. Surely no husband had ever kissed a wife where Mark's mouth now moved with such erotically languorous warmth. But I could not speak, I could barely breathe. I was slowly succumbing to that enchantment of the senses that is passion.

His slow kisses stopped for a few moments as he paused

to disrobe, and I dragged open my eyes and looked down at his long naked form. Unclothed, he was even more sinfully beautiful, like an Old Master's rendering of Heracles or Mars. His chest was covered with dark silky hair, his stomach was lean and flat, his legs, long and slender, were now entangled with mine. With a sigh I embraced him, pressed close to him. His bare chest met mine and his full length bore down on me, while his hands, like a sigh, stroked my quivering hips.

"Mark," I said faintly, then said nothing more as his mouth claimed my mouth and his legs parted mine and he slid himself smoothly inside me. For a time he lay still, then he lifted his head, and his dark slumbrous gaze rested warmly on mine.

"Lovely," he murmured. "How lovely you are." And with a finger, whisper-light, he traced the contour of my face.

His touch was hypnotic, a sorcerer's charm. I watched him, entranced, as he lifted me close and began to move inside me, his hard slender hips brushing smooth against my thighs. How gently he loved me, how sweet were his kisses, and yet fierce the heady passion that bound us as one. I was lost in a vortex of ecstasy, a dizzying universe where pleasure is primal and rapture reigns supreme. With each stroke of Mark's love this whirling world reeled more giddily, and with each kiss I sank deeper and deeper beneath his spell.

As he kissed me and loved me, I felt a fever of longing, a spiral of desire that tumbled full-tilt toward some glorious secret that was almost mine to grasp. But just as I teetered on the brink of discovery, Mark's body tensed above mine, he pressed me closer in his hold, and with a low, aching groan he released the hot passion that held me, yet unrelieved, in its breathtaking thrall.

At length he eased off me, but he took me in his arms, and he held me to his heart for the longest time. He did not drift off to sleep as Edward had always done. He stroked my back and kissed my brow as if he too wanted more than he'd had. I lay very still in his arms; there was an ache inside me, an unsated hunger that brought hot color to my cheeks. I wanted him again, I wanted him to fill the need

which he had aroused, a need which in all my years with
Edward I had never known existed.

"Mark," I whispered and I turned up my face to his.
"Mark." I kissed his strong jaw, the pulse at his throat, the
beguiling curve of his sensuous mouth. He stirred against
me, warm, hard, his skin smooth as silk brushing mine. I
was limp with desire, helpless with the need of him. He
leaned over me, took my face in his hands, but he only
watched me intently while I, in trembling anticipation,
stared longingly at his mouth.

"Joanna," he said, his voice low and strange, "why did
you marry me?"

"Why?" I said faintly.

"Yes, why?"

"I don't know," I told him honestly. "I don't know."

He digested this in silence; my answer, apparently, was
not the one he had anticipated. It seemed I had displeased
him again, and I thought for one horrible moment that he
would leave me, leave my bed, return to his own. But he
did not leave, he kissed me instead, a penetrating, sweet
kiss on the mouth, and then he trailed his kisses along my
neck and my breasts. His passion, I knew, was again as
aroused as my own, and I bit my lips to keep from begging
him to take me, to make me his, now, completely. But I
didn't have to beg—he rose above me, and looking deeply
into my eyes, he entered me with a tender yet animal urgency that made us both cry out. He pressed me to him until I no longer knew where my body ended and his began.
With quick, fierce movements we rose again to that terrible pinnacle, but this time I was lifted up, up and over, and
then I felt myself flowing outward in every direction at
once. I arched myself violently against Mark and heard a
long, wild, ecstatic moan. Only when it ended did I realize
it had come from me. . . .

After a time, when I lay in his arms, the soft beat of his
heart near my ear, I asked him shyly why he had married
me. I don't know why I asked. I would never have done so
but for the sweet euphoric intimacy of the moment.

At length he said simply, "Because I love you, Joanna. I
thought you knew that."

PART TWO
Alan

I loved him too much not to hate him at all.

JEAN RACINE
Andromaque

XII

HE MARRIED HER in January. He had asked me before I returned to New Haven if I should like to attend the ceremony. I told him no. I had told him earlier exactly how I felt about his marrying her. I had not minced words, and I thought for the first time in my life he might strike me. But he did not. He merely shrugged, called me an insolent brat, and left the room. God, how I hated him! And how I loved her.

I was sixteen when he first brought her to the house, and I remember thinking disgustedly: *Here's another of his trollops whom he'll take to his bed for a week, a month, before he goes on to another and another. . . .* But Joanna Sinclair was different. For one thing, she was a widow, which meant my father had broken his custom of seducing only married women. For another, she was as sweet, as pure, as heartbreakingly vulnerable as my mother had been, and I knew from the moment I saw her that I wanted her, wanted her for myself; wanted, in essence, to save her from my father.

She was older than I was, but she was possessed of an innocence, a shy reticence, which made her seem younger than her years. And she was lovely, her sweet, disarming loveliness not so much striking as it was endearing. The first night I met her I wanted to hold her, to shelter her. She was nervous and ill at ease, wary, I supposed, of my father's intentions. She was so clearly not one of his "women." No, quite the contrary: Joanna Sinclair was a lady.

I was not to see her again for a year; I imagined that he

had tried on that first night, without success, to seduce her. I could have killed him. Didn't he know the difference between a lady and a slut? Didn't he care that such a difference existed? Probably not, I thought bitterly. He had been married to a lady, and he had treated her as if she were the most common of whores. He was to blame for her death; he should never have got her pregnant again. She simply wasn't strong enough to bear another child. My mother had always been frail and of a delicate constitution. My father knew this but still he inflicted upon her his physical excesses, and invariably she acceded to his demands because, God help her, she loved him.

That was the only flaw in my mother's character, loving my father as she did. I would hear them sometimes late at night, talking quietly or laughing softly in her room, and as young as I was I would realize with a blinding rage what they were doing. Christ, how could she? How could she let him touch her, kiss her, share her bed, when he wasn't fit to share the same plane of existence on which she dwelt? My mother was a queen, a saint, a thing apart from other mortals. She had been everything to me: parent, mentor, ally, friend. My father, on the other hand, had always been too busy to pay much attention to his only son and heir. He was forever merging or manipulating or whatever the devil he did in that bloodstained world he called Eastern Seaboard Oil.

Once when I was eleven, he had said to me in a rare attack of conscience, "I realize, son, that I don't spend as much time as I'd like with you. But what I'm doing is, in the long run, for your benefit. Eastern Seaboard will be yours one day, and I intend that by the time it's in your hands, the company will be unchallenged in its field."

I told him contemptuously what he could do with his refineries. It was the first time I had scorned him openly, but I couldn't help myself. He had been in Pittsburgh for a month, and my mother had been ill in the latter stages of her pregnancy. When he returned from his trip she never said a word to him about her health and she implored me with tears in her eyes to keep silent as well.

"You'll only worry him, darling," she told me, "and he

has so much on his mind as it is. Say nothing to him, please, Alan. I'm perfectly well. I couldn't be better, I give you my word."

A week later she was dead.

I was with her at the end. They tried to keep me out of her room, but I pushed past them all—doctors, servants, friends—and stayed with her, helplessly holding her hand, till she died. She had just been delivered of a stillborn son; she was white as the pillow upon which she lay, and she was crying weakly and calling my father's name.

"Mama," I whispered, my eyes blind with tears, "I'm here. I'll stay with you."

But she wanted him. Over and over she called his name, moaned his name, till I thought I would scream with the monotony of it. But my father wasn't there. He was in Pittsburgh again, breathing life into Eastern Seaboard Oil while the woman who had borne his son lay dying.

It did not take her long. An hour or so after the stillbirth of the baby, she breathed a long sigh, her hand grew slack in mine, and she died.

I would not let her go. One of the doctors tried to take her hand from mine, but I simply would not let her go. I was crying openly, sobbing like a two-year-old, and when the second doctor and my godfather tried to separate me from my mother, I kicked and screamed and swore them all to eternal damnation until finally, mercifully, I suppose, they succeeded in tearing me away.

My godfather took me to my room. I loved Spencer Halston. He was a good friend to my father, which had always surprised me because they were so completely different from one another. My father was dynamic, volatile, a turbulent tempest of a man, while Spencer was as tranquil as a summer dawn.

Spencer sat with me a long time, saying nothing, allowing my grief to spill unrestrained. It was the wisest thing anyone could have done. If he had attempted to calm me, to soothe me, to assure me, for instance, that my mother was now at peace in the arms of her Creator, I think I might have killed him. But he said nothing, did nothing, until my sobs ebbed and my tears dried, and then,

in a hushed, ragged voice, he said, "Her pain has ended,
Alan, be thankful for that at least. Ours has only just begun."

At first I couldn't think why he had said such a thing,
but when I saw his eyes traced with red, and his pale tear-
stained cheeks, I knew with a wisdom beyond my years
that he had loved my mother, had loved her with a sweet
pure love unsullied by the carnal urges which characterized my father's love. And I knew too, in that singular moment of perception, that my father had murdered my
mother just as surely as if he had taken up a dagger and
plunged it into her heart.

When he finally came home, I never once saw him shed a
tear. He just stood like a stone at the side of the bier, and
even after the entombment he remained silent, dry-eyed,
and unmoved. During this period he did not attempt to
speak to me, which was just as well. If he had, I might have
told him just how thoroughly I despised him.

One evening several weeks later, Spencer Halston came to
call. My father received him in his study, a small room on the
second floor adjacent to my mother's boudoir, where I happened to be at the time, in morbid contemplation of her
absence. How I loved that room, redolent of her perfume,
reflective of her grace. She had decorated it herself with
fragile French chairs and a tulipwood desk and exquisite cu-
rios and *objets d'art* which reposed in shining magnificence in
a marquetry cabinet of ormolu-mounted kingwood. I had just
replaced a cunning Dresden shepherdess on one of the
shelves when I heard my godfather's voice.

"It wasn't true, Mark," I heard him say. "It was a pack
of lies from beginning to end, but it was the only way I
knew to make you let go. It didn't matter at the time what
I was doing to her; it seemed unimportant, irrelevant,
when measured against the eventual outcome."

He went on to say more but in a lowered tone inaudible
to my straining ears. What was he saying? What were the
lies to which he referred? And why was my father so un-
naturally, ominously silent?

For a time then I heard nothing else. I thought, after a
while, that Spencer might have left, but presently I heard

my father's voice. He was swearing in a low, brutal tone, words so obscene, so menacing, so utterly terrifying that a shudder of fear scurried up my spine. I heard Spencer plead, "Mark, for the love of God . . ." and then a stream of new obscenities from my father, the sound of the study door being opened and slammed shut, and then I heard Spencer running, fleeing in terror from the fearsome fury of my father's black rage.

I cowered in a corner, my brain racing, trying in vain to make sense in my mind of the precious few words I had heard. Lies, Spencer had said. What lies? And he'd said something about wanting my father to let go. To let go of what?

The door to my mother's room opened. Swiftly I extinguished the lamp and peered cautiously through the partially closed door which separated the boudoir from the bedroom. My father was standing at the foot of the bed, his hand clenched tightly on one of the tall posters. His face was ashen, his eyes were blank, vacant, as though he had just received a mortal wound. I saw his lips move, framing the syllables of my mother's name. Lenore, he mouthed soundlessly, over and over again. *Lenore*. It was the way she had called for him, before she had died, while I held her hand and wept.

A hot blast of hatred seared through me. "You bastard!" I cried and pushed open the door, flinging myself on my father in a crazed mindless rage. Through a mist of blind fury, I saw his startled face, and I reached up to strike him, to draw blood, to kill him, as he had killed the only thing in life I had ever loved. "Murderer!" I screamed as he grasped my flailing fists and pinned them firmly behind my back. "It's your fault she's dead! You killed her, you did it!"

"Alan, stop it!"

His voice shook with an emotion I saw clearly as guilt. His arms about me were firm yet gentle, like a father's loving embrace. But he was no father to me. I loathed and despised him, didn't he know that? He had all but ignored me from the moment of my birth. His only concern had been his interests, his holdings, his foul schemes, his nefarious empire. Nothing else mattered to him, and no one else. I cannot count the number of times he disappointed my mother, missing dinner, canceling engagements, absenting himself from functions he found tedious or not to his taste. But she never complained, not once in her life did she utter a harsh word against him. You see, she loved him. No matter how long his absences or how many times he disappointed her or how negligently he treated her, she loved him. More, I think, than she had ever loved me.

"Bastard!" I screamed again. "Filthy murderer! I hate you, I wish you had died instead of her!"

And then, to my complete mortification, I burst into tears and sagged heavily, helplessly against him.

"Alan, Alan," he said and held me close, as if he cared, the hypocritical bastard, as if he really loved me. "I wish it too, son. I would gladly have died in her place."

He brought me to a chair and sat down and cradled me like an infant in his arms. I was too weak, too anguished to protest. I kept thinking of my mother and of how she had held me when I was younger, nestled snugly against the soft fragrant warmth of her breast. I thought of her hands, slim and white, and of the mystic beauty of her face, the haunting, mellow sweetness of her voice. He had destroyed all that, and I could never, would never forgive him for that. I would neither forgive nor forget. And one day, if it took the whole of my life, I would repay him. One day, with the help of God or of Satan himself, I would punish my father for his abominable crime.

XIII

THE SECOND TIME Joanna Sinclair came to my house was on
the occasion of my seventeenth birthday. I doubt she would
have come had it not been for my highly presumptuous call
on her two weeks before, and God alone knows what impulse drove me to ask her, to *beg* her, to attend my party. It
had been almost two years since Edward Sinclair's death,
but Sally Monroe, Sinclair's niece through marriage, had
mentioned that Joanna still mourned her husband and
that she rarely, if ever, left the house. I could well understand such a grief; my mother had died six years earlier,
and not a day went by that I didn't think of her and long
for her dear presence.

In any case, when I spoke to Joanna and requested that
she attend the party she consented without hesitation, and
I couldn't have been happier. I knew from Mrs. Monroe
that Joanna had earlier refused my father's invitation, but
for some reason she had accepted mine. She was the very
first guest to arrive, and when my father entered the ballroom accompanied by Lavinia Winslow, his current whore,
I was further delighted to see that Joanna's presence had
come as a complete surprise to him.

How smooth he was, uttering his buttered phrases, concealing his astonishment behind the devious façade of his
courtesy. Joanna, however, was impervious to his specious
charm; she took my arm and indicated a desire to tour the
house. As I showed her through room after room of my
father's monument to his own ego, I knew with all cer-
tainty that I loved her and that I would for the rest of my
life.

She was so lovely, so sweet, in a pale yellow gown, with a cluster of yellow rosebuds in her hair. When we came to rest in the family room in the east wing I wanted to take her in my arms, to kiss her until she was breathless, but instead I was suddenly telling her about my father, of his avarice, and of his despicable neglect of my mother. I cannot imagine why I blurted out those things to her. She was quite understandably shocked, and as she strove desperately to sooth me in my hysterical raving, my father appeared at the door.

I turned like a Fury to face him. Had he heard what I'd said? I wished he had. I should have very much liked to listen to any defense he cared to offer. But he merely said calmly, "Your other guests have arrived, Alan, and are asking for you. If you'll go down to greet them I shall be happy to show Mrs. Sinclair the rest of the house."

I wanted to kill him. Dear Christ, how many times in my life I've wanted to kill that arrogant bastard. But from the corner of my eye I saw Joanna trembling, so rather than put her through more anguish, I excused myself in a voice I could barely control and fled.

Hot tears of rage stinging my eyes, I staggered down the hall, drawn like a magnet to the sanctuary of my mother's room. But before I had gone twenty paces, Lavinia Winslow stepped out of the shadows, and with a queer febrile look in her eyes, she placed a light hand on my arm.

I don't like to dwell on what happened next; it is something I prefer to forget, especially since my father very nearly caught us in the midst of the act itself. I have often wondered what dark motive prompted Mrs. Winslow to corner me in the hall, maneuver me somehow into my bedroom, and thereupon introduce me to a series of sexual practices the likes of which I have not encountered since. The woman was insatiable; she was as exciting an initiation into the heady realm of carnal knowledge as anyone, man or boy, could ever hope to enjoy. It was no wonder that her tenure as my father's mistress had lasted far longer than any of her less practiced and perhaps more inhibited predecessors.

At any rate, after she left me lying on my bed, half undressed, half bemused with the memory of her unexpected and totally deliberate seduction, my father entered the room. He knew at once what had transpired. I concluded that he had seen Mrs. Winslow emerge from my bedroom, and my state of dishabille along with the look of sheepish chagrin I gave him was evidence enough of my crime. My glorious afterglow soon vanished under the look he gave me. Quite frankly, I was frightened to death. I scrambled to my feet and attempted hastily to repair my attire. My legs felt like jelly, my hands shook so badly that I had to jam them into my pockets in an effort to still their trembling. I opened my mouth to speak, to try to explain what had happened, but no words came. Dimly I realized that no matter what I said he would only construe it as still another show of rebellion on my part. In retrospect I understand his feelings, but I shall never understand why, instead of beating me senseless, he merely characterized my actions with a few contemptuous words, then suggested coldly that I finish dressing and return downstairs to my guests.

I never saw Lavinia Winslow again. It would interest me greatly to learn how my father handled the situation, but, naturally, he didn't confide in me nor did he ever refer to the episode again. I suppose I should have felt grateful or guilty or at least apologetic, but I was none of those things. I despised him more than ever, and at the end of that summer, when I returned with my grandparents from Saratoga and learned he was seeing Joanna, my hatred for him increased to an almost unendurably painful intensity.

It never occurred to me that he wanted to marry her; my father was not a marrying man. In fact, I was convinced that the only reason he had married my mother was because she was sole heiress to Grandfather van Rensselaer's fortune. My father had had money of his own, of course, but it was only with my mother's very generous dowry that he was finally able to implement his schemes. With the added leverage of her virtually limitless funds he bought, cajoled, and coerced all opposition, then ultimately began his ascent to the precipitous summit of Eastern Seaboard Oil.

Was Joanna aware of these things? I wondered grimly. Had she married my father with full knowledge of his villainy? I couldn't believe, I *wouldn't* believe that a lady so fine would ever consent to wed a man such as he, had she known him for the ruthless, unprincipled scoundrel he really was.

My first full term at Yale ended in June, and I went home. Joanna and my father had been married six months and had only recently returned home themselves from a protracted honeymoon abroad.

"What a splendid trip!" Joanna told me as we dined together my first night home. "I never dreamed we'd be gone so long. I'm sorry we missed your birthday, Alan, but your father has planned a celebration for the end of the month. I shall have to peruse the list of this year's debutantes and cull four or five for your selection . . . unless," she teased, "you have a young lady of your own in mind."

She had changed since last I'd seen her. She was no longer timid; she was confident now, self-possessed, and supremely, nauseatingly happy. Throughout dinner her glance had wandered constantly to my father, and whenever he smiled, her face would light up with a radiant smile of her own. A blind man could see she loved him. And my father? What were his feelings? I neither knew nor cared about that.

"I have no young lady in mind, Mrs. Sinclair."

"Alan," she laughed, "I am no longer Mrs. Sinclair."

"Forgive me," I said in my silkiest voice. "Mrs. Van Holden then."

"Alan," said my father, his tone low but nonetheless peremptory, "if Joanna has no objection you will address her by her Christian name."

"Yes, Alan, please do," she said at once, and I noted with a twinge of conscience that my sardonic remark, intended to annoy my father, had only distressed her.

"I shall be happy to call you Joanna," I said as gently as I could. "I have wanted to do so for the longest time."

"Have you?" she whispered, her eyes growing luminous with what looked suspiciously like tears. Good God, was she going to cry? Had I upset her that badly?

"Yes, yes," I said emphatically. "I want you to know—if I haven't mentioned it before—that I'm delighted about your marriage. I'm sure my father told you"—I glanced at him desperately for support—"how pleased I was when he told me the news."

And incredibly she answered, "Yes, Alan, he did tell me that, but I thought—" She broke off, flustered, and looked helplessly toward my father whose dark, puzzled gaze rested openly on my flushed face. "I thought," she went on bravely, "that you might resent—"

"Never!" I said fiercely, out of my mind with guilt and misgivings. I could see now that she hadn't changed at all. She was still the same: shy, uncertain, and so terribly, heartbreakingly young. "Resent you indeed, Joanna! I'm not a child you know, that I would fly into a jealous rage over my father's marriage. I wish you much happiness, and I welcome you with all good wishes into the family."

There! I thought with a sigh of relief. *That should convince her—and my father—of my Simon-Pure sincerity.* And she believed me, thank God. She broke into a smile, but my father, I noted, his face grave and still, had not been so easily deceived.

"Joanna," he said when she prepared to withdraw to the family room, "we'll join you in a moment."

At the door she hesitated. "Mark . . ."

"In a moment, darling," he said softly, and when he gave her a reassuring smile, she trailed with reluctance from the room.

"Sit down, Alan." His smile was gone; he dismissed the servants, then closed the dining-room doors. "Smoke if you like," he said, indicating the chased silver humidor on the sideboard.

"You know I don't smoke," I said warily.

"Then you've picked up no new habits at Yale?"

"No, I haven't."

"Good," he said, resuming his seat at the head of the table. "I smoked my first year at Harvard. All of my friends did and it seemed, at the time, the manly thing to do. I never liked it though; cigars foul the breath and irritate the throat, and they're the devil of a nuisance to carry about in one's coat. In any case, I decided at the end of first term that smoking was neither practical, beneficial, nor even pleasurable, and so I gave it up."

Unaware of his direction, unable to formulate a line of defense, I kept silent.

"How do you find campus life?" he went on, and I thought to myself, *Get on with it, man! What is it you want to know?*

"I find it tolerable," I said at length, toying nervously with the nutcracker.

"Only tolerable?" He raised a dark eyebrow. "I had thought you'd be well content with your new independence."

"What independence?" I snapped. "My mother's legacy is tied up in trust until I'm twenty-five. How independent can I be living on your largesse?"

"My largesse, Alan? What an extraordinary thing to say. Don't you know that whatever I have is yours? I make you no gift of it."

"It's not mine!" I cried, losing the control I so desperately wanted to maintain. "Nothing of yours is mine, and I wouldn't want it anyway! I want only what my mother left me, what rightfully belongs to me."

"My money," he said deliberately, "my property, and all that I own, Alan, rightfully belongs to you."

"I want nothing of yours," I flung at him and rose, shaking, from my chair. "When I come into my inheritance I shall leave this house forever and—"

A look in his eyes stilled my words. If I hadn't known better I would have thought I had hurt him. But my father was too thick-skinned to be hurt, and moreover, why should he care if I left him?

"Sit down," he said again, and now his eyes were hard, his voice a threat. I subsided at once; my father's patience has its limits, and he was fast approaching those limits now. "I can see," he said tersely as I regarded him sullenly from across the table, "that a year at school has done little or nothing to change your opinion of me. It's unfortunate really that you should bear me an enmity the source of which exists only in your own mind. Be that as it may, I now have Joanna's welfare to consider along with your own, and for that reason I'm afraid I must insist that you alter your attitude toward me . . . even if it only be on the surface. Do I make myself clear?"

"Yes," I said contemptuously. "You want me to pretend I'm fond of you, is that it?"

"You needn't strain anyone's credulity, Alan. Simple courteous behavior will suffice."

He *was* hurt. His attempt at sarcasm did not quite conceal the injured disappointment in his tone. I stared at him openly, confused and astounded by a vulnerability of which I had thought him incapable.

"Under ordinary circumstances," he went on, his voice cold now, and bitter, "I would not impose so great a burden upon you. But our relationship, as you may have guessed, disturbs Joanna, and it is my wish at this time that she be completely free of any undue stress or anxiety."

"At this time?" I echoed, a suspicion forming in my mind.

"She's going to have a child."

"A child?" I clutched at the edge of the table with both hands. ".You've gotten her pregnant?" My stomach churned, the room spun dizzily before my eyes. He had touched her, kissed her, made love to her. Dear Christ, I couldn't bear it. "Couldn't you have waited?" I choked. "She's only a child herself. What if she—?" I broke off in terror as I thought of my mother lying white and lifeless on a bloody bed. "Oh, Jesus," I moaned and stumbled clumsily to my feet. "If she dies . . . Oh, Jesus."

"Alan, for God's sake, she's not going to die!"

"Let go of me!" I cried and flung off his hand from my arm. "Don't touch me, don't even talk to me unless she's in the same room with us. I'll do as you ask, I'll be the model son—for her sake. For her sake, you bastard, not yours!"

I started to leave, blind with fear and with a dark nameless rage, but just as I reached the door I felt his hand on my wrist and I was slammed with one swift, vicious movement against the walnut-paneled wall. My head pounded, my senses reeled from the unexpected brutality of his attack, and before I could recover my wits he had pinned both my arms in a bone-crushing grip behind my back.

"The next time you call me 'bastard' will be the last," he uttered savagely. "Do you understand me, Alan?"

His hold on my arms tightened, his dark face was inches away from my own. Stunned, petrified, I could only stare wordlessly into the deadly black depths of his eyes.

"I am tired to death of your insolence, your infantile rages, your irrational jealousy—"

"Jealousy?" I croaked.

"Yes, jealousy, goddamn you! I thought you would outgrow it, overcome it, but the years have only magnified it out of all proportion."

"What are you talking about?" I cried, twisting helplessly in his brutal vise. My arms were numb, bloodless from the elbows down, and I could almost feel the bruises starting on my flesh. "Why should I be jealous of you? I couldn't be, I'm not!"

"You could and you are," he grated, and then with a suddenness that startled me, he let me go and strode across the room, where he filled a glass with whiskey and downed it in one hasty swallow. His back was to me, but I could see he was trembling with rage. His hand on his glass tightened slowly as if it were about my throat. I could feel his anger as if it were a living thing; I was cold with fear but beyond that, another emotion danced dangerously in my brain.

"I'm not jealous," I said thickly when at last I could speak. "Why do you say such a thing? I could never be jealous of you."

For a time he was silent; the room itself rang with an ominous silence, and at length he said grimly, "Very well, Alan, you're not jealous. Perhaps I've been mistaken all these years. Perhaps you despise me on principle."

He turned to me then, and there was a look on his face that baffled me. His anger seemed gone, and in its place was another emotion, one which I found impossible to interpret. Was it loneliness? Sorrow? Contrition? Regret? Or, I wondered, as I thought bitterly of Joanna's condition, was it guilt?

XIV

SHE HAD A daughter on Christmas day. They named her
Noelle, and I couldn't have loved her more if she were my
own child. She hadn't a trace of my father in her; she was
all pink skin and velvet brown eyes and silky, fine brown
hair which framed her sweet cupid face. I couldn't bear to
leave her when school reopened. The term dragged interminably; I chafed at the bit like a bad-tempered horse, anxious to be home again, desperate to be with Noelle, and
with her mother.

The summer came at last and I went directly to Newport, where Joanna and the child awaited me. My father
was in Pennsylvania meeting with the state legislature in
an attempt to halt the proposed construction of the Tidewater Pipeline. My father now controlled all existing pipeline systems as well as the various other means of
transporting oil. In defense, the irate oil men had banded
together and had come up with a plan to build a new independent pipeline extending from the Alleghenies to the
sea, which would thus break the chains of Eastern Seaboard Oil which bound them. The newspapers reported
that all of my father's efforts to prevent this from happening would go for naught. The Pennsylvania legislature, it
seemed, had tired of dancing to Mark Van Holden's tune,
and it was almost certain they would approve construction
of the Tidewater Pipeline without delay.

Joanna appeared unaware of my father's difficulties in
this area, for when I arrived in Newport she welcomed me
warmly, chatted gaily about the baby and about the balls

and fetes scheduled for the season, and inquired at length after my health, my social life, and my future plans.

"Alan," she said as we strolled one morning in the garden, "you must not spoil Noelle so. You've been here only three weeks and already she knows you will pick her up at the first sign of a whimper. Do you know she waits for you every morning? She clutches the bars of her crib and peers out like a little prisoner, knowing that the instant you step into the room you will free her from her jail."

"Does she?" I laughed. "What a delightfully precocious child!"

"Oh, you're impossible. What am I going to do with her when you return to New Haven? Alan, I'm serious!"

"How lovely you look when you're serious."

"Alan!"

"Very well," I said solemnly. "I give you my word I'll not spoil her . . . not thoroughly, that is. I shall only instill in her the conviction that she's the most beautiful, most talented, and most intelligent child in the world."

Joanna sighed and shook her head in exasperation, and as I took her hand and tucked it snugly under my arm, I admired covertly the graceful fit of her white organdie frock. She looked no more than seventeen with her dark hair curling prettily about her cheeks, and her expressive brown eyes resting fondly and trustingly on mine. How I loved this woman, this child, who knew little of life and of love. Her goodness, her utter innocence, was a constant source of amazement to me. She had been married twice, had borne my father's child, yet she was as guileless, naive, and unblemished as the purest child herself.

"Doesn't the garden look grand this year? Will you be entering the roses in the flower show?"

"Yes," she told me, "and the gardenias too, from the greenhouse. Johnson has cultivated a particularly exotic strain this summer."

"I've seen them." I smiled, and noted with pleasure the gardenialike smoothness of her fair cheeks and brow. "And what about your social calendar? Have you planned a cotillion or two, and perhaps a *bal masque*?"

"Why, yes I have!" she exclaimed. "A *bal masque*, in

fact. But your father said that under no circumstances would he costume himself—"

"Will there be an America's Cup race this season?" I interrupted her. I did not wish to speak of my father.

"No," she replied, seemingly unperturbed by my abrupt change of topic. "Louisa Morgan told me that the Royal Yacht Squadron has sent a challenge on behalf of the Earl of Dunraven, but I believe the New York Yacht Club has expressed some objection to the conditions. I'm really not certain of what problems exist; when your father comes home he'll be better able to explain it to you."

My father again.

I decided to return to safer ground. "I shall take Noelle out in her carriage this afternoon. Perhaps we'll go down to the beach."

We had come to the end of the garden which bordered on the woodland of gnarled trees with their interlacing tangle of branches. I loved the grounds at Newport; I loved Newport itself with its gilded beaches, its vast argent sea, its shimmering days and still, fragrant nights. And never had I loved it more than this golden blessed year with Noelle and Joanna, and without my father.

"Alan," she said, releasing my arm, "you love Noelle very much, don't you?"

She looked up at me, her face dappled with sunlight, her mouth softer and pinker than any rose in the garden.

"Yes," I said softly. "I love her more than I can say."

"Alan . . ." She picked nervously at the folds of her skirt. "Don't you think you should start considering your future?"

"My future?"

"Well," she began hesitantly, "you're nineteen now. You must decide soon what you're going to do."

"What I'm going to do? About what?"

Her uncertain gaze wavered and fell. What was she thinking? And why was she suddenly nervous when only a moment ago we'd been almost as close as lovers?

"Don't you feel," she said at length, "that it's time you were thinking of a wife . . . children of your own? Of course you won't be marrying for several years, but you must give yourself sufficient time to make a wise and suitable choice."

"Why do you say that? Did my father put you up to this?"

"Oh, Alan, no!" she said at once, and I immediately regretted my harsh tone, for she hastened to add apologetically, "I did not mean to presume. I know I have no right to meddle in your life."

"Joanna," I said swiftly, "you have every right in the world. Forgive me, please, for snapping at you."

"No," she said sadly, "don't apologize. I should never have broached the subject. I forget sometimes that we are not truly related. And I always have the fear . . ." She paused, looked away self-consciously, then murmured with some reluctance, "that you don't quite accept me."

"That's not true!"

"No, I don't think it is true, but for a time I was afraid . . ." She paused again, searched for words. "What I'm trying to say, Alan, is that despite what you may feel for me, I've come to love you very deeply, and I had hoped you might learn to love me too."

"What?" I said. Had she voiced the emotion that, in my heart, in my soul, in my wildest dreams, I had hoped against hope she would one day admit to me?

"Oh, not as a mother!" she cried and turned anxious eyes on my incredulous face. "I should never want to take your mother's place in your heart."

But her last words fell on unhearing ears. "Joanna," I choked, "do you really love me?"

"Yes, of course," she answered, coloring. "Didn't you know that, Alan? How could I help but love you?"

"Oh, God," I uttered and took her, with a blind, fevered urgency, into my arms. "I love you too, Joanna. I've loved you for years, and I've hoped, prayed that you would . . ."

I couldn't speak, words failed me as I gazed fiercely at her suddenly startled face and felt the faint trembling of her slim frame against mine. Her lips were parted in helpless surprise, her hands lay limply on my arms. How sweet she was, how soft her fair skin, and how inviting her pink, pliant mouth. Slowly then, as I had done a thousand times in my dreams, I drew her closer, kissed the smooth line of her brow, and covered her lips with mine.

My mind whirled, my senses reeled. I wanted to taste, possess, devour her. I wanted her totally, completely. So often had I envisioned her thus: in my arms, in my power, and ultimately in my bed.

"Joanna," I groaned, "I want you so badly. Please let me love you. I want you, I need you."

"Alan! Oh, dear God!" she cried, but I heard nothing, felt nothing but her and my need and the fiery hot thrill of my scorching desire. I pulled her blindly into a leafy arbor and sank to the damp ground still holding her in my arms. The scent of roses enveloped us; time ceased to exist, my mind ceased to function while my senses sharpened with the sheer physical pleasure of her touch. I fumbled at her bodice. The buttons were small, infinitesimally small, and my task loomed infinitely large. "Joanna, help me," I whispered. "Help me." My hands touched her breasts, sweat poured from my brow. I had to have her now. Now. "Joanna, help me for the love of God."

And then, in one of those lightning-swift flashes of lucidity which brighten even the most abysmal depths of madness, I saw her face. It was as white as the face of a corpse, and she lay absolutely still beneath me, her eyes closed, a river of tears coursing freely down her cheeks.

"Oh, God," I said hoarsely. "Oh, God."

Dear Christ in heaven, what had I done? Burning with shame, I eased myself from her body and drew her, with the greatest of care, into my arms. "Please," I said, anguished, "I'm sorry. Forgive me. I didn't mean— I didn't want to— I love you, I swear it."

I held her tightly, desperately. I kissed her mouth and tasted her tears. She lay still as death in my embrace, and I wanted to die with the shame of hurting her, die with the torment of wanting her and not having her. "I love you so much," I kept saying, and my voice broke and my own eyes spilled over. "I've loved you forever, my dearest heart. I shall never love anyone but you. Joanna, speak to me, forgive me. I can't bear that I've hurt you."

For hours, it seemed, she lay motionless, and then at

long last she opened her eyes and gazed sadly at my grief-stricken face. "Poor Alan," she whispered, her voice dull and strange. "My poor, poor, darling Alan."

"Oh, God, don't," I said miserably. "Don't pity me."

"I don't pity you, my darling. I understand you. Don't cry, Alan. Don't cry, my sweet boy."

She touched my face with a soft slim hand. Her eyes glimmered with tears as she spoke in a queer, lifeless voice. "Poor darling. Always wanting, never having. I know what you're feeling, poor Alan. I know all too well what you feel."

She seemed drugged, dazed, and the slow hypnotic cadence of her voice puzzled and alarmed me. "Joanna," I said, my own voice rough with fear, "let's leave here. Let's go back to the house. Come, get up now. Joanna, let me get up."

But she lay heavily across my lap, her fingers tracing my cheek and outlining the curve of my mouth. "Do you know," she said softly, "that your mouth is like his? And your chin is like his—firm and strong."

"What?" I said hoarsely. "What are you talking about?"

I stared at her wildly, my mind in a chaos of love and bewilderment and unendurable excitement. She was dazed with shock, I saw that clearly, but just as clearly I knew that I still wanted her.

"Joanna. Let's go back. Get up, my darling. Let's go back to the house."

"It's strange," she murmured dully, still tracing the line of my mouth, "that you should look so much like him when you are not his son."

A shudder of fear trembled through me. What was she saying? And why did she stare so with those dull, tortured eyes? "Joanna . . ." My voice shook, my throat ached with a sudden insidious dread. "Joanna, what are you saying?"

"I didn't believe it at first," she went on listlessly as if I hadn't spoke. "I thought it was a lie, a vicious ruse to dissuade me from marrying Mark. But then I knew it was true. Why else would you hate him so? Why else have you set yourself against him and fought him at every turn? I know, Alan," she murmured sadly. "I know that you are not Mark's son."

"Joanna!" I grasped her arms and held her away from me. "What do you mean I am not his son?"

What was she saying? Not his son? Of course I was his son. I had only to look in a mirror to corroborate that fact. I had his slender height and his long slender hands, and though we differed in coloring I had the same narrow face and the identical uncompromising hard line of mouth. "I am his son," I insisted, and I shook her to emphasize my words. "I am his son."

I am his son. It was a truth I had abhorred all my life, but now, in the face of repudiation, it was suddenly of the most vital importance that it be so.

"Joanna, why do you say such a thing?" I asked in a voice cracking with emotion.

She was watching me quietly, her face drained and pale beneath the dusky, dark tangle of her hair. Her eyes were huge and sad and filled with the most heart-wrenching compassion. "No man," she said faintly, "has been a better father. No man has loved his son more than Mark loves you, and yet you've despised him as if the sin were his. It was your mother who transgressed, Alan, not your father. She is responsible for your illicit conception, not he. Why do you blame him for a wrong in which he took no part? Why have you refused his love, disdained his affection? Why do you hate him?"

"Are you mad?" I thrust her away from me and rose, shaking, to my feet. "Are you suggesting that my mother . . . ?" The words strangled me, I could barely speak. "Do you expect me to believe that she . . . ?"

I was going to be ill, I could feel the bitter bile rising in my throat. Joanna was staring at me, a new and frightened look in her eyes. She seemed puzzled at first, and then horrified. She uttered a choked sound, pressed both hands to her mouth. "Dear God," she said wretchedly. "You didn't know? You didn't know?"

She was no longer dazed and disoriented. Her eyes were alert now and wide with fear. She stumbled to her feet and reached out to touch me, but I struck away her hand with

one savage motion of my own. "Is that what he said?" I uttered fiercely. "Did my father tell you I wasn't his? Does
he hate me that much?"

"Hate you?" she cried. "Dear God, are you blind? He
loves you as he loves nothing else in this world!"

I swore bitterly and moved away as she took a step toward me. "He loves me, does he? Then why did he tell you
such a thing? Why did he tell you I was not his son?"

"He told me nothing! Someone else did. Oh, Alan,
please! I'm so dreadfully sorry I told you. I thought you
knew. I thought it was the reason you hated him. Don't say
anything to him, I beg you!"

She clutched at my sleeve with a cold, desperate hand,
but again I shook her off, too sick, too stricken to care
about anyone's feelings but my own. Not his son. I was not
his son. Why did the thought sadden me, grieve me? Why
did I feel betrayed, abandoned, bereft as I had never before
felt in my life? Why did I suddenly want to fall to my
knees, weeping with the irony of it, weeping and swearing
with the cruel bitter irony of not being his son?

I stood there like a stone, my thoughts an anguished torment in my brain. Joanna was speaking, begging me to
forgive her, but I was hardly aware of her as a thousand
painful memories rose like a spectre from the dark sepul-
chral recess of my soul.

I remembered a time shortly after my mother died when
I had called my father "murderer." I had fully expected
him to strike me, but he had not. He had cradled me in
his arms and had murmured softly against my hair, words
I could not hear, words I had no wish to hear, for I
had wanted no comfort from him. On that ghastly night,
I had fallen asleep in his arms. I remembered that now; I
had fallen asleep in my father's arms as he held me close to
the soft, hynoptic beating of his heart.

Why did I think of that? Why at this moment, when I
knew I was not his son, did I think of his strong arms
around me and of the low, tranquil murmur of his voice? I
had despised him then and I remembered my vow that he
would pay for his abominable mistreatment of my mother.

And yet I had fallen asleep, like a loving, trustful child, in his arms.

I remembered other things about that night, small things which for one reason or another I had pushed to the back of my mind. I remembered my father standing near my mother's bed, his eyes black as death, his lips helplessly forming the syllables of her name. Lenore, he had said though he'd uttered no sound, Lenore. Over and over again, Lenore, like a litany, like a plea, as if he had actually loved her. But he hadn't loved her. Had he?

I remembered an earlier time, a seemingly happier time. We were in Newport; I was nine or ten years old. I did not then hate my father quite so much as I later came to. I was sitting on the sand, gazing at the sea and my mother was telling my father she was "that way" again. I didn't know what she meant, but I could tell from her tone and from the faint furrowing of her brow that she was distressed. My father, however, was delighted. I saw him raise her hand to his lips, and his dark eyes shone. "My dear," he said, a restrained yet vibrant excitement in his voice. "My dear, I am so pleased."

"Mark," my mother whispered, "I'm afraid."

"Of what, Lenore?" he said swiftly, kneeling down beside her in the sand.

"That it will be like the first time: frightening, painful."

"Hush," said my father. "Hush, darling. It wasn't like that at all."

"But it was," she cried softly. "I was so afraid and you weren't there. Oh, Mark, I know you wanted to be there. I'm not complaining, my darling. I know you would have been with me if you could. But when I think of the pain, of the long hours I had to . . ."

"Be still, Lenore," he said sharply when he turned and took note of my attentive face.

I was staring transfixed at my mother. She was close to tears. I remembered thinking that my father was at fault, it was his harsh words that had made her cry. But had they?

I tried to think of a time when he had been deliberately cruel to me, and could not. He had always been kind in his brusque, moody way. He had always worried about me, cared about me; I realized that now as a tormenting kaleidoscope of memories tumbled dizzily in my brain. I remembered his patience, a thing alien to my father's nature, for he was an impatient man, a volatile, hotheaded, sharp-tempered man, but rarely with me. I remembered his eyes, dark and still, when I would defy him; I remembered his cautious silences when I was most contemptuously voluble. I remembered all these things and wanted suddenly to weep, though I couldn't, in my wildest imagination, think why.

You are not his son.

But I was his son. I had to be his son. It was absolutely imperative, it was suddenly of the utmost necessity, that I be Mark Van Holden's son.

XV

MY FATHER—at least, the man who for nineteen years I had thought was my father—came home on the Fourth of July. He did not go to our cottage on Bellevue Avenue but went instead directly to the cottage of John and Constance Chandler, who each year on the Fourth held a gala to which all of the Newport Four Hundred were invited.

A week had passed since that ghastly morning in the garden, and I had not had a cogent thought since. Joanna had tried to speak with me, to draw me out of my agonized contemplation, but I could not speak of it, I could barely think of it without succumbing to a welter of bewildered tears. My entire life had been upended. I was not Mark Van Holden's son. Who was I, then? What stranger had spawned me? What man had taken my mother in sin? Was it someone I knew?

I went to the Chandler party; I went because there was nothing else I could do. Life had to go on, didn't it? I couldn't lie down and die simply because I was now a fatherless bastard.

Joanna did not come. She had taken to her bed, and had sent me a message through her maid, which read: "I am unable to attend the party. Please give my regards to the Chandlers." I should have been worried; I knew I was the cause of her undefined malaise. I hadn't spoken to her, had barely looked at her since that ill-starred day.

At the party I felt like the guest of honor at a wake. Everyone about me was talking or joking or laughing uproariously while I, as pale and as still as a cadaver, stood silent and alone in a nook by the drawing-room doors.

"Where's Joanna?" they asked me.

"Home, ill," I replied.

"Too bad," they tsk-tsked.

"Yes, it is," I agreed.

"Why, Alan," said Constance, "are you all right? You look like death warmed over. Have some wine. Oh, I forgot, you don't drink. Well, eat something then, before you faint. John! Come look at Alan. I think he's ill."

"Constance, please . . ."

"Good God, Alan, what's wrong with you?"

"Nothing, John, honestly. I'm perfectly all right."

"John, dear, I really think he's ill. Alan, would you like to go upstairs to lie down for a while?"

"Please, Constance, no. I'm fine, I swear it."

I was beginning to truly feel ill now. My palms were sweating and there was a hollow, sick throbbing in the pit of my stomach.

"Are you sure?" she said doubtfully while black spots began to dance before my eyes. And as my nausea increased, my father walked into the room.

He was the only man in the room not in evening clothes, yet he looked like a prince of the realm. His linen was immaculate; the blue broadcloth he wore, rich and dark, bore not a trace of a wrinkle. Dimly I realized that he'd been traveling for hours, that he must have come to the Chandlers' directly from Harrisburg, but he looked bandbox-fresh, absolutely perfect. It was no wonder that every woman in the room was gazing at him in unconcealed admiration while their husbands fairly bristled with envious reproach. I, too, could not take my eyes from him.

"Mark!" Constance exclaimed. "What are you doing here?"

"I believe," said my father, "I was invited. Good evening, John. Alan." He gave me the briefest of glances. My hands, clasped tightly behind my back, began to tremble.

"Well, Mark," said John, "how did it go in Harrisburg? What did the legislature say?"

"They have decided in favor of the pipeline," said my father. His tone was low, measured. It had not gone as he had planned. I sensed his disappointment, his shattered hopes, and for some unlikely reason I wanted suddenly to weep.

"Goddamn them," John muttered. "It's final then, Mark? There is no recourse?"

"None that I'm aware of at this time. I learned too while in Harrisburg that the Reading Railroad has announced its intention to support the independents."

"What? The traitorous bastards! I beg your pardon, Constance. But, Mark, that means—"

"It means," said my father in that low, careful voice, "that the independent oil men may now flood the market or withhold their product at will. It means further an upheaval in the economy which will affect, unfortunately, far more than the oil industry."

My father then realized that Joanna was absent. He turned his dark gaze on my pale face and quietly inquired her whereabouts.

"She's at home," I mumbled. "She's not feeling well."

"Not feeling well? What ails her?"

His steady gaze unnerved me. I stared at my shoes, feeling sicker than before. "I don't know, sir. She wouldn't say."

"What's wrong, Alan? Are you ill too?" His tone had changed, it rang with concern, but I heard nothing as an inexplicable surge of guilt and remorse resounded clamorously in my brain. "Look at me, son. Are you ill?"

With the greatest reluctance I raised my head. His eyes, brilliantly dark, searched mine.

But I am not your son, I thought numbly. *I am not your son.* And I could feel all the color drain slowly and steadily from my face.

"He *is* ill," I heard Constance say. "Look at him, Mark. He's white as paste. Why don't you take him upstairs? I'll call Dr. Simon."

"There's no need for that, Constance," said my father. "I shall take him home. John, I think we should talk further, first thing tomorrow. Please call on me in the morning. Come along, Alan."

He took my arm with a gentle hand, but I wrenched away and said hoarsely, "No!"

It was not my wish to disobey him; for the first time in my life I wanted to do as he asked, but I couldn't face him alone. Not yet, not yet. "I don't want to go home. I'm not ill. Please, Papa, I don't want to go home."

Papa. Why had I so addressed him? I had never in my life called him Papa. It was a silly word, a childish word, and it implied a depth of affection I did not feel.

That damnable word silenced him. He was frankly astonished, and he regarded me with an intensity that frightened me, disarmed me, till my gaze wavered helplessly and dropped to the floor.

"I'm not ill," I repeated, my voice a faint plea. "I don't want to go home."

"You look ill, Alan," he said quietly. "I should like you to come home with me."

"No," I said again, my tone more belligerent. I did not want to be alone with him. If I were alone with him I should have to tell him. And I was not yet ready to tell him. . . .

A thrill of alarm darted through me. I raised my head abruptly and I said in a voice sharp with fright, "Let me alone! I don't want to go home!"

Not a muscle of his face moved. His eyes, shaded by thick lashes, were utterly expressionless. He watched me for what seemed an eternity. My hands, wet with sweat, knotted in anguish behind my back. When he spoke at last, his voice was as remote and as empty of emotion as the fathomless depths of his distant dark gaze. "Very well, Alan. If you're sure you feel well enough to remain."

"Yes, yes," I said quickly, averting my eyes from his. "I'm all right. You needn't worry about me."

"Yes, go on," Constance urged. "I shall keep an eye on him. What a stubborn child he is. He quite reminds me of my Deirdre."

She went on to say more, but I wasn't listening. My gaze had turned involuntarily, compulsively, toward my father. He was paying courteous attention to Constance while she prattled at length about her daughter, but I could tell by the cryptic dark veil of his eyes that he was troubled.

Feeling my scrutiny, he turned to me suddenly, and our eyes, dark and light, met and held. I could not look away. I stared at him silently, and as I scanned the contours of his moody, dark face I noted with faint surprise how tired he looked, and how drained. His eyes were shadowed with stress and fatigue, and there were harsh lines about his mouth that had not been there before. I had never seen him as now: weary, beaten, spent; and as I watched him in wordless fascination I felt all at once the strongest urge to touch him. I could not recall the last time I had touched him.

"Alan," he said softly, "come home with me, son. I want you to come home."

I almost said yes; I leant toward him, unaware that I had moved, and I was about to say yes when I heard John exclaim, "Good God, it's Spencer Halston! What the devil is he doing here?"

"I invited him," said Constance, her face defiant as she turned to my father. "For one thing, Mark," she told him crisply, "I had not expected you would be here tonight, and for another, you cannot expect me to shun Spencer simply because you and he have had a falling out."

"I expect nothing of the kind, Constance," said my father. "You're surely entitled to invite whomever you choose to your parties. Alan, shall we go?"

He was seething with rage, I could sense it, but only the clipped, precise intonation of his words betrayed it.

"Mark, I'm sorry," said John, throwing his wife a harsh look of reproach. "Don't go. You needn't speak to Spencer if you don't want to."

"Forgive me, John, but I was leaving anyway. My wife is ill, and my son too, it seems. Alan, please come along."

But suddenly I was frightened again, as I had been before, and I hung back as I looked across the room and saw my godfather talking to a young lady who looked young enough to be his daughter. He had hardly changed since last I'd seen him. His hair was as fair as my mother's had been, and his eyes were a delightfully merry shade of blue with laugh lines radiating outward like the rays of the sun.

"Alan, are you coming?"

"No," I said, my attention still focused on Spencer. I had loved him so much as a boy; I didn't realize until that moment how much I had loved him. "No, I'm not coming. I want to see my godfather."

It was absolutely the worst thing I could have said. I had forgotten about their quarrel. I had not stopped to think that my father despised Spencer Halston as intensely, I was certain, as I had despised my father. But I didn't despise him now. As he watched me for a moment with those weary, dark eyes, then said good night and walked slowly away, I wanted to go after him, to curl up like a child in the warmth of his arms, to beg his forgiveness for every wrong I had ever done him, to tell him that I *was* his son—no matter the circumstances of my conception.

I didn't say anything, though. I just let him leave without uttering a word. There was too much between us now, too many years, too many hurts. I could not mend a relationship which had never existed in the first place.

I turned my attention once again toward my godfather, who was talking still to his young lady. When he looked up at last and spotted me, he took his companion's arm and plunged through the crowd with a broad smile on his face.

"Alan, is that you?"

"Spencer!" My throat felt tight, my eyes stung. I flung myself unashamedly into his open arms. "God, how I've missed you!"

I could have wept as he embraced me, wept with joy and with a strange melancholy sadness.

"Lord, but you've grown!" He grasped both my arms and held me away for his inspection. He shook his head in disbelief. "You're a man, for God's sake! Where have the years gone? I feel like Methuselah! How old are you now?"

And when I told him, he shook his head again, and his eyes passed over me as if he could not have his fill of looking at me.

"Carrie!" he said, releasing my arms and turning to his companion. "This Adonis who stands before you is my godson. Can you believe it? I cannot!"

I turned politely to the young lady who was smiling uncertainly at Spencer. She was perhaps sixteen or seventeen, and looked charming in a simple white gown of the softest georgette. Her hair, fashionably frizzed on her brow, was the color of taffy, but her lashes, strangely, were dark and thick, shading cornflower blue eyes. She was quite the prettiest girl I had ever seen, and she reminded me, in an indefinable yet pleasurable way, of Joanna. And, beyond that, she looked vaguely familiar, although I felt if I had known such an enchanting creature, I could hardly have forgotten her.

"Have we met?" I asked straight out. "I'm Alan Van Holden."

"Yes, we have," she said shyly. "But it was years ago. I didn't think you'd remember me."

"I do remember you," I confessed, "but I'm afraid I've forgotten your name."

"Alan," laughed Spencer, "what a frightfully rude thing to do! This is Miss Caroline Monroe, Sally and Stephen's daughter."

"Of course! Carrie Monroe!" Now I remembered. We had met several years before at her twelfth birthday party. I must have been fourteen or fifteen then. "But, good Lord, the last time I saw you . . ."

"Yes, I know," she said, blushing in the most charming way. "My face was covered with freckles and I was thin as a scarecrow."

"But how delightfully you've changed!"

"Thank you," she murmured, her blush deepening, and once again I was struck by her uncanny likeness to Joanna. It was not in looks that she resembled her; in fact they were as different as night and day. No, the similarity was in nature, I thought, in their shy smile perhaps, and in their heartbreaking innocence of character. And as I thought of Joanna, the entire ugliness of my plight washed over me with renewed intensity.

"Will you excuse me?" I said thickly. I had to get out of there; if I stayed another minute, I would be ill.

"Alan, wait!" Spencer called, but I was already out of the room. I ran down the hall, flung open the door, and stumbled blindly toward my carriage which stood amidst a dozen others on the wide gravel drive in front of the house.

"Alan, wait!" he called again. He had been right behind me all the while, and as I pulled open the carriage door I felt his hand on my shoulder. To my absolute shock and chagrin, I turned into his arms and began to weep as though I were four years old.

I think he was more shocked than I. He stood statue-still, his arms at his sides while I sobbed in helpless anguish against his chest. I couldn't have been more embarrassed. I wanted to crawl into a hole and die, but I kept thinking of my father and of all the years I had scorned and defied him, and yet during all those bitter, hate-filled years, he had never once flung in my face the fact that I was not his son.

"Alan," I heard Spencer say, "get into the carriage. Every coachman in the yard is staring at us." He nudged me into the carriage, climbed in after me, then shut the door firmly behind us. "Now, what is wrong?" he asked, pressing his handkerchief into my hand. "Alan, why are you crying?"

I felt like a childish fool. I couldn't stop crying; I sat hunched in the seat, Spencer's handkerchief clutched in my hands, and wept. I was repelled and disgusted by my own behavior, shamed and embarrassed beyond endurance, but at last, by a supreme effort of will, I swallowed my sobs and dried my tears and looked up despondently into my godfather's kindly, caring eyes.

"I'm so sorry," I whispered hoarsely, "and so ashamed."

"Never mind that." He waved off my apologies with a short, impatient movement of his hand. "Tell me what's wrong. Let me help you if I can."

"No . . . no," I said miserably. "I don't need any help. I mean, it's nothing that can be helped."

"Well then, Alan, if I can't help you, at least tell me what the trouble is."

His voice was calm, his tone serene. I looked up and he was leaning back casually against the tufted upholstery, his legs crossed, one hand resting idly on his knee. I was suddenly reminded of the night my mother died when

Spencer had let me cry as he'd done just now. He hadn't said anything on that night either, he had just let me cry because he'd known then as he knew now that grief must first be spent before it can be dealt with. How wise he was, and how inordinately perceptive. But then again he had always known me so well—better, I think, than I even knew myself.

"Spencer," I said, my eyes on the floor, "do you know . . . ? Did my father ever tell you . . . ?"

"Tell me what, Alan?"

My heart began a sick, rapid beat. I felt suddenly warm all over; I could feel the perspiration dampening my shirt, and it was suddenly difficult to breathe.

"Do you know," I said in a whisper, the words sticking painfully in my throat, "that I am not his son? Did he ever tell you?"

"Not his son? What do you mean?"

Had his tone changed? I couldn't be sure. There was a pounding in my head like the uncontrolled pounding of my heart. The night was very still, and except for an occasional snorting of a horse and the faint sound of music from the house, all I could hear was that dull rhythmic pounding in my head.

"I am not his son," I said again, and to speak it out loud was far worse than the unspeakable fact itself. "Did you know, Spencer? Did my fa—did *he* . . . ever tell you?"

He did not answer at once. I heard him sigh. I looked up. He was looking out the window toward the house. His face was partly in shadow, but I was able to make out his expression which was all at once disturbingly grave, full of thought, and not in the least surprised.

"You know, don't you?" I blurted. "You've known all these years, and you've never—"

"It's not true," he said calmly, but he didn't turn from the window, he didn't look at me. "It's simply not true, Alan. You *are* Mark's son."

I didn't believe him. He was lying to save me pain. But it was no use his lying, didn't he see that? I knew the truth and I knew by the stillness of Spencer's pale face that he too knew the truth, that he had known it for nineteen years.

"Spencer," I said, my throat tightening with dread, "who is my father? I want you to tell me who he is. I know that you know, and I want you to tell me."

"Mark," he replied in a queer, toneless voice, "is your father."

"Spencer!" I cried. "For the love of God, stop saying that! I know he's not my father. You needn't lie any longer. I know the truth!"

"Do you?" he said. "Do you, Alan?" And he turned at long last to face me. "Then tell me," he said in that bone-chilling voice, "tell me the truth as you know it."

"I—I don't know the whole truth," I stammered, alarmed by that tone and by the eerie dark glow of his eyes. "I know only—"

"You know nothing." Now his voice was harsh, bitter, and his fair, friendly face was as harsh and as bitter as that voice. "Who said you were not Mark's son? What demon from hell resurrected that ancient tale?"

"What does it matter who told me? It's true, isn't it?"

"No, it's not true. I, more than anyone, know it's not true."

"But—"

"Have you talked with Mark about this? Does he know what you think?"

"No, I haven't said anything yet. But—"

"And you had better not, I give you fair warning."

He turned abruptly and flung open the carriage door.

"Spencer, don't go! I must know the truth!"

"You do know the truth," he said fiercely. "I have just told you the truth. You are Mark Van Holden's son."

He swung out of the carriage, but stood a moment holding the door, and his hand, I could see, was trembling.

What had happened? Why was he angry? But no, it wasn't anger that roughened his voice and drained all the color from his face. With startling clarity I realized that it was fear which held him in its icy clutches, as devastating a fear as I had ever witnessed in a man.

"Spencer, dear God, what is it? There's more to this than you're telling me."

"No!" He fired the word, shook his head emphatically. "I've told you what you wanted to know. You are Mark's son. That's all that need concern you." He paused a moment, and his hand on the carriage door tightened. "Alan," he said in a low, rapid voice, "give me your promise, swear on your honor, that you will not speak to Mark of this."

"But, Spencer—"

"Swear!" he demanded. "Swear it, Alan."

In the depths of my mind stirred a memory, something unpleasant, something that frightened me, and it had to do with Spencer, and with my father, and—dear Christ in heaven—it had to do with my mother!

"Spencer," I choked, "it's you, isn't it? You're my father. You—"

I broke off as a lightning-swift surge of realization illumined all the dark places in my mind. Spencer and my mother. Why hadn't I seen it? I knew he had loved her, I guessed it on the night she died, when he had let me cry, when in all probability he had been crying inside himself with the unendurable agony of having lost her. And then later, when he had quarreled with my father, when he had spoken of "unforgivable lies." Of course! That was it. Spencer had loved my mother, had made love to her, and had given her his child. And then when she had died, he had confessed to my father that I was the child of that love.

My father. But Spencer was my father. Spencer, whom I had loved as a father all those long years while I had despised the man whose name I bore, the man who for those same long years had openly and without shame acknowledged me as his son.

But I was Spencer Halston's son. How ironic to learn this. It was what I had wanted, it was something I used to dream about, for I loved Spencer. Then why did my eyes burn and my throat ache with hot, anguished tears as I comprehended the inescapable fact that I was not Mark Van Holden's son?

XVI

I THINK I might have gone mad that summer if it had not been for Carrie Monroe. I began to see her, out of desperation, I think, for I could no longer even look at Joanna, let alone confide in her the nightmare of anguish I was suffering. My father had returned to Harrisburg in an attempt, I imagined, to reverse the legislative decision concerning the proposed pipeline. It was just as well he was gone, for if he had stayed in Newport he would undoubtedly have perceived that all was not as it should be between Joanna and myself.

She no longer attempted to speak to me. Though we dined together almost every night, she uttered not a word, and had I not been blinded by my own torturous thoughts I would have seen the remorse and the helpless despair behind her silence.

It never for a moment occurred to me that I should apologize to her, that I had shamed and debased her by my inexcusable conduct on that day. I had almost made love to my father's wife. . . . But he was not my father. How strange that I should keep forgetting that fact. I was Spencer Halston's son. Except that Spencer would not acknowledge me as such, whereas Mark Van Holden, for the past nineteen years, had allowed me to believe I was his.

Why? Why would he do such a thing? He didn't love me, he hadn't loved my mother. In fact, he must have hated her, knowing of her infidelity. And he must have known of it. Why else would he despise Spencer? And what else could Spencer have meant when he'd spoken of "lies" on the night they had quarreled?

145

I tried not to think of my mother's part in all this, but of course it was impossible not to do so. My beautiful mother, my perfect mother, had lain with another man. I had to stop thinking of it, I had to put it out of my mind or else go mad with the thought of it. Which was why—out of frustration or desperation or some dark, perverted feeling of guilt which I dared not analyze—I began to call on the daughter of Sally Monroe.

I didn't like Carrie's mother. I hadn't any idea why, but I had always disliked her with the same fierce aversion I had to my father's whores. Mrs. Monroe had never been intimate with my father, not that I knew of, at any rate, but the feeling persisted nonetheless. Perhaps this feeling was heightened by the fact that she and Joanna were no longer speaking to one another as a result of a falling out, the details of which Joanna would not discuss. I never questioned her about the reasons for this breach; I only knew that she now disliked Sally Monroe, as intensely, I was certain, as I did.

Carrie, however, was a different matter entirely. What a pretty girl she was with her taffy-colored curls and her enormous blue eyes shaded strikingly by that thick tangle of dusky, dark lashes. She was the most attractive member of her family. Her sister Mary was a snub-nosed, flaxen-haired chit, not nearly as lovely as Carrie, and her brother, who was a year older than Noelle, looked nothing at all like his sisters, nor for that matter did he resemble either of his parents. They were a close family, a loving family, but it surprised me the amount of freedom Mrs. Monroe allowed Carrie, a freedom which I knew would not have been extended had her father been in Newport rather than busy at his brokerage house in New York. The girl, after all, was only seventeen, yet I was permitted to escort her unchaperoned to Bailey's Beach or for drives about town or to the continuous round of parties that were as much a part of Newport as the magnificent cottages within which they were held.

In no time at all, I knew Carrie was falling in love with me. Although I wasn't at all sure of my feelings for her, I couldn't help but hold her and kiss her whenever we were alone—which was often, thanks to her mother, but which was undeniably dangerous in light of Carrie's growing feelings for me and my own unsettled emotions. Whenever I held Carrie I would think of Joanna, of that day in the garden, and of the sweet but momentary joy of thinking she loved me. Whenever I kissed Carrie I would feel Joanna's mouth, soft, warm, and pliant, and the rapid, frightened flutter of her heart pressed close to mine.

"Alan," Carrie would whisper, "please don't. You mustn't."

But it was Joanna's sweet voice I heard, like a rapturous song in my ears.

"Please, Alan, no," Carrie would beg, and I would want her all the more, want her for not having had Joanna, want her with a passion which became increasingly more difficult to control.

I decided to stop seeing her. I was frightened of hurting her—she was so very young—and I was frightened too of the love she bore me, a love I didn't want, a love which I felt I would never be able to return. I wrote her a letter. I explained very carefully and very gently that our relationship had entered a phase for which neither of us was prepared. I pointed out her youth, her inexperience; I stressed the fact that I cared for her deeply and for that reason I did not wish to limit her prospects at so early an age. "See other men," I advised her. "I haven't the right to monopolize your time as I've been doing of late. I'm older than you; be guided by my judgment. I want more than anything to do what's right, and for you to be happy."

But I never sent the letter. I never stopped seeing her. I couldn't, I didn't want to. I was so desperately confused, and so lonely too. There was no one in the cottage now except for the servants and myself. My father was still in Harrisburg, and Joanna had accepted the Chandlers' invitation to cruise down to Florida in search of some suitable property for a winter home which John planned to build in Dade County. She had taken Noelle with her, of course, and I couldn't have felt more abandoned.

One night toward the end of July, I took Carrie home with me. We'd been at a party, one of those never-ending affairs which begins with a banquet, is followed by a ball, and then culminates spectacularly with a seven-course "midnight" supper at dawn. I was bored with it all, and abysmally depressed. At eleven o'clock I seized Carrie by the arm and told her we were leaving, that I'd had enough, that if I heard another waltz or saw another morsel of food or spoke with one more satin-swathed, diamond-dripping matron, I would vomit.

She was quietly submissive as I led her from the house and handed her into the waiting carriage. I admired her for that. In the carriage she even said with a hesitant smile, "I'm glad you decided to leave, Alan. I was terribly bored, but I didn't want to say anything in case you were enjoying yourself."

"Enjoying myself?" I said sullenly. "I hate those bloody parties. I bloody hate Newport."

As a matter of fact, I hated neither. I loved Newport and I thoroughly enjoyed a party of any description, be it a fete, a ball, a *thé dansant*, a full-blown cotillion, or a casual picnic in the park. But of late I hated everything. It was as if I were denying myself, punishing myself, though I had done nothing wrong. It was Spencer Halston who had sinned, who was worthy of punishment, not I. And my mother; she too had . . . Dear God, I couldn't think of my mother. Not in that way. Not in Spencer's arms, in his bed—Oh Jesus, I really did feel sick.

"Carrie!" I gasped. "Talk to me. Say something. Anything!"

I groped for her hand, crushed it in mine. I needed to touch her, to touch someone, to prove to myself that I wasn't alone.

"Alan," said Carrie, "what is it?" She stared at me, startled, her splendid blue eyes wide with alarm.

If I didn't love Joanna, I would surely have loved Carrie, for she was everything any man could want. She was warm, good, and kind; she was sweet, she was pure. And she loved me. In the midst of my grinding despair I could see that unlike Joanna, unlike Spencer Halston, and unlike the man I called "Father," this dear, gentle girl loved me.

"Carrie," I whispered, "come home with me. Stay with me awhile. I don't want to be alone tonight."

"Oh, Alan, no," she cried softly, and I realized at once that she had misinterpreted my meaning. At that moment, sexual activity was the furthest thing from my mind. I wanted only companionship, human contact, a soft voice.

"Carrie, please," I implored. "I cannot face an empty house tonight. Just stay until midnight. One hour, no more, and then I'll take you home."

But she was afraid. She knew what to expect when we were alone together. I saw her fear, her sad indecision. She began to tremble and, like a child, she lowered her gaze and plucked nervously at her skirt.

Poor darling. She *was* a child, so painfully innocent, so heartbreakingly young. She was just like Joanna; she hadn't any comprehension of life and its evils. She had trusted me initially, as Joanna had trusted me, and I had betrayed them both with my lust. I had wanted Joanna because I loved her, and I wanted Carrie because I couldn't have Joanna. That I had had neither of them did me little credit; I would have taken them both if they had let me.

"Please," I persisted, "I won't touch you, I promise. Carrie, I need you. I need you to be with me tonight—just to talk. Please, won't you stay with me one hour?"

She raised her head slowly and rested her blue gaze on mine. Her trembling had ceased and her hands now lay placidly on her lap. She watched me for a time, without emotion it seemed. God knows what was going through her mind, but at last she said softly, "Very well, Alan. I shall stay with you an hour. And then I should like you to take me home."

I dismissed the servants as soon as we arrived. Kelsey hovered about a few moments longer, his disapproval patent in his dour, lined face. Kelsey was a strict adherent to the old school of decorum. To his mind, young ladies did not accompany gentlemen to their homes, nor for that matter did they appear in public, anywhere, at any time, unchaperoned.

"Good night, Kelsey," I said pointedly when he stood

like a stone in the hall. "I won't be needing you anymore this evening."

"Perhaps," he suggested with a stolid determination which irked me, "the young lady would like some refreshment."

"No," Carrie murmured, and I could see she was embarrassed, for she would not meet his reproachful eyes but only stared self-consciously at the floor. "Thank you, Kelsey, I don't want anything. I won't be staying long and I . . ."

She trailed off and fell silent, and at last, having played out all pretense to stay, Kelsey left.

"Don't mind him," I told Carrie as I took her arm and directed her gently down the hall. "He's just a foolish old man. I don't know why my father doesn't pension him off."

I took her into the sunroom. Tall open windows looked out on the lawn, and the scent of night flowers and damp, new-cut grass mingled lazily with the soft evening breeze. A stone fountain stood in the center of the room, surmounted by a fetchingly carved nymph bearing a graceful jug from which water cascaded into the surrounding reservoir at her feet.

As a child, I used to sit in this room for hours and wonder how a jug so small could contain an endless flow of water. I remember once asking my father if the fountain were magic. He explained patiently, and in great detail, the entire mechanics of the water supply system!

How curious, I thought as I settled beside Carrie on the cushioned divan, that I had hated my father for so many years and yet the discovery that I was not his, learning that no ties of blood bound us together, had grieved me more profoundly than had even my mother's death. I couldn't begin to understand my feelings.

I saw him now as a different man, an entity apart from all that touched me; and yet he *had* touched me, had made me, in essence, all that I was. As much as I hated him, I *was* him. I had his arrogance, his volatility, his occasional brutality, and the hotheaded, passionate temperament which both of us struggled to control. No natural father and son were more alike. I used to despise this similarity, but now I felt . . . I felt . . . I didn't know what I felt. I only knew that I was no longer certain of my feelings for Mark Van Holden. In fact, I was no longer certain about anything at all.

"Carrie!" I blurted and reached again for her hand, for the comfort of her touch. Here was truth: this young girl, her love for me, her sweet, aching, unreturned love. Of this I was certain, and only of this. Carrie, sweet Carrie. Why couldn't I love *her,* and not Joanna?

"Carrie, I wish . . ."

"Yes?" she said quietly. "Tell me what you wish, Alan."

"Carrie," I asked like a young witless fool, "do you love me?"

Why had I said that? Was I losing my mind? I was well aware of her feelings for me. I released her hand and rose from the divan and began an aimless pacing about the room.

"Don't answer that," I told her. "Forgive me for asking. I don't know what's the matter with me tonight. I'd say I was drunk, but I haven't had a drink in weeks. And that's ironic, you know. My father prefers that I abstain from alcohol until I'm twenty-one, but I've always drunk on the sly . . . until recently. I haven't touched liquor in a month."

I stopped at the fountain and gazed quizzically at the nymph. Why had I stopped drinking? At school I had drunk like a fish. The few friends I'd made at Yale had cautioned me repeatedly against this habit:

"You'll be chucked out of school if you're discovered," said one. "Why do you drink so much anyway? You don't enjoy it."

"Who said I don't?"

"I say you don't. I've never seen an unhappier drunk than you."

"I'm not a drunk!"

"You're damned well on your way to becoming one!"

In characteristic defiance, I had disregarded the well-intentioned comments of my friends as totally as I'd ignored my father's wishes. To hell with them all, I'd thought angrily. I would drink as much as I pleased. It was my affair and no one else's.

But my friend was right: I didn't enjoy drinking, I never had. I'd only done it to hurt my father. Except lately I hadn't the slightest desire to hurt him. Quite the contrary, in fact. Lately I wanted only to—

"Alan." I turned with a start. Carrie had come up behind me.

"I want to answer you," she said, whisper soft. "I do love you. I love you terribly. I know you don't love me, but it doesn't matter, I love you just the same. I know what you think of me, what you want of me. I know . . ." She faltered and paused, then went on in a faint voice. "I know you brought me here tonight because you want to make love to me, but that doesn't matter either. I love you. I'll do anything you ask."

I stared at her, stunned, her astonishing words reverberating in the cavernous depths of my mind. I'd had no such intention, I truly hadn't; but with her slim form so close to mine, I suddenly found I wanted very much to make love to her.

"That's not true," I said hoarsely. "I didn't bring you here for that reason. I would never hurt you in that way. I care for you too much."

"Do you?" she whispered. "Do you, Alan?"

"Yes," I said, being especially careful not to touch her. "Of course I care for you. Don't you know? Can't you tell? You're very important to me."

"I think not," she said sadly. "I think another girl might serve your purpose just as well, but you have involved yourself with me at the moment, and therein lies my importance."

"You're wrong," I insisted, but she was right. I had wanted her because she was there, conveniently there. I had wanted a woman—any woman—because I couldn't have Joanna. Knowing this, I should have avoided her, for I did care for her and I didn't want to hurt her. But I hadn't avoided her, I couldn't though I'd tried, and now we were alone, really alone without fear of intrusion, and I wanted to make love to her.

"Carrie," I said in a low husky voice, "let me take you home."

I touched her arm, turned her toward the door, and she said nothing, only followed my lead, but her sad, submissive silence broke my heart.

"Perhaps," I said with difficulty, "it would be wiser if we don't see each other after tonight."

"Oh, no," she cried softly. "Don't say that."

"Carrie." I stopped at the door. "Please. You said you'd do anything I ask. Do this then, for your own sake. Stop seeing me."

"No," she said faintly. "Anything but that. Alan, no."

God, she was lovely! She gazed up at me, her face revealing her passion, her azure eyes bright with tears, and I took her in my arms. I realized it was dangerous but I did it, unmindful of the consequence, because she was going to cry. She wept as I held her, she wept as I kissed her, she wept when, without conscious thought, I drew her to the divan and lay down beside her, my mouth warm on hers and my hand moving slow on the curve of her breast.

I made love to her then, I couldn't help myself. I tried not to hurt her; I had never made love to a virgin before, and I tried very hard to be as gentle as I could. But she wouldn't stop crying. At first I was nervous, and frightened of her tears. But after a while, it didn't matter. After a while, nothing at all mattered.

XVII

I MADE LOVE to her every night, sometimes twice a night, for a month. God knows how she escaped pregnancy, for I was taking no precautions. It simply didn't occur to me.

Each evening I was at her home promptly at seven, and after an obligatory chat with her mother, I would collect Carrie and we would trot off to the nearest party, circulate conspicuously to ensure that our presence had been duly noted, after which we would take furtive flight, return to my house, make love in my bedroom for an hour or so, and then I would take her home.

She never cried again as she had that first night; she was always very quiet when I made love to her. She was compliant enough, and as ardent in bed as any man could wish, but she was sad sometimes, and ashamed too, I think. I suppose I should have considered her more, inquired about her feelings, but I was not of a mind, at that time, to explore motives or to indulge in "deep thinking" of any kind. I was content to simply turn off my thoughts and luxuriate fully in the exquisite rapture of physical gratification. As a result, my problems now seemed remote. I no longer thought of Joanna, and I had almost stopped thinking of my father.

One night we attended a ball at the cottage of the Robert Defoes. The Defoes were recently married; Bobby was the son of a friend to my father, and Eileen, his wife, had been a favorite partner of mine, years before, at Miss Lydia's School for the Dance. I always took Carrie to the younger set's parties, as we were less likely to encounter anyone who knew our parents and who might possibly comment on our early departures.

The Defoes gave exceptionally fine parties. Their cottage was new, a gift from Bobby's father. The marble alone—staircases, balustrades, statuary—cost six million dollars, and the house itself was worth twice that much. Bobby loved to flaunt his wealth—his father's wealth, that is. Mr. Defoe was a banker. He had supported many of my father's endeavors—at an exorbitant rate of interest since my father's ventures were usually quite risky and not altogether legitimate. But my father routinely surmounted risks and eluded the law, and Mr. Defoe's return on his investments was considerable. And when Mr. Defoe profited, Bobby, being the eldest and best-loved son, profited too. Hence the twelve-million-dollar cottage and the townhouse in New York and the villa in Capri and the house on Long Island with its full stable of purebred Arabian horses which had all come into Bobby's possession on the day he married Eileen.

"Happiest day of my life," Bobby said as he led me from the ballroom to his oak-paneled study, where he immediately lit a long Havana cigar. "I only wish I had married sooner. What about you, Alan? Is it serious with you and Carrie? And by the way, where do you two disappear to every night? Yes, I've seen you tiptoe away from the parties like a pair of sneak thieves. You haven't been misbehaving yourselves, have you?"

He laughed uproariously, then choked on a mouthful of smoke, and I watched him in silence, fervently wishing he would choke to death.

I didn't like Bobby. I didn't know him well—he was five years older than I—but what little I knew of him, I disliked.

"I think you're mistaken, Bobby," I said with tight politeness. "I may have taken Carrie home early once or twice, but we generally stay late at the parties."

"Oh, come now," he said, leering, "be honest with me, Alan. Are you sleeping with her?"

My nerves tightened, my stomach lurched. I took a step toward him, then stopped abruptly and shoved my hands deep into my pockets. "No," I muttered at length, "I'm not sleeping with her."

"You're not?" he said skeptically. "More's the pity. She's a neat little package, she is. If I weren't a happily married man, I would seriously consider bedding her myself."

"Bobby," I warned, "you'd better shut up."

"Alan!" he laughed. "You're all your father, do you know that? Mark was close-lipped about his conquests too. Everyone knew he was sleeping around like a satyr, yet no one ever knew with whom."

"Goddamn you, shut up!"

"Oh, very well," he said petulantly. "What a bore you are, Alan."

"I'm not sleeping with her," I was compelled to repeat. "I respect her utterly."

"If you say so." He shrugged, then suggested that we rejoin the party.

Jesus, I thought as I followed him from the room, *was it obvious then?* If Bobby, that dim-witted lummox, suspected I was sleeping with Carrie, did everyone else think so too? And what if her family caught wind of it? Her father would kill me.

God, what a mess! What had made me think I could keep such a secret in the fishbowl of Newport society? There were no secrets in Newport. Everyone's activities were common knowledge, communal property. You couldn't spit in Newport without a dozen people discussing it the same day. Christ, I thought miserably, soon everybody in town would know I'd slept with Carrie: her mother, her father, my father . . . and Joanna.

Oh, no, I groaned inwardly, *not Joanna.* If she knew what I'd done, if she learned I'd dishonored Carrie . . . Joanna. How strange I should think of her now. I hadn't done so in weeks. I'd completely forgotten about her. I had even forgotten I loved her.

"Alan! Bobby! Where have you been?"

Eileen descended on us in a sweep of green silk and a heavenly cloud of expensive perfume.

"You've been smoking," she accused, catching scent of

her husband's breath. "Bobby, really! You promised you
wouldn't."

"Forgive me, Eileen," he said with a grin. "I know I
promised, but indulge me just this once, won't you? You
know I can't resist tobacco . . . just as I can't resist you, my
little temptress."

His arm went round her waist and he nuzzled her cheek,
then whispered suggestively near her ear. She blushed
scarlet and tried to pull away, but when he wouldn't release her she smiled resignedly, leaned close against him,
and gave him a swift, loving kiss.

I excused myself and walked away. Carrie was sitting on
a window seat where I'd left her. Her gloved hands were
folded on her lap and she was gazing wistfully at the swirl
of laughing dancers. She wore a dress of white voile, simple yet becoming, and there were pretty white flowers entwined in the masses of her coppery curls.

I did not approach her. I watched her awhile from across
the room, wishing I could change things, wishing I hadn't
hurt her. I had done to her what I had always despised my
father for doing. My father and his women; how I hated
him for his women. Each one, it had seemed to me, had
been a deliberate insult to my mother's memory. But now I
knew better. Now I saw that a man's need was a thing
apart from himself, an insidious force which drove him to
commit unforgivable infamies against those he loved,
against those most innocent, like Joanna, like Carrie.

Reluctantly, unwillingly, I moved toward my victim.
She smiled when she saw me, a heartbreaking, trusting
smile; and my guilt and shame suddenly became a burden
I could barely support. If only I could turn back the clock,
undo what I'd done. If only I had cared more about her feelings and less for my own. Perhaps, I thought briefly, I
should marry her. But no, I couldn't marry her. I loved Joanna. I would never love anyone else. There was no one I
would marry if I couldn't have her.

"Alan," said Carrie, "you were gone so long. I thought
you'd forgotten me."

"Carrie," I said, my voice low, "come, dear. Let me take
you home."

"Home?" she asked, puzzled.

"Yes, home. I know it's early, but I—"

"Oh," she said with a sigh of relief, "you mean to *your* house. For a moment I thought—"

"No," I corrected her. "Not to my house. To yours."

"But, Alan . . ."

"Come," I said curtly, guilt roughening my voice. "Get your wrap. I want to leave now."

"I—I haven't a wrap," she stammered. "Alan, what's wrong?"

"Nothing's wrong, for Christ's sake. I want to go home, that's all. If you want to stay, by all means do so, but I'm leaving. Are you coming?"

I glared at her angrily, hating myself and suddenly hating her for no earthly reason I could think of. Why did she stare at me with those huge tear-damp eyes? Why did she permit me to insult and abuse her, for I'd done nothing else since the day we'd first met.

"Well?" I demanded. "Are you coming?"

"Yes," she said faintly, "I'm coming."

She rose slowly, her head lowered, her shoulders drooping dispiritedly, and followed me from the room. We did not bid anyone good night; we were not in the habit of announcing our departure.

In the carriage I fell grimly silent. Carrie huddled against the door, and I could feel her eyes on me, but I did not return her desolate gaze. I couldn't face her. I was too angry, too confused, and desperately at odds with my conscience. I wanted to do the right thing but I hadn't the courage. If I married her, I would he hurting her as well as myself. In other words, I was still placing Carrie's needs second to my own.

"Please," she said presently, and her voice was so soft, so hesitant, that I almost couldn't hear her. "Please don't take me home."

I did not speak. I couldn't, if I had wanted to.

"Alan," she whispered, "what have I done? Why are you angry with me? Please tell me what's wrong. Please tell me what I've done."

God forgive me, I ignored her. I stared out the window,

my face set like stone, and ignored her. She began to cry. It was the first time she'd cried since that infamous night, and for some unlikely reason it reminded me of when my mother lay dying; when, as I held her hand, as hot tears scorched my cheeks, she had wept for my father, had called my father's name.

A cold bitter rage such as I had never felt swept through me, and I turned to Carrie and said harshly and cruelly, "Be still!"

She stared at me, her eyes bright with tears, trembling with hurt and surprise. I too was shaking, with a fierce dark emotion that frightened me. I wanted to strike her, to hurt her. . . . No, I wanted to kiss her, to make love to her, to dispel the icy aura of my strange and lonely rage in the restorative warmth of her loving embrace.

"Carrie," I muttered, and took her in my arms, pressed my cheek to hers, felt her tears on my tears, for I was crying now, with a silent torturous grief I could not explain. "I love you," I said, but my lips spoke the words, not my heart. I kissed her, and then again, and after a time my grief mellowed, my tears dried, and I was no longer sad or angry or lonely, nor even afraid.

I did not take her home. I instructed the coachman to take us to my house, and when we arrived and I had dismissed the servants, I took Carrie up to my room and made love to her.

Afterward, as we lay together in the dark, I began to think again of my mother, but somehow my thoughts were puzzlingly interspersed with images of Joanna. I saw my mother lying pale and still on her deathbed, and then she became Joanna, lying pale and still in my arms in the garden. I thought of earlier summers, of my mother in the full bloom of health and perfect beauty. She'd been a queen in the kingdom that was Newport, and I had been her most loyal subject. Then Joanna again: successor to the throne, a younger, shier queen, but worthy all the same of my unwavering fealty.

"Alan."

I heard Carrie's voice and I felt her light touch, but we couldn't have been farther apart.

"Yes?" I said softly. "What is it?"

"Alan," she whispered, "did you mean what you said? Do you love me? Do you really?"

I turned my head slightly. Her eyes blazed with love, her pale face glowed in the dim, moonlit room. I watched her in silence and thought of Joanna. I envisioned Joanna and remembered the touch and the taste of her mouth against mine. I could feel her, see her, hear her; she was more vivid a presence than the sweet, loving child I embraced. I wanted her still though I had lost her. I wanted her more for not having her. I thought of Joanna, I longed for her, ached for her. But it was to the girl in my arms that I said, "Yes, I love you."

XVIII

JOANNA CAME HOME the next day. I was delirious with excitement but at the same time numb with fear. What if she hadn't forgiven me? What if she found out what I'd been doing with Carrie? What if she'd told my father what I had done to *her?* I had seen him after that infamous day, and although he'd been moody and irritable and more short-tempered than usual, I knew he'd been preoccupied with his difficulties in Harrisburg and not specifically angry with me. Still I was worried. There was always the possibility she might yet tell him.

I hid in my room until dinner. I was too much of a coward to face her alone. At least at the dinner table, the servants would afford some distraction; she could hardly upbraid me in their presence, nor could she ignore me, which was what I feared more than her rightful reproach.

She was already seated when I joined her. She looked absolutely breathtaking in a new Paquin dress of rose-colored silk, her only adornment a simple gold chain from which hung suspended a small gold heart minutely inscribed with the letters J. S.

She had worn my locket. She wasn't angry then. She couldn't be angry and have worn my locket.

"Joanna," I said, my voice shaking with gratitude. "Joanna, welcome home."

"Thank you," she murmured, her face flushing slightly. "I'm glad to be home. I—I've missed you, Alan."

She lowered her gaze from my incredulous face and began to fuss distractedly with her napkin.

She had missed me? Had I heard her correctly? She had *missed* me?

"Joanna." I sat down swiftly and covered her hand with mine, unmindful of the footman's astonishment and of Kelsey's coldly disapproving stare. "Can you ever forgive me?" I blurted, but she withdrew her hand in a fluster of embarrassment and implored me with her eyes to keep silent.

The footman, young Hendrick, stood avidly attentive, the platter of steaming chops forgotten in his hands. Kelsey's white brows were lowered ominously and his great brush of a mustache literally quivered with reproof.

My face grew hot, my collar was suddenly strangling me.

"Hendrick!" I snapped. "Serve the meat, if you please. Kelsey, fill Mrs. Van Holden's glass!"

They fell to their tasks in one motion, Hendrick quickly, clumsily, and Kelsey with the dignified disdain I deserved. But I ignored them both and stared at Joanna. She was home. She had missed me. She'd forgiven me. My heart raced and leaped; I couldn't have been happier.

"How is Noelle?" I managed to say while I poked aimlessly at my food. I couldn't eat. I could barely breathe for the unutterable happiness that rose in my breast in great joyous waves.

"She is well," said Joanna, and she too was not eating. "She cut another tooth while we were at sea, but she never fussed once. She is such a good baby."

"Yes. Yes, she is." I toyed with my vegetables but left them untasted. "Did John find his property? Will he build in Florida?"

"Yes," she replied. "He purchased several hundred acres in Miami, fronting on Biscayne Bay. The land is quite wild, but very beautiful. John plans to clear four or five acres at the waterfront for the house and grounds, but he intends to leave the remainder of the land in its natural state. The foliage is lovely, Alan, so exotic and graceful. And the palm trees and tropical flowers are magnificent." She paused, then asked with a hesitant smile, "And you, Alan? What have you done this past month?"

I lowered my gaze as a sharp stab of guilt pierced my conscience. "Nothing," I said. "I've done nothing."

"Nothing?" she echoed worriedly. "But surely you've done something in my absence."

My guilt chiseled deeper. I stared like a dolt at my dish. At long length I mumbled, "I've gone to some parties . . . with Carrie Monroe. I've been seeing her—with no special intent, you understand. She's a sweet girl and I like her, but—"

"Carrie?" she exclaimed. "Alan, how wonderful! She's a darling, isn't she? Carrie Monroe! Oh, I couldn't be happier!"

I looked up abruptly. Her eyes shone, her face was radiant.

"Alan," she urged, "you must bring her to tea one afternoon. I should so like to see her. It's been ages since—"

"I don't know about tea," I said quickly. "I doubt if Carrie would—I mean, there's nothing serious between us."

"Of course you're not serious now. You're both so young."

"It has nothing to do with age. I like Carrie well enough, but I shall never marry her."

"How can you know that?" she laughed. "Oh, Alan, I can't tell you how pleased—"

"Joanna, there is absolutely nothing to be pleased about. Carrie means nothing to me." And then, realizing how callous that sounded, I added quickly, "I'm very fond of her, of course, but not in that way."

"Very well," she said with another laugh. "You'll never marry her. You're very fond of her. I think I understand the situation."

But I could see that she understood nothing, and that she was determined to ascribe to my relationship with Carrie an importance which did not exist.

We had our coffee in the sunroom. Joanna began to talk of her trip, of the Chandlers' hospitality, of the fair weather and mild seas they had experienced. She described Miami in great detail as if she had stored in her mind great funds of information upon which to draw in order to avoid any discussion of a personal nature with me.

I stared at the fountain while she spoke. I wanted to apologize. I longed to tell her how sorry I was for having hurt her. I wanted to say, too, how desperately lonely I had been in her absence, how I'd thought of her, yearned for her, and that I had never for a moment stopped loving her. But I knew if I spoke of those things, I would only be hurting her anew. And so I kept silent. And stared at the fountain. And ardently wished I were dead.

The hall clock struck ten.

We rose from our chairs like twin puppets on string.

"Good night," I said glumly, and waited for her to precede me from the room.

But she remained near her chair, watching me with the oddest expression on her face, and when I eyed her questioningly, she said with much reluctance, "Alan, before we retire, I should like to say something to you. I've been putting it off all evening because, to tell you the truth, I was . . . afraid. I know you don't want to talk of it, I know it hurts you to even think of it, but you must know how sorry I am for . . . telling you what I did. And more importantly, you must, I beg you, realize how deeply and completely Mark loves you."

"Be still," I said hoarsely. "Don't talk of that."

I was suddenly trembling with the same lonely rage that had plagued me for weeks.

"Please," she said rapidly, "you must hear me out: I've thought of nothing else for weeks. I've agonized over this every waking moment I've been away. That day . . . that day in the garden when you tried . . . tried to make love to me, I blamed myself for that. I thought perhaps I had led you on in some way, led you to believe that I cared for you as other than a son. But then I realized the reason for your—"

"Enough," I implored her. "I don't want to hear any more."

"Alan, listen to me, please! It's of vital importance that you see things as they are. This . . ." She paused, drew a steadying breath, then went on: "This all has to do with your mother. You've never been able to accept the fact that you've lost her. And you hate Mark, you *blame* Mark, not for her death, but because she loved him."

"What?" I said sickly. *"What?"*

"It's true," she insisted. "That's why you think you love me. You don't really, you know, not the way you think you do. You're only jealous of my love for Mark, as you were of Lenore's love for him. You wanted her love exclusively, and now you want my love exclusively. You don't want to share me, least of all with Mark, who you feel stole your mother's love."

"Shut up!" I cried hotly, and I moved toward the door in a panic. "You don't know what you're talking about. Shut up! Get out of here! Don't speak to me of my mother. Don't ever speak to me of my mother!"

I stared at her violently, my hands clenched at my sides. I was strangling with frustration and with the terrible torment of a grief that had never died.

"Alan," she persisted, "if you would only realize that Mark stole nothing from you. Your mother loved you. And Mark loves you too, he always has. You must put aside your childish insecurities and recognize the truth once and for all. You must reconcile yourself to the fact that your mother is gone and that no one can replace her. Blaming Mark for her death will not bring her back. Loving me as a substitute will not bring her back. And . . . and . . ." she faltered, "what's of paramount importance is that the circumstance of your conception makes no difference to Mark. It's so obvious, Alan. It's so painfully obvious that he loves you as his own."

Why didn't she shut up? What did she know of fierce, aching passion and uncontrolled need, of brutal betrayal of the foulest kind? What emotion had ever stirred her? What adversity had ever touched her? Had she ever in her life known a driving love, a vital loss, or a hopeless, ruinous sorrow? She had lost a husband. What of it? The loss had been negligent and her love for him too had been of no account, for hadn't she found a speedy replacement? She had married again, had loved again, an insipid spiritless love, which was fathoms away from my own love for her.

"Alan," she whispered, and she dared to draw near me, dared to try to console me with her traitorous touch.

My mind spun with rage. Incoherently I shouted, "Stay away from me, don't touch me, don't speak to me! He doesn't love me, he never did. And neither did my mother. No one loves a bastard, don't you know that? My own father, my *natural* father has denied me; he won't even admit I am his. And you expect Mark Van Holden to love me? He doesn't, I tell you. He couldn't possibly love me. And he never will."

"Alan, oh, wait, listen!"

"Don't touch me!" I cried when again she reached out with a quivering hand. "Don't touch me, don't pity me!"

I stumbled away, flung open the door, and raced up to my room.

She followed me, rapping at my door and frantically calling out my name. I think I swore at her, I can't remember, but after a while I heard her walk away; a door closed at the end of the hall, and then I heard nothing at all.

I pulled off my clothes and crawled into bed, where I curled up in a ball and drew up the bedspread to cover my head. I was still shaking, I couldn't stop shaking, and I was cold, icy cold, though the air in the room was dead still, close and hot. The sound of the sea was a din in my ears; the waves roared and broke and it seemed that the sound was contained in my skull.

I might have slept then, I'm not sure. I kept seeing images, cruelly clear and hurtful: Joanna in my arms, yet maddeningly unattainable; my mother in Spencer's arms, damp limbs intertwined, kissing, touching, moaning with pleasure, and conceiving a baby in the rapture of that love. I saw myself as a child, falling asleep in my father's arms, my head on his breast, the beat of his heart a balm on my soul. I saw Noelle in his arms. He had sired Noelle, had given her life. She was his own, the child of his body, his true flesh and blood. I was not.

Toward dawn, the images faded. I saw nothing more; my thoughts seemed suspended in the dark, tortured cells of my brain. The room brightened slowly, a gray light first, tentative, soft, a silvery portent of day. I had tossed aside the bedclothes, in my sleep perhaps. For some reason I was reminded of Carrie, of the nights she had lain with me, of the love she had given me. Only Carrie, of all who knew me, loved me. Strange she should love me when no one ever had, strange and incredible and ineffably sad. Carrie loved me and, I daresay, wanted to marry me, to bear my children, children who would love me as all children love their fathers.

I sat up suddenly, peered into the pellucid light of dawn. *All children love their fathers.*

The thought intrigued me, fascinated me.

I rose from my bed, rang for my man. My mind had long ceased to function in a rational manner. Reason and logic had no place in my thoughts, but my purpose was clear. I would call on Carrie immediately the day dawned and I would ask her to marry me. She would of course say yes; I hadn't the least doubt on that score. We would marry quickly, without pomp. We would have many children, it was absolutely imperative that we have children. And the children would love me.

That I didn't love Carrie, nor ever would, mattered not. That I loved Joanna and always would was of no relevance at the moment. I had made up my mind and nothing would change it. I would marry Carrie, give her my children, and the children would love me. Because all children love their fathers. It is a simple law of nature that all children love their fathers.

XIX

COULD IT BE she had read my thoughts? Or was it possible she had known all along that our clandestine relationship would eventually bring us to this pass? For she was waiting for me that morning, waiting on the loggia, dressed in white as always, and bathed in the drowsy light of the shimmering morning sun.

She ran down the steps when she saw me, and oblivious to the coachman and to a pair of gardeners who were clipping the flowering shrubs, she threw herself into my arms.

"Alan!" she greeted me, breathless and laughing. "Alan, I'm so glad to see you."

She clung to me tightly, her arms round my neck. I saw the gardeners smile, I saw my coachman shake his head, then tactfully turn his gaze from the scene.

"Carrie." I disengaged her arms, held her gently away. "Carrie, let's go into the house. I want to talk to your mother."

"To my mother? Why?"

Somehow I think she knew.

I had decided to say nothing until I had seen her mother. Stephen Monroe was still in New York; therefore I should have to ask Sally Monroe for her daughter's hand. I wanted to do the right thing. For some reason it was extremely important that everything be done according to the strictest code of propriety. I was well aware of the wrong I had done Carrie; perhaps there lay the reason I was determined that matters henceforth should be conducted properly and with the utmost decorum.

But Mrs. Monroe had not yet arisen.

"My mother is a late sleeper," Carrie told me. "Especially in Newport. She never rises till ten or eleven. The sea air, she says, enervates her. Why did you want to talk to her, Alan?"

She had taken me into her father's study. It was a marvelous room, dramatically furnished with small Tudor chairs and Carel chests, an Isfahan carpet, and an exquisite Gothic settee of black oak. The mantelpiece of the darkened fireplace was of African rose marble, and on the opposite wall, a van Eyck rendering of the Virgin and Child gazed down in solemn splendor from a dimly gilded frame. I have always particularly liked that room. Unlike my father's study in New York, which was his sanctum sanctorum and which I was never permitted to enter unless specifically invited, Mr. Monroe's study was accessible to all, especially to his children, which had somehow imbued the room with an aura of warmth, and of family unity and love.

"Alan," Carrie said as I studied a detail of the saintly van Eyck, "why do you want to talk to my mother?"

I turned from the painting. Carrie was watching me with an expectant smile. Her cheeks were rose pink, her eyes were the deepest, purest blue under a fan of inky lashes. Impulsively, I touched her face, petal smooth under my hand, and she closed her eyes and rubbed her cheek against my palm like a graceful and contented kitten.

"How pretty you are," I was compelled to say. "I am always astonished at how pretty you are."

"Do you think so?" she said softly. "Do you really think so?"

"Yes." I assured her. "I really think so. You are the prettiest girl I have ever seen."

"Oh, Alan, I want to be pretty for you, only for you. And I want to make you happy in every way I can."

"You do make me happy."

"Do I?" she whispered. "Do I really?"

"Yes." I smiled and dropped a brief kiss on her brow. "Yes, really, my little skeptic."

"Alan." She moved away from me, lowered her gaze, and began to fidget with her skirt. "You don't think . . . ?"

"Think what, Carrie?"

"You don't think me . . . bad?" She threw me an anguished look, then said in a rush, "You do realize, don't you, that I would never let any man but you make love to me? You must give me your word that you believe me. I should die if you ever thought I—"

"Sweet girl," I said gently and drew her into my arms, "don't think about that. Don't torture yourself with shameful and distressing thoughts."

"Shameful?" she cried softly. "You think my love shameful?"

"Carrie," I said at once, "you misunderstand me. The shame is in me, not in your love. I was wrong to coerce you into a relationship which bears neither social nor moral sanction. I am at fault for inducing you to act against your conscience."

"Oh, don't," she begged in an agonized voice. "Don't make it ugly. Don't despise it, don't regret it."

"Regret it? My good child, I regret only your pain, the humiliation I have caused you."

"Oh!" she cried and burst into tears and attempted to wrench free of my arms. But I held her fast, cursing myself for a blundering fool, for I had expressed myself badly; she did not understand me. She thought I despised her, her love, when in fact it was myself I held in the deepest, most loathsome contempt.

"Carrie," I soothed, "don't cry. Everything's all right. I'm going to make it right. I want to marry you."

She raised her head, a sob caught in her throat. "Marry me? You want to marry me?"

"Yes," I said firmly. "I want you to be my wife. I hadn't meant to tell you now; I wanted to speak first to your mother. But it doesn't matter. We're going to be married—right away—before I go back to New Haven. You do want that, Carrie? You do want to marry me?"

"Oh, yes. Yes, I do. But, Alan, so soon? I cannot prepare in that short a time. There are things to be done: invitations, the church, the caterers—"

"I don't care," I stopped her. "I don't want all that. We'll be married simply, quietly, as soon as possible. I don't want to wait. I will not wait."

"Oh, Alan," she sighed, misinterpreting my intensity, "do you love me that much? Do you want me that badly?"

"I want," I said fiercely, "to marry you. And I want your children. You must give me children."

My arms tightened painfully about her. She gave a soft gasp and her eyes widened in sudden alarm. "Alan," she cried, "you're hurting me."

"I'm sorry," I said and released her at once. "I'm sorry, but it's very important that we marry immediately. You see that, don't you, Carrie? You do understand?"

"What's this?" came a voice from the door. "Wedding plans? Do I hear talk of wedding plans?"

I looked quickly toward the speaker. Mrs. Monroe, that tiresome woman, had decided at last to rise from her bed.

I shuddered involuntarily. My dislike for her had not lessened in the past month; on the contrary, it had grown till I could barely conceal it. Those nightly chats with her had almost been my undoing. Every evening when I called for Carrie, I had been forced to endure the tedium of Sally Monroe's conversation, punctuated with coy innuendoes and arch, sidelong glances. I had the distinct impression she was aware of what was happening between her daughter and myself, but I had told myself guiltily that she couldn't possibly know what we were doing.

And whenever I called, Mrs. Monroe was always dressed to the nines, bejeweled within an inch of her life, and she invariably exuded a cloud of the most nauseatingly musky perfume. I would have given my soul to tell her exactly what I thought of her, but instead I always continued to nod pleasantly while she babbled, or I would smile obsequiously, or compliment her gown while she preened like a peacock, her shapely bosom and wasp-thin waist proudly on display for my view. What a ridiculous woman she was—attractive but ridiculous—and I would often wonder wearily how she could ever have produced a charming and intelligent daughter like Carrie when she herself was so fatuous and absurd.

"Alan," she said now, "dear, *dear* boy. Did I hear correctly? Is there to be a wedding? Carrie, you sly thing, you might have confided in me."

"But, Mama, I didn't know till just now. Alan wanted to . . ."

"I wanted to speak to you first," I interjected. "Mrs. Monroe, I apologize for not broaching the subject in the proper manner, but I . . ."

"Don't apologize, Alan," she said airily. "Good heavens, I knew all along that your intentions toward my daughter were honorable."

She gave me one of her knowing looks, and the hairs began to rise on the back of my neck. God, I disliked her!

"Well then," she said, turning to her daughter, "when shall we announce the engagement?"

Carrie said nothing; she looked to me helplessly for support.

I cleared my throat, tugged at my shirt cuffs.

"Mrs. Monroe," I said, "with your permission I should like to marry within the month, before I return to Yale. I've discussed this with Carrie, and we are agreed on this point."

"Indeed?" said the woman, her bird-bright, blue eyes scanning mine.

"An engagement," I explained, "serves only to prolong the inevitable. Why should we wait months or even a year to marry? We're not children. We both know our minds and we're both of us certain of our decision."

"My daughter," she reminded me, "is only seventeen, Alan."

"But, Mama," the girl exclaimed, *"you* married at seventeen!"

"Be quiet!" commanded her mother. Then turning to me: "Why do you wish to marry in haste? No, let me rephrase that: Is it *necessary* that you marry in haste?"

"Mama!" cried Carrie.

"Be quiet, Caroline! Alan, I want an answer."

"No," I said stiffly. "It is not necessary. I wish to marry immediately for reasons of my own. I have not compromised your daughter, if that's what you're implying."

How smoothly the lie rolled off my tongue, and how hard the cold glitter of Sally Monroe's eyes.

"I am implying nothing," she said at length. "Your wish for an immediate marriage merely puzzles me. One would naturally assume a reason lies behind all this inexplicable . . . urgency."

She eyed me significantly; I chose to say nothing.

My lack of defense appeared to disarm her. She smiled after a moment, an oddly humorless smile, and said with apparent resignation, "Well, I suppose I cannot dissuade you since it's obvious your mind is made up. Frankly, I've always been in favor of early marriages, but my husband, I fear, may not share this opinion where his daughter is concerned. She is his favorite, you know. But not to worry. I'm reasonably certain I can override any objections he might raise. By the way, Alan, what does Mark say about all this? Is he reconciled to losing his only son?"

I think she stressed the word *only*, though I cannot be sure, for my thoughts had careered wildly at the mention of my father's name. I hadn't even stopped to consider what his reaction might be. What would he say when I suddenly announced I had decided, without consulting him, to marry?"

"Alan," she pressed, taking note of my uneasiness, "you *have* told him?"

"Yes. Yes, of course," I lied. "He's delighted with the idea. He's always been fond of Carrie."

"Has he?"

"Yes. He's told me so a hundred times."

"And he doesn't think you're too young, or that the responsibilities of marriage will interfere with your schooling?"

Jesus, that's exactly what he would think. He would never permit me to marry at nineteen, and somehow I had the feeling Mrs. Monroe knew this. But like a fool I replied, "No, he doesn't think I'm too young. Well, perhaps he does, but he has no real objection to my marrying at this time."

What was I saying? Why was I constructing a cage of lies from which later there would be no escape?

"Alan," the witch persisted, "I was under the impression that Mark was in Harrisburg and that he's been there for the past several weeks. How then did you discuss your plans with him?"

"How?" I said blankly.

"Yes, how?"

"Well, I wrote him," I told her, compounding my stupidity, "and he responded to my letter, indicating that he did not oppose the marriage."

"I see."

"Naturally, we could not fully discuss in a letter the many aspects and ramifications of such a decision. I'm sure though that when he comes home . . ."

I paused and fell silent in a hot, sick sweat. What would I do when my father came home?

I looked at Carrie. She smiled uncertainly, realizing, I think, that I had neither spoken nor written to my father of my plans. But she said nothing, and I was grateful for that; my admiration for her increased a thousandfold.

Mrs. Monroe, however, did not have her daughter's tact. She said with a smirk, "I don't know that I believe you, Alan. I rather doubt Mark would sanction a marriage at your age. You are, after all, his *only* son. A man tends to dote on his *only* son, while at the same time imposing more severe restrictions than he would if he had *other* sons."

She had done it again: She had specifically stressed the word *only*. What was she driving at? Did she know I was not his son and was she, in a cruel oblique way, trying to tell me she knew?

My nausea increased as a sickening rage shuddered through me. I swung round to face this odious woman, and said in a cold, hostile voice, "Whether or not you believe me is immaterial, but if you like, when my father comes home I shall ask him to pay you a personal visit and to inform you firsthand of his consent."

"I should very much like that," she murmured.

She left us alone then, and soon I bid Carrie good-bye; I was too agitated to listen to her happy chatter.

All I could think of now was Mark Van Holden. When my father came home I knew there'd be hell to pay. What would he do? Shout at me? Strike me? He was a hard man, to be sure, hard and dangerous and sometimes even violent, but he'd never been that way with me. He had been tolerant with me, and patient, though patience was not one of his strong points. I had never before realized the cautious, easy way he handled me. I had neither seen nor cared that when dealing with me he had always been kind, lenient, almost indulgent. Under ordinary circumstances I might have thought he loved me. But he didn't of course. I was, after all, another man's son.

What a puzzle he was, this man I had thought was my father. I had thought I knew him, but I did not. I had thought I hated him, but I did not.

Now wasn't that strange? I suddenly realized I no longer hated him. I no longer hated a man I had hated for all of my life. I felt purged, cleansed, renewed, and restored. I felt better, saner, happier than I had in years. My nausea vanished, my rage was dissipated, and the cold, empty sadness that had plagued me for weeks was miraculously gone.

I hated my father no more. And I couldn't for the life of me think why.

XX

I HAVE ALWAYS preferred the house in Newport to the town-house in New York because my mother, with the help of Richard Morris Hunt, designed it. It was my mother's wish to recreate in her summer home the style and tone of an earlier time, and to this end she prevailed upon Mr. Hunt to execute a suitable setting for the antiques and furnishings and magnificent works of art she had already begun to purchase.

Mr. Hunt did not fail her. The house, of Indiana limestone, rose three stories high overlooking the sea, and the interior was exquisite with its great Gothic ballroom and Versailles dining room, and its spacious stately hall of breccia marble and richly carved oak. Into this glorious shell my mother had introduced *fleur de pêche* mantelpieces, Louis Seize woodwork, Tiepolo-inspired murals, and a bronze and marble Allard staircase, so that the house literally sang with grace and grandeur. It was the showplace of Newport, a fitting tribute to my mother's memory; but when my father returned from Harrisburg he told me at breakfast, in the most infuriatingly conversational of tones, that he intended to sell it.

He had come home late one night, following Joanna's return from Florida. He had failed again in Harrisburg; the Pennsylvania legislature had not and would not change its position regarding the proposed pipeline. I had read of his defeat in the *Newport Daily News,* and according to that newspaper, "He had exhausted all possibilities, and the control of the oil refining marketing which he had held autonomously with no regard to the havoc wreaked in the industry would not long be his."

His mood was murderous. He did not acknowledge my murmured greeting but went straight to his room and slammed his door; I did not see him again until the next morning at breakfast.

We were alone in the morning room; Joanna had chosen to breakfast upstairs, which was just as well, for I knew when I spoke to my father of my impending marriage, there was bound to be a quarrel, and I did not wish to distress her any more than I already had.

"What the devil's wrong with you?"

I looked up from my dish with a start. My father was watching me, his piercing, dark gaze holding mine, and I realized sheepishly that I had been staring at my plate since I'd sat down.

In a fever of embarrassment I lowered my eyes. "Nothing's wrong," I mumbled.

"Why aren't you eating? Are you ill?"

His tone was sharp but his concern was clearly evident. How many other times, I wondered, had he spoken to me in this way, disguising his concern with a harsh angry voice?

"No," I responded. "I'm not ill. I—I have something to tell you." But I did not speak further, and still I would not raise my gaze.

"Well?" he said impatiently. "What is it?"

I looked up at last, really looking at him for the first time since he'd been home. The legal battle in Harrisburg had left its mark on him: His face was thinner, harder, and his dark eyes were shadowed with fatigue. Dimly I realized how alone he was and how he had always been alone, struggling single-handedly against monumental odds, yet ever maintaining the rigorous standards he set for himself.

I wanted to touch him, to smooth the weary lines from his brow. And then I thought frantically: *What's happening to me? Why do I want to comfort him? And why, whenever I remember I am not his son, do my eyes sting with hot angry tears?*

"Well?" he demanded again. "Are you going to tell me

what's on your mind or are you going to stare at me mutely
for the remainder of the day?"

"Sir," I began in a low voice that shook, "I have asked
Carrie Monroe to marry me."

"Carrie Monroe?" He frowned, obviously trying to recall
who she was.

"Stephen Monroe's daughter," I reminded him. "I have
asked her to marry me and she's accepted. I'm sorry I
haven't mentioned it to you before now, but you've been
away most of the summer. . . ."

I trailed off feebly, and he watched me a moment in silence. Apparently my news surprised but did not anger
him. At last he inquired, "And when do you plan to marry?
After graduation? That is a long time hence; are you certain you won't change your mind by then?"

"Sir," I said nervously, "I plan to marry before I begin
my fall term."

"Next fall?" he said with another frown.

"This fall."

"That's out of the question."

"But, sir . . ."

"You will not marry this fall, or next fall. You will complete your studies first, and if at that time you are still determined to marry your young lady—"

"But, sir—"

"Listen to me!" he snapped, and I could see the intense
effort he was making to curb his temper. "I am neither so
insensitive nor so old that I have forgotten the passion of
first love. There is nothing in life quite as fierce, and as illogical. I fully understand your needs, your feelings, but I
can neither sanction nor support them. You do yourself a
disservice by making so crucial a commitment at so tender
an age. This is a time for introspection, for self-discovery;
you must delve into your nature, learn who you are, what
you are, before contemplating a lifelong alliance. You're
far too young to marry, to even think of marrying. We
shall talk of it no more."

Talk of it no more? What was he saying? We had to talk
of it, he had to give me his consent! Didn't he realize how
vital it was that I have children?

"Please!" I burst out. "I must marry her, I have to marry her!"

"What?" he said, stunned. "Have you gotten her **pregnant**?"

"No, no, it's not that!"

"Alan, I want the truth. Is she pregnant?"

"No, I swear it!"

His dark eyes searched mine. He saw my fear, my desperate need, but he saw too that I had answered him truthfully. With a curt, impatient gesture of dismissal, he said, "In that case, I see no reason for you to marry her at this time."

"But you must let me marry!" I cried. "You cannot forbid—"

"I do forbid it!" he said sharply. "And you will obey me, Alan. Now let's drop the subject, if you please. I have had my fill of disagreement this summer."

I subsided in frustration, my hands clenching impotently in my lap. In the back of my mind I realized I had approached him at the worst possible time and that given other circumstances he might have been more willing to hear me out. But I was angry and hurt; I cared less for his problems than for my own wounded dignity, and I could only think now that he was the most obstinate, pigheaded, arrogant man alive. I was suddenly glad he wasn't my father! I should have told him I knew, I should have told him how delighted I had been to learn I was no son of his. He didn't care about me, about my feelings, he never had. He cared only for himself and for his self-centered, self-serving interests.

"Alan," I heard him say, "if you will stop brooding for a moment and give me your attention, there is something rather unpleasant I must tell you."

Unpleasant? I thought bitterly. As far as I was concerned, anything he'd ever had to tell me had been unpleasant.

And when I gave him no answer but only glared at him resentfully, he said with a shrug, "I have sold the house."

I glared at him, still without comprehension.

"I'm selling the house," he said again, and he watched

me and waited till at length I asked sullenly, "Which house?"

"This house. I'm selling it to the Simpsons."

Comprehension came to me like the report of a rifle. I sat bolt upright in my chair. "Why?"

"I need money," he said, his voice low, his words clipped. "I need the devil of a lot of money and I need it now. Grace Simpson has always admired the house, and her husband has offered me a fair price for it—in cash."

"But you can't sell it!" I cried. "It's my mother's house. Everything in it is hers. I know she would want me to have it."

He at least had the good grace to look uncomfortable. He picked up a fork, turned it over in his hands, then placed it very carefully near his dish. "Alan, I don't want to sell, but I must. All of my funds are tied up in the refineries, and the approval of the new pipeline has—"

"I don't care about that! Sell something else. Sell the townhouse. I hate the townhouse!"

"Yes, I know you do."

"You don't have to sell this house. You're doing it purposely," I accused. "You're deliberately trying to eradicate all trace of my mother."

"Don't be a fool!" he said harshly. "Why should I want to do that? I need money, I tell you, and it's available to me now if I sell this house."

"I don't believe you. You're a bloody liar. You're only doing this because . . ."

I choked back the words that rose to my lips. I couldn't say it, I simply couldn't tell him I knew I was not his son. I don't know what stopped me. Perhaps it was the memory of Spencer's denial when I had accused him of being my father. "You are not my son," he had insisted. "You are *Mark's* son." And if Mark Van Holden, too, were to say to me: "You are not my son," I don't know if I could have borne it.

"Alan," he said, his voice patient, restrained, "I'm selling this house because I need money. That is the only reason, believe me. It would be senseless to sell the townhouse; I must live in New York. And besides, this house is worth four times as much as the townhouse."

I said nothing. I sat rigidly upright, staring blindly at the table, and I could feel the carved edges of the chair digging painfully into my back. My mother had chosen these chairs, and the long table, and the Gobelin tapestry on the wall, and every last lovely piece in the house. And now he was going to sell it. He didn't need money, he couldn't possibly need money. My father was one of the wealthiest men in the country, if not *the* wealthiest. There had to be another reason he was selling my mother's house and it must have to do with the fact that I was not his son.

"Why are you doing this?" I heard myself say, and it was as if another being, not my own, spoke the words. "Is it because of Spencer Halston?"

My father's eyes, black and hot, scorched mine.

"What do you mean?" he demanded.

Again that being spoke, that alien being who slumbered in stealth within the uncharted chambers of my brain. "Are you selling this house," said my voice, "because of Spencer? Are you taking vengeance on me for a wrong he did you years ago?"

I saw his eyes change. I saw the shock of disbelief and then a swift, bitter pain he could not hide. I tried to look away but could not. I stared at him fearfully while he stared, with terrifying deliberation, at me.

"Explain yourself," he said in a deadly quiet voice. "Explain yourself at once."

"You know what I mean," I said faintly.

I was afraid now, afraid of his voice and of his ominous dark gaze. I had said too much; I had unleashed the demons of my father's private hell, and I was afraid.

"Explain yourself, Alan," he said once more. "I will not ask you again."

"Don't threaten me," I said, trembling. "You haven't any right to tell me what to do. You're not my—"

I broke off in mid-sentence, silenced and quenched by the terrible stillness in his eyes. A long moment passed, and then he rose and came toward me. Instinctively, blindly, I scrambled to my feet and backed away. I knew he would strike me if I spoke another word.

He must have seen my fear, for he stopped suddenly and his dark face changed, grew puzzled at first, then oddly apprehensive. He looked frightened, strange as it seemed, frightened by his anger and by the violent act he had almost committed because of that anger. He stared at me in the most peculiar way, as if he didn't quite recognize me. But no, that wasn't it. It was more as if he were looking past me, beyond me, to a private, dark memory which he had tried but was unable to forget.

A moment might have passed, or an hour, I couldn't say which. At last I said hoarsely, "What can I tell you that you don't already know? Spencer denied it, but I know it's true."

"Spencer?" he said. "Spencer told you what happened?"

"No!" I cried, my fear returning in force, for his face had gone ghastly with a fierce and violent rage. "Spencer didn't tell me. Someone else did."

"Someone else? Who?"

"No one! No one told me! I overheard it," I lied desperately. "On the night you quarreled with Spencer I overheard everything."

"You overheard?" he said, stricken. "You've known all these years?"

I perceived his shame, the agony of humiliation I was causing him, but I had to lie. I couldn't say Joanna had told me. Some remaining shred of sanity told me I couldn't, shouldn't, tell him that Joanna had uncovered a truth which for years he had tried to conceal.

"Yes," I replied, my voice heavy with a shame of my own, "I have known all these years."

He said nothing for a very long time. I watched him in silence as he returned to the table and slumped tiredly in his chair. He seemed dazed, disoriented, as if he had just been dealt a severe physical blow.

Suddenly then, as I had before, I wanted to touch him. Flesh of my flesh. Where was that from? The Bible? Did it pertain to man and wife or to man and child? But I was not of this man's flesh. I was not his child, and the thought suddenly struck me as ludicrously, insanely funny. I heard myself laugh, a strangled half-sob of a laugh, and my father looked up, his startled, dark eyes searching mine.

"I'm sorry," I said, unable to control the inexplicable burst of humor that curved my mouth into a ridiculous smile. "I don't mean to laugh, but it's funny, don't you think, that Spencer should have denied it? Because it's true, of course, a blind man could see it. But I suppose you're going to do the same thing now: tell me it's all a lie, that it isn't true at all."

And as the absurd laughter trembled treacherously on my lips, I realized that it was exactly what I wanted him to do. I wanted him to say, "Yes, Alan, it's a lie. Of course I'm your father. It was all an unspeakable lie."

But he did not say that. He watched me a moment, his eyes dark with a memory and with the insupportable pain of that memory, and he said at length, "No, Alan, I won't deny it. It would be pointless, wouldn't it, since you've been aware of the truth for eight years. I can see now . . ." He paused and lowered his weary gaze to the table. "I understand now why you feel toward me as you do. I should have guessed it—what a fool I've been!—but I think I knew all along that you knew, and out of cowardice I suppose, I preferred to bury that truth along with . . . the other."

He fell silent, picked up a napkin and began to turn it round and round in his hands. I was too stricken to speak; he had confirmed indisputably what I had hoped against hope wasn't true. So it was final then. I had the facts from the most unimpeachable of sources.

I moved toward the door. "What a joke," I said bitterly, dangerously close to tears. "What a contemptible twist of irony that for the past eight years I have constantly called you bastard when in reality *I* am the fatherless bastard."

He raised his head abruptly; the napkin dropped from his hands. "What the devil are you talking about?"

"Don't you think it's funny?" I said, my voice rising. "Don't you think it's hilarious that I have called you that name for years and yet I am the true bastard? How you must have laughed each time I said it! How it must have amused you! But what I don't understand is why you haven't tossed me out on my ear. Why do you let me live here? Why do you feed me, clothe me, shelter me? Why have you made me your heir? Why would you want all that is yours to pass into my hands? Why do you do these things for me when I am not your son?"

The room reverberated with my words. I glared at him defiantly while the hot sting of tears pricked humiliatingly behind my eyes. He stared at me in silence for fully three minutes, and then, to my everlasting gratitude, he said, "For Christ's sake, Alan, what sort of nonsense are you talking? You *are* my son, *my* son, do you hear me? And I do all those things for you because I love you."

PART THREE
Mark

Men in rage strike those that wish them best.

WILLIAM SHAKESPEARE
Othello

XXI

I REALIZED AT last that we had been talking at cross-purposes. It became clear to me that Alan had not overheard my quarrel with Spencer Halston, but instead had been told by some prattling fool the cruel piece of gossip that he was not my son. My anger at this senseless and inexcusable act was mitigated by the monumental relief of realizing that Alan knew nothing of what had actually transpired between his godfather and myself, and that I could still hope, by the grace of God Almighty, he never would. Because God alone could forgive the outrage I had committed, with Spencer Halston's help, against my wife. God alone, if a God existed, had the wisdom and the infinite compassion to exorcize the relentless ghost of guilt which haunted me still. Only a Supreme Being, unfettered by the chains of mortal weakness, unblemished by the passions and jealousies which distort the mortal mind, could pardon my unpardonable sin. For I had murdered my wife, I had murdered her as deliberately as though I had laid violent hands on her, and only God in his limitless mercy could forgive me that cold-blooded crime.

I looked on the face of my son, and there was my eternal punishment in the exquisite eyes and the fair, perfect face of Lenore. He was she come to life to condemn me, for he had all of his life borne me the hatred which in her perfect goodness my sweet, loving wife never had.

But he hated me no more; I saw it in his uncertain gaze and in the faint, tremulous quiver of his mouth. It was the same look I had seen the night of the Chandler party, and I had been puzzled by it then and unable to discern its sig-

nificance. But now I saw the insensible fear giving way to
the newfound hope. Now I saw the love, the incredulous
and not quite certain love, as he comprehended the truth
that he was indeed my son and that I welcomed and re-
joiced in the fact.

"I am your son?" he said shakily, and I saw the telltale
brightness of his eyes and knew that if he spoke another
word he would weep.

"Good Christ!" I said in my angriest voice. "How could
you think otherwise? Would I have endured your sneers,
your contempt, your reprehensible conduct, were you not
my son? God knows I've wanted to chuck you out of the
house a dozen times over, but you're mine and I'm stuck
with you, and that's the sad truth, whether it pleases you
or not."

My show of anger, as I knew it would, restored him. His
young mouth hardened, and secure now in the knowledge
of my paternity, he said with all of his old insolence, "It
pleases me very little to be your son. I only thought it
strange—if I weren't your son—that you didn't tell me."

"How," I asked irritably, "could I have possibly known
what was on your mind? Why didn't you tell me what you
thought? Why did you keep such a thing to yourself? And
who in Christ's name told you this lie?"

His gaze wavered under mine; he shifted nervously on
his feet and said with a shrug, "What does it matter who
told me?" But then, realizing a more important consideration, he looked up and asked, bewildered, "If it's not true,
if I *am* your son, why should anyone say that I am not?"

He watched me intently, his fear returning. It was more
expedient, I decided, to put his mind at rest than to discover the identity of the bearer of that scurrilous tale.

"Who knows?" I replied, and now I was the one who
shrugged carelessly. "A man in my position has many ene-
mies, I'm sure you know that, Alan. Perhaps some de-
mented fool thought to hurt me through you. But you may
rest assured you are my son."

I saw him relax, the lines of stress and fear vanishing
from his brow. He smothered a sigh, and with a sorry
attempt at flippancy, he remarked, "It doesn't matter,

you understand. I wasn't the least bit concerned when I
thought I wasn't yours. It's just a bloody nuisance not
knowing who your father is."

And giving me one last impertinent look which did not
quite disguise his enormous relief, he turned and saun-
tered casually from the room.

I very much wanted to go after him. I longed to embrace
him while at the same time I wanted to crack him soundly
on his brazen, ill-tempered, irreverent jaw. He was surely
the most exasperating son a man ever had. His discour-
tesy, his utter disregard for all feelings save his own, knew
no bounds. I realized the fault was largely mine; I was perhaps more lenient a parent than I might have been under
normal circumstances, but I simply could not bring myself
to discipline him. What wrong had he ever done, what
crime had he ever committed to equal mine? The boy was a
rascal, of that there was no question; he was rude and un-
civil and quite the most irritating little barbarian I had
ever encountered, but his conscience was clear, his soul
still unstained. Unlike mine, to be sure, unlike the blood-
spattered, filth-laden conscience that was mine.

I did not sell the house in Newport. I found another, less
than legitimate way to raise the money I would need. The
Tidewater Pipeline had temporarily suspended my control
of the oil refining industry, but I have learned from experience that every man, no matter his ethics or ideals, has his
price. It was therefore my intention to simply buy all of
Tidewater's oil, thus regaining the control of which the independent oil men sought to deprive me. But they refused.
Despite the inflated rate I offered them, they were determined that Eastern Seaboard Oil, myself along with it,
should fall into ruin. This eventually seemed hardly likely
in light of the fact that the Eastern trust agreement, au-
thored by my attorney Randolph Harper, encompassed
forty-five corporations, each a separate entity, yet interre-
lated in such a way as to combat effectively any assault on
one or more of its brother branches. But the independents
were resolved I should fail. They felt they had knuckled
under long enough to the anaconda, as they called it, of

Eastern Seaboard Oil. Now was their opportunity, once
and for all, to crush the stealthy serpent as it lay dying.

They very nearly succeeded. My cash flow was at its lowest ebb; the Pennsylvania legislature, in further support of
the independents, decided to prosecute the principals of
Eastern Seaboard, naming me as chief conspirator; and
the public outcry against monopolists was at its zenith.
The future looked bleak. But my entire adult life has been
a struggle against seemingly insurmountable odds, and I
was reasonably certain that this present setback would
prove temporary, as had all the others.

The hearing in Pennsylvania was scheduled for early
November, but thanks to Randolph Harper's legal skill, it
was soon thereafter concluded, with all charges dropped
for lack of sufficient evidence. I was guilty of each and
every charge brought against me; the legislature knew I
was guilty, everyone in the oil industry knew I was guilty,
but because of the ingenious and convoluted structure of
the trust agreement, it was never quite clear to anyone, except to those within the corporations, exactly where own-
ership began or indeed where responsibility lay.

The newspapers, however, did not trouble themselves
with anything so insignificant as proof. They glibly reported every last iniquitous deed of which I had ever been
rumored, believed, conjectured, or alleged to have perpe-
trated. That they were, on the whole, surprisingly accurate did not trouble me. Today's news is tomorrow's trash
wrapper, and, moreover, Mr. Hearst and Mr. Bennett were
not without blots on their respective escutcheons. What
did trouble me was the effect of this notoriety on Joanna.
She was understandably shocked when Thomas Nast, in
one of his more vituperous cartoons, depicted my brush
with the Pennsylvania legislature as Lucifer's fall from
grace, the legislature naturally in the role of the Deity,
and myself, complete with horns and cloven hooves, in in-
glorious descent to the oil-slicked pits of Hell. Although
Mr. Nast's popularity had waned considerably in the past
several years, his acrimonious doodles still held the power
to rouse public sentiment against his unfortunate tar-
gets, and when that particular cartoon appeared in *Once a*

Week, Joanna broke one of her self-imposed rules and spoke to me for the first time regarding my affairs.

What a strange little creature she was. Throughout the hearing itself she had said nothing, but this did not surprise me, for she was not in the habit, even in the best of circumstances, of questioning my activities. In fact, she seemed little interested in anything at all that concerned me, and as a result I often wondered why she had accepted my proposal of marriage. She so obviously deplored all that I was; I knew this from the moment we first met. Even later, when she consented grudgingly to marry me, I more than expected that she would ultimately change her mind.

Joanna reminded me very strongly of Lenore. This likeness in nature astounded me, for I had thought never to discover again the virtue, the honor, the unpretentious modesty which had so characterized my first wife. When Lenore died, I vowed to myself that I would never remarry. I should not have married in the first place—mine is not the temperament for the conjugal life—but I wanted Lenore, I wanted her with the fierce, unreasoning passion of first love, and so I married her. That the union was disastrous surprised no one, least of all her father, who had opposed the match from the beginning. Lenore's father was a Van Rensselaer of the Castleton-on-Hudson Van Rensselaers, and although Van Holden was as fine and as revered a name as his own, the precarious state of my finances at the time rendered me unsuitable, in his estimation, to court, let alone marry, his daughter. His objections proved futile; Lenore and I eloped six months to the day after our first meeting, but it was not until Alan was born that Philip Van Rensselaer recognized his daughter's marriage, and, with ill-concealed distaste, accepted it.

He was extremely generous thereafter. In Lenore's name he presented me with a dowry, the amount of which astounded me. I knew he was rich. I shall even admit that his wealth was one of the initial reasons I had pursued Lenore; but I expected nothing so prodigious as the sum of money he placed at my disposal on the day my son was christened.

"Use the money wisely," he told me, his patrician face

grave and disapproving, for his dislike for me had not diminished. "You now have the means to live comfortably
and honorably for the rest of your life. To this end, I
strongly suggest that you disassociate yourself from industry and from all that it entails. Only ill can come of your
present endeavors. Leave Eastern Seaboard to the vul-
tures who manage it. You don't need it. As a gentleman,
you shouldn't want it."

But he was wrong on both counts: I wanted Eastern Seaboard and I needed it with a driving urgency he could
never begin to understand. I forbore to contradict him; it
was useless to try to explain what I myself did not fully understand. I knew only that I had set myself a goal and that
I would not be at peace until the reins of Eastern Seaboard
were in my hands.

If Lenore was unhappy in the years that followed, those
long bloody years while I attacked, besieged, and ultimately annihilated all competition, she never said so. She
was the most loyal of wives: submissive, unquestioning,
and totally loving. Nothing swayed her love, no amount of
neglect or coldness or downright cruelty on my part lessened the intensity or the heartbreaking purity of that love.
She was always there when I needed her, although I regret
to say I needed her very little. My needs, my interests, lay
elsewhere. Lenore was my wife and she should have been
one of my prime concerns, but my energies at the time
were expended in different directions. It never occurred to
me that she might have needs of her own, needs I had
never bothered to fulfill; and I suppose, in the end, my rec-
ognition of those needs was one of the reasons I found it so
easy to believe Spencer Halston's lies.

I cannot speak, I cannot *think* of Spencer Halston without experiencing the most violent and vengeful rage. His
treachery was that more detestable in light of the fact that
he had been my friend, my confidant, the brother I never
had. We had grown up together in Ravena, a sleepy hamlet
near the banks of the Hudson. We had been schooled together at Exeter and at Harvard; we had gone everywhere,
done everything, together. We had even lost our virginity
together during a gloriously memorable evening in a

much-touted brothel on the outskirts of Cambridge. And
years later, when my star began to rise at Eastern Seaboard, I quite naturally took Spencer with me and named
him chief counsel of my little band of fox-shrewd attorneys.
Unfortunately, Spencer's own star did not shine in that
particular sphere. He was charming, to be sure, and as intelligent and imaginative as anyone in my organization,
but he simply was not cut out for the complexities of corpo-
rate chicanery. Thus, when it came time to draw up the
trust agreement which would establish Eastern Seaboard
as the most powerful and impregnable of monopolies, I
chose Randolph Harper, without qualm or reservation, for
that intricate, devious, and vitally important task.

Harper was infinitely more suited, by nature and experience, for the job. He had been formerly connected with that
gang of jackals at Tammany Hall, and his reputation for
flawless legal duplicity was without parallel in the state of
New York. I had no difficulty in wooing him away from the
Tammanies; I merely offered him treble his salary plus a
hefty block of Eastern Seaboard stock, and when he was
comfortably ensconced in the luxurious offices which ad-
joined mine on Broadway, I informed him with droll gravity that his fortune would increase commensurate with his
performance and, of course, with his unwavering loyalty to
my interests.

What a wonder he was! What a consummate artist in his
field! The Eastern Seaboard trust agreement would stand
forever as testimony to his skill, to his utter gift for organi-
zational cunning. I was sorely tempted, because of his bril-
liance, to raise his rank along with his salary; however,
this would have meant further embarrassment for Spencer, whose feathers had already been ruffled by Harper's
unqualified triumph with the trust agreement. I merely
suggested to both of them that any negotiations or trans-
actions which had formerly been engaged in indepen-
dently should henceforth be conducted jointly—a mistake,
I realized later, on my part, for Spencer's feelings toward
me were never the same thereafter.

I sensed at once the change in him. He was cooler, distant, he began to refuse my social invitations, and even

during business hours he spoke to me rarely and at an absolute minimum. I knew I had angered him and, perhaps, hurt him, and finally I asked him point-blank if he was growing unhappy with his work, and more importantly, if he resented Randolph Harper.

"No to both questions," he replied in his soft, cool, untroubled voice. "I am content with my work as always, and I could not possibly resent someone who so obviously benefits the company. But perhaps," he added quietly, "you are growing dissatisfied with me. If that be the case, by all means say so, and I shall tender my resignation without delay."

"Don't be a bloody fool!" I snapped, guilt roughening my voice. "Did I say I was dissatisfied? Have I ever given you any indication . . . ?"

I stopped and turned away from the silent indictment in his eyes. Of course I had given more than an indication of complaint. I had, in effect, cast doubt on Spencer's competence, and it was evident from his attitude that he was neither ready nor willing to forgive me that insult.

Eventually, he excused himself courteously and left my office to return to his. It was only a month or so later that the rumors about Lenore began to reach my ears. But it never for a moment occurred to me to link the origin of those rumors with my good friend Spencer Halston.

XXII

"MARK," SAID JOANNA, "have you settled your difficulties with the Pennsylvania legislature? I know the newspapers say that charges have been dismissed, but I saw the most disturbing cartoon today in *Once a Week*."

We were in bed; I had just made love to her, and as always, her response had been warm but wary, as if she feared to give herself to a man she did not completely trust.

"Disturbing?" I said, drawing her closer in my arms. "In what way disturbing?"

For a moment she was silent. Then, with reluctance, she said, "The artist did not flatter you."

Her attempt at tactful evasion both touched and amused me. Suppressing the smile that tugged at my lips, I commented dryly, "I have seen the cartoon in question, and you are quite right: It does not flatter me. Mr. Nast seldom flatters his subjects, which accounts, I think, for his ambiguous success. I shouldn't worry though if I were you. Notoriety of that sort is unpleasant, I agree, but it's inevitable, darling, and you must learn to ignore it as I do."

"I cannot," she whispered, and she turned to me abruptly and buried her face in my chest. "I cannot ignore such a contemptible slur on your character. And I will not abide it!"

She clung to me tightly, almost protectively, and so startled was I by this totally uncharacteristic burst of emotion that for several long moments I was simply unable to speak. Joanna was not a demonstrative woman. In that

way alone she differed from my first wife, whose feelings
had always been exceedingly easy for me to read.

"My dear," I said softly and turned up her face to mine,
"I appreciate your loyalty and I value it, but you must not
distress yourself on my account. I care nothing about the
propaganda of satirists and scandalmongers, nor should
you mind what they say, for to do so will only cause you
greater distress."

"But I do mind," she insisted. "I mind very much what
people say about you."

"Do you?" I smiled, and once more I was ineffably moved
by her fierce and unexpected concern. "Why is that, darling?"

"Because . . . because you're my husband," she faltered.
"And because I . . ."

"Yes?" I urged with interest. "Go on, Joanna."

"That's all," she whispered, and her lashes lowered and
brushed charmingly against suddenly flaming cheeks. "I
wasn't going to say anything else."

"How delightful you are," I laughed softly. "After two
years of marriage you're shy of me still, and uncertain too,
I suspect."

"Uncertain of you?" She raised her head and gave me a
puzzled look.

"You have never once confided in me your feelings, your
fears, your likes and dislikes, nor even any of the endearing and intimate details which a wife normally shares
with her husband. I begin to think, my reticent darling,
that you don't quite trust me."

"That's not true, Mark!" she said at once. "I do trust
you. Of course I trust you."

"Do you?"

"Yes, yes." She moved away from me and sat up against
the pillows and regarded me anxiously. "I trust you without question. And I . . ." She paused uncertainly, then said
in a swift breathless voice, "And I care for you."

"You *care* for me?" I smiled. "In what way, darling? As a
brother? As a dear friend?"

I was teasing her, baiting her. Any mention of affection
seemed to confuse and embarrass her, and it absolutely de-

lighted me when she stammered and blushed like the innocent child she was.

"No, Mark," she murmured and lowered her gaze once again. "I care for you more deeply than that."

I drew her into my arms, moved beyond words by her unexpected admission. "My dear wife," I said softly, "are you trying to tell me you love me?"

She did not answer. Her lips brushed my chest as she moved closer, shyly closer, in my embrace.

"Joanna." I kissed her gently, and with a hand I traced the contour of her breast. "Do you love me? Do you, darling?"

She quivered under my touch and moved even closer, but still she did not reply. What an odd little creature she was; there were times I could swear she loved me, and there were times too when I wondered if she had any feeling for me at all.

How differently she behaved with Alan, however. With my son she was always warm and outgoing and loving, but perhaps that was because she was much closer in age to him than she was to me. And yet there had been a good many more years between her first husband and herself. Age had not seemed to matter in that case, for Joanna had informed me on the very first night we met how deeply and completely she loved Edward Sinclair.

Did she love him still? I sometimes wondered. Did she think of him, did she compare me with him, and did I suffer by the comparison? That she had been devastated by Sinclair's death I had realized at once when I had seen her at the funeral; and afterward she had gone nowhere, had done nothing, for an inordinately long period of time. In all truth, I think she accepted my proposal simply because she had been too shy, too polite, to do anything else—and because, of course, she was so very fond of my son. They had got on well together from the beginning. Joanna had never been shy with Alan. From the start she had been . . . comfortable with him, which is something she had never been with me.

"I wonder," I said now, and I released my wife and lay

back against the pillows. "I really wonder if you care for me."

"But, Mark," she said, puzzled by my tone, which was sharper, I think, than I had realized. "I've told you I do."

"Yes," I said pensively, "you've told me."

For a while I said nothing else. I gazed at the ceiling and thought of my wife and of her *comfortable* relationship with my son.

"Joanna," I said presently, impelled by a curious and disturbing unease, "do you recall that night last summer when I returned from Harrisburg? The night of the Fourth of July? You were ill, you told me, and that's why you hadn't attended the Chandler party. And when I mentioned to you that I had seen Alan at the Chandlers' and that he too looked ill, you became alarmed for some reason, and defensive. In fact, if you remember, we subsequently had a rather heated row, for which I took full blame—until the next morning when I was less angered, less involved, and able to think more clearly, and then I realized that you had deliberately picked a quarrel in order to avoid answering a specific question I had asked you."

She grew very still beside me. Long moments passed, but she did not reply. I turned my head; she was staring at me nervously and plucking at the sheet with a visibly shaking hand. At length she whispered, "I don't remember the question."

"I do, Joanna."

She swallowed convulsively and her hand closed tightly on the sheet in an obvious effort to still the trembling. "What was it?" she asked faintly.

"I merely asked you if you knew of any reason Alan might be distressed. He had behaved somewhat oddly at the Chandlers', and I thought at the time he might have confided in you whatever was troubling him—for something was decidedly troubling him—and I was inclined to believe, in light of your own curious behavior that evening, that you knew what it was."

"But I didn't," she said pleadingly. "I promise you, Mark, I knew nothing."

"You needn't promise me, darling. An answer was all I

wanted, and now that I have it I shall of course take you at your word."

I turned on my side, away from my wife, and absently drew up the quilt. I couldn't imagine why I had brought up that particular happening, five months in the past, nor why it should have disquieted her as it did. I hadn't given it much thought when it occurred, for shortly thereafter I had gone back to Harrisburg, and upon my return to Newport Alan had confronted me with the charge that I was not his father. Quite frankly, after that astonishing announcement, Joanna was the last thing on my mind, and even afterward, in the months that followed, I was far too busy to give any consideration to what had seemed, at the time, an insignificant incident. I did notice, however, that Joanna was quieter, less communicative than usual, and I attempted on several occasions to speak to her about this, but soon I was too wrapped up in my own problems to even begin to think of anyone else's. My mind was occupied with other matters, more important matters, namely the survival of Eastern Seaboard Oil. During the same period while I was embroiled with the Pennsylvania legislature I was also conceiving a plan to combat the Tidewater Pipeline by constructing a pipeline of my own. The terminus, I decided, would be in New Jersey at the site of Eastern's great coastal refineries and storage tanks. It was an easy matter to convince the town council of Bayonne to grant a franchise, but exceeding haste and secrecy were required, for the Reading Railroad, catching wind of my proposed plan, was preparing to seek a blocking franchise, which eventually they did. But too late. Within a matter of weeks the Continental Transit Company, the newest Van Holden enterprise, was in operation as the leading pipeline system in the nation; and the control of the oil refining industry was once again safely and indisputably in my hands.

But now, with the worst of my struggles behind me and with the smoke and blood of battle beginning to fade, I saw more clearly what I had not seen before, what in my characteristic absorption with only my own pressing concerns, I had not bothered to see before.

"Joanna," I said as a half-forgotten memory rose suddenly foremost in my thoughts, "after that night, the night of the Fourth of July, I seem to remember that Alan went out of his way to avoid speaking with you. Had you quarreled with him perhaps? Was that the reason you were both so upset?"

She did not answer. I turned and she was lying against the pillows, tense, apprehensive, watching me with fearful dark eyes. The minutes ticked by. The house was very still. The windows were closed against the midwinter chill, and all was quiet. I looked down at my wife, at the sensuous, naked outline of her form beneath the sheet; I looked at her hair, curling darkly in a charming tangle on her brow; and finally I looked at her face turning pale with a sudden shame and guilt she could no longer control.

"Darling," I said softly, "I think you should tell me what happened between you and my son while I was away."

She stared at me mutely, her face growing even whiter, and when I drew her slowly, reassuringly, into my arms, her arms crept round my neck and she leaned heavily against me with a weary, disconsolate sigh.

"Joanna"—my voice was low, careful—"is it possible that you are the one who told Alan he was not my son?"

Her body grew tense; she tried to move away but I detained her gently, firmly, in my arms. I could feel her heart pounding rapidly under mine. I awaited her reply with an apparent calm I was far from feeling. At last she admitted, her voice a shamed whisper, "Yes, Mark, I told him. I told Alan he was not your son."

I drew a deep breath. My hands on her back closed unconsciously into fists.

"Why?" I asked slowly. "Why, Joanna?"

Her arms tightened about me. She sighed again. Her lips, when she spoke, brushed my chest. "I thought he knew, Mark. I would never have said it otherwise. I was sure he knew. Why else would he . . . ?" She drew a ragged breath. "I have wanted to tell you for the longest time but I was afraid . . . and ashamed. I know Alan hates me now. I tried to speak to him, to apologize, both before I left for Florida and after I returned. But he wouldn't listen, he refused to speak of it. And," she added mournfully, "he has not answered any of my letters since he's been back at school."

She trailed off and fell silent, and I could feel the faint tremors of shame and remorse that shook her. I drew her closer, kissed her tumbling hair, all the while repressing the most violent urge to choke the breath of life from her throat. Why had she repeated that despicable rumor to my son? A remnant of logic told me she very probably believed the rumor herself, but God Almighty, that still did not explain why she had told him.

"Joanna, look at me." I lifted her chin, smoothed the hair from her brow. "Why did you tell him? No, don't be frightened, darling; I'm not angry. Just tell me why you told him."

"I—I don't know," she said faintly, but she was lying, she who had never before, to my knowledge, lied to me. And she was afraid.

"Come now," I coaxed her. "There has to be a reason you told him. Discussions of that nature are not generally conducted over teacups, are they? Tell me why you told him, darling. I won't be angry, I give you my word."

But I *was* angry, deeply, fiercely angry that this shy, timid creature should have so disrupted my son's peace of mind.

"Joanna," I said patiently, although my patience was fast wearing thin, "did you quarrel with Alan? And in the heat of the quarrel, did you think to hurt him by—?"

"Yes, yes!" she blurted with a desperate and curious relief. "That was it. We quarreled."

"You did?" I regarded her closely, searching her face and the deliberate evasion of her eyes. "About what did you quarrel?"

She looked away; I saw her mouth tremble. When she replied at long length, her voice trembled too.

"I don't remember, Mark. It was so long ago."

"Five months," I said evenly, "is not a long time, Joanna. And moreover," I pointed out, withdrawing my arms from around her, "if your quarrel was so intense as to have precipitated your telling Alan he was not my son, then I daresay you could hardly forget the particulars of that quarrel."

"Oh, please," she said miserably, "you mustn't question me, Mark."

"I mustn't question you? My dear girl, you've told my son the cruelest, most inexcusable lie, and you have the temerity to say I mustn't question you?"

"Lie?" she echoed blankly. "What do you mean 'lie'?"

"It's a lie," I said harshly. "Alan *is* my son. But there are some people who think otherwise. Because years ago someone started a rumor, an odious, scurrilous rumor—"

I broke off, breathless with a sudden killing rage. I cannot speak, I cannot *think* of Spencer Halston without experiencing the most savage and devastating rage.

"Who told you Alan was not my son?" I demanded, and I took hold of her wrist with a hard brutal hand. "Was it Halston? Have you seen that bastard, talked with him? By Christ, I'll kill him!"

"Mark!" she cried. "No, no! He did not tell me. You know who told me. We talked about it. You even said . . . Oh, please, Mark, you're hurting me."

"We talked about it? Are you mad? We've never talked of such a thing."

"We did, we did! Don't you remember? It was before we were married. You were so terribly angry. And then on our wedding night you wanted to discuss it further but I couldn't talk about it. I couldn't bear to, Mark. I didn't want to hurt you."

"What the devil are you saying? We've never talked of Alan's paternity. What insane, perverted game are you playing?"

My hand tightened savagely on her wrist. She cried out in pain and tried to pull away, but I held her without mercy and with no regard for the desperate fear I saw leap into her eyes.

"Mark," she begged, "you must remember! Sally Monroe told me about Alan, and I told you that same night. I wanted you to know it didn't matter, that I—"

"Sally Monroe?"

"Yes, it was Sally. Don't you remember?"

My hand dropped from her wrist and she flung her arms about me and began to tremble incontrollably. I was numb with bewilderment. Sally Monroe? Sally had told Joanna that Alan was not my son? And Joanna and I had discussed it? But we had never discussed such a thing. In fact, the only time we had talked about Sally was when Joanna had told me—

"Oh, good Christ," I groaned as a sickening wave of recollection flooded my thoughts. "Joanna!" I grasped her arms and held her away from me. "Joanna, look at me, listen to me! It's very important that you remember her exact words. Darling, I'm sorry I frightened you. Joanna, look at me! Tell me what Sally said."

"I don't remember!" she cried. "I don't remember her exact words. I was so outraged when she told me. I wanted to strike her, to kill her!"

"Yes, yes," I said impatiently. "I can see that you'd be angered. But, Joanna, you must try to recall her exact words. Did she actually say Alan was not my son, or did she only intimate it in some way?"

"I don't remember! I can't remember! What does it matter?"

She wrenched away, gasping, shaking, and I pulled her back into my arms and strove to calm her, to bring her under control, for she was hysterical now, and telling me in a wild, almost incoherent voice how dreadfully sorry she was for hurting Alan and for hurting me. And as I held her and caressed her and murmured words of love and comfort in her ear, I thought of Sally Monroe and of her little boy, Stephen, who was a year older than my daughter. We were his godparents, Joanna and I, despite the fact that Joanna and Sally were not as close as they had been before our marriage. I had never questioned my wife about this obvious rift in the friendship. For reasons of my own I preferred that she have as little to do with Sally as possible. Fortunately, as time passed, we began to see less and less of the Monroes socially. Of course I continued to meet with Stephen on a regular basis since he was my broker and I saw no reason to sever the relationship in that respect. But

Sally was another matter. I wouldn't have cared if I never saw Sally again; in fact, I would have preferred it.

"Darling, forgive me," I said to my wife. "I'm sorry I spoke harshly to you. Let's talk of this no more. It's over now. No one's been hurt. I've spoken to Alan. He knows it's not true, he knows he's my son, and that's all that really matters."

"But why, Mark?" she asked. "Why did Sally lie to me? Why did she tell me such a terrible thing?"

"I don't know," I replied in my sincerest voice. "But regardless of her reasons, Joanna, I think it might be wiser if you don't see her again."

"I won't!" she said fiercely. "I shall never see her again, I give you my word!"

I held her in my arms and said nothing more. At length she quieted; her trembling abated, and then, carefully, so as not to disturb her, I eased away from her, doused the light, and attempted to sleep. But I lay awake all night long, intensely aware of each breath she took and every movement she made, for she too was awake the entire night through. She huddled against me like a contrite little puppy. Now and again, thinking I slept, she would whisper my name and sigh a sad sigh; and once, toward dawn, I felt her mouth on mine, her soft, sweet, innocent mouth on mine.

"Mark."

Beside me, she stirred, her body, soft and warm, brushing mine. She reached for my hand and clung to it, and reluctantly, with the greatest of effort, I turned and opened my eyes.

"Mark," she said meekly, "I'm sorry I woke you. I couldn't sleep. I've been awake all night, worrying."

"There's nothing to worry about," I assured her. "You mustn't think of it anymore. I've already told you that Alan knows the truth."

"Yes, I know you did but, Mark, I think you're angry with me—and well you should be," she added swiftly. "But if you could only forgive me . . ."

"Don't," I said softly. "I'm not angry, I swear it."

"Mark . . ." Her voice was hushed yet urgent. "I remember now why Alan and I quarreled."

"Do you, darling? Would you like to tell me about it?"

"Yes, yes," she said rapidly. "It was about Noelle. I had scolded Alan for spoiling her, and he became angry, and then one word led to another. . . ."

She trailed off into silence and watched me apprehensively, her hand still on mine, clutching it tightly in a desperate effort to elicit my trust. Her face was very pale, her eyes shadowed from lack of sleep. She looked so young, so utterly defenseless—like a child, a penitent, guilt-ridden child.

"That's the truth," she persisted when I said nothing and my hand lay, unresponsive, in hers. "You do believe me, don't you?"

"Yes," I said at length. "I believe you, Joanna."

But I didn't believe her. And I wondered if I ever would again.

XXIII

I SHOULD NEVER have married her. I should never have married anyone, ever. I am not suited to the married life. I haven't the temperament for it, nor the patience, nor any of the other qualities requisite to a successful wedded union. When my first wife died I vowed I would never remarry, and to this end I decided to associate myself exclusively with ladies who were already committed, a decision, I might add, which led to the severance of an exceptionally fine relationship with my sister Adele.

Adele was seven years younger than I, not a vast difference, but she had always seemed a child to me, my baby sister, my charge. My parents had married late in life: my mother at thirty, my father at forty-five. When Adele was ten, my mother succumbed to a long and painful illness, and my father, lonely, bitter, and heartbroken, survived her by only one year. At the age of eleven Adele was solely in my care. My father had left a modest estate, but we had no close relatives who might have taken Adele into their homes. In any case, I would not have abandoned her to the charity of virtual strangers, for she was mine and I intended to raise her, though I was not far from childhood myself.

My father's small legacy saw me through Harvard and even stretched so far as to provide a suitable selection of nursemaids and governesses for my sister. During those years, though Adele and I saw comparatively little of each other, we were close, for my summers and holidays were spent exclusively with her—my days, that is; my nights were spent in less impeccable company. It pleases me to relate that despite my youth and a less than moral life of my own, I was able to instill in Adele all of the honesty, honor, scruples, and ethics which I myself lacked. By no means was she a saint; on the contrary, I had spoiled her outrageously and she was a willful little minx, stubborn, opinionated, and patently aware of her creamy-skinned, sable-haired beauty.

She married young, which did not surprise me. She married a banker, Wesley Kendall, a man just my age, as slender and as dark as I, but there the resemblance ended. Kendall was something of a puritan, as staunch a Presbyterian as the Good Lord ever welcomed to his fold; and marriage to this paragon served to intensify in my sister the virtuous qualities and strength of moral fiber which I had done my best to foster. My duty done, I was well pleased. But I was totally unprepared for the awesome consequences of my success.

Adele had lived in my house, of course, until the day she married. Her relationship with my wife had been of the closest keeping, and when Lenore died Adele had been almost inconsolable. Lenore had been to her a mother, a sister, the dearest friend. She had filled a void, the need for feminine companionship which I, as a brother, never could. It was only natural, then, that after Lenore's death when I began to see other women, women who in my sister's opinion were an affront to the memory of my wife, we would quarrel.

On the second Christmas following Lenore's death, Adele and her husband and her two charming daughters were overnight guests in my house. We lived less than five blocks apart, but spending the holiday under one family roof was a custom originated by my wife and perpetuated in her honor by her loving and dutiful sister-in-law.

Over the past several months I had had a number of short-lived but satisfying relationships, the most recent being with a young matron who, unbeknownst to me, was cousin to a woman who chaired every charitable and religious committee in the city, each of which could count my sister as a member. I had made the grave error of calling on my "friend" one afternoon while her husband was upstate on business, and as I was leaving the house I encountered this redoubtable cousin, who no doubt surmised the reason for my visit, and immediately reported it to Adele.

On Christmas Day, after a stupefyingly huge dinner, while the children napped upstairs and Wesley dozed in a fireside chair, Adele drew me into my study, closed and locked the door, and demanded an immediate explanation of my unseemly behavior.

"I cannot believe it," she said, her superb, dark eyes ablaze with indignation. "Lenore has been gone little more than a year, and you have the gall, the audacity, not only to commit the most shameless indecency, but to commit it in broad daylight for all of New York to witness. How could you, Mark? Have you no pride, no sense of honor? I looked up to you, worshiped you; you imparted to me all that I had thought was inherent in you. But it was all a farce, wasn't it? You preached moderation but practiced excess. You bade me be chaste while you were promiscuous. I couldn't be more hurt . . . or revolted."

I stared at her in astonishment. Was this Adele, my own heart, my dear sister, who had blushingly confided to me at the age of fifteen that she would never love anyone as much as she loved me? I had erred, I admit it, but I had committed no act so reprehensible as to incur such a heated and hostile tirade.

"Look here," I said sternly. "I won't be spoken to in that manner. And what's all the fuss about anyway? I called on a lady. Does that brand me promiscuous?"

"You not only called on her, Mark, you very probably made love to her, as you've been doing to half the married women in the city. Your escapades are the talk of the town. The gentlemen are placing wagers as to who your next conquest will be, while secretly praying it won't be one of their own wives. The wives themselves vacillate between tittering anticipation and fascinated revulsion; it seems they cannot decide whether to be spectators or participants in this disgusting charade."

"Good God!" I exclaimed, shocked to the core that my sister should know, let alone speak, of such matters.

"And the worst," she went on, "the ultimate degradation occurred on Tuesday last when Minna Walters told me, with a positively prurient smile on her face, that in one week alone you had had five different partners."

I couldn't believe my ears. I could not believe that my sister was telling me these things.

"What's got into you, Adele? Do you realize what you're saying? Do you actually believe those salacious stories?"

"Yes," she said. "I do. And what's more, Mark, I don't know that I can ever forgive you."

"Forgive me?" I flared. "I've done nothing that needs forgiving. What gives you the right to sit in judgment on me? Everything you've heard is an exaggeration. I've had women, yes, but certainly not five in one week. But even if I had, how dare you presume to tell me how I should conduct myself? What would you have me do, live celibate the rest of my life? I am a widower, not a corpse. My God, if I'd known I was raising a self-righteous little prig, I would have packed you off to the nearest charity house!"

"I don't think so," she said with a calm that enraged me. "You need me, Mark. You've always needed me . . . and used me."

"Used you? What are you talking about?"

"You've made me your conscience, your better self, a part of your nature you choose to ignore. It's too inconvenient for you to have a conscience of your own; you've always done what you've wanted, right or wrong, and at times—those rare times when you pause to reflect on your sins—you seek me out, as if proximity to morality might purify your soul, wash clean your transgressions. It's the same reason you chose Lenore for a wife. She too was everything you are not. She was your one fragile link with virtue and truth. And now that she's gone, you've come back to me, to your honor, to your conscience."

My self-control snapped; I shouted in a rage, "What a damnably idiotic thing to say! I have no conscience? *You* are my conscience? That's hardly likely and hardly accurate. A millstone round my neck is what you are and what you've been for the past eighteen years! I haven't used you, nor ever needed you. Christ Almighty, I've never needed anyone less!"

She gazed at me quietly, my exquisite, regal, impeccable sister, and said nothing. I waited for her to speak, to upbraid me, to reproach me, but she did none of those things. It was I then, impelled by a rage out of all proportion to its cause, who broke the silence.

"Why are you staring? Why don't you say something? If you find me so base, so totally revolting, why don't you leave? Why don't you take your eunuch of a husband and your immaculately conceived children and get the hell out of my house!"

Her face went white; she drew a sharp breath. She stared at me a moment longer, then she turned abruptly, went to the door, unlocked it, and opened it. She didn't turn, she didn't stop. She left the room without ever looking back.

I should have gone after her, I should have apologized. But I did not. I had said things I shouldn't have said, words which in anger I hadn't meant. Adele too had spoken angrily, unthinkingly. But it occurred to me later that much of what she had said had not been too far from the truth.

I went to her house on New Year's Day. I was told by her butler she was not at home. Annoyed but undeterred, I called the following day and the day after that and for a week thereafter, but she was never at home to me. I wrote her a letter, several letters, none of which she answered. A month went by, then two, and I called on her again, once more without success.

I couldn't accept the fact that she had deliberately estranged herself from me. Very well, we had quarreled, but all family members quarrel; they do not, as a consequence, stop seeing one another. Adele was just being obstinate, and foolish. What did she expect of me? I was not a saint; I had never purported to be anything other than what I was. If I had taught her virtue while taking a different course myself, it was only natural. Women are expected to be virtuous; it is their duty, their obligation. A man cannot afford such a luxury, for virtue is indeed a luxury—and a rarity—in a man's world. Were I scrupulous, truthful, and just, the control of Eastern Seaboard would long since have passed from my hands. Were I less ruthless, I would be in the gutter, down at heel, a cipher, a failure; in short I would be nothing. I had had to succeed after my father died. He had left us precious little, and were it not for my "excesses," my "lack of conscience," I—and Adele along with me—would have rotted in the dust of the obscurity whence we sprang.

I neither excuse nor mitigate what I am. I did what I had to do. I regret nothing. I did, however, regret my break with my sister. And I regretted too the profane wrong I had done my first wife—but that is another matter. Adele was the one who concerned me. I needed to mend the breach in our relationship.

Adele, however, went out of her way to avoid me. She went so far as to inform herself at all times of my where-abouts in order to eliminate the possibility of even a chance encounter. I shall never know how she did it. We lived in a city approximately thirteen miles long and mea-suring only two and one half miles at its greatest width, and yet not once did our paths cross.

I should have been angry with her. I should have re-sented the unreasonable and arbitrary manner in which she had cut off all lines of communication between us, but I was only hurt and puzzled by her actions, by her apparent disregard for all we had been to one another. Our years to-gether, the kinship that bound us, obviously meant noth-ing to her; she could not otherwise have allowed a simple quarrel to drive us apart. Therefore, when a year passed and all my efforts to contact her were still being rebuffed, I conceded defeat. If this was what she wanted, so be it. I loved her still, I would never stop loving her, but I told my-self reasonably that there was little sense in continuing to bash my head against a stone wall. My sister had made her position clear. She was done with me, and there wasn't a blessed thing I could do about it. It wasn't easy. I missed her unbearably. She had been right on that one score at least—I did need her. My God, how I needed her.

My break with Adele did virtually nothing to change my life. I continued to see married women. I was still deter-mined that I would never remarry, and for the most part, such an arrangement was mutually satisfying since there were many young matrons who looked to me, as I did to them, for diversion only and not for any lifelong entanglement of the heart. Sometimes, however, as in the case of Sally Monroe, I would misjudge the motives of my partner and I would misjudge as well the lengths to which a lady would go in order to preserve a relationship which should never have existed in the first place.

That I had even considered bedding Sally was an absurdity of the first order, for despite her pert, pretty face and an exceptionally fine figure, she was vacuous and dull and quite the most offensive little social climber it had ever been my misfortune to know. But as I said, I was not in the market for a wife, and Sally Monroe was possessed of certain attributes which perfectly suited my particular needs.

Our affair was brief, but unfortunately it lasted long enough for Sally to conceive my child. When she told me she was pregnant I couldn't have been more stunned. I was always extremely careful when I made love to a woman. My method of contraception has its origin in the annals of antiquity, but it had proven nonetheless effective in my experience. Until Sally, that is.

At first I denied the possibility. "It is your husband's child," I said coolly. "It cannot possibly be mine."

But just as coolly, Sally pointed out that her husband had been in Schenectady when conception had occurred, and that there was no doubt in her mind as to whose child she was carrying.

"How," I inquired casually, "do you propose to explain this discrepancy to Stephen?"

"I propose," she replied with an unconcerned smile, "to explain nothing. I'm sure you don't want your child to bear another man's name, therefore I am perfectly willing to divorce Stephen and marry you."

"Really?" I said. "But I have no wish to marry."

"I know that, Mark, but under the circumstances . . ."

"Forgive me, Sally, but no circumstances on earth will ever induce me to marry you. You've been a most charming and diverting companion, but I told you at the outset—and you agreed—that our relationship would impose no obligations on either of us."

"That agreement," she said, "would now appear logically inconsequent in view of my condition. You must marry me, Mark. You cannot expect me to present my husband with a child not his."

"My dear Sally, I expect nothing from you. It is you who expect something from me. But I'm afraid I cannot accommodate you in this instance. It's certainly regrettable that we've conceived a child; I can only tell you again, however, that I will not marry you."

She was not at all pleased by my decision. She told me, in words I had thought never to hear on a lady's lips, exactly what she thought of me. I accepted her abuse with a serenity not in keeping with my character only because she was, after all, a member of the gentler sex. If she were a man, I would have broken her jaw.

Our affair, I assumed, had come to an end. Which was just as well, for while I was seeing Sally, I had been mulling over in my mind the possibility of marrying Joanna Sinclair. I had met Joanna two years earlier while her husband still lived, and I had thought when I first saw her how different she was from the smart, sophisticated, world-weary, jaded ladies of my acquaintance. My first instinct was to take her to bed; but when we were dancing and she said in a swift, breathless voice, "My husband and I are very much in love!" I folded my tent, as Longfellow wrote, and silently stole away.

Not long thereafter, her husband died.

I went to the funeral. She was prostrate with grief. I gave her some time, and then I called on her. Her grief was still evident, but I could not restrain myself from asking her to dine with me. Anticipating a refusal, I mentioned Alan. Most women cannot resist children, and I knew Joanna would adore Alan.

She accepted. We dined together. As I had hoped, she was entranced with my son. She gaped when she saw him, for he was an exceptionally beautiful child at sixteen; and throughout dinner, while I carried on a one-sided conversation, Joanna stared at Alan while he stared rudely, remotely, at his dish.

He excused himself soon after dinner and, coincidentally, Joanna decided at that time that she should like to go home. I was convinced I had offended her—I had asked to see her again, and she had replied stiffly, "I am in mourning."

Very well, she was in mourning. I took her home. I left her alone. For a year. And then she accepted Alan's invitation to his seventeenth birthday celebration, after repeatedly refusing the invitations *I* had extended, through Sally Monroe.

I had no intention of proposing to her that night; she so obviously hadn't the slightest interest in me. In fact, if anything, I would say she actively disliked me. But I did propose, and when she hesitated, while she cast about in her mind for a suitable manner of refusal, I mentioned Alan again. It was unfair of me, I suppose, to use my son in an effort to gain my own ends. But I wanted her, and I felt she would only marry me for the boy's sake. I had counted on it, banked on it. I would have staked my life on the fact that she wouldn't refuse my suit providing she thought it was Alan who wanted her, needed her, as a "substitute mother."

And I was right. She married me.

But I knew she didn't love me.

XXIV

SHE WAS A good wife, warm, considerate, and, in her shy quiet way, touchingly responsive to my needs. Within three months of our marriage she was pregnant. I wanted a daughter, she gave me Noelle. She seemed happy. We got on well. And then I learned she told Alan he was not my son.

Sally Monroe had no doubt intimated to Joanna that young Stephen was mine. Joanna had misunderstood her and had then related her misinformation to Alan. This raised three questions in my mind: Why, apart from bitchiness, had Sally done such a thing? Why had Joanna told Alan? One does not impart information of that sort unless an extremely personal relationship exists between the two parties. And if that were the case, what was the exact nature of the relationship between my wife and my son?

I considered putting these questions to Joanna, then quickly dismissed the idea. She had already lied to me: first, when she said she did not recall the events only five months past, and secondly, when she told me that she and Alan had quarreled about Noelle. I never for a moment believed her. She is not a good liar, my second wife.

Alan came home for the holidays. His attitude toward Joanna had curiously changed, for he spoke to her barely at all, while his attitude toward me had taken a spectacular turn for the better. He was bursting with news about school: He had joined the fencing club and the polo team; his grades were excellent; he had been invited by a classmate, a young Italian count, to summer in Rome—did he have my permission to do so? And when I said no, he would have to wait until graduation and his grand tour to see Rome, he merely shrugged, grinned, and said good-naturedly, "I knew you'd refuse. You always do."

I was unprepared for such amiable behavior. He was open, expansive, almost affectionate, and he even asked, somewhat deferentially, if he could visit my offices while on holiday because he would very much like to "learn the ropes," as he phrased it, of the oil refining "mess." His slang appalled me, but his new and unexpected conduct intrigued and pleased me enormously.

During the course of all this companionable chatter, he never once mentioned Carrie Monroe, which I found odd, to say the least, since he had been so determined to marry her only four months before. I decided to question him; he was more than willing to share his thoughts with me.

"Oh, yes, Carrie," he said. "Well, you were right, of course. I am too young to marry now. I explained this to her and she agreed, reluctantly, that we should wait until I've completed my schooling. Which is just as well, really, because when her father learned we wanted to marry so quickly, he absolutely forbade it. Mrs. Monroe went along with her husband's decision, although at first she had had no objection to my marrying Carrie as soon as I'd wished. But now we've all agreed that Carrie and I should consider ourselves unofficially engaged until I graduate, after which time we can begin to give serious thought to a wedding."

"And are you satisfied with this arrangement?" I asked.

"Indeed, yes! Immensely so! I cannot think why I pressed so strenuously for marriage last summer. It was a foolish, adolescent thing to do. Don't you agree, sir?"

I smiled and said nothing.

"Perhaps," he said pensively, "I was prompted by boredom . . . or loneliness. I was awfully lonely last summer. Everyone was away. The house was so empty. Do you think that had something to do with it?"

"What do you think, Alan?"

He laughed self-consciously. "Why, I don't know what to think! I was a bit off my head last summer. I actually thought I'd gone mad. You see, I couldn't endure the thought of not being your son—"

He stopped suddenly, aware all at once that he had finally admitted a long-repressed truth to himself as well as to me. He looked away, flushing with embarrassment, his young face contorted with a dozen different emotions. I watched him struggle vainly to make clear in his mind the bewildering turmoil of his conflicting thoughts. He was a child still, despite his nineteen years, a lonely, uncertain, and desperately confused child. For years he had hated me and had found some measure of comfort in that hatred. But now that his feelings had changed, now that he was beginning to question all which hitherto he had believed, he was simply unable to deal with it.

He turned back his gaze to mine, shook his head, groped for words. "What I mean—well, you can see how shocked—"

"Alan," I said, "I think I understand what you're trying to say. A man likes to know who he is. Certainly you'd be upset to learn after nineteen years that you were not who you thought you were."

He breathed a soft sigh. I saw him relax. "Yes. Yes, that's exactly what I meant."

I rose from my chair and wandered about the room, then stopped near the fireplace and stared moodily into the flames. The room was quiet save for the muted crackle of the fire and the rhythmic ticking of the Berthoud clock on the mantel. I was silent a long time; Alan too said nothing. I wondered vaguely if Joanna had retired for the night. She had been uncommonly subdued at dinner and had excused herself immediately after the meal. Although Alan had not addressed more than two or three casual remarks to her at the table, he had watched her leave the room with so rapt an intensity that it had appeared he could not bear to see her go.

I turned from the fire and looked for a time on the slim, perfect form of my son. He was leaning back in his chair, his face half turned from the fire, his elegant feet in narrow boots resting on an eighteenth-century footstool, the new cover of which Joanna had industriously fashioned. I could see the smooth line of his brow, the curve of his cheek, the fine delineation of his jaw and chin. His hair shone pure gold in the lamplight; his lashes, long and straight, cast silky shadows on the planes of his face. He was a handsome boy, an exceptionally handsome boy, and I wondered momentarily if the friction between my wife and my son had anything to do with the irresistible attraction of his looks or with the ever-present temptation of his clean, pure, untainted youth.

"Alan," I said in a low, neutral voice, "what happened between you and Joanna in Newport?"

He looked up with a start. His eyes—Lenore's eyes— were wide and alert, and brilliantly, exquisitely gray. "What do you mean? Nothing happened."

"Something happened," I said calmly. "Something which led Joanna to tell you you were not my son. And I should very much like to know what it was."

"She told you?" he uttered. "She told you what happened?"

"She told me only that she was the one who had informed you inaccurately of your parentage. She did not elucidate the events leading up to this rather extraordinary revelation. Perhaps you will enlighten me in that area, Alan."

His mouth paled; his voice, when he replied, was almost inaudible. "Nothing happened. Nothing, I swear it. She just told me, that's all."

"You swear it. How interesting. Joanna, too, promised that nothing whatever had motivated her disclosure. Now let me see if I understand the situation correctly: One day last summer, you and Joanna were chatting pleasantly— about your grades perhaps, or about her newest frock—and she mentioned in passing that you were not my son. Is that how it happened?"

He stared at me, pale-faced and still.

"Or was it at a party?" I suggested. "The orchestra was playing a waltz. You asked Joanna to dance, and as you took her in your arms she said with a smile, 'You are not Mark's son.' Was that how she told you?"

His face grew paler, and still he did not speak.

"There are other possibilities of course. But how much

simpler it will be, Alan, if you yourself tell me exactly what happened between you and Joanna last summer in Newport."

He looked lost, frightened, and completely vulnerable. He resembled Lenore at that moment, more than ever before in his life. That one fact alone should have stopped me, but it didn't. I merely waited patiently until he collected his wits about him and gathered the courage to speak.

"I cannot," he managed to say. "I cannot tell you what happened."

"Why not? Is it so terrible?"

"Yes," he said sickly, "it is terrible."

"Come now," I coaxed him. "Nothing is so terrible that you cannot confide it in me. Believe me, son, I am quite unshockable. Tell me what happened; you'll feel better for it, I promise you."

I could tell from the strained expression in his face that he wanted to tell me, he longed to tell me. The need to unburden himself was very evident. How ironic, I thought grimly as he struggled for words, that now, of all times, he should trust me.

"Last summer," he said in a low halting voice, "I . . . insulted Joanna."

"Insulted her? In what manner?"

"I said some things I ought not have said."

"What things?"

"I cannot tell you."

"I want you to tell me, Alan."

"Sir, I cannot . . . and I will not." Defiantly, he raised his chin, but his mouth, I could see, was trembling.

"Very well," I conceded. "You insulted her. What happened next?"

"She became angry. She wept."

"She wept? How curious. I have never known her to weep but once."

"She was very angry."

"I daresay. Go on with your story, son."

"We quarreled."

"Ah, yes, I rather expected a quarrel at this point. And then?"

"One word led to another . . ."

"One word led to another. A catchy phrase, that one."

"Sir?"

"A passing thought, Alan, nothing more. I did not mean to interrupt you. Please continue."

"And then she told me I was not your son."

"Oh."

"That's how it happened."

"Of course."

"I swear it."

"Again you swear it. Very well, I am convinced. But tell me, Alan, is there any possibility of my learning the exact manner in which you insulted Joanna?"

He said nothing. I waited. He watched me.

"Alan?"

"No, sir."

"Is there anything I can do to persuade you to tell me?"

"No, sir. It is . . . a personal matter."

"I see."

But I saw nothing more than I had prior to this devious, contrived, and utterly pointless conversation. Alan was lying, as Joanna had lied. And that they had both of them lied was, to my mind, proof in itself. But proof of what? What had actually transpired between them? What had they done that they should go to such lengths to conceal it?

"Sir," said my son, "may I go now?"

He rose to leave; I stopped him with a look.

"Yes?" he said, wary. "Is there something else I can tell you?"

"The truth," I said quietly. "I should very much like to be told the truth."

"Sir," he maintained, "I have told you the truth. Joanna and I did quarrel last summer in Newport. I give you my solemn oath."

"You needn't give me your oath on that score. The quarrel has already been established. I want further truth."

"Sir, there is no further truth. . . . But, yes," he reconsidered, "there is one more thing."

"Yes?"

"Joanna thinks I'm still angry with her—about the

quarrel. But I'm not; I was never angry with her. I was shocked naturally when she told me I was not your son, but once I learned the truth it didn't matter anymore what she had said. The only thing is, I haven't been able to convey this to her, do you know what I mean? I feel so guilty about treating her the way I did—I all but ignored her after she told me—and now, whenever I try to bring up the subject, to apologize, I find I can't talk of it." He paused indecisively, regretting this sudden and extremely revealing admission, but then, realizing he had gone too far to retreat, he blundered on: "The reason I'm telling you all this is because now that you know about . . . the quarrel, perhaps you can speak to Joanna, tell her how I feel, tell her I'm not angry and that I never was. I don't like to use you as an intermediary, but I so want to make my peace with her. I can't bear being at odds with her. I simply can't bear it!"

His gray eyes blazed, his voice rang with passion; and as the full import of his words reached my brain, I suddenly realized what I had half suspected, half discounted for years. He loved her. My son was in love with my wife. But no, I thought on closer examination, he *wanted* her, as I had once wanted her: totally, physically, and with no regard to the fact that she belonged to another man.

I went rigid with rage.

For one ghastly instant I envisioned him in her bed, touching her, kissing her, his body on hers; and worse, I envisioned Joanna, her arms clinging tightly about him, and her mouth turning hungrily to his. He was everything I was not, my young unsullied son, and Joanna loved him. Just how deeply and to what degree she loved him I did not know. Nor, I thought with a sudden blinding fear that surpassed my deadly rage, did I wish to know.

I swore suddenly, a particularly foul oath, as a fresh wave of anger assailed me along with another new emotion I dared not name. Alan gaped at me in a panic, but I was not concerned with him at the moment. It was Joanna who filled my thoughts. Joanna, my wife, my shy, proper wife, with her shy, proper kisses and a maidenly restraint of which I had goddamned well had my fill.

I slammed out of the room, impelled by a force I was neither willing nor able to control. I strode down the hall with one purpose in mind, and pushed open my wife's bedroom door. She was in bed, the lights extinguished, but she was awake, for she turned when she saw me and gave me a sweet, drowsy smile.

"Mark," she murmured, "I was almost asleep." And then, seeing my face, guessing my intent as I shed my coat and tossed it on a chair, she colored like a schoolgirl and drew the quilt up to her chin.

I finished undressing, got into bed, and with one abrupt movement took her in my arms and kissed her hard, roughly, driven by a dark need I neither recognized nor understood. I knew only that I wanted her, wanted her as though I had never before had her, wanted her with a swift, savage passion I had never before shown her: As I pressed her down against the pillows, my mouth hot on hers, my hands on her skin, her arms came round my neck and she returned my brutal kisses with a swift and heady passion of her own.

She strained urgently against me, as if she could not have her fill of touching me, and the unexpected eroticism of her actions aroused me more than anything in my experience ever had. She was a fire in my arms; she was a tempest, a temptress. The more brutal my kisses, the more she strained near me; the rougher my touch, the more fevered her response. When I shifted above her, she reached down to take hold of me, and I caught my breath sharply as, with hot insistent hands, she directed my passion where it would most pleasure her.

I took her at once in a turbulent excess of excitement. I took her fiercely, absolutely, forgetting she was my wife, forgetting the distinction I had always made between the women I loved and the women I bedded. I climaxed so quickly and so violently that I thought I had hurt yer, yet she clung to me tightly and moaned with pleasure, and would not let me go until I grew hard again inside her and brought her to the culmination she desired.

She released me at last, falling back against the pillows with a soft and sensual sigh. Her eyes were closed, her face flushed, and her pink, proper mouth was deliciously curved in the most charmingly naughty of satisfied smiles. Feeling my scrutiny, she opened her eyes and her smile deepened and she whispered my name so ardently, so seductively, that had I the strength I would have taken her again, taken her with passion and with the deepest love I had ever known.

What a puzzle she was, this shy, quiet girl I had married. She didn't love me, on that I would stake my life, yet she still delighted me and pleased me and surprised me as no other woman ever had. No wonder Alan loved her. How could he help but love her? But she was mine, not his. And she would remain mine for the rest of our lives.

XXV

THE MOST CURIOUS change in our relationship ensued. After that night she became warmer, closer, and more loving than she had ever been. Every evening she would greet me at the door, and slipping her arm through mine, she would accompany me to the family room, prepare my whiskey and soda, see that I was comfortably settled in my favorite chair. Then she would sit back contentedly with a scrap of needlepoint or a basket of delicate mending, and ask how I had passed my day.

Formerly, she had not spent that time with me; she might be dressing at that hour, or tending to Noelle, and we would not see each other until dinner. But now it seemed, she *made* time for me, went out of her way to be with me every moment I was home. The fact that Alan had returned to school may have had something to do with this inexplicable metamorphosis. She seemed happier now that he was gone, more relaxed. She smiled often, she became a veritable chatterbox, and she even laughed gaily at my silliest jokes.

But it was the nights that astonished me most. Each night when we retired, if I did not join her, she would come to my room—something she had never done before—and she would slip into bed and curl up in my arms as if it were the most natural thing in the world. At first it did not occur to me the reason for these nocturnal visits, so I would merely hold her gently till she drifted off, somewhat restlessly, to sleep. But after several nights of uncommonly restrained behavior on my part, I gave in to my instincts, pulled her hard against me, kissed her until she was breathless, and made love to her until we both collapsed, panting and exhausted, amidst the tangle of damp, twisted sheets.

"My God," I said softly when at last I could speak. I had never in my life been so shaken, so thoroughly moved by an act of love.

I turned to my wife. She was lying on her back, uncovered and unashamed, and she gave me a smile and reached for my hand and pressed it with a sigh to her cheek.

Fascinated, I watched her. I could not take my eyes from her. Incredible as it seems, I wanted her again. Though I had just had her, I wanted her. I ached with desire just to look at her. I felt that if I took her in my arms, that if I so much as kissed her, my passion, like an undisciplined boy's, would release itself in a hot, incontrollable flood.

"What are you thinking?" she asked, and she smiled that sensuous, inviting, provocative smile.

"I am thinking of making love to you again. Would you like that?"

For a moment she was silent; her cheek under my hand grew warm. Then: "Yes, Mark," she said in a soft, breathy voice, "I would."

Her response, as well as her previous question, surprised me. Joanna was not in the habit of casually inquiring the direction of my thoughts, nor had she ever freely admitted a desire to make love. But I was far too aroused to analyze this startling change of character. And moreover, at that moment, I could not have cared less about the workings of her mind.

I drew her close, kissed her brow, her eyes, her ivory cheek. Her arms wound round me as my wandering mouth came to rest at the curve of her breast. I shivered with pleasure at the mere touch and scent of her. No one in my experience had ever thrilled me as she did; no lover, no wife had ever filled me with such love as did this woman whose very nearness quickened the tempo of my pulse.

I raised my head, and she was watching me pensively, her fingers at play in the hair at the nape of my neck.

"Why do you look at me?" she asked softly. "What is it you see when you look at me?"

"I see all that I want," I answered, as softly. "All that I shall ever want, in this world or the next."

"Mark," she whispered, and taking my face in her hands she reached down to kiss me with a tender, aching sweetness I cannot describe. Her mouth beneath mine was a trembling flower, petal soft, gardenia smooth. Her hands on my face were fragrant with her scent, a faint rose aroma, like the arbor at Newport, whose perfume fills summer nights with its heady intoxicant.

I moved her closer, gently closer in the circle of my arms, and with infinite love I began to make love to her. She received me with a sigh, a goddess accepting tribute, and her hands brushed my sides, then came to rest at my hips, approving the rhythm of my love. I took her slowly this time, savoring the feel of her, aware of every contour of her body under mine. How sweet her slender throat where my lips sought the pulse which echoed my own; how tender her pink-tipped breast, a gentle dove in the captivity of my encircling hand.

I could have loved her all night; my passion sought no release, only infinite duration. And it appeared, by her response, that her wishes were identical to mine. She kept whispering my name and kissing me, touching me. She kept pressing me closer, as if to sustain for eternity the physical union which joined us as one. Yet it was she who succumbed to engulfing desire, moaning in my arms for consummation, satiation. And as she clung to me tightly and cried out at last in passion, my own, like a deluge, discharged itself hotly to mingle with hers.

At great length I eased off her and lay down beside her. My mind hummed with pleasure. And as I lazed drowsily in the luxurious aftermath of love, I said to my wife, "It amazes me how much I love you. I had thought I'd lost that ability years ago, along with my youth. But you've revitalized me in a hundred different ways. I've a new life because of you, new vistas to contemplate with you at my side. I love you so much! Lord, it frightens me sometimes to love you so much. I love you so deeply, so fiercely, that at times I grow faint with the intensity of it. You're on my mind night and day. I think about you constantly: at my offices, during board meetings, on the floor of the Stock Exchange. It's strange"—I laughed softly—"I had thought that once I married you, this disconcerting obsession would fade, but it has only grown stronger. I love you too much, my darling. I love you far, far too much."

She sighed, then moved closer and kissed me. But she did not find it necessary to reply. This lack of response was somewhat unnerving; in fact, it downright embarrassed me. I had proclaimed my devotion like a lovestruck swain; she had reciprocated with silence. And the longer her silence lasted, the more my embarrassment grew.

"Joanna," I said at length, "you *are* happy, aren't you? You have no regrets about marrying me? I wonder about that, you know. You seldom tell me how you feel."

She did not answer at once. Perhaps she was unsure of her thoughts. But presently she replied, "I am happy, Mark. I only regret . . ." Again she paused, longer this time. Then, softly, uneasily: "I regret only some of the things I have done."

"What things, Joanna?"

"Well, my difficulties with Alan, of course."

My skin prickled; I felt suddenly cold, and I moved away from my wife and drew up the sheet, unconsciously creating a barrier between us. "Alan," I said quietly. "Of course."

"I don't know if I ever mentioned this," she went on, oblivious to my sudden distance, "but we had not been on the best of terms after I told him he was not your son. In fact, when he returned to school in the fall, I wrote him several times—to apologize—but he did not answer any of my letters. Had I mentioned that to you, Mark?"

"Yes, you mentioned it."

"And when he came home on holiday, he barely acknowledged my presence. I thought surely he was still angry, that he would never forgive me. But before he left again for New Haven . . ."

"Yes?"

"He spoke to me one day. He explained that he wasn't angry, he said he was sorry if he had distressed me by his conduct. Mark, he apologized to me. I was speechless! And I felt so guilty."

"Guilty? For what reason?"

"Because *I* had hurt *him*, don't you see? I had hurt him so badly, and there he was, asking my forgiveness. It was a terrible thing I did to him, Mark, all the more so because I love him."

"You love him."

"Yes, I do. I love him as if he were my own. I love him as dearly as I love Noelle. Poor, lost child. I remember the first night I met him. What a sad, lonely little boy he was. He reminded me so much of myself at that age. I felt his loneliness, I shared his sadness. And as I grew to know him better, I saw how dreadfully he missed his mother and that there lay the cause of his unhappiness. I tried to fill the void in his life, I really tried, Mark, because I knew that's what you wanted of me. And for a while I thought I had succeeded. But then . . ." She trailed off dejectedly with a great mournful sigh. "It all went for naught," she concluded. "I failed miserably. Loving him was not enough; it hadn't been nearly enough."

I need hardly have commented on her discourse; to my mind she had said it all. But unlike my reticent wife, I felt that a remark of some kind was only courteous in light of such an intimate and revealing confession.

"Perhaps," I said tersely, "you loved him 'not wisely, but too well.'"

The irony of my suggestion was lost on her, for she merely protested, "Oh, no, Mark! One can never love a child too well. Although," she admitted sadly, "I'll grant you my love was not wise."

I wondered if she knew what she was saying. I wondered if she realized how easily, how readily, she had expressed her love for my son after pointedly refusing to verbalize her feelings toward me.

"I'm so sorry, Mark," I heard her say. "I failed you too, and I'm heartily sorry for that."

"Failed me? What do you mean?"

"I know what you wanted of me; I know you expected me

to help Alan, to see to his welfare, to draw him out of himself, but I'm afraid I wasn't equal to the task."

"I expected," I said stonily, "a wife for myself, not a mother for my son."

"But, Mark," she stammered, nonplussed by my tone, "before we were married you said—"

"I said many things before we were married which you chose to interpret in that peculiarly circuitous manner characteristic of your sex. It has been my unfortunate experience with women that they hear only what suits their purposes. And you, my dear wife, have fallen neatly into that pattern."

I heard her gasp softly in injured surprise, but I was too angry to care that I had hurt her, and I was far too exhausted to pursue this infuriating discussion even one word further. I turned on my side, signaling an end to the conversation, and after a time, when she lay a wary, imploring hand on my arm, I shrugged it off and moved farther away from her, putting as much distance between us as my narrow bed permitted.

She subsided quietly. I half expected she would leave my bed in a scramble of outraged dignity, but she only settled with a sigh on the pillow, being especially careful that no part of her body should touch mine. She whispered a good night but I did not answer. I lay like a stone on my side of the bed and thought of my son.

So she loved him. I was not surprised. I had known of her love, I had even fostered it to some degree, but to hear her speak of it was a different matter entirely. How glibly she prated about loving Alan, hurting Alan, feeling guilty about Alan, yet her feelings for me remained privileged information known only to her and God. I realized, of course, that her love for my son was of the purest nature, but it enraged me nonetheless. If she loved him and could discuss it so freely, then why, by the same token, could she not freely discuss her feelings for me?

Unless, I thought grimly, she *had* no feelings for me.

Goddamn her, I thought in a dull, weary rage, Goddamn her and every last bloody member of her sex. I'd had nothing but trouble with every woman I had ever known. And the more high-minded, the more principled and virtuous the woman, the more havoc she wreaked with my life. My sister had disowned me, Joanna had spurned me, Lenore . . . well, Lenore was another matter; but one and all, the women in my life had done more to disrupt my tranquillity than the combined efforts of every opponent, detractor, and enemy of Eastern Seaboard Oil.

I burrowed into my pillow, desperate for sleep, anxious to rid my mind of these tiresome thoughts. So she loved him; what of it? Let her love him if that's what she wished. I no longer cared. It no longer mattered to me.

I finally slept. But I tossed all night, awakening and dozing intermittently; not until the roseate dawn began to vanquish the night, did I succumb to deep slumber and dream of Lenore, my first wife.

She was walking in the garden in Newport, and she carried a straw basket heaped high with pink and red and white roses. So vivid was the dream that I could feel the heat of the sun, could even smell the fresh scent of flowers and feel the tickle of new-cut grass beneath my unshod feet.

I was watching Lenore from the edge of the lawn. She wore a green dress of the sheerest voile, and small fragile flowers were wreathed in her hair. She appeared unaware of my presence; her attention was focused on her companion, a tall, fair-haired man who took the basket from her hand and placed it with care on the ground. I saw Lenore smile. The man, whose back was to me, bent to kiss her. It was a long kiss, a passionate kiss, and as strongly as I felt the sun and smelled the flowers, I could feel the hot intensity of that kiss.

The stranger began to undress her. In the dream, I did not think this odd. His movements were leisurely yet erotic; he removed each article of clothing with careful, caressing hands, and Lenore watched him, smiling, while I watched them both with a curious lack of emotion of any kind. When this interminable act of disrobing was complete, the man, whose identity remained unknown to me, shed his own clothes, and though I stood a considerable distance away from him, I could see plainly the texture of his skin and the lean smoothness of his back, the lithe supple muscles in his long, slender legs.

He bent again to kiss Lenore. She received him eagerly, her arms wound round his neck and she pressed her naked body close to his. And it was most extraordinary that when they sank to the ground and began to make love, Lenore became Joanna and the stranger in her arms was my son.

I awoke with a start, perspiring and sick. The memory of the dream clung tenaciously to my brain.

"Good Christ," I groaned softly.

"Mark."

I felt her hand on my arm—Joanna's hand, Lenore's hand—I could not be sure. In my befuddled and groggy state, they seemed one and the same, inseparable, interchangeable.

"Mark," she said, frightened, "what's wrong?"

I swung my legs over the side of the bed, and I sat in a stupor, my elbows on my knees, my sweat-drenched face hidden in my hands. I was afraid to move, afraid to speak; if I did either I would be sick.

"Mark," said my wife, "please tell me what's wrong. Are you ill? Let me help you."

I looked up at last, swallowed with difficulty. She was kneeling beside me on the bed, clutching the sheet about her to cover her nudity, but I saw her as in the dream; unclothed, with virginal flowers of white in her hair, her arms and legs entwined about my son, his eager young form pressing her down, pushing into her, thrusting into her again and again.

"I'm fine," I said hoarsely. "I'm all right."

But I was far from fine, light-years away from all right. I stumbled to the bathroom, and closed and locked the door. Blindly I doused my face and neck with water, but the memory of the dream lingered on. I heard my wife's voice calling my name. My stomach heaved and I retched several times, but the vile, bitter taste that was the dream lingered on.

XXVI

WHEN I FINALLY emerged from the bathroom that morning, Joanna begged me to return to bed, insisting that I spend the day at home.

"Impossible," I said as I rang for my man. "I am meeting with Trevor Winslow today. There's talk of a strike at the Bayonne facility—groundless talk, I'm sure—but all the same, I should like to ascertain firsthand the mood of the workers."

"But, Mark," she persisted, "at least spend the morning at home. Please! You look so dreadfully ill. Let me telephone Dr. Feldman."

"No," I said shortly. "I'm fine. Nothing's wrong. It was a touch of indigestion, nothing more. Now go to your room, Joanna, if you please. Sanders will be here in a moment, and I'd rather he didn't see you swathed only in a sheet."

She glanced down self-consciously and pulled the sheet closer about her naked form, but this act of modesty merely served to draw attention to the youthful curve of her breast and the sensuous line of her slim, curving hip. As I watched her, I could see, in my mind's eye, her bare flesh, her smooth, ivory skin. I could almost feel it beneath my hands, taste it cool and sweet against my mouth. As I watched her, as I envisioned her cool, silky skin growing warm against mine, an emotion stirred within me—not desire, but an emotion as fierce as passion and twice again more violent.

"Joanna," I snapped, "get dressed, for God's sake!"

I took her arm roughly and directed her toward the communicating door to her room. She stumbled against me with a soft, startled cry, and the sheet slipped from her grasp and fell to the floor. I let go of her arm. Mutely, she stared at me, helpless, bewildered, the sheet in a heap at her feet: The sight of her nude body reawoke in my mind the revolting details of my sinister dream, as well as my slumbering, murderous rage.

I tore open the door, literally pushed her into her room, and slammed the door closed behind her. At the same instant, Sanders tapped on my door and let himself into my room. I swung round to face him; my expression must have been deadly, for he mumbled a brief greeting, then disappeared into the safety of the next room and began to draw my bath.

For several long moments I remained motionless near my wife's door. I was seething with anger, but at the same time I wanted to go to her, to beg her forgiveness, to crush her in my arms and rain kisses of love and remorse on her dear face and mouth. She had done nothing to incur hostility. She was guiltless, an innocent victim of my unreasonable rage. Why should I be angry with her? Was it because she loved my son? But it couldn't be that. I had always known she loved him. Was it the dream then? Was that what had angered me? I doubted it; no. I am not a believer in dreams.

"Mr. Van Holden, your bath is ready."

"What? Oh yes, thank you, Sanders. Let's hurry, shall we? I've wasted the whole of the morning, and I haven't a moment to spare."

As usual, my absorption with Eastern Seaboard banished all other considerations from my mind. Even before the ferryboat docked in Bayonne, I had relegated Joanna to the back of my thoughts. And as soon as I spoke with Trevor Winslow, I saw that his fears were ill-founded; the men were discontent with wages and working conditions, but no more so than usual. To assure myself further, however, I decided to go directly to the men—or rather to the all-important man who controlled the others.

I went to the yards and met privately with the current labor representative, one Morris Llewellyn, a Welshman from Cardiff, who, though not long in this country, possessed an exceptional grasp of American industry. He was a big man, as tall as I, but thirty pounds heavier, and he had a coarse brutish face which concealed a mind as intricately devious as that of any executive in my employ.

"Mr. Van Holden," he said, "the refineries are operating at peak efficiency, with an output of fifteen thousand barrels a day, which is double and treble the output of your Cleveland and Pittsburgh refineries respectively. Your men are hard workers, but their loyalties lie with me, if you follow my drift, sir. You might say I hold the future of Eastern Seaboard in the palm of my hand."

And so saying, he extended his hand, palm upward, in a gesture universal in its significance.

"Mr. Llewellyn," I replied, "I take your meaning. And I am fully aware of your personal contribution to the high standard of performance at this facility. Such a contribution will not go unrewarded. I have already spoken with Mr. Winslow, and he agrees that you have merited a raise in salary, plus a biannual bonus in . . . shall we say four figures?"

"Yes," he said thoughtfully, "that sounds equitable. Four figures biannually, five figures a year. Is that what you mean, sir? I don't like to seal a bargain unless I'm certain in my mind of the particulars."

"Then let me speak plainly, Mr. Llewellyn. Five thousand dollars in cash will be paid you on January first and June first of each year, totalling ten thousand dollars a year. Your weekly salary will increase by fifteen dollars."

"Yes, good," he agreed, "that is extremely satisfactory. May I have your hand on it, sir?"

"Of course." I shook his hand. "By the way, Mr. Llewellyn, Mr. Winslow tells me the men are somewhat disgruntled, and that rumors of a strike have reached his ears. Should I place any faith in these rumors? Need I take precautionary measures to offset the possibility of a work stoppage?"

"On no account!" he exclaimed. "Discredit all such talk, Mr. Van Holden! The men would never dream of striking the refineries. Why, how would they support their families? Who would put bread on their tables? A strike? Unthinkable! You have my word on it, sir. I personally guarantee there will be no strike at this facility." He paused momentarily, then added with a fatalistic shrug, "But of course I cannot promise what conditions will be like a year or two from today. I'm not a prophet, after all."

I could not resist smiling at the sheer gall of the man. He was threatening me in his pseudo-obsequious manner, and the very idea amused me immensely. Didn't he know, this clever coyote, that I had been threatened by forces far more powerful than he and that no threat had ever been successfully effected against me? At the present time it suited my purposes to pay for his services; I had no wish to involve myself directly with the workers. But Morris Llewellyn would do well to keep in mind that he could be as easily replaced as his predecessor, a man whose greed had exceeded his performance and who had suddenly found himself unemployed despite his seemingly inviolable position with the union.

"No one," I said wryly, "can predict the future. And it is not my intention to extract any long-range promises from you. I am more than willing to discuss the situation again at the end of two years, but if in the interim I develop the slightest doubt as to your competence, or if I begin to wonder where *your* loyalties lie, I shall have no alternative but to reconsider your value to the company in general, and to me in particular. Do you follow *my* drift, Mr. Llewellyn?"

"Yes," he said gravely, "I do, Mr. Van Holden. I'm not as stupid as I look, sir, and I like to think I have more sense than to bite the hand that feeds me."

"I have never questioned your intelligence, Mr. Llewellyn, only the extent of your ambition."

"Sir," he assured me, "ambition has its limits, and loyalty its rewards. I shall never betray you if that's what you're thinking."

"Yes," I said frankly, "that's precisely what I'm thinking."

"Don't worry about it, sir."

"I don't worry about it, but I do think about it. I think about it all the time. One of my faults, Mr. Llewellyn, is an unrelenting single-mindedness. A concept, once established in my mind, remains implacably rooted to plague me."

"I see," he said cautiously.

"I hope so," I said with my friendliest smile. And then shaking his hand once more, I left him to ponder my words.

I was reasonably certain I had put the fear of God in him; toward the end of our interview he had looked a bit green about the gills. He would not betray me, I had paid him too well for that, and yet in the back of my mind an uneasiness lurked, a disquiet I could not quite dismiss. I didn't like him, I didn't trust him. But then again, there were very few people I trusted.

Before I left Bayonne, I stopped in again to see Winslow.

"Trevor," I said, "make a note to give Llewellyn the usual retainer. But keep a close watch on him, will you? There's something about him that rubs me the wrong way."

"He's a good man, Mark," he said too quickly, too emphatically. "I chose him myself for the position."

"Did you now?"

"Yes. And he came highly recommended from the most reliable sources."

"Well, that's comforting to know, but all the same, I want him watched."

His gaze dropped from mine, and he bent his head and began to move papers about on his desk. I pulled up a chair and sat down, all the while taking note of his atypical tension. Trevor Winslow was by nature a tranquil man, an imperturbable man, but he seemed incongruously nervous this day.

"How is Lavinia?" I asked casually. "It's been ages since I've seen her, or you, socially. I remember she was quite the theatergoer; in fact, I first met her at the Lyceum. I was with Marianne Gormley, and the four of us bumped into each other at the end of the second act. Do you recall the night, Trevor?"

"Yes, Mark," he answered, "I do."

"God, we had some good times together! Do you remember those dinners at Delmonico's and that evening at Canfield's? I do believe your wife was the only lady Dick Canfield ever permitted inside his establishment. What a stir she created at the gambling tables."

"Lavinia was always venturesome."

"Indeed she was," I laughed. "I shall never forget that Sunday in the Park when she appeared in your son's trousers and proceeded to ride her horse astride. Christ, the audacity! But she certainly cut a fetching figure in boy's clothing."

He lifted his head and gave me a smile. I did not like the look of that smile.

"Trevor," I said, "what's wrong?"

"Wrong? How do you mean?"

"What's troubling you? Your hands are shaking, do you know that?"

He looked down at his hands, then clasped them together and interlaced the fingers. "I'm tired," he said. "That's what's wrong. I haven't been sleeping well lately."

"Why not?"

"I don't know."

"Is it your work?"

"My work?"

"Are you working too hard?"

"I like to work hard."

"Then what is it? Are you having problems at home?"

He faced me unwaveringly, his handsome brown eyes very frank and very clear. "No," he said quietly. "Everything's fine at home."

Trevor Winslow was a few years my senior and one of my most invaluable associates. He was a gentleman, with money of his own, but he was very much like me: He loved to work, he wanted to work, he needed to work or go mad. When I took his wife for a mistress I did not do it out of malice; on the contrary, I liked Trevor. As a matter of fact, I thought twice about entering into a relationship with Lavinia Winslow, for although she was extremely beautiful and came of impeccable family, she was a queer, wild girl, with the instincts and soul of a whore. I could not imagine why Trevor had married her, that is until the first time I made love to her. Then I understood everything. I had never before encountered a lady of good breeding who performed so uninhibitedly the particular sexual practices Lavinia favored. The woman was incredible, insatiable. Sometimes I think she would still be my mistress today—if I hadn't married, that is, and if she hadn't seduced my son.

I wondered now, if by some cruel twist of fate, Trevor had learned we'd been lovers. I had always been exceedingly discreet about my affairs, but at times even the most carefully hidden secrets are uncovered.

"Trevor," I ventured, "if there's something you'd like to discuss with me . . ."

"About what, Mark?"

"About anything at all. I know something's bothering you and I'd like to help if I can."

"I appreciate your concern, but nothing whatever is bothering me. I've become something of an insomniac, that's all. It will pass. Everything passes in time."

He rose from his desk and took a leatherbound ledger from a shelf on the wall. "Would you care to see this month's figures? Our profits have risen again."

Puzzled by his coolness, then hurt, and finally irritated by it, I rose to leave. "No," I said brusquely, "I haven't time today. Send me a copy and a full analysis of sales. And Trevor"—I stopped at the door, my hand on the latch—"see that your insomnia doesn't interfere with your good judgment. I want you to watch Llewellyn, despite his recommendations and despite the fact that you personally chose him for the job."

An emotion flickered briefly in his eyes, one that I could not name, and he was silent for so long a time that for a moment I thought he was not going to respond. But at length he said stiffly, "Very well, Mark, I'll watch him if that's what you want."

I did not like his tone, nor the cool, measured look he gave me when I bade him good day. I assumed he had learned about my affair with his wife, but there was precious little I could do about it now. If my assumption was correct, if Trevor did know that Lavinia and I had been lovers, I sincerely hoped it would not adversely affect our relationship. He was a good man, an asset to the company; I should very much hate to let him go.

I spent the remainder of the day and the better part of the evening in my offices at 18 Broadway. It was past ten o'clock when I returned home. I hadn't had dinner, I was tired and cross, and to add to my annoyance, Joanna was nowhere in sight. Muttering and grumbling, I climbed the stairs and looked in on the family room. It was empty, the lights were extinguished, and a fire had been laid but not lit. For some reason, the oddest sense of foreboding struck me, but I shrugged it off and went down the hall to my room.

At my door, I hesitated. The sense of foreboding returned. I stood statue-still, waiting, listening, as though my unlikely apprehension would somehow manifest itself as a palpable presence in my path. The house hummed with silence; the stillness droned loud in my ears. Slowly then, as if compelled, I turned from my own room and moved toward my wife's bedroom door.

The door was closed. I opened it and stepped inside. The bed was made, the covers had not been turned down. I went into the boudoir; it too was empty, but on the dressing table a letter lay in the circle of light cast by the lamp, and as I drew closer, I saw my name on the envelope, written in my wife's fine hand.

I picked up the envelope and, none too neatly, tore it open. The letter was brief, the message concise.

XXVII

Mark, I'm leaving you. I don't know what else to do. We should never have married; I've never understood you, nor have I ever really understood what you want of me. I blame myself for our difficulties. I've made you unhappy, but I am unhappy too. I shall stay with the Chandlers until I find a small house for myself and Noelle. Try, please try, to forgive me for unsettling your life.

Forgive her? By God, I would kill her!

A faint glimmer of logic told me she was right in saying we should never have married, and I knew without doubt that I was absolutely the worst man in the world for her. But I loved her, didn't that matter to her? I loved her and wanted her and needed her, and I would never under any circumstances let her go.

I left the house without my hat and coat and walked, almost ran, the seven and one-half blocks to the Chandler house. The windows were dark; I assumed that all within slept, but that did not stop me from pounding like a madman at the door. Presently, an alarmed servant, clad in slippers and robe, answered my summons and reluctantly let me in.

"Where are the Chandlers?" I demanded. "Where is my wife? Awaken her at once. Tell her I've come to take her home."

"Mark, for heaven's sake!"

Constance, also attired in nightclothes, descended the stairs, dismissed the frightened servant, then firmly took my arm and steered me to her husband's study.

"Sit down," she said, lighting the lamp on the desk. "I'll pour you some whiskey."

"I don't want whiskey, Constance, I want my wife."

"You fool," she said harshly. "You're in no position to want anything where Joanna is concerned. Now sit down and drink this."

She thrust the whiskey into my hand, then waited stubbornly till I sat down and raised the glass to my lips.

The whiskey burned hot in my throat and scorched a path down to my empty stomach. My eyes teared and I almost gagged, but after the initial shock I began to feel better and I drank a bit more, then finished the rest in one swallow.

"Do you want another?" she asked.

"Yes," I said grimly. "And fill it this time."

Constance was an old friend, one of the few women in my circle whom I genuinely respected and admired. She was a handsome woman of thirty-five, with silky brown hair and laughing, vivacious brown eyes. Her figure was perfection: full in the breast, narrow in the waist, but despite these alluring endowments I had never slept with her, nor ever wanted to. I liked her too much for that.

"Now then," she said when I had disposed of my second whiskey, "you look sufficiently calmed down to carry on a rational conversation."

"Where's John?" I asked, sullenly ignoring her barbed remark.

"In Baltimore. Mark, what's happened? Why is Joanna here?"

I threw her a suspicious look. "She didn't tell you?"

"She told me she's left you, nothing else. She was in rather a state when she arrived; I thought it best not to question her. And if I were you, I'd let her alone until she's had some time to collect her thoughts. Honestly, Mark, you are the limit! Charging in here like an enraged bull, demanding—*demanding*—to take her home. I daresay your temper is one of the main reasons she left you. And I can't say it surprises me. She's not Lenore, you know."

"What the devil is that supposed to mean?"

"Lenore permitted your tantrums, your childish outbursts, although only God knows why. She tolerated too much, overlooked too much, and as a result you've not mellowed with age but hardened into habit all that is execrable within you."

I sprang from my chair like an uncoiled spring. "Goddamn it, I don't have to listen to this! Get my wife down here or by Christ, I'll—"

"See what I mean?" she said irritably. "You're forever flying into a rage at the least provocation. Good grief, if I were your wife I'd have left you ages ago. You've given me quite a severe headache."

I did not sit down, but I did subside, none too gracefully, and shoving my hands into my trouser pockets, I waited testily for Constance to speak her piece. I did not have long to wait.

"The trouble with you," she commenced her attack, "is that you've always been more attractive than is good for you."

"For God's sake, Constance—"

"No, listen to me, Mark. For as long as I can remember, you've always had your way. You wanted Lenore, her father objected, but she married you all the same. You wanted Eastern Seaboard, the fates were against it, but you ultimately gained control. It's your mesmerizing good looks—certainly not your charm—which has opened many doors to you, and all of your life you've taken shameful advantage of anyone foolish enough to fall under the spell of your physical sorcery."

"Constance, don't be absurd. My 'mesmerizing good looks' aren't worth a tinker's dam in the business world. And if you don't mind, I can do without your left-handed compliments."

"Compliments? My dear Mark, I never compliment accidents of nature or, if you will, gifts of God. You had absolutely no hand in forming your physiognomy, therefore I do not compliment it, left-handed or otherwise. And perhaps it had little to do with your success at Eastern Seaboard, but a handsome face does have its uses, doesn't it?"

"What are you driving at? Get to the point, won't you?

I'm tired and hungry; I want to go home and I want my wife."

She eyed me askance, then commented acidly, "Yes, I know you want her, but do you deserve her?"

I swore in frustration, then began an angry pacing about the room.

"Mark, I'm sorry," she said. "That was cruel of me. But you're so thoughtless sometimes, so insensitive to those who love you. You've hurt Joanna, I could see that at once, and you've frightened her too, I think. Lenore was better equipped to deal with your temper, with your rages, but Joanna is—"

"For the love of Christ, will you stop talking about Lenore! I know how abominably I treated her; you don't have to rub my nose in it. And I know I should never have married again. I know it, Constance, but I love Joanna, I love her, do you understand me?"

"Yes," she replied as calm as you please, "I understand you. And I know why you married her. Everyone in New York knows why you married Joanna."

"Yes, yes," I said impatiently, "I know what you're going to say. I married Joanna because she is the personification of Lenore."

"Lenore?" She stared at me in astonishment. "Are you joking, Mark? Joanna is nothing at all like Lenore. Adele is the reason you married her. Joanna is just like Adele."

Now I was the one who stared in astonishment. Adele? Impossible! Joanna was as different from my sister as night from day. There was a vague physical resemblance perhaps; they were both dark-haired with creamy, fair skin and great, velvet brown eyes, and there was a certain similarity of form, both of them being slimmer than fashion decreed stylish. But that was coincidence, nothing more. As far as likeness of character was concerned, they couldn't have been more dissimilar.

"Mark," Constance said, "are you serious? Do you actually think Joanna is like Lenore?"

"Yes. Yes, of course I do. Can't you see it?"

"No," she said, frowning. "Quite frankly, I can't."

"Jesus!" I snapped. "What difference does it make who—

she's like? And what is the point of this ridiculous conversation?"

"The point, Mark," she answered, "seems to be that you don't know your women very well. Which is probably the reason Joanna left you."

I went ice cold with rage; I could almost feel the blood congeal frostily in my veins.

"Listen," I said in a low, shaking voice, "I have had just about enough of your senseless theories and your offensive remarks. I want you to shut up. I also want you to go upstairs and tell my wife I'm here. If you don't do as I ask, if she's not down here in five minutes, I'm going to go up those stairs and drag her bodily from whichever room you've secreted her in. Now which shall it be, Constance? Will you fetch Joanna, or shall I do it myself?"

I think she was frightened. I think the mere fact that I hadn't raised my voice frightened her more than anything I had said. I wasn't sure what I had said; I was so furious, so totally spent with frustration and rage, that my mind was only fragmentally rational. If Constance had objected, if she had opened her mouth to even attempt to protest, I think I might have strangled her. But fortunately for both of us she just turned on her heel and left the room with a haste no doubt instigated by my lethal mood.

I poured myself another whiskey, bolted it down, and refilled the glass with a none too steady hand. The liquor no longer burned my throat nor affronted my stomach; instead, it quieted my nerves and tempered the ferocity of my rage.

I was tired to the bone, and drinking only increased my weariness, but it was a blessed weariness, a respite from unrest which I sorely needed if I was to present myself to my wife in the best possible light. I knew Joanna would not want to come home. I realized, with a sudden and painful clarity, how appalling my behavior had been the night before and this morning. I conceded her right to be angry, but by no means did I sanction her leaving. She shouldn't have left me, I did not understand her leaving me, nor was I going to permit it.

"Mark."

I swung round with a start at the sound of my name. She was at the door, her dressing gown buttoned modestly to her throat, her hair tucked childishly behind her ears, falling free down her back to the waist. She looked no more than sixteen and so touchingly vulnerable that I could barely restrain myself from enfolding her protectively in my arms.

"Joanna," I said in a calm neutral voice, "please sit down. I'd like to talk to you."

She came into the room slowly, reluctantly, her great, dark eyes apprehensively watching my every move. She did not sit down, but stood at a safe distance from me.

"Darling, please," I said quietly, "I'm sorry about this morning. I never meant to hurt you, either physically or emotionally. There's no acceptable excuse I can offer you, but I do apologize, I want you to forgive me, and I promise that nothing of the kind will ever happen again."

Joanna did not speak, and for a long uncomfortable time, neither did I. I searched my mind for an appropriate way to approach her. It was vitally important that I not alienate her any more than I already had.

"Your note," I said presently, "surprised me on several counts. First of all, I want to assure you that you have in no way 'unsettled my life'; on the contrary, I have never felt more content and at peace than these years we've been married. Secondly, and most importantly, I was not aware that you were unhappy. I should like you to tell me—that is, if you please, Joanna—exactly why you feel this way."

She was now sitting tensely on a Sheraton chair near the desk. Her face was in shadow, I could not discern her expression, but every muscle in her body seemed rigid, poised for immediate flight.

"Joanna," I said as gently as I could, "can you tell me why you're unhappy?"

She shook her head and lowered her eyes, her hands twisting nervously in her lap.

"Darling," I persisted, "we can only solve our problems if we discuss them. I realize you're upset now, but perhaps this is the best time to express your true feelings. Come now," I coaxed her, "tell me what's wrong. I know I am at fault, but I should like to know in precisely what manner I have made you unhappy so that I might never do it again."

A long moment passed and then, slowly, she lifted her head. The look on her face broke my heart.

"I am only unhappy," she said faintly, "because I cannot make you happy. You are not at fault, Mark. I am to blame for our difficulties."

"No, Joanna, you're wrong about that."

"I have never known you," she said, ignoring my words. "I have lived with you, shared your bed, borne your child, yet I know less of you now than I knew on the night we first met. In the beginning, when we were first married, I thought time and proximity would change that; I felt sure that as your wife I would reach an understanding of you which had eluded me always when you were courting me. A husband, I thought, has less need for poses, for pretenses, than a suitor. But as time passed, I saw that as a husband or as a suitor, you were the same: I still didn't know you, and I felt I never would, because what I had thought was the enigma of a man I hardly knew was really you."

She looked up at me briefly. "Do you understand?" she asked haltingly. "Do you know what I'm trying to say?"

I did not reply at once. The truth of the matter was I did not understand her at all. But at length I ventured tentatively, "Yes, I think so, Joanna. When we married, you weren't quite certain of your feelings. Is that it?"

And incredibly she answered, "Yes, Mark, that was part of it. I wasn't sure how I felt about you, and I wasn't at all sure I should marry you. I knew I didn't suit you; I was so different from . . . the women whose company you enjoyed. I used to wonder why you wanted me, what it could possibly be you saw in me. I never flattered myself that you might love me; and then when you told me on our wedding night that you did love me, I couldn't have been more stunned. Strangely though, learning you loved me only reinforced my belief that we shouldn't have married. I knew I could never live up to whatever expectations you might have of me, and I realized for the first time in my life what an awesome responsibility love is."

She paused. I said nothing.

"You see," she went on, "when you told me you loved me
. . . well, it imposed an obligation on me which I hadn't anticipated and which ultimately I learned I could never fulfill."

"An obligation? Of what nature?"

Her eyes met mine squarely, and she sighed deeply as if
facing at last an inevitable and inescapable truth.

"To love you," she said. "I felt obligated to love you, and
I knew I couldn't. I knew I was incapable of loving you as
you should be loved, as you expected to be loved. We are so
different, you and I, I knew this at the outset, but when I
thought you only wanted me because of Alan, I felt I could
deal with being your wife under those circumstances, and
so I consented to marry you."

"I see," I said blankly, but I saw nothing, felt nothing
save the most wretched, overpowering, and soul-shatter-
ing despair. "Is that why you're unhappy then? Is that
why you left me? Because you do not—cannot—love me?"

"No," she answered, "that's not it at all. Please let me
finish, Mark. I know I'm explaining myself badly, but it's
so hard to finally put into words what I've kept in my heart
all these years."

"Of course," I said politely. "Do go on. Forgive me for in-
terrupting you. I am only trying to understand. . . ."

I trailed off and fell silent as a semblance of reason was
restored to me. She could not be saying what I thought she
was saying. This woman, who had only the night before
trembled with passion in my arms, could not now be saying she did not love me. Surely I had misinterpreted her
meaning, surely my heightened emotions had blunted my
innate perception. I knew people so well; I knew what
moved them, what frightened them, what elated or saddened them. But not Joanna, not this shy, perplexing puzzle I had married. Of the legion of liaisons in my varied
experience, I loved this woman best, and yet I knew her
the absolute least.

"I knew," my wife went on, "that our marriage would
not survive unless I changed my way of thinking. And I
wanted it to survive, Mark, it was terribly important that

this marriage succeed since I had failed so disastrously with my first."

I tried to respond and could not. It struck me as odd that she should refer to her first marriage as a failure, but it was impossible for me to comment. I could only think how easily she had admitted she didn't love me, as easily and as freely as she had told me, the night before, that she loved my son.

"I began to think," she went on, "that if ever I was to make you happy, I should have to pattern my behavior on the ladies with whom you had associated yourself before we were married. It occurred to me that the physical side of a relationship is the one most appealing to you, and so I tried to—"

I swung round abruptly as her incredible words slashed like a sword at my consciousness. "What?" I said fiercely. "Do you mean to sit there and tell me you thought for even a moment that I compared you or classed you with my whores?"

"Oh no," she cried softly. "That's not . . . I never . . . Please, Mark, don't be angry. It frightens me, your anger; it's so intense, so *internal.* You're never so distant from me as when you're angry. I don't understand it, I cannot fathom the reasons for your rage. Last night you were angry—I didn't know why. It was when I was talking of Alan; you were watching me so oddly—whenever I talk of him you look at me in that same cold way. I had thought it was because you still had not forgiven me for telling him he was not your son, but it's not that, it's more than that, and I cannot endure it, Mark, I cannot combat what I don't understand. And then, this morning . . . this morning"— she rose from her chair, trembling and pale—"when you pushed me from the room . . . as if you were casting me out of your life."

"My God, Joanna, that wasn't it at all!"

"What was it then?" she said wretchedly. "Why did you look at me as if you despised me? Why did you let go of my arm as if my touch repelled you? Was it because I've come shamelessly to your room night after night? Was it because I wanted you, *encouraged* you, to make love to me?"

"Jesus, no!" I insisted. "It wasn't any of those reasons." But in the emotion of the moment, the full import of her words eluded my understanding. I knew only that I had to comfort her, to hold her in my arms, and to banish at the same time her fears and my own. But as I moved to embrace her, she evaded my touch, putting distance between us, a distance so small and yet a gap as immense as infinity.

"Don't," she said wretchedly, "don't touch me. I cannot think clearly when you touch me. Everything is confused when you're near me. In your arms I forget our differences, nothing separates us, we are one in spirit as well as in flesh. In your arms I am happy, but it is a transitory joy, an elusive bliss, which evaporates with first light of day. When you make love to me I am sure, then and only then am I sure of who I am, of what I mean to you, of why you married me. But when it's over I am certain of nothing. I am only frightened and bewildered."

"Jesus," I groaned and pulled her close, uncaring of her protests. "Joanna, forget this morning. Forget everything, please, except that I love you. If you're happy in my arms, I shall keep you there forever. If your doubts fade with my love, I shall love you continuously from morning till night. Stay with me, darling, don't leave me. Stay with me, stay with me."

"Oh, don't," she moaned, "don't touch me, don't hold me. Mark, no . . ."

"Yes," I insisted, "yes. Come home with me, stay with me. I love you. I refuse to let you go. Darling, look at me. Look at me! I love you, do you believe me?"

"Yes," she said faintly. "I believe you."

"I can make you happy. I *will* make you happy. Do you believe that too?"

She shook her head, struggled feebly in my arms. "No, Mark, no. It is *I* who cannot make you happy. Don't you see? Haven't you understood what I've been trying to tell you?"

"Joanna, stop it, don't fight me, listen to what I'm saying. You do make me happy, you always have. Trust me, believe me, and grant me the chance to make you happy too. I'll never hurt you again, I swear it, nor ever give you cause to leave again. Stay with me, please. I want you, I need you, I love you so much."

I was wooing her purposefully, with my voice, with my hands. She had made it clear, in her own ingenuous way, that she welcomed my physical love. If that was what she wanted, if that was the only way to ensure she not leave me, I would be more than happy to accommodate her.

I drew her closer, so close that I could feel the rapid beating of her heart. She struggled for a moment: struggled against me, against herself, against the baffling inner conflicts of her conscience. But when I kissed her, when my mouth closed on hers and my hand brushed the curve of her breast, her struggles ceased, she permitted my touch, and she reached up her arms to embrace me.

XXVIII

I NEVER DELUDED myself that our troubles were over. She came home with me, she slept in my arms the entire night through, but we had resolved nothing; our relationship was still as tenuous, as endangered, as it had been before. I was still not certain of the exact nature of our difficulties. Joanna had said she could not make me happy. But that was nonsense; she did make me happy. Why did she find that so hard to believe?

The following day, I remained at home. It seemed wise as well as practical to hear my wife out, to question her further, for on the night before, she had said very little I understood. Only one thing stood to the fore: She did not love me, she never would. That, and that alone, she had made unequivocally clear to me.

"Joanna," I said at breakfast, "do you mind if we talk more about what's troubling you? You'll have to forgive me, darling, but I didn't quite grasp what you were trying to explain to me last night."

We were alone in the dining room. We always take breakfast buffet style, as I dislike the formality of solicitous servants first thing in the morning.

Joanna was clad in a smart morning gown of creamy cambric, with an ethereal webbing of white Irish lace at the throat and the wrists. Her hair was curled and caught up with combs off the nape of her neck, and there was a faint blush of color on her cheeks and her mouth. She looked utterly enchanting.

She put down her cup when I spoke. "Mark," she said

evasively, "I'd prefer not. I'm afraid if we talk more, we'll quarrel."

"Darling, no, I assure you I won't."

"Please," she implored, and impulsively, she reached across the table to cover my hand with hers. "I cannot make clear to you what I myself don't understand. It's so difficult for me to share my feelings; it's a failing, Mark, a terrible failing which I've tried unsuccessfully to correct. And it is one of the things which convinces me that we are ill-suited to one another."

"Don't say that," I said, scowling. "We are not ill-suited. It's simply not true."

"Please," she repeated, her hand clutching mine. "Don't question me, Mark, I implore you. It's impossible to convey to you what I'm thinking, and invariably, whenever I try to explain myself, you take the wrong meaning, and then . . ."

"Very well," I conceded. "I won't question you. We'll speak of it no more if it distresses you. But, Joanna, you must promise me . . ."

"Yes?"

"You must promise you won't leave me. I want your word on it, darling. I want to be sure you won't leave me."

"I won't leave you," she whispered, her voice faint with shame. "I'm sorry about yesterday. I never meant to hurt you. I thought I was doing what was best for you."

"Joanna, *you* are what's best for me."

"Oh, Mark, I hope that's true. I pray I won't hurt you by staying."

"Don't talk nonsense. If you stay, I'll be happy. That's what you want, isn't it, to make me happy?"

"Yes," she said earnestly. "It's what I want more than anything else in the world."

"Then stay."

"I'll stay."

"You'll never leave? Not for any reason?"

"I won't. I promise."

"Very well then. It's settled."

I rose abruptly, unable to contain my enormous relief. I

prowled about the room, stopped near the buffet, then finally returned to my chair.

"I love you, you know," I said gravely. "I love you much more than you realize."

"Mark . . ." she said, troubled.

"Yes?"

"Why do you love me?"

Her unexpected question brought me up short. The reasons for love are not easily defined. "Why do you ask, Joanna?"

"I . . . I don't know. Perhaps if I knew why you love me, I might find it easier to please you."

"You do please me, darling."

"In every way, Mark?"

For a moment I hesitated. I was thinking of Alan. And I was thinking how little it pleased me that Joanna loved him. But I only said gently, "Yes, Joanna, you do. You please me in every way."

She gazed at me anxiously, as if not quite convinced by my answer. I doubt she believed me. I'm certain she knew I was lying.

Despite its numerous flaws, the marriage endured. Joanna was wary for a time, wondering, perhaps, whether or not she had made the right choice in remaining my wife. But we quarreled no longer—I was making a concentrated effort to restrain my unholy temper—and for a year or so following the night she had left me, we lived peaceably, serenely, together.

Oddly, because of Constance Chandler's remarks, I suppose, I began to liken my wife to my sister. As each day passed, I began to see more and more the similarities between them which had never before caught my notice. Adele and Joanna, they were cut from one mold. They were chaste, refined, modest, well-bred, and both of them took what they felt was their due without feeling the need to give in return. I recognized this fact, but I did not resent it; on the contrary, I have never expected much from women, for they are a reticent species, the more timorous

of God's creations, and it is a man's duty and joy to give to
a woman without thought or regard to requital.

Adele and Joanna, the women I loved. Both of them had
deserted me, both had left me at a time when I needed
them most. Not that I blamed them; they'd been wiser, and
luckier, than Lenore. Lenore had not left me. She had
stayed—to her misfortune. Perhaps if she'd left me, as
Adele and Joanna had left me, she might still be alive today.

Coincident with the abatement of my marital difficulties, my occupational concerns were faring peaceably as
well. Every branch of Eastern Seaboard Oil was operating
smoothly, at top efficiency, and virtually unhampered by
competition. The workers seemed content, or so I was informed with punctilious regularity by Morris Llewellyn
and Trevor Winslow. My uneasiness about Llewellyn,
however, had not diminished. I still didn't like him, I still
didn't trust him, and I was beginning to have my doubts
about Trevor Winslow as well. I was now convinced that he
had learned of my affair with his wife, and I was further
convinced he was planning a fit retribution. I wasn't
worried though. I am not a worrying man. But I thought
about Trevor a great deal, and I made it my business to
personally investigate every transaction, no matter how
trivial, with which he was directly involved.

In 1891, my son was graduated from Yale. And in Newport that summer, he became officially engaged to Caroline Monroe. I couldn't very well oppose his choice; Carrie
was a sweet child, more like her father than her mother,
but it disturbed me that Alan had chosen for a wife the
daughter of Sally Monroe, thus binding my life inextrica-
bly with the life of a woman I abhorred. I tried to avoid
Sally as best I could that season, but since our children
were planning to marry in the fall, she had a perfectly legitimate reason to seek me out at parties on pretext of discussing "the lovely couple" and "the eminently suitable
match."

"What beautiful sons they'll have," she would say
archly, her meaning clear to me if not to Joanna, who

would hang on my arm and say nothing, for she disliked Sally now, disliked her with an intensity of which I had not thought her capable.

At the end of July, Sally invited us to dinner. My first impulse was to refuse, but I realized I could not do so without raising a host of questions I preferred not to answer.

"But, Mark," Joanna protested when I showed her Sally's note, "I don't want to go. Please make some excuse. I cannot sit at her table. I will not!"

"I feel as you do, darling," I said calmly. "But we shall both have to bear it for Alan's sake. He'd be terribly disappointed if we refused, and curious as to our reasons. You don't want him to know, do you, that Sally was responsible for . . ."

"No, no," she agreed quickly. "We'll go if we must. But, Mark, don't leave me alone with her. I won't be responsible for what might happen if you leave me alone with her."

I gave her my promise, of course. The last thing in the world I wanted was for Sally Monroe to be alone with my wife.

On the night of the dinner, Alan was dressed and ready an hour beforehand, while Joanna, gloomy, disconsolate, and nervous as a cat, kept us waiting in the hall a full thirty minutes past our intended time of departure. The wait was well worth it, however, for when she finally appeared at the top of the stairs, her dark hair curling about a flushed, anxious face, and her slim form clothed splendidly in a gown of ice blue moiré, I was strongly tempted to forgo our dinner engagement and take her to bed to make love to her all through the night. Naturally, I did no such thing. I merely took her arm as she ended her descent, but I fear my eyes betrayed my feelings, for when she looked up at me, startled by the hard possessive pressure of my hand, I saw in her eyes, for just a fraction of an instant, an ardent and loving response.

In the carriage, Alan chattered like a monkey. He was anxious to marry, he told us. He was longing for children, how happy he would be when he had children. This struck me as odd, as I had not been aware that Alan particularly liked children.

"Carrie and I have discussed it," he said. "We are agreed that we shall have at least six, and we shall have them as soon as possible. I want a house filled with children, I want so many children that I shan't be able to recall all their names. Perhaps we'll have more than six. Carrie and I are young; if we start now and have a child a year . . ."

"Alan," I laughed, "have some consideration for your young lady. Wait a while, enjoy yourselves first, and then in a few years you can start your family and have a dozen children, if you wish."

He regarded me solemnly in the dim light. "Sir," he said simply, "I want children now. It's important I have children now."

"Why, son?" I asked. "Has yours been a lonely life? Have you missed having brothers and sisters?"

"No," he said slowly, his gaze moving from mine to my silent and watchful wife. "I have had Noelle. I am grateful for her."

I turned to Joanna and covered her hand with mine. "Did you hear that, darling? Without even realizing it, you have made both the Van Holden men happy."

She glanced up at me swiftly, with an odd, alarmed look I could not interpret. But before I could think to question her strange reaction, the carriage had stopped and Alan was reaching impatiently past me to push open the door.

The Monroes greeted us in the hall: Carrie, angelic in a white frock with lace appliqués; Stephen, looking more distinguished than ever in evening clothes; and Sally, dressed to the hilt, a choker of emeralds and pearls the perfect complement to her green velvet, pearl-studded gown. I was not surprised when Sally was tactless enough to comment on our tardiness. And feeling Joanna's hand pressing anxiously into my arm, I volunteered, "You'll have to blame me for that, Sally. In my old age I've become shamefully vain about my looks. After I was dressed tonight, I spent all of an hour peering into my mirror and plucking gray hairs from my head."

"Really, Mark?" she drawled. "I've never noticed any gray in your hair."

"That, my dear Sally, shows you how thorough I am."

"Yes," she said with an unpleasant smile, "I'm fully aware of how thorough you are."

I swallowed a swift surge of anger, and choked back a cutting retort. Silence, I decided, was the only safe course when dealing with Sally Monroe.

"Carrie," said Alan, "how lovely you look! Is that a new dress?"

And when she blushed and smiled and nodded her pretty head, he remarked with a fond, teasing grin, "It looks like a wedding gown, sweetheart. Are you trying to rush things by any chance?"

"Oh, Alan," she laughed, "I think I can wait three more months."

"Well, dinner won't wait," said Sally peevishly. "Come along, everyone. And let's hope that the meal isn't ruined."

The meal—baked chicken crepes Mornay, wild rice with mushrooms, and potatoes in cream sauce—was by no means ruined, but as far as I was concerned, the dinner was a total disaster. Talk was spare. Stephen is not the most voluble of men; Carrie and Alan were wrapped up in each other, oblivious of all else; Joanna had become a veritable sphinx; and I was still seething with anger. Which left the full burden of conversation on our fool of a feather-brained hostess.

Fortunately for Sally, society discourse, with its tedious invariability, is easy to maintain. One, as a matter of form, speaks only of yachting or of riding or of current fashion or of past dinner parties. One never speaks of business or of—perish the thought!—ideas. This dubious convention suited Sally perfectly, for I doubt she had ever consciously entertained an original or intellectual thought in her entire life.

"I do not care much for the new direction in dress," she was saying as dessert was served. "The hourglass contour of the form is unnatural and uncomfortable. Why, the waist is cinched so tightly, one can scarcely breathe! I vow I shan't adopt the fashion. What do you think, Joanna?

You've become *très chic* of late. I simply adore that dress.
Is it a Worth? I knew it! His designs flatter even the
plainest women. \. . . Oh, I don't mean to imply that *you're*
plain, my dear. I was simply trying to make a point."

I saw my wife flinch against Sally's deliberate barb; I
saw Alan look away from Carrie and his young face turn
hard with protective anger. "Mrs. Monroe," he said in a
low, caustic voice, "I think it is Joanna who does credit to
Mr. Worth's gown. No amount of design or fine fabric can
disguise an unattractive woman . . . or a woman of advanced age." And his gaze rested pointedly on the unmistakable creping of Sally's white throat which even her
jewelled collar could not fully conceal.

His arrow had found its mark. Sally flushed a deep and
unbecoming shade of red, and she asked him sharply, "Are
you an expert, Alan, on *haute couture?* One would not expect a gentleman to be conversant in that exclusively feminine field."

"Sally," suggested her husband with a patience and for-
bearance I envied, "I believe Mark is ready for his port.
Why don't you take the ladies into the drawing room?
We'll join you shortly, my pet." And he nodded significantly toward the door.

Bristling with indignation, Sally rose like a shot and
swept from the room. Her daughter, bewildered by the pro-
ceedings, slowly followed, and Joanna, glancing anxiously
in my direction, had no recourse but to leave the table as
well.

Immediately the ladies left, a decanter of port was produced, along with an assortment of sweetmeats and nuts.
As soon as the servants had withdrawn, Stephen said
quietly, "She can be such a shrew at times."

The aptness of his observation required no comment. I
picked up my glass, admired the clarity of the wine, and
drank, all the while watching, from the corner of my eye,
my silent and tormented son. His quick defense of Joanna
and the anguish now apparent in his face confirmed all my
wildest conjectures. He loved her, he wanted her. That she
was married to me, and that he was shortly to be married
himself, seemed not to concern him. He would make her

his own if she would but let him. And I wondered, with a sudden and blinding irrational rage, if eventually she would.

"Tell me, Alan," I heard Stephen say, "have you given any thought to a career? Will you be entering the ranks of Eastern Seaboard now that you've graduated, or have you other irons in the fire?"

"I'm not sure," Alan mumbled, his thoughts evidently elsewhere. And as Stephen continued to question him, I watched my son as I would an adversary: guardedly, searchingly, and with every defensive instinct in my body on ready and total alert.

I took note of his beauty—the elegant features he'd inherited from Lenore enhanced by his own youthful masculinity. I beheld his fair skin, his golden hair, his ingenuous eyes, his sensitive, sensuous mouth. What woman could resist him? What woman would want to resist him?

"I have been spending some time in my father's offices," he was telling Stephen, "and have involved myself to a small degree in the operation of his refineries." He turned to me suddenly, feeling my scrutiny perhaps, and added in a hushed, nervous voice, "But I daresay he thinks me clumsy and inexperienced."

I made no response. I was afraid to speak, afraid of my thoughts, afraid of the emotion that trebled the tempo of my pulse. I kept thinking of Joanna and of the way Alan had watched her and of a certain look in Joanna's eyes when, at times, she would watch him. She loved him too, that much I knew. But in exactly what way did my wife love my son?

The conversation droned on. After a time I found myself making an occasional appropriate response, but it soon became evident to Stephen that I had had my fill of after-dinner discourse.

"Shall we join the ladies?" he said, rising, and my son rose too, more anxious than I, it seemed, to return to the woman he loved.

Upon entering the drawing room, we found young Carrie absent, Sally stiff-backed and pale on the settee, and

Joanna, who stood near the French doors which led to the balustraded terrace, as alarmingly white as Sally.

"Sally," said Stephen, "what's wrong? What's happened? Where's Carrie?"

His soft, patient voice had gone harsh with command. He approached his wife, whose own voice, when she replied, quavered with a profound and fearful guilt.

"Nothing's wrong, Stephen. Caroline had a headache, that's all, and has retired. Alan"—she turned to my son—"Caroline sends you her regrets. . . ."

She trailed off tremulously under the silent indictment of her husband's scrutiny. Her gaze darted about the room, avoided Joanna's still figure, then came to rest, as if compelled, on the horrified suspicion in my eyes.

Good God, had she told her? Had that stupid, addle-brained, social-climbing slut told Joanna that I, and not Stephen, had sired her son?

"Joanna." I went to my wife, put a hand on her arm. Although the night was warm, her skin was cold, icy cold, and her eyes, when she turned to face me, sent a spasm of fear down my spine.

"I want to go home, Mark. I want you to take me home." She moved away from me, her face colorless, her spine ramrod-straight. "Stephen," she said in a faint, toneless voice, "would you ring for our things?"

"Joanna," he insisted, "what's happened? Have you quarreled? Joanna!"

"Please," she said weakly. "Please, Stephen, I want to go home."

He began to protest but stopped when he saw the intense look of anguish in her eyes. Mystified, frustrated, he shook his head angrily, strode across the room, and gave a hard sharp tug to the bellpull.

I saw Sally leave the scene, quietly, stealthily; I saw the puzzled bewilderment on my son's face; I saw Stephen, that patient, gentle man, yank a second time at the bellpull almost ripping it from its mooring; and then I looked at my wife.

She seemed about to weep, she who never wept. Her mouth trembled and her eyes were fever bright. Again I moved toward her, reached out to touch her; and again, in deliberate evasion of my touch, she moved away.

In the carriage, she would not speak. She stared out the window, her hands clasped tightly on her lap, her slender shoulders tense and stiff, quivering visibly beneath the rich silk of her cloak. I longed to be home, to be alone with her, to explain the unexplainable, to set right that which I realized could never be set right. And at the same time I wished the journey would never end, for when it did I would have to speak to her, would have to discuss what I had thought was an issue long dead, long buried, and long forgotten.

All too soon though, the carriage drew up to the house. I alighted at once and held out a hand to my wife, which she pointedly ignored. She swept past me, my son in her wake, and when he opened the front door, stepping aside so she could enter, she lifted her skirts, rushed into the house and flew up the stairs before I even had a chance to cross the threshold.

"What is it?" Alan cried, turning to me abruptly as I stepped into the hall. "Why is she like this? What's happened?"

"I don't know," I said grimly. "I just don't know."

I left my son and climbed the stairs with the slow, heavy tread of doom and defeat. Whether or not he followed I did not know, for I was aware of nothing but my own dismal thoughts. What had happened? he'd asked. All hell had broken loose. My past, my shoddy despicable past, had reared its ugly head to irrevocably destroy my future.

Presently I found myself in my wife's room—that is, my first wife's room—which remained as she had left it, an exquisite reflection of her exquisite taste. The marble floor gleamed dully underfoot. The canopied bed, the *chinoiserie* screen, the Marie Antoinette chaise, all reposed in tranquil splendor within the elegant proportions of the cream and gilt walls. My son had been conceived in this room —my second son, a son who had not lived; and for his death too I was guilty, for he would have lived and Lenore would have lived, were it not for my sin.

I remembered so clearly the night I had committed that

sin. As I gazed at the bed where I had lain with Lenore, I remembered the night that had directly precipitated her death. I could still see her eyes, wide with terror, and I could feel her smooth skin as my hands slid deliberately, without mercy, about her soft throat. What I said to her, the filthy abusive words I said to her, I could not recall. But I remembered her face and the warmth of her flesh as I cursed her, reviled her, and accused her unjustly of a wife's most unforgivable sin.

How she pleaded with me on that night. How she pleaded and wept and protested her innocence. But I was beyond compassion, beyond reason. I flung her away from me. And I called her a whore. A whore. My sweet darling. I called her a whore.

She died because of that outrage. Days later she died, giving birth to a stillborn son. She had never been strong, and my brutal accusations, my fierce physical abuse, had sapped the last vestige of her strength.

It was shortly after the funeral that Spencer Halston unburdened his conscience to me, confessing the lie that I had so easily believed. Spencer, my friend, and Lenore's. He admitted the lie that had become the bloody instrument with which I had murdered my wife.

Dear God, I couldn't think of it anymore. I left Lenore's room and, numb with pain, sick with grief, I stumbled down the hall to my own. I passed my room, not knowing I had done so, and I stopped, in a stupor of disorientation in front of Joanna's door.

The drone of voices, low and indistinct, reached my ears, and then I heard the soft mournful sound of her weeping. She was weeping, my wife, as my first wife had wept, as my first wife had suffered the injustice of my sins.

My pain increased, my shame became a constricting thickness in my throat. I pushed open the door in a torment of guilt. I had to apologize, I had to beg her forgiveness. I was determined to spare this woman the misery I had inflicted on another.

But as I stepped into the room, the penitent phrases fled from my mind, and rage more violent than any I had ever experienced burst like an explosion in my brain. Joanna was standing at the foot of the bed, her hair in disarray about her shoulders, her thin nightdress revealing the sweet, slender curve of her body. At her side, his arms tight about her, his hands on her skin, his mouth near her trembling mouth, stood Alan, my treacherous son.

PART FOUR
Joanna

Farewell, happy fields, where joy for ever dwells!
Hail, horrors, hail, Infernal world, and thou,
profoundest hell

JOHN MILTON
Paradise Lost

XXIX

FEAR HAS MANY facets. I have known fear often in my life, but then again I was a timid child, and the years which have passed since my youth have not changed me to any appreciable degree. I knew fear when my mother died, but Edward's proposal soon banished that fear; and I knew fear again when Edward died, for I was convinced I had caused his death. But then there was Mark.

"I love you, Joanna," he had said on our wedding night. "I married you because I love you."

And I believed him. And I began to think that I had seen the last of fear. As Mark's wife I felt that nothing and no one could harm me. Who, after all, was as rich as Mark or as influential or as powerful? Surely all fear was behind me, surely all things good and happy would now be my lot, for I was Mark Van Holden's wife and he had said he loved me, and when one is loved, one has nothing to fear.

Our first years together were an idyll of bliss. We honeymooned abroad, and when we came home I learned I was carrying Mark's child. How I wanted a daughter! It was somehow terribly important that I give Mark a daughter. And when she was born I could barely contain my joy, for I had given Mark Van Holden something which he had never had before.

He was pleased, I thought, when Noelle was born. He had never expressed a desire for a daughter, but I thought he was pleased nonetheless. Yet he rarely visited the nursery and he seldom spoke of her, either to me or to anyone else; and when I mentioned his odd and unpaternal behavior, he only said gravely, "I love her dearly, Joanna, as I

love you, and I apologize for causing you concern in that regard. I shall make it a point to spend more time with her if
you wish." But he never did, and after a time I mentioned
it no more, and I began to wonder, in the deepest regions of
my mind, if Mark really loved anyone.

Oh, he was kind enough to me, and affectionate and
thoughtful, and his generosity knew no bounds. He was
forever showering me and Noelle with gifts. On her first
birthday, in fact, he presented her with a virtually price-
less pearl necklace, almost as long as she was, which she
promptly popped into her mouth. When I commented on
his extravagance, pointing out the unsuitability of such a
gift, he gave a soft laugh, embraced me warmly, and said
in a wry, amused voice, "It is for her debut, my darling. I
realize that's a long time hence, but I like to plan ahead, as
you may have noticed, for didn't I plan years in advance to
win you and make you my wife?"

Mark was such a complex man, far too complex for my
naive comprehension. He controlled a great empire, he entertained and was entertained on a grand and royal scale,
and yet his tastes, his needs—those which he showed me,
at any rate—were unembellished, straightforward, almost
spartan in their simplicity. His eating habits, for example,
were very plain, very spare. I daresay this contributed to
the hard, slender look of his form. And his attire, though
fashionable, was always understated, a perfect dark back-
drop for the portrait-perfect contours of his face. He was
such a beautiful man, such a beautiful, sophisticated man.
Yet he had chosen me, had "planned for years to win me
and make me his wife." Why? Because he loved me? It became easy, as time passed, to believe that he did.

I realized, of course, that his love for me differed from his
love for his son. Alan was Mark's life, his chief interest, his
main concern. I understood that love, and quite frankly, to
a smaller degree, I shared it. Alan Van Holden was easy to
love. As he grew older, he became a fair-haired, gray-eyed
edition of his father. He was all that Mark was, and more:
the slender grace, the languid gaze, the hard line of jaw,
and that hypnotically seductive mouth. Yes, I loved Alan,
and I can even admit, though not without a tremor of guilt,

that after he tried to make love to me in Newport, I thought of his kisses for months.

It puzzled me and shamed me, how often I thought of those kisses. Especially in Newport, directly after that day in the garden, while Mark was away on one of his many business trips. I would lie awake nights, alone in my bed, reliving the episode, feeling again the heat of Alan's mouth and the hard relentless pressure of his body crushing mine. "Let me love you," he had whispered, as his hands had stroked my breasts. "Joanna, I want you," he had groaned, and his tongue had pushed past my lips, and I had felt his hard desire throbbing against me.

Why, I would wonder, did the memory of Alan's passion haunt me, and worse, why did it fill me with a curious guilt? Surely it was sinful to think of his kisses, to re-create in my mind the very movement of his body pressing fiercely against my own. Mark had never touched me in that way, not until later in our marriage, not until that incredible night when he had burst into my room and had taken me with a passion he had never before shown me. On both occasions—with Alan in Newport and on the night Mark had loved me with an ardor approaching violence—the memory had aroused in me certain feelings that both confused and shamed me. Perhaps it was my innate dislike of excess in any form, though I could not in all truth tell myself that excess, in those particular instances, had displeased me.

At any rate, after that day in the garden, he avoided me completely. I had told him, you see, that he was not Mark's son, but the bitter irony of the situation was that he *was* Mark's son. Sally Monroe had lied to me. Or so I had thought until the night we dined at her cottage in Newport, and she told me then, in the midst of the most revolting tirade, that in my abiding stupidity I had misunderstood her those long years ago. She hadn't been speaking of Alan on that ghastly day we had quarreled. She had been talking of her own child, young Stephen, *her* son . . . and Mark's.

We were alone in the drawing room when she told me. I thought she had gone mad. She had been an absolute witch at dinner, insulting me, insulting Alan. When her husband suggested tactfully that the ladies should withdraw, Sally stomped from the room, and as soon as we had entered the hall she ordered her confused daughter to leave us, as there was "a matter of vital importance" she wished to discuss with me alone.

I should have left then and there. I should never have followed her like the spineless coward I was and have permitted her to tell me—to *scream* at me—that I had married a man who for years had loved her and who had given her his love child in proof.

I didn't believe her. I didn't want to believe her. But she shrieked on, describing the most intimate details of their relationship until I realized with anguish that no one but a lover could possibly know those things about Mark.

She fell silent at last and glared at me triumphantly as I clutched at a chair for support. I felt drained, totally spent; I felt as though I had been beaten physically. I stood frozen, immobilized, for what seemed an eternity, and I thought of Mark making love to Sally, giving her his child. Dear God, I thought wretchedly, if he loved her, why in the name of all that was holy had he married me?

When the gentlemen joined us a short time later, they saw immediately that something unpleasant had transpired. I think Mark realized at once what Sally had told me. He came toward me, his eyes anxious, searching, and when he took my arm I moved quickly away, so disturbed and offended was I by the mere touch of his hand. I looked then toward Stephen. Poor Stephen. Poor trusting, unsuspecting Stephen. How good he was, and how cruelly he had been betrayed. His son, his only son, had been fathered by another man. I prayed silently that he didn't know; I prayed as I have never prayed before that God would spare him the devastating knowledge I now possessed.

We left the house immediately. The carriage ride home was an ordeal. I could feel Mark's eyes on me, I sensed his distress, but all I could think of was Sally's face, contorted with hatred, as she told me shamelessly the intimate details of her shameless affair. Mark had made love to her—

many, many times, she'd said malevolently—and even after he had asked me to be his wife, he had gone back to her again and again.

"He couldn't stay away from me," she had gloated. "He would have married me if I'd been free, he told me so a dozen times, but instead he gave me his child. He only married you because he felt sorry for you. I can imagine how you must have played the shy, helpless widow in an effort to entrap him. But he doesn't love you; don't flatter yourself that he does. He pities you, you doltish girl, as everyone who has ever known you has pitied you. Edward felt the same way, you know: obligated to protect you. What a sly little schemer you are! A trait inherited from your mother, no doubt, whose own dubious talents lay in that same direction. You're as clever as she was, and as vulgar. And the fact that you married your men makes you no less a harlot than she."

It's not true, I kept thinking as the carriage bore us home. Edward had loved me, I knew that now, I had known it for years. And my mother, in her own careless, perfunctory way, my mother had loved me too. It was only Mark's love I questioned now. How could Mark love me, yet have slept with Sally, have given her his child? I couldn't believe he didn't love me, I didn't want to believe it, yet the facts Sally had presented to me seemed, at that moment, irrefutable.

When we finally reached home I scrambled unassisted from the carriage and sped into the house and up to my room. I had to be alone, I had to think. After undressing, I trailed to the window to stare blindly at the sea that pulsated restively and shimmered with light beneath the brilliant glow of a full summer moon. A moment might have passed, or an hour. I was unaware of time, unaware of anything but my own agonizing thoughts. And then my door opened. I did not hear it. Nor did I hear someone enter the room and walk slowly, noiselessly, to my side.

"Joanna."

The low voice startled me. I turned abruptly, expecting to see Mark, but it was Alan who stood before me, Alan Van Holden, my beautiful sensitive stepson, and in his eyes was all the concern and all the love I so desperately, at that moment, needed to have.

"Alan," I said, in a faint shaking voice.

"Oh, Jesus," he groaned. "What's happened? What is it? Joanna, let me help you."

He reached out for me, but I lurched away, frightened suddenly by my own uncontrollable need. I wanted him to hold me, I wanted *someone* to hold me and to show me his love—but not Alan. For some reason I did not fully understand, it mustn't be Alan.

I moved toward the bed, fearful, confused. Dimly, I heard him follow, and then I felt his hands on me, his hard, strong, comforting hands, and without thinking, without stopping to consider the awesome consequences, I turned, as if it were the most natural thing in the world, into the warm, loving shelter of his arms.

"Oh, Jesus," he groaned again. "Tell me what's wrong. I can't bear to see you this way. I love you, Joanna. . . . No, no, don't be frightened. I don't love you like that. I know now you were right. I never wanted you in that way. It was just— Oh, God, Joanna, don't cry. I only want to help you. Trust me, please, I won't hurt you."

His arms were crushing me, his hands scorched my skin. I suddenly found I was unable to speak, unable even to think with his young slender form pressing so close against mine. I tried to protest, but no words came. I attempted to move away but his arms held me fast, and as I struggled feebly in his hold, the door opened, and I looked up with a start into the dark and deadly depths of my husband's murderous eyes.

For several long moments there was neither sound nor movement in the room. Stunned, petrified, I stared at Mark while he stared, in blood-chilling silence, at his son. I wanted to scream, to run, to flee from the fury in his terrifying gaze, but I could only watch numbly as he moved at last and came toward us both like the inescapable onslaught of Death.

"Get away from her," Mark said, his voice unrecognizable, and I felt the warmth of Alan's arms leave my skin.

I leaned weakly against the bed. My legs were shaking,

my throat was parchment dry. I heard Alan speak, his voice a hoarse whisper, and then I saw Mark strike him, closed-fist, lightning-swift, across the face. The boy reeled back against the wall. I screamed Mark's name, clutched at his sleeve, but he pushed me away and advanced once again toward his son.

"Mark, no! Oh, dear God!"

I stumbled after him, propelled into action by the greatest fear I had ever known. Alan stood dazed, unmoving, against the wall. There was blood on his mouth and on the immaculate white linen of his shirt. With a blind, protective instinct, I flung my arms about him and turned frantically, fearfully, to confront my husband's rage.

"Don't touch him!" I cried with a courage I little felt. "Don't dare touch him again, Mark!"

"Joanna, get out of the way," Mark rasped.

"I won't let you hurt him. He's done nothing wrong. You had no right to strike him. He was only giving me comfort—as you should have done. But you were too ashamed, weren't you? Too guilty to face me now that I know your guilty secret. How dare you inflict punishment, you who have gone unpunished all your life for the most detestable crimes? And how dare you attribute your own base motives to a boy whose only intention was to ease the pain you have caused me?" The words tumbled out, hot and cruel, from some part of me where fear did not rule.

"How valiantly you defend him," Mark said through clenched teeth.

"His actions need no defense," I answered hotly. "You are the culprit here. You have violated every code of decency and morality, yet you have the colossal arrogance to sit in judgment on your son. His crime was compassion; his sin love and understanding. Do you know even the meaning of those words?"

I glared at my husband, my arms locked tight about his son, and as I did so, Alan stirred and straightened, his eyes still dazed and bleary from Mark's attack.

"Joanna," the boy mumbled, "don't say any more. I can speak for myself. Leave us, please. I want to talk to my father alone."

His words were dull, disjointed, his movements slow. Mark had hurt him with that blow, had hurt him badly. I reached out to touch him but he moved awkwardly away, and there was more dignity in that stumbling, slow movement than I had ever before witnessed in my life.

"Please," he said again, "please, Joanna, I must talk with him."

"Don't bother," said Mark, his voice hard and cold. "I believe everything has been said tonight that needs to be said. I expect you will both want to leave as soon as possible. Don't bother about that either; I shall be packed and out of here first thing in the morning. This house is yours, Alan. You may do with it what you wish: live in it, sell it, or burn it to the ground. And as for you, my dear . . ." Mark turned to me, his eyes black with rage and with another emotion I was far too distressed to perceive.

"Your own definition of love and understanding leaves much to be desired, for you have 'loved' and 'understood' only one member of this family. My son has been your sole concern for as long as you've known him. You have championed him always, disregarding the fact that when we wed, you pledged yourself to me. I, on the other hand, have been loyal to you. Any outside relationships I may have had were discontinued on the day you consented to be my wife. Can you honestly say you have been as faithful? Can you tell me in truth that you love me . . . as you love my son? Or indeed that you love me at all?"

I didn't answer; he did not deserve an answer. Mark was a stranger to me, this dark, frightening, dangerous man. He had struck his son in a brutal rage, he had said he was leaving me as if he and not I were the wronged party, and now he was asking me, with all the bitterness of a betrayed husband, if I loved him.

"Mark," I said weakly, "you are unfair."

"Unfair?" he snapped, and his voice shook with injury. "*I* am unfair? You, my dear girl, have added a new dimension to the term. You have demonstrated just now your unswerving dedication to my son, which surprises me less than it disgusts me. You have also reinforced a choice which I realize fully was made years ago. If that is your answer, so be it."

"Mark!" I cried as he turned and strode angrily to the door. "My first loyalty is to you, don't you know that? But Alan—"

"But Alan," he echoed bitterly. "Always Alan."

And his fierce gaze turned for a moment on his strangely silent son, then he swung open the door and closed it behind him with a great, thundering crash.

XXX

HE LEFT IN the morning. I was awake and dressed at first light of dawn, but when I went into his room at seven o'clock, he was already gone. His clothes and his papers, the voluminous memoranda pertinent to Eastern Seaboard which he always kept with him, were gone too. There was a note on his bureau, addressed to me.

> You may continue to draw from my account at your discretion, and the townhouse is yours for as long as you need it. If it is your wish to legalize our present situation, please let me know and I shall speak to my attorney who will then speak to you regarding terms.

He had written two more lines but had obliterated them with several bold strokes of his pen. I tried to make out the words but could not. That unfinished message bothered me. Mark was so unpredictable, and the tranquil tone of his note had in no way eased my fears. He was angry and he was hurt. That he had hurt me too seemed of little consequence to him; the fact that he had fathered another woman's child had never once been mentioned during the course of our quarrel. I should have been angered by this further display of total disregard for my feelings, but, unaccountably, I was not. I was only saddened that he should think I favored his son over him, and I was grieved beyond words that he had left me.

I stared at the note for a long time. My marriage had failed and I felt at fault. I had been incapable of keeping a man such as he. In the back of my mind I had always been

aware of this inadequacy; I had always felt that eventually
he would lose whatever passing interest he may have had
in me. Perhaps that was still another reason I had kept my
emotions in check. I loved Mark, but I had always been
afraid to make known my feelings. I was afraid to expose
myself to the danger of losing him. I could not explain this
conviction; it was groundless, ridiculous. Why should I
lose him if I loved him? But I clung to the thought nonetheless.

Mark absolutely terrified me at times, yet there was no
place I would rather be than in the warm, hard haven of
his arms. How curious that this should be so. I continuously encouraged his embraces, I yearned for his nearness,
for his kisses, for his love. It embarrassed me how much I
wanted him. No lady, no *proper* lady, should want a man
physically as much as I wanted Mark.

But my worries in that area now seemed moot. Mark
had left me. Whether or not I wanted him was no longer an
issue of consequence.

"I'm sorry," said Alan later that morning. "I'm truly
sorry for what happened last night."

He had found me in my sitting room. He spoke quietly,
his head lowered, and when he raised his gaze to mine, I
saw the bruise on his face, the vivid discoloration, a
ghastly reminder of his father's awesome rage.

"Alan," I whispered, the word a choked sound. "Alan."

"Don't," he said hoarsely. "Don't pity me. I cannot endure your pity. That's why you defended me last night,
isn't it? That's why you've always sided with me against
my father. I used to think it was love that motivated your
loyalty. I used to think . . ." He paused for a moment, drew
a deep painful breath. ". . . I used to think so many things
that just aren't true."

He shook his head and lowered his gaze once again. It
was as if he couldn't bear to look at me. It was as if he
blamed me, in the same way Mark blamed me, for failing
him.

"Alan," I implored, "what are you saying? I don't pity

you. I do love you. And if ever I've defended you, it was not a denial of your father. I care for you both very deeply."

"Yes," he said softly, "I know you do."

But when he looked at me again, I felt more than ever that I had failed him.

"Oh, what is it?" I cried. "Why do you look at me like that? Isn't it enough that I have lost your father? Am I to lose you as well?"

"Lose me?" he said. "Joanna, you'll never lose me. I'll always love you, always. Not in the way I used to think I loved you, but in the proper way—as a friend . . . or as a son, if you will. But don't you see, *I've* lost my father too. Just when I'd found him, just when I'd come to realize how much I love him, I've lost him. He thinks . . . oh, Jesus, he thinks the worst of me now. He'll never forgive me. And if I try to explain the innocence of the situation, I know he won't listen. He's convinced that I . . . that we . . . Oh, God, what am I going to do?"

He stumbled away from me, his face white with torment, a torment for which I alone was responsible. I had told him he was not Mark's son. I was the reason Mark had left him. I was at fault. I was to blame for ruining his life, and for ruining Mark's life as well.

Burning with guilt, I went after him, caught hold of his sleeve, and at my touch he turned and looked helplessly into my anguished face. "Joanna," he choked, "what shall I do? How can I convince him that there's nothing like that between us?"

Nothing between us? But there had been something between us. Alan had wanted me, had tried to make love to me, and I wondered dimly if Mark had known this, if he had sensed that all was not as it should be between his wife and his son.

"Joanna!" cried Alan when my silence endured. "What am I going to do?"

His eyes shone with tears, his lips trembled. I watched him in a daze and, irrelevantly, I thought how beautiful he was, and how like Mark's was his sensuous mouth.

"Please," he said desperately and took hold of my arms.

"Help me, please. You must convince my father that we have never . . ."

Suddenly, he stopped speaking and stared down at me intently. His face changed, and I watched him, transfixed, as he returned my mute gaze with a fierce, hungry look I knew well.

"Joanna," he said in a hoarse, shaking voice, and his grip on my arms tightened painfully. "Joanna," and then, as if compelled by a will not his own, he took me in his arms, pressed me to his heart, and as his mouth grazed my cheek, I could feel his breath quicken, hot, against my skin.

"Oh, no," I said faintly. "Oh, no, Alan, no."

When his mouth covered mine, I thought of Mark's mouth and Mark's arms and of Mark's hard, strong body that would never again join with mine. *Mark*, I thought, *Mark*. I endured his son's kisses, and succumbed to the touch of his son's urgent hands. And when he drew me to the chaise, I did not resist, for it was Mark's need I answered. I had never before realized that Mark needed me with a violent intensity I could not begin to fathom.

"Joanna," said Alan in his father's low voice, and his mouth against mine and his hands on my flesh were as Mark's. "Joanna," he breathed, "I love you, I want you. Joanna, my love . . ."

He kissed me again, pressing me down with the urgent, young strength of his limbs. He was all heat and passion; he was holding me, touching me, creating a need which one man alone could fulfill.

"I love you," he whispered. "I love you with all my heart. I shall never love anyone as I love you."

But it was Mark's voice I heard, Mark whose love I craved, Mark whom I had loved since the very first night we had met. What perverse fear had stifled my love, sending my husband out of my life forever? Why had I held him at arm's length, denying him that which he fully accorded to me? For Mark *did* love me, I knew that now. Sally had lied. Mark didn't love her, he had never loved her. How quick I had been to condemn my husband, how easily I had doubted his word, insulted his honor. How foolish and

childish I had been to deny myself and this man the love I
had felt for him always. No wonder he had left me.

A sharp tapping at the door froze my thoughts, and as
Alan leaped to his feet, hastily straightening his attire, I
heard Myrna's frantic voice calling, "Mrs. Van Holden,
are you in there? Open the door, please! It's Noelle. She's
ill. Mrs. Van Holden, open the door!"

Before I could get to my feet, Alan had flung open the
door, his hands trembling, his face turning ashen with
fear.

"What is it?" he demanded. "What's wrong with her?"

"Master Alan!" cried Myrna. "She's sick something awful. She's vomiting and choking, she won't stop. I've sent
for Dr. Simon. Oh, please come! Peggy's frightened to
death; she can't do a thing for the poor child, and she's
blaming herself. Master Alan, Mrs. Van Holden, come
quickly!"

She rushed out of the room, but we did not follow immediately. I needed Mark; Noelle needed Mark.

"Alan!" I said. "Go after your father. Tell him Noelle is
ill. Tell him I need him. Alan, hurry!"

"Joanna," he said, his voice hoarse with shame, "forgive
me, I'm sorry. I never meant to touch you in that way. Please
don't tell my father—I've already hurt him so much—"

"Be quiet!" I screamed, out of my mind with worry and
fear. "Don't speak of that now! Do as I tell you, Alan. Go
after him, bring him back. He left because of me, not you,
you foolish child! He left because of my coldness, my neglect, and now God is punishing me through Noelle."

I didn't really believe that, not intellectually at any
rate. God is not in the habit of meting out such punish-
ments, as he has considerably more important matters to
attend to. Edward had told me that. I had ruined his life
too—because I hadn't been able to show him my love
either. Poor Edward, poor Alan, poor Mark. I had destroyed the life of each and every man who had ever had
the ill luck to love me.

Noelle's affliction, thank goodness, passed swiftly. Dr.
Simon, an elderly physician whose practice in Newport

was limited to occasional cases of sunburn and indigestion, would not give a definite diagnosis.

"A transient indisposition, dyspepsia perhaps. Bedrest is prescribed, and a bland diet. No cause for alarm. You may put your mind at rest, young lady."

But Mark, when he returned with Alan the following day, thought otherwise.

"I want her examined by a specialist," he told me. "That old quack Simon hasn't had a bona fide patient since the Mexican War. Pack her things, Joanna. I shall take her to New York at once."

"Mark," I wavered, grateful that he was even speaking to me, "I want to come too. I want to be with her."

"Come then," he said, "but be quick about it." Then turning to his son: "And you?" he asked brusquely. "Will you come too?"

"No," Alan answered, his remorseful eyes turning toward me. "I doubt I shall be needed there."

Mark was watching us both. God alone knew what he was thinking.

We returned to New York on Mark's yacht, the *Lorelei*. She was a grand vessel, over three hundred feet in length, with mahogany paneling and shining brass fittings throughout, and she was fully staffed with a crew of sixty-five and a pudgy French chef from Cherbourg. The chef, however, had been engaged solely for the benefit of our guests. Mark himself ate very simply, and Monsieur Moreau was forever attempting, without success, to beguile the palate of his austere employer.

As we steamed home that day, I was treated to a veritable feast of *soupe au Geraumon*, bouillabaisse Marseillaise, and an airy soufflé citron served delectably with apricot sauce. Mark's meal consisted of one small chop, a tossed green salad without dressing, a cup of black coffee and, of course, no dessert.

He had not spoken to me since we boarded. He seemed tense, distracted. I knew he was worried about Noelle; he had carried her himself from the house and only when she was peacefully asleep in her cabin did he relinquish her to her nanny Peggy's care. His unexpected concern was immensely touching. I had always felt that Mark cared very little for his daughter, but I saw now that in that regard as well I had misjudged him.

"Mark," I said timidly after the steward had cleared the table, "I should like to talk to you about . . . about . . ."

His expression silenced me. He had never before looked at me in that way: indifferent, remote, uncaring. Had I lost him forever, then?

"Mark," I braved, "I know you're angry with me, and I know I've—"

"If you don't mind," he said distantly, "I think you should concern yourself at the moment with our daughter's health, and nothing else. I think further that if I hadn't come back to Newport, you would have accepted old Simon's diagnosis without question, being that your mind was preoccupied with . . . other matters."

"Oh," I cried softly, "you are unfair, Mark."

"So you've already told me."

"Please, we must talk about this. You must allow me to explain—"

"Explanations," he stopped me, "are superfluous under the circumstances. I am fully aware of your feelings for my son, and of his for you. If it is your intention, however, to discuss a divorce, save your breath. I shall consult with my attorney in New York, and he will advise you of your rights in the matter."

"But I don't want a divorce!"

"No? What *do* you want then? The semblance of a marriage for the sake of convention?"

"Mark," I implored, "if you would only listen to me."

"I listened," he said coldly, "most carefully the other night when you made crystal clear your innermost thoughts. I concede that you were shocked, outraged, by what Sally told you, but if you recall I had tried to discuss that particular incident with you before we were married, and again on our wedding night. I realized much later that you had misunderstood Sally's words, but by that time I had no desire to disinter a corpse which had lain buried for so many years. And moreover, Joanna, you have never been especially interested in my past, my present, or my future, for that matter. You've made it a point since the night we first met to disassociate yourself mentally and spiritually from anything even remotely connected with me or my interests. You've never listened to me, you have never had the least interest in anything I had to say. You closed yourself up in the cloister of your contempt; you held yourself away from me as a saint avoids sin. And when our daughter was born, you infused in her the same aversion to me which you have practiced unstintingly since the day we were wed."

"That's not true! It's not true!"

"It is true," he grated, his eyes black as death. "I used to delude myself into thinking it was just your way. You were young, you were shy, you were a lady. It had been so long a time since I had associated with 'ladies' that I had literally forgotten how to approach one. I did everything in my power to change, to win your love, your respect, but it all went for naught. It was Alan you respected, Alan you loved. You've loved him from the beginning, for his honor, his purity, for all of the virtues I have long abandoned. No doubt it was in his arms you pretended to be when you responded so ardently to my lovemaking. And it was Alan whom you taught Noelle to love as well. You created your own family, exclusive of me. You were complete in yourselves, the three of you. I kept waiting for—dreading—the day when you would come to realize—"

He broke off suddenly and turned quickly away, but not before I saw the pain, the profound, bitter pain I had caused him.

"Mark," I whispered. "Oh, Mark."

"Leave me alone," he said harshly. "Let it end. Leave me alone."

He rose from his chair, shaking with emotion, unable and unwilling to speak. I had hurt him, but he still loved me, I could see that so clearly now. But it was too late. He had closed the door of communication between us, a door I had never before bothered to really open.

"Mark, I beg you, you must let me speak. I understand your feelings, your anger. I know why you think what you do about Alan and me, but it's not true, I swear to you it isn't true. And I know you think I never cared for you, but I do, more than I can tell you. I was so terribly afraid to let you know how I felt. You've always said you love me, but you once told me you married me because you wanted me, and I thought—"

"You little fool!" he said fiercely. "I wanted you because I loved you! I have *wanted* dozens of women, but I didn't marry them. I married *you,* Joanna, because I loved you. But you loved my son. He was the reason you condescended to marry me."

"No, that's not true! You must hear my side of it! If you would only try to understand what I myself did not realize until recently. Mark, I love you. I think I have loved you from the first night I saw you, but I felt I had no right to love you then, and as a consequence I have always associated guilt and shame with whatever feelings I've had for you. And I was afraid too that you would consider me just another of your . . . women. I was even more afraid that once you had . . . got what you wanted, you would tire of me and divorce me, or worse, we would remain married but you would go back to your old ways."

I wavered and paused, stunned by my own unrestrained candor. I had never in my life bared my thoughts, my emotions, to anyone. But this was no time for modesty; I wanted my husband, and if it meant exposing the deepest secrets of my soul, I would do it.

"And then," I blundered on, "when Sally told me about young Stephen, I saw that my worst fears had materialized. She told me, you see, that you loved her and that you had . . . been with her even after you proposed marriage to me."

"That's a lie," he uttered. "I have been faithful to you. Whereas *you,* Joanna, have always given your undivided loyalty to my son."

"Oh, but you're wrong!" I cried. "I do love Alan, but, Mark . . . Oh, Mark, I love you too!"

His face grew very still. He watched me in silence for a long time, and then wearily he said, "Joanna, spare me the crumbs of your affection. I know you love Alan, and I know you loved your first husband; you were most anxious to impress that fact on me when we first met. But you don't love me, you never have and you never will. I'm not surprised, you know. I never actually thought you would love me. I know what I am. I know my world is poles apart from yours. It was unrealistic of me to think you might change it all, that you might somehow integrate into my nature a portion of your own purity and incorruptibility. No, it doesn't surprise me at all that you have chosen my son over me. He is everything I am not: He is honor and virtue, and I think I have always known that you would never accept anything less in a man. Very well then, I am reconciled. You want Alan, you have chosen him, you shall have him."

"Mark," I said desperately, "I don't want Alan. I want you."

"Forgive me, Joanna, but your eleventh-hour reversal lacks a certain credibility."

"You must believe me!" I cried. "I love you, Mark, I do love you. What can I do to convince you?"

"My dear girl," he shrugged, "you have already convinced me that you don't love me. In fact, no one in my life has ever done a more thorough job convincing me of something I preferred not to believe. Now let's leave it at that, shall we?"

XXXI

NOTHING I SAID would dissuade him. He was leaving, he told me, as soon as he had satisfied himself that Noelle's health was unendangered. A battery of specialists examined her. She was fine, thank the Lord. And on the day the final physician's diagnosis concurred with each of the five preceding it, Mark did as he had promised: He left me.

"If necessary," he said before leaving, "you may reach me at my club or at my offices. I have not as yet had an opportunity to speak with my attorney, but I shall do so today, and you should be hearing from him within a week or so."

"I don't want a divorce, Mark," I said faintly. "You're my husband, I love you."

"Joanna," he said tersely, "I very much doubt that you know what you want . . . or whom you want in a husband."

And with those humiliatingly significant words ringing in my ears, he left me.

What did he mean? What had he been driving at? On the yacht he had said, "You have chosen Alan, you shall have him." He couldn't possibly think that I wanted Alan, loved Alan in that way. I knew he thought I favored his son and loved him perhaps more than I should. But to suggest that I—oh, he couldn't have meant that! Alan would always be a child to me, Mark's son, someone I loved dearly, but only in the purest sense. That day in the garden when he had tried to make love to me, that morning in my sitting room when he had held me and kissed me, meant nothing, nothing! They were isolated incidents, regrettable occurrences which in no way reflected the true essence of our relationship. Alan had never really wanted me in a physical way. He wanted a mother's arms, a mother's love, a love of which he had been too soon deprived. Couldn't Mark see that? Didn't he know that if a love existed between Alan and me, it was only the love of a mother and son?

The news of Mark's departure soon spread through the city, and as summer neared its end and the Newport crowd returned to New York, I was deluged with notes and letters and callers, all posing the same questions: "What happened?" "Where is he?" "Is it final?" "Aren't you crushed?"

Crushed? I was shattered, devastated. For the first time in my life I knew a genuine and passionate love, and I had lost it with its discovery.

Only Constance Chandler, dear, dear Constance, understood, to some degree, my anguish.

"I know what you're feeling," she said calmly one day in September. "John left me once, early in our marriage, over an issue I prefer not to discuss. He was well within his rights in leaving, and I should not have blamed him if he never returned. But he did, Joanna, he came back to me and he forgave me, as Mark will you. Mark and John are cut from the same cloth. They're self-willed, stubborn mules, the pair of them, but they share another trait which far outweighs all others: They are unrelentingly loyal to those they love. Don't you remember, Joanna, how Mark came chasing after you when you left him? Good heavens, I thought he would tear the house apart! He loves you, my dear, make no mistake about that. He loves you, and he'll come back to you."

"He did love me," I mumbled. "I doubt if he still does, Constance."

"Hogwash," she said. "Mark is no schoolboy whose emotions change with the seasons. He married you, didn't he? That alone is proof positive of his love. I'm sure I don't have to remind you that before you met Mark he was quite the Lothario-about-town."

"No," I said morosely, "you don't have to remind me."

"And I daresay marriage was the last thing on his mind."

"I daresay."

"He had his pick of every last woman in New York, you know, single *or* married."

"Yes, I know."

"In fact his numerous affairs were the prime topic of teatime discussion in every drawing room on Fifth Avenue."

"Constance, please!"

"My dear friend," she said gently, "I am only trying to impress upon you the fact that Mark could have had any woman he wanted. But he chose you, Joanna. He chose you."

"But, Constance," I protested, "you don't know what I've done to him. You don't know—"

"Nor do I want to know," she said briskly. "Marital spats bore me to tears. Despite the variety of causes, it invariably converges on one point: misunderstanding. You quarreled; heated words were spoken. He meant one thing, you meant something else. Lord, the futility of it! If people would only learn to *listen* to one another. Tell me truthfully, Joanna, now that you've had a chance to think about it, aren't you remembering certain things Mark may have said which were not all that clear to you during the course of the quarrel?"

You have loved and understood only one member of this family.

"Yes," I said glumly.

"And don't you wish you could retract some of the things you said to him?"

How dare you inflict punishment, you who have gone unpunished all your life for the most detestable crimes?

"Yes," I said with a shudder. "Yes, I do."

"Mark is having those same thoughts, I'll wager. I'm sure he regrets half the things he said to you, and has forgotten much of what you said to him."

"No." My voice dropped to a shamed whisper. "He will never forget. And he'll never forgive me for betraying him."

"Betraying him?" Constance sat bolt upright in her chair. "Joanna, you didn't?"

"No, no," I said quickly. "Not that way, of course not. But there are other ways, crueler ways, of betraying a man who loves you."

"Oh, good heavens, what a fright you gave me! Joanna, you have just proved my point! For a moment I thought you had . . . Well, don't you see what I mean? People only half listen to what they hear, which results in the most appalling misconceptions. Why don't you telephone Mark, ask to see him? If you talk this thing out and really listen to one another, I'm certain you'll be able to iron out your differences in no time."

She went on to say more, coaxing me, urging me, to talk with my husband, to insist that he listen, and to open my mind and heart to what he would say to me. It all seemed so easy, so sensible, so sane; but Mark, I soon learned, was not of a mind to comply.

"I'm sorry," he said when I telephoned him later at his offices, "I cannot see you today. I am leaving the city in an hour. A salary dispute has arisen at the Bayonne refineries and it is imperative that I open negotiations with the labor leaders at once. I foresee a long period of bargaining, and there's a good possibility I may have to do the same at the Pittsburgh and the Ohio refineries, for I've been told similar problems are expected there also. I haven't any idea when I'll be free to meet with you."

"Mark, must you go now, today? Surely someone else can deal initially with the labor people in Bayonne. Couldn't you ask Trevor Winslow to—"

"I have discharged Winslow."

"Discharged him? But why?"

"Joanna, your sudden interest in my professional activities is extremely gratifying, but I'm afraid I haven't the time now to discuss the subject."

"Mark," I persisted, undaunted by his coolness, "I think it's important we see each other as soon as possible."

He said nothing.

"Please," I implored when his silence lengthened. "I

must see you, talk to you. I want to explain. I want you to know the truth about Alan and me."

He was cryptically, frighteningly silent. If only I could see him, embrace him, tell him with my kisses just how deeply and completely I loved him.

He answered at last, his voice low and cold, "No. It's impossible. I cannot see you today."

And then I heard him ring off.

The labor dispute in Bayonne proved even more troublesome than Mark had anticipated. His initial proposals were rejected by the workers, and weeks of heated negotiations wrought nothing but ill feelings on both sides. The men were determined that their union should set a standard throughout the country for resisting the "slave wages" offered by the "malevolent captains of industry," and Mark remained adamant in his refusal to increase salaries above what he saw as a reasonable level. In the meantime, thousands of gallons of crude oil lay untouched in great storage tanks, unrefined and useless, while public resentment grew against Eastern Seaboard, encouraged no doubt by the searing editorials of James Gordon Bennett, an admitted archenemy of Mark's.

"The serpent strikes again," wrote Mr. Bennett in the *Herald.*

The anaconda that is Eastern Seaboard Oil is attempting to crush, devour and annihilate the very source that gives it life. The good men who labor unceasingly at Eastern Seaboard's mighty Bayonne facility are seeking a well-deserved wage increase, but Mark Van Holden, the Viper-in-Charge, has refused to meet even a single demand of his loyal and valiant employees. This newspaper is not in the least surprised. Van Holden, whose fortune is conservatively estimated in the vicinity of two-hundred-million dollars, has always cared more for turning a profit than he has for the welfare and well-being of his workers.

But Mr. Bennett's appraisal was untrue as well as unfair. Mark had offered the men a fifteen percent raise in salary and had agreed to supplement the hourly wage of the night-shift workers as well. However, his proposals were again rejected, and when it became clear that the labor leaders were not bargaining in good faith but rather were attempting to draw public attention and support to their cause, Mark immediately broke off negotiations and recommenced operation of the refineries, employing a workforce of nonunion men. The riots which resulted were inevitable. Union men and scabs alike were beaten and battered until the huge refinery yards in Bayonne resembled nothing more than a bloody Civil War battlefield. But after two violent weeks, the workers capitulated. The men wanted their jobs, and a few of them even admitted to the newspapers that they had been more than willing to accept Mark's terms but had followed the dictates of the union representatives who had virtually commanded them to reject all offers on principle.

The fight was over. All refineries resumed operation, and Mark found it unnecessary to go to either Pittsburgh or to Ohio, for it was reported that the workers there had been advised by union officials to "accept all terms as set forth by the Company." I couldn't have been happier; I had been frightened to death for Mark's safety throughout the ordeal. It had only lasted a month, but it had seemed like a lifetime.

With the cessation of hostilities in Bayonne, I telephoned Mark at his offices but was told he was not available. I left a message. Several days passed. I did not hear from him. I telephoned again. I telephoned twice daily for a week, but he never acknowledged any of my calls.

Caught up as I was in my own nightmare world, I was scarcely aware that the day of Alan's wedding was drawing near. He had had very little to say to me since that unfortunate morning in Newport, and I, anxious and worried about Mark, had had little to say in return. I would ask him occasionally if he had seen his father, for he was working with Mark now at 18 Broadway, but invariably he would mumble, "No, I haven't seen him."

And after a while I stopped asking.

Carrie began to visit me in the afternoons. She was such a dear girl, so completely different from her mother. She knew Sally and I were at odds, and I was certain she knew that Mark had left me, but she had the tact and the good sense to refrain from broaching either subject.

How excited she was about her wedding! We would spend hours poring over the pages of the latest fashion magazines, choosing tea frocks and lingerie and day wear and ball gowns for her trousseau, and discussing possible coiffures for the wedding day, and planning on places to visit when she honeymooned abroad, and deciding on a suitable house in which to live when she returned to New York.

"I'm so happy!" she would exclaim out of a clear blue sky. And then she would laugh and blush and stammer an apology.

But I knew how she felt. I had felt much the same when I married Mark, though I had never been as freely able as Carrie to express my feelings. How fortunate Alan was in choosing a wife who would give him her love without a qualm. If only his father had been as fortunate. If only Mark had married an ardent, passionate, and totally uninhibited woman . . . instead of me.

They were married on the twenty-fourth of October, an exceptionally beautiful day, with a brilliant white sun in a radiant, cloudless, blue sky. Carrie wore satin, a simple tasteful gown, with a trimming of seed pearls and *point de Venise* lace; her veil was of the finest, sheerest tulle, caught at the crown with a coronet of orange blossoms, and sweeping grandly and gracefully to the floor. As she came down the aisle on her father's arm, I was hard put not to weep, so lovely a picture did she make. Alan waited at the altar, his hands clasped before him. His bearing was somber, his fair face expressionless. I wondered what he was thinking. I wondered worriedly, fearfully, if he loved the young girl he was making his wife.

Mark stood at my side, and his eyes too were on the elegant face of his son. Mark had telephoned me finally on the day before the wedding and had told me simply that he would be attending the ceremony but that he would not be present at the home of the Monroes afterwards.

"But, Mark," I had said, "why not? You must come to the reception. What will people think?"

"They will think," he said shortly, "that we are estranged, Joanna, which happens to be the case."

"Oh, don't, Mark," I said. "Don't do this to Alan. He's done nothing to deserve such an insult. If you're angry with me, I accept it, but please, please, don't hurt him in that way."

For a time he said nothing. I was naive enough to think that he might be having second thoughts. But then he said coldly, "Still defending my son, are you? I see nothing has changed in my absence."

His hard, bitter tone unexpectedly enraged me. My patience snapped. A lifetime of stolid reserve and reticent constraint suddenly dissolved in a turbulent fury of uncontrollable wrath.

"How dare you!" I cried. "How dare you allow a vile and unfounded suspicion to ruin the most important occasion of your son's life? You self-centered, obstinate man! You have no right to hurt him, to *humiliate* him, because of your stupid, blundering, irrational misconceptions. There is nothing, *nothing*, between Alan and me. There never has been and there never will be. And if you allow your baseless distortions of the truth to disrupt your son's wedding day, then I hope never to see you again as long as I live!"

I slammed down the receiver with a crash. The telephone teetered precariously toward the edge of the table, then toppled and fell to the floor. I stared at it numbly, heartsick and dazed. What had I done? Why had I screamed at him? I had never in my life raised my voice to anyone, and to have done so now to the man whose love I was trying desperately to win back . . . Oh, what had I done? I had ruined it all. He would never come home to me now.

But the next morning at half past nine, just as Myrna was putting the finishing touches to my hair, Kelsey knocked at the door, and when I bade him enter, he said in a queer, joyous voice, "Mrs. Van Holden?"

"Yes?" I said, turning away from the mirror at that unnatural sound.

Kelsey was as staid a servant as I had ever encountered. He never smiled, and he spoke only in the most tiresomely lifeless of monotones. But he was smiling now, and his voice, when he spoke again, was as gay and as melodic as a lark's. "Madam," he all but sang, "Mr. Van Holden is in the drawing room, and is waiting to escort you to church."

Mark? Mark was here? Home? My heart leaped and pounded. I clutched at the vanity for support.

"Mr. Van Holden," I whispered, "is here?"

I could not believe it. I was tingling with joy, with indescribable happiness.

"Thank you, Kelsey," I said breathlessly, and barely able to contain my excitement, I rushed out of the room, hurried down the wide staircase, and threw open the drawing room door.

Mark was at the fireplace, his watch in his hand, checking the time against the clock on the mantelpiece. How beautiful he was, more astonishingly beautiful than I had even remembered him.

"Mark." My voice was barely audible.

He turned when I spoke, and I could only stare in silence at the midnight-dark mystery of his eyes.

"Joanna." He nodded.

"Mark," I said again, and wanted to touch him, to hold him, to never let him go. "I'm so glad you're home."

He watched me quietly and gave no response. His face was unreadable. My own, I knew, was an open book.

"Please," I said, trembling, "sit down."

"Thank you, no," he said politely. "I think we should be going. Will Noelle be coming with us?"

"Noelle? Coming with us? Coming where?"

"To the church," he reminded me, and I could not be sure, but I thought I saw the ghost of a smile dart briefly across his face.

"Oh, yes. The church. Of course. Yes, Noelle will be coming. Shall I fetch her?"

I started nervously toward the bellpull on the wall, but Mark stopped me with a lightly restraining hand.

"Joanna, a moment, if you please."

The instant I turned to him, his hand left my arm.

"Before we leave," he said, "I should like to apologize for my attitude yesterday on the telephone."

"Oh, no, please don't. It was I who—"

"No, Joanna, I was the one who spoke out of turn. And you were right, of course: It would be wrong of me to spoil Alan's wedding day by not attending the reception. I shall go if you like."

"Oh, yes," I blurted. "Yes, do!" And then realizing how childishly eager I sounded, I added in a more subdued tone, "I know Alan would want you to be there."

He watched me for a moment with an unlikely look of disappointment, as if having expected a somewhat different reaction. But when I only returned his gaze in embarrassed silence, he turned away, went to the bellpull and gave it a tug, summoning a servant to bring him his daughter.

Noelle entered the room several minutes later, a Botticelli angel with gossamer hair, pink cheeks, and a pink rosebud mouth, clad charmingly in white eyelet with a blue satin sash at the waist.

"Papa!" she cried in delighted surprise. "Papa!" And flung herself into his arms.

He lifted her up, his dark eyes glowing, and she encircled his neck with two plump, dimpled arms, and gave him copious kisses which he returned, laughing. Then finally, with obvious reluctance, he set her down and said rather shakily, "We'd best be going, Noelle. Your brother is to be married this morning, you know. We don't want to be late for the ceremony, do we?"

"Papa," she demanded, ignoring his words, "where have you been? Mama told me you were busy at your work, but I missed you! Why didn't you come home?"

She glared up at him possessively, her hands planted on her hips, her silky brow knit in a fierce baby frown. She looked such a tyrant, such an utterly comic and endearing young tyrant, that Mark burst into laughter, whereupon Noelle promptly burst into a welter of mortified tears.

"Darling!" he exclaimed, sweeping her up in his arms and holding her close as he pressed remorseful kisses on her tumbled curls. "Noelle, please don't cry. Darling, look! Look what I've brought you."

He searched through his pockets with his one free hand and finally located a small gold bracelet which he held up for her inspection, but she only clung to him tighter, her wails growing louder and more pitiful than before.

Mark's eyes, dark and pained, lifted and met mine over our daughter's tremulous head. My throat ached with emotion. How could I ever have thought he didn't love her?

"Noelle, please," he said gently, "don't cry, dearest child. I'm home now, I'm here. Come now, dry your eyes. You don't want Alan to see you in tears on his wedding day, do you? There, that's better. Give me a smile now . . . a big one. How pretty you look when you smile. Why are you giggling, darling? You are pretty, you know, as pretty as your mama, and some day soon, she and I will be attending *your* wedding, and everyone will say you're the most beautiful bride who ever walked down an aisle. . . ."

As I watched Carrie Monroe become Mrs. Alan Van Holden, I thought of Mark's words, and I thought of the pain in his eyes when his daughter had wept, a pain he could not hide, a dark, bitter, devastating pain which I, in my selfish absorption with my own foolish fears, had caused.

I turned to them now, my husband and our child. She was resting her soft cheek contentedly against his sleeve, gazing up at him with eyes brimming with love.

"Papa," she whispered, "you won't go away? You're finished with your work? You'll stay with me now?"

"We'll see, darling," he said softly. "We'll see."

At the conclusion of the ceremony, we stood in the vestibule on one side of the bridal couple, the Monroes on the other, to receive the congratulations of the many well-wishers who had filled the church to capacity. I had seen Stephen earlier and had greeted him warmly while merely nodding stiffly to Sally. I wondered fleetingly what lie she had told her husband about that ghastly night we had quarreled.

Noelle clung to her father's leg like a little vine despite all of Peggy's efforts to disengage her, and everyone smiled and commented to Mark on the touching devotion of his daughter. They smiled at me too, arch, meaningful smiles. I daresay they thought Mark's presence at my side consti-tuted a reconciliation. I myself had no such illusions; I knew that when this day ended, the brief, bittersweet truce with my husband would end as well.

As the crowd began to dwindle, I noticed, near the end of the line, an attractive woman in her thirties who kept star-ing intently at Mark. She was obviously a lady; her patri-cian face showed centuries of good breeding, and she wore a Révillon gown and a sable-trimmed cloak in that easy, indifferent, perfunctory way of the immensely rich. Her hair was dark brown, her eyes dark and heavily fringed with the longest, most luxuriant lashes I had ever seen. She had a cool, regal posture, almost arrogant, her glossy head held high as if bearing a crown; and her complexion was flawless, gardenia-fair and smooth, the appropriate setting for those startling, sultry dark, lushly lashed eyes.

She continued to stare at my husband.

Mark was unaware of her scrutiny, as he had inclined his head to catch some remark of Carrie's, and moreover, his attention was further diverted by the constant tugging at his hand and at his coat by his petulantly demanding daughter. As the woman approached, I saw that she was accompanied by a tall slender gentleman, apparently her husband, and two extremely pretty girls whom I took to be her children.

The woman suddenly seemed nervous; her gloved hand, tucked under her husband's arm, began to loosen and tighten convulsively on his sleeve. At one point I saw the gentleman lean down to whisper something in her ear—a word of reassurance, I imagined—and this seemed to calm her. She glanced up at him with a brief, cool smile, then looked once more toward Mark, who at that particular mo-ment turned away from Carrie and looked directly into the woman's eyes.

"My God," I heard Mark utter. "My God."

"What's wrong?" I said, alarmed, but immediately fell silent when I saw the shock, the surprise, the love and joy that flamed a dark fire in the lean contours of his face.

The woman drew closer. Mark made a move toward her, then stopped as if fearful of confronting her. The woman stopped too; she started to tremble. And as she gazed at him silently, helplessly, he stepped forward again, with a low aching groan, and gathered her into his arms.

"Mark," she said brokenly. "Mark." And then she began to weep.

I could not see Mark's expression, his back was to me, but I could see plainly the woman's face, no longer cool and haughty, but suffused with a fever of love. I watched them, transfixed, unaware that everyone else present was doing the same. I was enraged, and thought: *Who is this stranger that she can evoke such emotion in my husband? Who is she, and what gives her the right to weep in his embrace when I, his wife, yearn so desperately for the comfort and warmth of his arms?*

"Good heavens!" someone said. "What's she doing here? I thought they'd parted company years ago."

"Well, for pity's sake," said another, "you didn't think she was going to miss her own nephew's wedding, did you? *She* has a sense of propriety, even if her brother does not."

Her brother? Mark was her brother? This was the sister, then, with whom he had quarreled so long ago. How tightly she clung to him and how closely he held her as if he would never let her go. I stared at her jealously, envying her the touch of his hands, the clasp of his arms, envying her the love he so obviously bore her. I wanted it too, I wanted his love. More than anything else I had ever wanted in life, I wanted my husband's love.

XXXII

THE MONROE DRAWING ROOM was a grand, spacious room with frescoed ceilings and gilt-trimmed, mirrored walls which endlessly reflected the great crush of guests who pressed into its luxurious confines. The Chandlers were there and the Morgans and the Goelets and the Mellons and the Fricks, all of the "Robber Barons," as the newspapers had dubbed the influential men of Mark's sphere. They were a vital, energetic lot, these powerful men. They prowled the room like sleek, restless cats, stopping here and there for a casual word, a polite nod, but it was plainly evident that they were out of their element and that they would much prefer to be back in the exhilarating vortex of their turbulent industrial and financial pursuits.

Mark, however, seated in an alcove with his sister, seemed perfectly content and at ease, and if he were longing for the environs of Eastern Seaboard Oil, it was not apparent in his tranquil posture nor in his frequent smiles. Not wishing to intrude on this intimate reunion, I had drifted away from them toward one of the tall, fretted windows overlooking Fifth Avenue. From this vantage point, I could see my husband clearly, and I watched him jealously, hungrily, begrudging his sister every precious moment she was spending with him. Though I had talked with Adele only briefly in the carriage, I had found her gracious and charming and totally likable, but she was taking Mark away from me at a time when I wanted him to myself. Not that I had charted any plan of action for this day; on the contrary, I had not even expected Mark to attend the reception. But now that he was here, now that I had the chance to talk with him, to explain . . .

"Mrs. Van Holden, may I get you a glass of champagne?"

I turned abruptly, an impatient refusal springing to my lips, but the words died in my throat for it was Adele's husband who stood at my side, and he looked just as lost and forlorn as I.

"Thank you, no, Mr. Kendall," I said at length. "I have already had two glasses and I'm afraid that's my limit. But please don't let me stop you."

"I don't drink," he said solemnly. "As a boy, I had quite an unpleasant experience with a bottle of Napoleon brandy, and I haven't had the least desire for either wine or spirits since." He smiled then, an unexpectedly engaging smile, and I found myself smiling in return.

Wesley Kendall was a handsome man, as dark and as slender as Mark, but without Mark's intensely striking magnetism. His aspect was grave, but when he smiled his dark eyes gleamed, not unlike those of a mischievous boy, and his stern mouth relaxed, showing his perfect, white teeth. I could well understand why Adele Van Holden had married this man. Though I barely knew him, I very much liked him. In a vague, pleasant way, he put me in mind of my first husband.

"Did the brandy make you ill?" I teased.

"Oh, very ill indeed, Mrs. Van Holden," he said with a grin. "My mother was distraught. She was convinced I had been afflicted with some exotic and incurable disease. In a panic, she dispatched a servant to summon my father from his bank. The servant no doubt led my father to believe that I was at the point of expiring, for he rushed home in a trembling fear, burst into my room and, much to his mingled relief and rage, found me lying on my bed in the most wretched throes of advanced inebriation. I cannot describe to you my terror. I suddenly found myself completely sober. But the damage had been done. My father hauled me from my bed by the scruff of the neck and thrashed me so soundly that even now, thirty years later, I wince at the very memory of it."

"Oh, my word," I said, smothering a laugh, for he was watching me glumly as if the memory of his chastisement were indeed physically painful. But his eyes danced with amusement, and I laughed out loud then, so heartily in fact that several people in our vicinity turned their heads and stared.

"Good Lord," he whispered in mock horror, "I hope no one overheard me. I should not like that incident to become public knowledge. Promise me, Mrs. Van Holden, that you'll never repeat a word of what I told you."

"I promise," I said, still shaking with mirth, and it suddenly occurred to me that this thoughtful, perceptive, considerate man had deliberately set out to distract my thoughts and lift my spirits, and he had fully accomplished both.

"Thank you," I murmured as the last of my laughter faded. "Thank you for being so kind."

He shook his head, somewhat discomfited that I had guessed his intent. "Mrs. Van Holden," he said, adroitly diverting the conversation, "where is your daughter? What a beauty she is! She resembles my girls, had you noticed? One can tell at a glance they are cousins."

"My husband thought it best to send Noelle home," I told him. "She was overstimulated by the wedding ceremony and by . . ." I paused, remembering her tears, remembering Mark's eyes. ". . . and by the excitement," I finished lamely.

"Yes, of course," he agreed. "The excitement."

"She does resemble your daughters," I said pensively. "They are such lovely girls. How old are they?"

"Celia is sixteen and Helen is seventeen. I think daughters are so much nicer than sons, don't you? I have never felt the need for a son."

I did not answer at once, for at that moment I caught sight of Alan across the room. He was talking with friends, his new wife at his side, but he was watching me with an odd look that for some reason worried and alarmed me.

"Yes," I said at last, returning my gaze to Wesley Kendall. "I too prefer daughters to sons. I don't know that

I could successfully rear a son. Men, at any age, are rather a mystery to me."

"Do you really think so?" he said, smiling. "I believe just the opposite. Women are the mysterious species. As much as I love my wife and daughters, they continually baffle me."

He paused then, his smile slowly faded, and his dark eyes grew suddenly grave. "Mrs. Van Holden, do you mind if I ask you a personal question?"

"No, I don't mind."

"Forgive me, but do you know the details of the quarrel between my wife and your husband?"

"No. No, I—"

"I'm sorry," he said at once. "You needn't answer that. I'm truly sorry for presuming—"

"No, don't apologize, please. I don't know why they quarreled. I never— Mark and I never talked of it. Don't you know the reason? Didn't your wife ever tell you?"

"No," he said grimly, "she never did. All I know is, one Christmas day I was dozing in a chair, Adele woke me, told me she had quarreled with her brother, that we were leaving his house, and that she never wanted to see him again as long as she lived."

Oh, how cruel those words sounded, and how familiar.

"But, Mr. Kendall, did you never talk to Mark, ask him what had happened?"

"Yes, I talked to him. On several occasions. He was most anxious to make up the quarrel with his sister, but he too would not say what had caused it."

"And your wife? You never questioned her?"

"Adele was rabid on the subject. If I so much as mentioned her brother's name, she would fly into a towering rage. They have much the same temperament, you know. Adele is more controlled than Mark, a great deal more civilized, but at heart she is as headstrong and as emotionally violent as he."

I couldn't think what to say to this man. His marriage, it seemed, was almost as troubled as mine.

Incredibly then, as if sensing my thoughts, he said quietly, "So you see, Mrs. Van Holden, all married people disagree for one reason or another. And as you can further see," he added, nodding toward Mark and Adele, "reconciliations are indeed possible, no matter the length of separation."

"Oh!" I cried softly, and I lowered my eyes, unable to face him, unable, as always, to honestly confront my feelings.

"I'm sorry," he said again. "I don't mean to distress you, but I think you should know that your estrangement from Mark is what more or less motivated Adele to make her peace with him."

I looked up quickly, my heart thudding painfully. "What do you mean? Why would she do that?"

"She loves him, you know. Whatever happened between them that Christmas Day has never changed the fact that she loves him. When she learned he had left you, she was staggered, aghast. I cannot convey to you the overwhelming anguish that engulfed her. She was absolutely unapproachable for days, weeks. I had the strongest feeling she blamed herself in some way. . . ."

"Blamed herself? Why?"

"I don't know. I just don't know. There's a bond between those two that I can neither explain nor understand. It's more than family ties. Perhaps it's because Mark raised his sister almost single-handedly from the time he was eighteen. You know, of course, that they were orphaned when Adele was still a child."

"No," I said, ashamed that I knew practically nothing of my husband's past. "I didn't know."

"Well, in any case, I'm convinced that your separation from Mark is what prompted Adele to return to him. It's as if . . ." He paused, then said slowly, "As if she did not want him to be alone. As if she were terrified of his being alone."

A cold shudder went through me and I shivered involuntarily. I did not know why, but the thought of Mark alone frightened me too. And that was strange because Mark had always struck me as a man who needed no one, who sought nothing to sustain him, for his strength and his sustenance seemed to dwell solely within himself. But perhaps, I thought dimly, even the strongest man needs someone to love him, to support him, to stand as a barrier between him and the intolerable emptiness of a lonely life. Mark had no one now. He hadn't a wife or a son or a daughter. I had seen to that. I had alienated my husband from all he loved and truly needed.

"Mr. Kendall," I said in a faint shaking voice, "please excuse me. I must—"

"Mrs. Van Holden, are you all right? You're awfully pale. Shall I fetch Mark?"

"No, please. Don't disturb him. I'm fine. I must leave you now. I want to see Alan."

I left Wesley Kendall and made my way slowly across the crowded room. Mrs. Stuyvesant Fish stopped me midway, a tall, gaunt, autocratic dowager who felt compelled to comment on Mark's presence, and who questioned me unmercifully about the status of our marriage. She detained me with a ring-studded, clawlike hand, and swallowing my revulsion, I smiled automatically, answered her questions as courteously as I could, and after what seemed an eternity, she dismissed me with a nod and moved away.

At the long buffet table, Hermann Oelrichs caught my arm and extracted my promise to visit his Tessie who, several months earlier, had given birth to their first child. We talked for a while—Hermann is an extremely witty man—and I remember laughing quite a lot, a bit hysterically, I think; then finally, Hermann turned for a moment to greet Pierpont Morgan and his wife, and I took this opportunity to slip stealthily away.

Alan, when I joined him, was alone. The French doors leading to the garden were open to the splendid fall day, and I had seen him leave the drawing room as if the swarming sea of guests had suddenly become unendurable. He was standing beneath a tree at the far garden wall. The leaves were aflame with color, and near his feet, a similar riot of color blazed brilliantly from a prancing row of red and yellow and amber-gold zinnias. He regarded the flowers with a rapt, pensive look; his hands were sunk deep in his trouser pockets and his fair head was bent as he stared intently at the gently swaying blooms.

I spoke his name softly, with a profound and fearful reluctance, for I was afraid to face him, afraid of being alone with him, though a houseful of guests were but a few yards away.

He raised his head. His smoky gray eyes met mine, and my uneasiness increased, but I forced myself to say, "Alan, have you talked with your father? Have you made your peace with him?"

The strangest expression transformed the smooth planes of his young, perfect face. "Yes," he said evenly, "I've talked with him. And no, I have not made my peace with him."

"Oh, but you must! You must make it a point before you leave—"

"Joanna," he stopped me, "it is my father's decision, not mine, to prolong the dissension between us. I have tried innumerable times to talk with him, both at his offices and at his club, and on all occasions he has turned a deaf ear to my words. Today, at the church, I asked him if he could spare me a few moments alone at the reception—I did not want to go abroad without trying one last time to settle our differences. But he just shook his head and turned away from me. It's finished between us, can't you face that? He wants nothing to do with me now."

"No," I said firmly, "that's not true. Mark loves you, he always will. And he needs you desperately."

"Needs me? What are you talking about? My father needs no one, he never has."

"You're wrong, Alan, he does need you. He needs you and me and Noelle, but he's just too proud and too stubborn to admit it, even to himself. Have you been watching him today? Have you seen how heartbreakingly happy he is that his sister has returned to him? A man who needs no one could not have reacted in that way. He needs us both, I tell you, he needs our love. And the burden of responsibility lies on both of us to convince him and assure him of that love."

"Joanna, be realistic, won't you? How can we convince him of anything when he has totally closed off all lines of communication?"

"I don't know," I said frankly. "But we must find a way.

There's so little time; your ship sails tomorrow. Perhaps if you approach him again, now—"

"No."

"Alan—"

"I said no! What possible purpose can it serve? He doesn't want to talk, he doesn't want explanations. I've hurt him beyond forgiveness. I loved you, I wanted you, and I'm sure he's aware of that fact even though the night he came upon us in your bedroom was perfectly innocent. Nothing I say can undo what I've done. I cannot admit to him that I physically desired his wife. But if ever he asks me straight out, I cannot deny it."

"But of course you must deny it!" I cried. "Would you hurt him afresh by giving substance to his suspicions? You must never, *never*, admit to him what you felt for me. If he ever— Oh, dear God, if he knew . . ."

"Of course I won't tell him!" he snapped. "I don't want to hurt him any more than I have. But it doesn't matter whether or not he knows the truth. He believes the worst, he believes I still love you. And we will never succeed in convincing him otherwise."

I returned to the drawing room alone. I felt certain that Alan blamed me for all that had happened. He had behaved so strangely in the garden, so coldly, as if my very presence offended him. If he had ever loved me, I had no doubt he no longer did.

"Joanna, I've been looking for you! Where did you disappear to?"

My heart began an erratic beating as Mark approached me, caught hold of my hand, then circled my waist with an arm. He seemed to have forgotten we were at odds; he was flushed and smiling, his hair curling damply on his brow, and as he drew me close, guiding me skillfully past the frankly curious guests, I feared I might weep from the sweet, aching joy of his nearness.

"My sister has asked us to dine with her tonight. As soon as Alan and Carrie leave, we'll be going to her house. . . ."

He stopped near the drawing room doors, looked down at

me, frowning. "What's the matter? Wesley said you looked ill. You're very pale. Are you all right?"

"Yes . . . yes, I'm all right."

"You're sure? Nothing's wrong?"

"Yes, Mark, honestly. Nothing's wrong."

He watched me a moment as if he weren't quite sure he believed me. His arm was still around me, I felt it tighten for just an instant, then he released me, stepped back, and said neutrally, "Come along then. Freddy Brentwood has been asking for you. He wants you to meet his new wife."

The afternoon passed swiftly. At precisely six o'clock Alan and Carrie announced their intention to leave, but it was yet another hour before all the good-byes and final congratulations had been tendered by the guests. Carrie had changed into a fetching blue cashmere that exactly matched her eyes, and as the guests filed past, she clung to Alan's arm, smiling shyly.

Mark and I were standing to one side, waiting for the others to leave. As I surreptitiously watched his dark face, I hoped against hope that when he said his good-byes he would intimate to Alan in some way that he was willing to suspend hostilities and that a future reconciliation was possible. But when the moment came, after Mark had kissed Carrie and offered his hand to his son, he only said distantly, "Good luck to you, Alan. Have a safe voyage." And then he moved brusquely away.

I saw Alan pale. His eyes turned to mine, and as I stepped forward to bid him good-bye, his young mouth hardened and bitterly he said, so that only I could hear, "So much for his needing me."

I reached up to kiss him, lingered a moment near his ear. "Be patient," I whispered. "Give him time. He loves you, he needs you. He'll come back to you."

He did not answer. I drew slightly away to see his face, but he was looking over my shoulder, and when I turned my head, following the direction of his glance, I saw Mark watching us.

XXXIII

MARK'S SISTER'S HOUSE on Fifth Avenue was almost as exquisite as his. The Kendalls were obviously a family of wealth, one could see that from the sixteenth-century Brussels tapestries, the Renaissance mantels, the Boulle and Caffiéri tables and chests, and the spectacular staircase of Numidian marble and bronze. The dining room was especially impressive with its great chandelier of Baccarat crystal, casting light and luster on silk-papered walls that boasted paintings by Hals and Van Dyck and Boucher. As we ate our dessert, a heady concoction of fresh fruit and rum, I could not help but remark to Adele that her elegant taste was strikingly similar to her brother's.

"Do you think so?" she said with a most charming smile. "I feel I am somewhat heavier handed than Mark when it comes to decorating. My preferences, I fear, run to the opulent, the baroque, while Mark has always favored the more aesthetic and classical designs."

"Nonsense, Adele," Mark protested at once. "This house is perfection; I have always admired it."

"I am complimented," she said, directing her attention to her brother. "If you admire the house, then it is indeed perfection, for your standards permit nothing less."

Unsure of her meaning, he gave her a puzzled smile. "What an extraordinary thing to say, Adele. Wherever did you get such an idea?"

"My dear," she said softly, "have you forgotten that you reared me to those standards?"

Their eyes met and held in a spellbinding testimony of

mutual love and regard. I looked quickly away, embarrassed by and envious of so fierce a display of emotion.

"Joanna," said Wesley Kendall, "did you happen to read in last week's *Times* the account of Mrs. Ingersoll's mudless gown?"

"Why, yes," I said, and turned to him. He had noted my embarrassment and was seeking, in his kind way, to allieviate it. I was grateful to him.

"What do you think, Joanna? Would you wear such an ensemble on a rainy day?"

"Good heavens, no!" I exclaimed. "The *Times* said Mrs. Ingersoll's skirt measured only thirty-six inches in length, and that it showed all but the tops of her opera-toed boots. I should be mortified to be seen in public that way."

He nodded approvingly. "I daresay Mrs. Ingersoll was seeking a bit of cheap notoriety with her antics. It's true that ladies' gowns tend to collect mud on rainy days, but to clothe oneself in an indecently short skirt is surely sacrificing modesty for convenience, don't you agree?"

"Oh, indeed," I replied. "Indeed, yes." And then I fell woodenly silent.

From the corner of my eye, I could see Mark and Adele in deep and serious conversation. His dark face was grave as he listened intently while his sister spoke, then he gave a brief response which caused her to lay a slim hand on his sleeve. He took that hand and raised it to his lips. Adele smiled, her eyes grew very bright. I felt stifled, suffocated, breathless with a primitive fever of jealousy and rage.

"Are you a theatergoer, Joanna?" asked my brother-in-law.

Slowly, dully, I forced myself to respond. "I enjoy the theater."

"Had you planned on seeing Lillian Russell this season? She has formed her own company, you know, and is putting on a production of *La Cigale* at the Garden. Perhaps we can make it a foursome. Adele loves the theater, and Mark—"

He stopped abruptly, having suddenly remembered the tenuous status of my marriage. "I do beg your pardon," he said after a pause. He spoke very softly as if fearful that

Mark might have heard him. But my husband, I noted, was rapt in conversation with his sister.

Wesley Kendall cleared his throat. "My dear," he addressed his wife, "will you take Joanna into the drawing room so that Mark can have his brandy?"

"Wesley," laughed Adele, "don't be so formal, please! We are all family here. And besides, I'm sure Mark doesn't care to drink alone. Let us all retire to the drawing room; Mark can drink his brandy there, Joanna and I will have sherry, and you, my dear teetotaler, can watch us and wait for your coffee."

She rose without waiting for her husband's answer. Mark rose too and presented his arm. Adele took it with another laugh, beckoned to Wesley and me to follow, and the four of us repaired to the drawing room.

Mark had his brandy—several brandies—while Adele sipped at her wine. Conversation lagged, for while Mark and Adele exchanged frequent glances of silent communication, Wesley Kendall and I had fallen morosely silent. My sherry sat untouched on a table at my side. I have never liked the taste of sherry; my mother used to drink it.

"Joanna," said Adele when the coffee service arrived, "have you made any plans for Christmas? I should like you and Mark and Noelle to be our guests this year. Mark, did I mention to you that we bought a house in Pleasant Valley? It's a hunting lodge actually; Wesley has had the grounds stocked with deer and pheasant and whatever else it is you men like to stalk. So cruel really, killing some poor, defenseless creature just for the sport of it. But if that's what makes men happy . . ." She shrugged gracefully and turned to me. "You will come, won't you, Joanna? Mark?"

Neither of us answered. Mark rose from his chair, refused the cup of coffee which his sister held out to him, and refilled his snifter with brandy.

"Mark?"

He stood near the table upon which reposed the crystal decanter of liquor, and drank.

"I don't know."

"Mark, I insist."

"I don't know, Adele. I shall give you an answer. . . ."

"When?"

"Soon," he said distantly. "Soon."

I could feel myself pale. His meaning was clear. He had only to tell me he wanted a divorce, that our marriage was finished, and then he could answer his sister: "*I* will be with you this Christmas," he would tell her, "but Joanna, my former wife, will not." Oh, the shame of it. The unendurable shame.

"Joanna, your coffee."

Adele stood over me, the cup in her hand, and when I raised my head, I saw in her sad, long-lashed eyes that she too had taken her brother's meaning.

My throat went dry. Unable to speak, I shook my head.

"Please, my dear," she urged gently. "I have fixed it just the way you like it. Mark tells me you have an incurable sweet tooth."

In an agony of embarrassment, I meekly accepted the cup. I couldn't bear her pity. I wanted only to leave this house, to return to my own, to bear my disgrace in undisturbed solitude.

"Mark," said Wesley after a long and uncomfortable silence, "are you still a member of the board of directors of the Metropolitan Opera House?"

"I am," Mark replied.

"Then I take it you had something to do with the importing of Signore Verdi's *Otello*. What excitement it has caused abroad! I'm most anxious to see it. Is it true that Emma Albani and Jean de Reske have been cast in the lead roles?"

"I believe so, Wesley."

"The premiere is set for the eleventh of January, is it not?"

"Yes, that's right."

"Did you make the arrangements, Mark? I know that you have imported several of Verdi's operas in the past."

"No," said my husband, his voice low, restrained. "As a matter of fact, I was against it."

"Against it? But why? The critics have called it a masterpiece, a work of pure genius. And they say it is completely faithful to Shakespeare's play."

"So I've heard."

"Then why are you against it?"

"I have always disliked the theme of the play. I therefore assume I would have much the same aversion to the opera."

Mark drained his glass, set it down on the table, and directed his attention to me. "Joanna, shall we go?"

"Mark, so soon?" said Adele. "It is not yet eleven. Won't you stay awhile longer?"

"No," he said curtly. Then realizing the harshness of his tone: "Another time perhaps, Adele. It's been a full day, and I think my wife is tired."

My wife. He had called me his wife. How much longer, I wondered painfully, would the designation apply?

At the front door, Adele embraced me warmly, called me "dear sister," and said with a sad, anxious smile, "I have so enjoyed this evening, Joanna, and I want to see you again very soon. Shall I telephone Mark and arrange another engagement for some time next week?"

"If you like," I evaded, "but I don't know his schedule. He's been so involved with his work lately."

"Yes," she agreed, her smile fading. "Mark is always involved with his work, sometimes to the exclusion of matters far more important. You must try, Joanna, to see what you can do to change his priorities."

Change Mark's priorities? What an odd thing to suggest. I was the last person on earth with the ability to change anything at all about the hard, willful man I had married.

In the carriage, Mark asked me, "What do you think of my sister?"

Although he sat as far from me as possible on the plush seat, he was watching me closely, his eyes brilliantly dark in that beautiful Florentine face, and it took all of my willpower not to fling myself shamelessly into his arms.

"I like her very much," I answered, taking care to keep my tone as even and as unemotional as his.

He sighed, turned away from me, and directed his gaze to the sparse flow of carriages along Fifth Avenue. "I've missed her," he admitted, his voice low. "I've missed her sorely. I wonder . . ." He paused, sighed again. "I wonder what made her come back."

The glow from the streetlamps we passed alternately illumined and darkened the flawless configuration of his profile. It seemed symbolic, that change from light to dark, it seemed somehow to delineate the bewildering variability of his moods.

"Mark," I ventured boldly, "what happened between you and Adele? Why did you quarrel?"

He turned to me slowly, his expression suddenly unreadable. "It was a foolish quarrel," he said at length, "as all quarrels are foolish in retrospect. I've agonized for years over the cruel, vile words I flung at her that day, but the irony of it is she has forgotten most of them . . . or has chosen to forget them. When I reminded her of one of the less reprehensible things I had said to her, she just laughed and said it was tedious as well as futile to rake up the past, and why didn't we simply apologize to one another, forget all that transpired before this night, and commence our relationship anew. She also said—"

He stopped, regarded me intently for a moment, then shrugged and turned away.

"Yes? What else did she say, Mark?" I pressed him, for I dared to presume she had spoken of me.

But he only responded, "She said nothing else."

And then he fell silent for the remainder of the short journey home.

At the front door, I said to him, "Will you come in with me? I should like . . ." I paused nervously, averting my eyes from his probing look. "I should like to talk to you about something."

I could feel him watching me; I sensed his indecision, and fearful of a refusal, I raised my head and blurted like a child, "Please, Mark, don't say no!"

He continued to watch me, his dark face grave, his eyes thoughtful, and at great length he answered, "I hadn't any intention of saying no. As a matter of fact, Joanna, I wanted to talk to you too."

Once inside the house, Mark promptly dismissed the servants. I took heart at this act of domestic authority; perhaps it meant— But no, I thought glumly. He had only acted out of habit.

We climbed the stairs in silence, passed my bedroom door and his, then entered the family room. Nervous and ill at ease, I trailed to the mirror under pretext of inspecting my appearance. My face was white with tension, my eyes were bleak, and tendrils of hair had escaped from my chignon to curl in haphazard disorder on my pale brow and cheeks. I looked a fright. But thank heavens for my gown. The dress was not new—it had been purchased in Paris at La Maison Rouff while Mark and I were on our honeymoon—but it had hung unused in my wardrobe, for I had always felt I was not attractive enough to rival the beauty of the sherry-colored brocade, and moreover, the bodice was cut so indecently low that I had never had the desire, nor the courage, to wear it. Tonight though, I mused, it might well serve a purpose. And then my face flushed scarlet as I realized the direction of my thoughts.

"The house looks wonderful," Mark said from the door.

I watched his reflection in the mirror; his eyes traveled the room as if he had been too long gone from this place, from his home. I so wanted to speak, to beg him to come back and to urge him to make his peace with his son, but I couldn't think how to begin.

Restlessly, I turned away and moved toward the liquor cabinet. "Would you like something to drink?" I offered.

"Thank you, no. I have had more than enough to drink tonight."

"Would you like something to eat, then? Shall I ring for—? Oh, I forgot. You've dismissed the servants."

"Joanna," he said quietly, "does my presence distress you? Would you rather I left?"

"Oh, no, Mark, don't go!"

"Are you sure? You've been nervous as a cat all day. I know this has been difficult for you."

"Difficult?" I choked. "Oh, Mark, my only difficulty is . . . is . . ."

"Yes, Joanna?"

"I am only distressed because . . ."

"Yes?" he urged. "Because?"

"Because of Alan," I blurted. "Because I so want you to speak to him, to make up your difference. . . ."

I should not have said that. Too late I realized I should not have mentioned Alan at all. Mark's face had changed; his gaze, bent on mine, was distant, remote. "If you don't mind," he said, "I prefer not to discuss my son at this time."

"But Mark," I blundered on, "his ship sails tomorrow. You can't let him leave without—"

"Is that what you wanted to talk to me about?"

His low tone alarmed me, and at the same time it enraged me. I wanted to speak, how I longed to confess that it was Mark and only Mark who mattered to me now. But as always I was silenced by the wretched restraint which had driven him away from me. I looked at him wordlessly, held mute by my own crippling inability to express the emotions that most mattered to me. How long, I wondered grimly, would this childish fear persist? How much must I lose before finding the strength to speak bravely the truth as I knew it?

As my silence endured, Mark turned away. He slipped his hands into his pockets and began to roam moodily about the room. Finally he stopped and faced me, his expression unreadable.

"My sister is of the opinion that you and I should reconcile," he stated.

My heart leaped and pounded. I took a step toward him, then stopped when his cool gaze met mine.

"I told her," he said, his words measured, "that it was out of the question."

"But why? Mark, why?"

"Because," he said evenly, "it seems you are determined to go through life acting the intermediary for my son. It's clear what you want: to defend him, to protect him. But tell me, Joanna, do you intend never to let him fend for himself? He's a man, not a boy, you know. Or have you already discovered that fact for yourself?"

"Oh, how can you?" I gasped.

"How can I?" he grated, his long-suppressed anger unfettered at last. "How can you not face it? Are you blind?

Are you truly the innocent or are you the slyest woman God ever created? What do you want of me? Why do you cling to me, torture me, when it's him you love, him you want?"

"No, Mark, no! I love only you. But Alan—"

"But Alan," he mimicked cruelly. "Always there is Alan."

"Mark, don't do this," I begged him. "Don't shut him out of your life. He needs you, he has no one else. Carrie will never be able to fill the emptiness inside him. She can't begin to understand what he wants, what he needs. He has already lost a mother; will you deprive him of a father as well?"

"Be still!" he commanded. "I will not hear you plead for him."

"Mark, please, if you love me. If ever you loved me—"

"Shut up!" he said fiercely. "I do love you. I'll never stop loving you."

He caught hold of my arms, dragged me close, kissed me once, hard and brutally, on the mouth. Instinctively, blindly, I reached up to embrace him, but he stepped back so quickly that had he not held out a steadying hand, I would surely have fallen at his feet.

His hand crushed my wrist; I tried once again to embrace him, but he held me away from him, his eyes narrowing hungrily, his slender frame trembling with rage and desire.

"Listen to me," he said hoarsely. "I love you, I want you, but it's over between us. Do you understand me?"

"No, oh, no . . ."

"Yes, Joanna, yes. It's over, finished. I have nothing to give you."

"Your love. Mark, please, give me your love."

"You have that, Joanna. No woman has ever had it more. But you never returned it, never even accepted it. Goddamn it, Joanna, why did you marry me? Why in Christ's name did you marry me?"

I stared at him numbly, this hard, angry, beautiful man, and suddenly I knew why I had married him, and I knew too why I had never before been able to tell him. I had married him because I wanted him. It was that simple. As he had wanted me, I had wanted him. And for the first time in our marriage, because I mortally feared losing him, I told him the truth as I knew it.

His hand dropped from my wrist. "You wanted me?"

"Yes, Mark," I whispered, "I wanted you."

"Physically?"

I could not speak.

"Joanna, answer me!"

My face grew hot. I tried to look away, but he captured my chin and directed my shamed gaze to his.

In my eyes was his answer, in my sick, anguished eyes was the infamous answer he sought.

"My God," he said, staggered. "My God."

He took a step backward, as if filled with the deepest contempt, but in the next instant he reached out for me roughly, pulled me into his arms, and his mouth came down on mine with a swift, brutal passion that arrested my breathing and quickened the beat of my heart. My arms circled round him, my lips gave way to the deep probing onslaught of his. I felt his hands at the fastenings of my dress, and then I was aware of nothing else but his mouth on mine, his breath hot and quick, a rustle of clothing, the rough scratch of fabric against my bare back as he pressed me down on the couch. My eyes were closed, but with the touch of my hands I could feel his body strong and hard and leanly muscled as it moved against mine, moved rapidly, urgently, filling me, crushing me, hurting me, pleasing me, till I ached with excitement, till I moaned with the rapture of his hot, savage, violent love.

If I had died then, in his arms, I would not have cared. My life was complete, I desired nothing else. My husband could not leave me now. A pledge had been made on this night.

When it was over, he did not withdraw. He lay heavy upon me, breathing rapidly, raggedly, his sweat-covered body a welcome encumbrance on mine. A long time passed and then he stirred. I looked at him, smiled, took his face in my hands and kissed his straight mouth and the hard curving line of his jaw.

"I love you," I murmured. "I love you so much."

But he did not reply. He only watched me in silence, his eyes half-veiled by a thick brush of lashes, and presently he said, in an odd, listless voice, "Do you?"

Startled, confused, I released him, and he rose slowly, then turned away from me to repair his disordered attire. I watched mutely as he picked up his coat from the floor; as he knelt down at my side and wrapped the coat about my suddenly trembling shoulders.

The most awesome suspicion took shape in my mind. The tremors that shook me increased.

"Forgive me," he said, his hand on my cheek. "I shouldn't have said that. I suppose you do love me . . . in your own way. But . . ."

"But?" I trembled, knowing he had left the worst unsaid.

"But I'm not going to stay."

"Mark," I said, stunned, "you must stay. You cannot leave now, not after—"

"It is all the more reason to leave."

"Why, Mark? Why?"

"Don't you know?" he said tiredly. "Can't you see why? Shall the success of our marriage be based solely on physical need? We are truly compatible on that score, my darling, on that and nothing else. 'In your arms I forget our differences.' Do you remember telling me that? Do you remember saying that in my arms you were happy, but that the happiness evaporated with first light of day? Do you also recall my telling you that if that were the case, I would keep you in my arms forever?" He smiled grimly, shook his dark head. "But it wasn't a very practical suggestion, was it?"

Bereft beyond words, I could utter no sound as he walked away from me.

"I won't apologize for making love to you. I love you, I wanted you. But you wanted me too . . . didn't you, Joanna?"

He was waiting for an answer I was too humiliated to give him.

I had wanted him, yes. I had always wanted him, even

while my first husband lived. I had wanted Mark, and almost from the beginning I had led him on like the lowest of whores, tempting him, baiting him—in my own proper way, of course—because I wanted him to love me, because I wanted him to want me as men had always wanted my mother. I could face the truth now. Tonight I had been unmasked. Mark had seen me, and I had seen myself, without illusion. I was my mother's daughter after all, and my true self had surfaced. Sally Monroe had been right: I was as base and as immoral as my mother had been, and the fact that I had married my men made me no less a harlot than she.

I sat up in a daze. "I don't want you to leave," I said numbly. "I shall die if you leave me. I want nothing in life but your love."

"My physical love, you mean."

"That too," I admitted. "But I love you, Mark. I am your wife, you cannot abandon me. If you love me, you'll stay with me."

"I do love you," he said, "more than you'll ever know. But love notwithstanding I have hurt you, and I shall continue to hurt you by simple virtue of my presence. You see, I cannot countenance your love for my son, nor his for you. . . . Wait, let me finish. When I think of it rationally, I know there was never anything improper between you. But I know how I am, I will never let it rest. I shall see you always in his arms, and I shall know you belong there."

"Mark," I said, desolate, "I belong in your arms, nowhere else. I know it must have seemed to you that I cared more for Alan than I did for you, but it's not true, it's just not true. You cannot leave me for that reason; you cannot arbitrarily end our marriage. If I've hurt you, you must forgive me. If I've hurt you . . . Oh, Mark, I *know* I've hurt you, but have you never hurt someone who loved you? Have you never committed a cruelty against someone you held dear?"

He grew frighteningly still. His eyes were dark with a memory. I ached to go to him, to assuage his dark pain, but my own was so fierce, my own was so blindingly fierce.

"Yes," he said finally, "I have hurt someone I loved, and

I regret it as I regret nothing else in life. I had promised myself that I would never repeat that cruelty, but it seems I am destined to commit an endless succession of acts of cruelty against those I hold dear and love best. No, please—don't say anything. I know what I am, I'm not blind to my faults, but I know I can't change. If I stay with you, if I allow our marriage to continue, I shall only keep on hurting you, and more than anything else in the world, I don't want that."

"But, Mark," I whispered, my throat raw with pain, "if you leave me, you'll hurt me."

"Not as much," he said bitterly, "as if I stay."

XXXIV

IN LATER MONTHS, I would come to see Mark's side of it. But on the night he made love to me and left me, I went into his bathroom, picked up one of his razors, and held it poised, for fully one hour, above the fast-beating pulse at my wrist.

I could see no reason to go on with my life. Surely death was preferable to this agony, this torment, the anguish of losing him, the prospect of spending the remainder of my days on earth without him. That he had chosen a particularly cruel manner of leaving me did not enter my mind. I knew only that he was gone, that I was alone, and that life was not worth living unless I shared it with Mark.

I cannot recall what brought me to my senses; the thought of Noelle perhaps, the terrible probability that she would suffer forever the stigma of my suicide. I could not inflict so loathesome a legacy on my baby. My own mother had not stopped to consider the effect her mode of conduct might have on her daughter in future years. I could not, in good conscience, do the same to Noelle.

I put down the razor, trailed dazedly to my room, and crept into bed. Presently, I fell into a torpid sleep. I dreamed all night long of my husband. I cannot recall the details of the dreams; I remember only a sadness, an overwhelming aura of desolation and despair. Intermittently throughout the night, I would waken with a start and a soft, frightened moan. And when dawn finally broke and I opened my eyes to a gray, cheerless day, I was weeping.

Adele telephoned me later in the week. She had talked with Mark, and although she did not relay to me the gist of the conversation, I had the distinct impression he had told her our marriage was finished.

"I needn't tell you," she said graciously, "that Mark is buried in work this week. You of all people know how hopelessly entangled he can become in his endless web of refineries. In any case, there's no reason why you and I shouldn't see one another in the meantime. I am having a tea on Thursday next to benefit the survivors of the Delancey Street fire. Yes, it was an awful tragedy, wasn't it? Those disgraceful tenements aren't fit to house animals, let alone human beings. My husband has formed a committee to protest living conditions in that area . . ."

She went on, stopping now and again to ask my comments, chatting as warmly and as amiably as though we had been lifetime friends. I knew what she was doing. I knew she was merely trying to keep open the lines of communication between her brother and me. But didn't she know it was useless? Couldn't she see that any hope I had ever had of saving my marriage was dead?

I went to her tea. In the empty, desolate weeks that followed, I went to more teas and bazaars and art exhibits than I had ever before attended in my life. The Kendalls were active in or associated with every known charitable organization in the city, and from the frequency of Adele's invitations, it appeared she was intent upon eliciting my participation in each and every one of them.

"You must keep busy," she would tell me frequently. "Mark is busy; you must be busy too. If you'll forgive my saying so, Joanna, a woman's life simply cannot revolve around her husband. The benefits reaped from such an endeavor are spare, to say the least, as I'm sure you've discovered being married to Mark."

She never directly referred to our estrangement. In fact, she behaved at all times as if Mark and I were the happiest of couples, and that his awkward absences could be easily explained or excused.

"Isn't it too bad," she said in November, "that Mark is in Pittsburgh this week? He would so have enjoyed the exhibit of Mr. Carolus-Duran's early works. But you'll be there, won't you, Joanna? Elinor Mendelssohn is down with *la grippe,* and I'm counting on you to share hostess duties with me."

I complied, of course. I did everything Adele asked of me. I served on committees, passed tea and cakes on Fifth Avenue, ladled soup on the Bowery, sang hymns in her church, taught Bible lessons to the children of the poor on Sundays. I didn't mind. I would have laid bricks and dug ditches if it meant I might see my husband again. But I never did. After the night he made love to me and left me, Mark vanished from my life just as totally and irrevocably as if he had died.

Several weeks before Christmas, Adele and I were in Lord & Taylor's, shopping together for our girls. The gaily decorated store was filled to bursting with holiday shoppers; in fact, Broadway itself was congested with pedestrians and with a riotous flow of vehicular traffic. I had just purchased a cunning music box in the shape of a swan and was waiting for the salesclerk to wrap it when Adele said abruptly, "Do you know Spencer Halston?"

"Yes, I've met him," I answered, somewhat taken aback by the sudden intensity of her tone.

"He wants to see you. He has asked me to arrange a meeting at your convenience."

"For what reason, Adele? What does he want of me? I hardly know him. And besides, Mark . . ." I stopped, disconcerted, unwilling to impart information about which I myself knew almost nothing.

But Adele said, "Yes, I know. Mark despises him."

"How do you know that? Did Mark—?"

Adele frowned, shook her head. "Mark tells me very little, Joanna. I hope you realize that. I question him continuously about his . . . problems, but he refuses to discuss them. I have tried . . ." She paused, looked about us at the bustling jostle of shoppers. "Let us talk of this later," she suggested quietly. "I don't want—"

"Yes, of course," I said at once, more reluctant than she to speak on so intimate and distressing a subject.

We concluded our shopping, then walked a bit on Broadway. Adele said she needed fresh air, and so the coachman trailed slowly behind us, keeping tight rein on the horses, who strained at their bits and snorted and pranced impatiently. It was a chill, sunless day, with a brisk, bitter wind, and my cloak, though warm, provided little defense against the cold. Adele, however, in a chic beaver hat and a beaver-trimmed coat, seemed impervious to the weather. Her cheeks glowed red, and her magnificent eyes were a radiant light beneath the dark fan of her lashes. How lovely she looked, and how I envied her. Oh, not her beauty, of course. I envied her only that she saw Mark, spoke to him, while I could not.

"My brother," said Adele, as we paused at a busy intersection, "has not changed in the long years we've been apart. He remains a man of intense loyalties, of fixed convictions, neither of which can be shaken, and which mostly account for his difficulties. In a word, he is stubborn. His loyalty, of course, is an admirable trait, although in some cases, it is ill-placed. His convictions, too, are often misguided, and this adamant refusal to yield, to unbend, has unfortunately been his undoing. It's obvious to me that Mark loves you, and what's far more important, he needs you, yet for some obscure reason he is firmly convinced that you and he are better off apart. I can't help thinking that this decision is directly related to our estrangement—his and mine, I mean—and as a result, I feel personally responsible for yours."

"Please," I said guiltily, "don't blame yourself. You had nothing to do with it."

"Joanna, forgive me, but I think I know Mark rather better than you do, and I also think my appraisal of the situation may be somewhat more valid than your own. When I quarreled with my brother, I said certain things to him which I'm afraid he took too literally and too much to heart. At the time, I was smugly certain that all I had told him was the absolute truth. But as the years passed, I came to realize that there is no such thing as absolute truth, and I realized too that much of what I had said to Mark was cruel and unfair and potentially damaging." She paused, and a shadow fell across those lovely eyes as the past haunted her thoughts.

"There were so many times I wanted to return to him, to

ask his forgiveness," she continued, "but I had rebuffed Mark's overtures for peace for such a long time that, to be perfectly honest, I was afraid he would rebuff mine. When I learned he had married you, I began to breathe easier. You are well liked, Joanna, do you know that? I've received many favorable reports about you, and I began to think: Thank heavens. He's found a good wife. He'll be happy now. But when I learned of your separation . . . Well, that's when I knew I had to shelve my sinful pride and put my brother's feelings above my own."

She glanced over at me, then slipped her arm through mine and gave me a gentle smile. I wondered why she was talking of my problem with Mark when previously she had not even acknowledged that a problem existed.

"My dear," she said softly as if sensing my thoughts, "I know it must have seemed to you that I was completely ignoring the situation, but believe me, I have thought of virtually nothing else since the day I learned my brother had left you. I had hoped against hope that your estrangement was only temporary, but the more I talk with Mark, the more I am convinced that he intends it should be permanent."

My stomach contracted; I could feel myself pale.

"Joanna, are you faint? Oh, I'm sorry! I shouldn't have . . ."

She grasped my arm firmly and directed me toward a quaint gypsy tearoom tucked tidily between two tall brownstones. The tearoom was empty save for an elderly gentleman munching scones in a corner, and the exotically clad proprietress who showed us gracefully, albeit languidly, to a neatly set table for two.

Adele ordered tea and croissants, and after we were served, she said anxiously, "Have something, please. You'll feel better if you do. I'm sorry for shocking you like that, but you've been so very complacent throughout this ordeal that I thought . . . Well, it doesn't matter what I thought. I can see now you're as distressed about the situation as I am."

"But of course I'm distressed," I said sickly. "Why should you think I wasn't?"

"Quite simply, Joanna, because you haven't shown the least hint of emotion in all the time we've been spending together. I had not expected hysterics, mind you, for Mark has intimated on several occasions that you are of a restrained nature. But you haven't once asked about him, or even mentioned his name. Except for today, that is. Except in connection with Spencer Halston."

Spencer Halston. I had forgotten that the impetus of this entire unlikely conversation had been Spencer Halston. "Adele," I demanded, "why are you telling me these things now, today? What does it all have to do with Spencer Halston? Why does he want to see me? And why does Mark hate him?"

"I don't know," she said frankly. "I don't know the answer to any of those questions except, perhaps, the first. I had to speak out today; I could no longer keep silent on the subject. You see, I'm very much afraid that Mark is going to divorce you, and I'm even more afraid that if he does divorce you, it will utterly destroy him. Spencer feels as I do. He telephoned me yesterday—I couldn't have been more stunned, for I haven't heard from him in years. In any case, he was most insistent that I speak to you and arrange a meeting. He told me he was concerned about Mark, and that he thought he might be able to help you both. At first, I hesitated. I know how Mark feels about him, though I don't know the particulars of their quarrel. That's what I meant before when I spoke of Mark's loyalties. He loved Spencer once, as dearly as a brother, and despite what has transpired between them, he will not speak ill of him. . . . Perhaps that's a good thing, keeping one's own counsel in such a situation, but in Mark's case, it frightens me. His emotions are much too turbulent to suppress. I shudder to think what he keeps locked in his heart."

She stopped suddenly and gave me a harried look. "I'm sorry, Joanna, it's just that I'm so terribly worried about Mark."

She was worried? Dear God, I was terrified.

"Adele," I asked, "what can I do? How can I convince him—"

"You can convince him of nothing against which he has

set his mind. I've tried, and it's useless. I don't know what else to do. Perhaps Spencer's call, coming when it did, was the work of divine providence. Perhaps he can help Mark where you and I have failed."

"But how, Adele? How can Mark possibly be helped by a man he despises?"

"I don't know," she said grimly, and at that moment her resemblance to Mark was both astonishing and frightening. "But if you love my brother, Joanna, and if you want him back, you had best shed your shield of dispassionate restraint . . . and do something about it."

XXXV

DISPASSIONATE RESTRAINT! Was that the image I projected? Did Adele really think I was so cold, so unfeeling, that my husband's leaving had not distressed me? It angered me, her cursory assessment of my character, it absolutely enraged me. And yet, I thought later, perhaps she was justified in thinking as she did. Perhaps my wretched inability to properly express my emotions had alienated still another member of the Van Holden family.

I agreed, though reluctantly, to see Spencer Halston. Adele had suggested that we meet at her house—on neutral ground as she put it—but I told her I would see him in my home, or not at all. I needed the security of familiar surroundings.

I received him in the drawing room. He arrived a full twenty minutes before the appointed hour of eight, but I had been dressed and waiting since seven. The gown I had chosen was new, a slender tube of magenta cashmere, trimmed from collar to waist with magenta passementerie braid. Mr. Halston's attire was likewise *soigné;* he was dressed in dark blue, and his handsomely folded cravat was held neatly in place by an exquisite sapphire and gold stickpin. He was very attractive. His fair hair gleamed flaxen, his eyes were a fine azure blue, and his mouth was hard and straight and remarkably similar to Mark's.

"Mr. Halston," I said, "do sit down. Would you care for some coffee? No? Something stronger, then?"

I daresay he thought me cool, unconcerned, but I was shaking inside like a terrified child, and in fear of his visit,

341

I suppose, I had been struggling all day against a faint but persistent nausea.

"Thank you, no," he replied. "I have been trying in the past several weeks to discontinue a pattern of drinking which has become . . . somewhat unmanageable."

I flinched at his candor. What a strange thing to say. What was his purpose, I wondered, in making such a personal and embarrassing statement?

Discomfited, I said rudely, "Mr. Halston, would you mind telling me why you wanted to see me? My sister-in-law said that you felt you could help Mark. May I know in what way you propose to do this?"

"Mrs. Van Holden," he said with a quick smile, "how refreshingly direct you are. I had formed an altogether different impression of you from the first time we talked. I remember thinking at the time how inordinately unsuited you were to Mark, and what a devil of a life you could expect if you married him."

"How dare you!" I blazed. "How dare you say such a thing?"

"My dear lady," he said in the calmest of tones, "your present situation tends to support my theory. Your marriage is in jeopardy; I am not surprised. I am only surprised it has lasted this long. Mark, I fear, is not the ideal husband."

A hot retort rose to my lips, but Mr. Halston went on before I had a chance to speak.

"Mrs. Van Holden, believe me, I am not denigrating Mark. I was merely commenting on his unyielding obstinacy, a characteristic which has caused him—and those he loves—considerable anguish."

"What are you saying?" I demanded. "You insult my husband, retract the insult, then reinforce and embellish it. Who are you to speak of the anguish he has caused others, when you have hurt him so monstrously that the very mention of your name sets him trembling with rage!"

"Yes, I have hurt him," he conceded. "But he does himself and you and everyone he loves a far greater injury by refusing to bury the past, by clinging to a guilt which is mine alone."

"Guilt?" I said impatiently. "What do you mean?"

"That," he explained, "is the reason I wanted to see you. I doubt Mark will ever be happy until he exorcizes the ghost of that guilt; however, the difficulty here is that he cannot do it alone. I think I can help him, but not directly, you understand, for Mark will accept nothing from me ever again."

He paused, eyed me steadily, then said in a tense, low voice, "I hope I don't have to tell you that everything I am about to say to you tonight is of the utmost confidentiality. If Mark ever learns—"

"Oh, do get on with it!" I snapped, my nerve ends rubbed raw. "What guilt are you talking about? And why do you say it's yours?"

He sighed heavily and leaned back in his chair. "Mrs. Van Holden, Mark blames himself for his first wife's death. The truth of the matter is that *I* am to blame."

"But how could anyone be to blame?" I asked. "She died in childbirth."

"Yes," he said slowly. "But I loved her, you see. And that was the reason she died."

I stared at him mutely, having heard but not comprehended his words.

"I loved her," he said again, "but she didn't love me. She loved Mark, loved him more than any man deserves to be loved, and sometimes I would wonder why that should be so, but then I came to realize that there's never a reason for love. Why, for example, did I love Lenore when I knew many women as beautiful and as accomplished as she? Why had I chosen her, a married woman—for she was already married when I met her. . . ."

He trailed off in thought, and his eyes clouded over with memory.

"She was a vision," he said presently, "a dream come to life when I first saw her. I had been abroad for a year, and when I returned to New York, I stopped in to see Mark, and there she was: his new wife, as lovely a creature as God ever made. They were on their way to the theater, I remember, and Lenore wore a pearl gray gown threaded with silver, and her eyes shone silver gray from her perfect face that gleamed like polished ivory. I cannot describe my feelings as Mark presented her to me and she took my hand with a warm, gracious smile.

"At that very moment, I fell in love with her. I wanted Lenore as I had never in my life wanted anyone. That she was Mark's wife meant nothing to me. I loved her, I wanted her, and regardless of the obstacles, I was determined to have her."

He rose suddenly and moved unsteadily to the window, as if his unholy thoughts were a punishing thorn in his side. I saw him draw back the curtain and stare blindly into the inky night. At length, he let the curtain fall and returned with a sigh to his chair.

"We could not avoid seeing each other," he continued. "Mark gave many receptions early in his marriage, and of course I attended them all. I don't know how I survived those months; I was mad with jealousy—the sight of his hand on her arm was enough to send me into a paroxysm of rage. I used to devise ways of being alone with her, but that was worse. We might be alone, but she wasn't mine, I couldn't touch her, she belonged to him— God, how I hated him! No, no," he amended. "I never hated him. It was only that I loved his wife and wanted her—"

"Stop it," I said, as a swift surge of repulsion rose in my throat. "What's wrong with you? Why are you telling me these dreadful things?"

"Mrs. Van Holden," he said, "allow me, if you will, to say what I must, and then judge for yourself the reason I am telling you . . . 'these dreadful things.' "

He awaited my comments, but I was too numb, too confused, to reply. What possible reason could he have for reviving this old memory, for telling me, a stranger, of his futile and illicit love?

"May I continue?" he asked at length, and when I nodded helplessly, he took up the thread of his tale.

"Despite Lenore's love for Mark, she was never quite confident of his love for her. He is not an ardent man, as you may know, despite the reputation he gained following her death. His emotions are volatile, to be sure, and violent at times, but he has always been impatient with

women, abstracted, as he was with Lenore, and I daresay
this added to her insecurities and to her conviction that
the primary reason he had married her was to avail himself of her extremely generous dowry."

"That can't be true," I choked. "Mark wouldn't—"

"Excuse me, Mrs. Van Holden, but I'm fairly certain
that when Mark was contemplating marriage to Lenore,
the Van Rensselaer fortune was very much the deciding
factor."

"What a cruel thing to say," I said. "What a cruel and
vicious thing to say."

"Perhaps," he responded. "But it is nonetheless accurate. Which was all the more reason I felt little or no guilt
for wanting Lenore. I felt, in fact, that I deserved her,
whereas Mark, with his mercenary purpose in marrying
her, did not."

His eyes turned briefly to the glorious portrait of Lenore.
The hopeless love he bore her was painfully evident on his
face.

"I was with her," he said softly, "when that portrait was
painted. She had commissioned it as a surprise for Mark's
birthday. The artist was a friend of mine, a talented devil
but a miserable wretch of a human being. I did not want
Lenore to be alone with him; she was to sit for him every
day for a week, and she gladly agreed when I offered to accompany her to the studio. We grew very close in that
week. We talked incessantly, totally oblivious to the artist
who, fortunately, was equally oblivious to anything we
said, for it was there in that studio that I first told Lenore I
loved her.

"I knew it was wrong, hopeless. I knew how much she
loved Mark, but my own love had reached a point where I
could no longer keep it to myself. She was startled by my
confession, but she was very kind, she didn't laugh—I was
terrified she might laugh at me—but she did not. She
merely explained, gently and patiently, that she loved
Mark and that she simply couldn't conceive of a life without him. But I would not be put off; I rejoindered angrily
that Mark, on the other hand, could not conceive of a life
without the Van Rensselaer fortune. I went on to point out

his many shortcomings, his absorption with his work, his increasingly prolonged absences from home. I even inferred he was seeing other women, when I knew for a fact he was absolutely faithful to his wife. And, God forgive me, I succeeded. Lenore's worst fears were—she thought—substantiated by my lies. She believed all I told her; she broke down and wept. In torment because she had no one else, she turned to me. But she still loved Mark. She would always love Mark. At the end, when she died, I was there at her side. But it was Mark she wanted, Mark's name she called, and not mine."

Once again, Spencer rose from his chair and moved, as if drugged, to the window. The silence in the room was as ominous as his story. He turned to me, and continued. "After Alan was born, she stopped seeing me. Just like that, she stopped seeing me. I was out of my mind with a cold, helpless fear. I loved her—and I was naive enough to think she had come to love me—and here she was, refusing to see me, returning my letters unopened; I thought she'd gone mad. But finally she wrote to me, a brief, chilly note telling me it was over, that she loved only Mark, and that anything she had thought she felt for me was misguided, unsanctioned, and dead. Dead? I would not accept that. I attributed her attitude to postpartum insanity, to guilt, to anything but what it truly was. When years went by and every effort I made to approach her was inexorably snubbed, I had to admit it was over, that I had deluded myself, that it was her husband she loved and would till the day she died.

"It was then I decided I would force the issue. I wanted Lenore, and with or without her consent, I would have her. Though she had said she loved Mark, he did not, in my estimation, love her, and I considered it almost my moral duty to take her away from him, to make her my own. But it was clear to me too that Mark would not relinquish his hold on his wife simply because he didn't want her. Mark is not that kind of man. And so, out of desperation, because I could think of no other way to free her, I let it be known about town that Alan . . ." Spencer paused for a moment and his gaze faltered and fell. ". . . that Alan was not his son."

"You?" I said, stunned. "You are the one who spread that vicious lie?" He stared at me oddly, as if puzzled, perplexed. He started to speak, but I cried in a rage, "Don't you dare attempt to justify—"

"I'm not," he said hoarsely. "There is no justification for what I did. It was a despicable thing to do, wicked, depraved. But I loved her, you see. I loved her and I wanted her, no matter the cost, no matter who suffered."

"What manner of monster are you to have done such an abominable thing?"

"There's more," he said grimly.

"I won't listen! I won't hear another word of—"

"Please!" he insisted. "I am telling you these things for the sake of your future happiness."

"What?" I cried. "What has my future happiness got to do with it? You are only attempting to ease your own conscience!"

"Yes, all right," he admitted. "That's partly true. I have borne this burden in silence for too many years. Telling you all this is my catharsis, I suppose, a purging of guilt, if you will; but it's more than that, Mrs. Van Holden. Believe me, I implore you, it's more than that. I want to help you and Mark."

"Haven't you 'helped' him enough?" I snapped.

"I deserve that," he conceded. "I deserve far worse than anything you could ever say to me. But I want you to try to believe this: Despite what Mark feels for me I am deeply concerned for him. We were closer than brothers, he and I. We shared much that I cannot forget, and he has helped me in ways that can never be repaid."

"You have a strange way of expressing your gratitude," I said bitterly.

"Gratitude," he said quietly, "was the last thing on my mind when I wanted his wife."

He looked away for a moment, his face white and strained, in recollection of his pain. But if he was seeking to gain my sympathy he was wasting his efforts. I could see now why Mark despised him. Spencer had betrayed him in the foulest way. He had taken all the kindness and affection Mark had to give, and in return he had—

But hadn't I done the same thing? I thought suddenly. Hadn't I abused my husband's love in much the same manner? No wonder he didn't want to come back to me. He had given freely of his love, his loyalty, once to his friend and once to me, and both times he had been betrayed.

"The disclosure about Alan," said Spencer Halston, "is the least of my atrocities."

I looked up slowly, my tortured thoughts numbing my brain. "What are you talking about?"

His eyes, dull blue in color, met mine. His face was haggard, etched heavily with memory and remorse.

"The disclosure," he said, "was only the beginning. When Mark finally heard of it, he and I were somewhat at odds because of the Eastern Seaboard trust agreement. He had assigned that rather important piece of work to another of his attorneys, and I was angered and hurt by this flagrant insult to my competence, though in all fairness, Randolph Harper was more qualified than I for that particular task. But I wasn't feeling very fair at the time; I had another, more pressing, matter on my mind: I was waiting for the rumor to reach Mark's ears.

"Several days later he summoned me into his office. I knew at once that he had not heard the entire story, for his manner, though agitated, was civil. He bade me be seated, but he himself kept pacing the room like a caged jungle cat, and at length he said tersely, 'Have you heard the latest gossip, Spencer? Are you aware of the scurrilous story that's making the rounds?'

" 'No,' I told him coolly, 'I've heard nothing new lately. To which story are you referring, Mark?'

"He wouldn't come right out with it. He hedged and evaded; he began to talk of something else, then he asked me again if I'd heard the filthy rumor that was now common knowledge in New York.

"I told him no once more, but I said it in such a way that he would think I was lying. I have rarely been able to successfully deceive Mark, he knows me too well. But his personal involvement, his ferocious emotions, had distorted his judgment, rendering him incapable of seeing through my pathetically simple ruse.

" 'You've heard then,' Mark said in a soft, yet deadly voice. 'It's true what they're saying about Lenore.'

"For just an instant, I knew fear. I was too well acquainted with Mark's murderous rages, and for a brief moment, I trembled with fear. But then I remembered Lenore. I remembered her face in all its perfection; I remembered her lambent eyes, her petal-soft mouth, her figure, her grace . . ."

Spencer paused, looked up at me dully. He seemed to have forgotten I was there. His fair face was blank, devoid of expression.

"I could have stopped it there," he said emptily. "It would have been an easy matter to convince Mark that all he had heard was idle rumor, a tissue of lies. But I didn't. I let him believe it. I even said pointedly, 'I haven't any idea what you're talking about, Mark. Are people really chattering about Lenore? What are they saying? No, don't tell me. I make it a point to disregard gossip, even though ninety percent of it is usually true.'

"And then I left him. I left Mark, knowing that he believed, beyond a shadow of a doubt, that his wife had betrayed him. It was done now, I thought, she was mine. Mark would leave her, I had only to wait until the divorce decree was final, and then she would be mine. She was pregnant at the time with her second child, but even that had not deterred me. In fact, to my eyes, she was more beautiful in that condition than she had ever been before.

"I heard from her several days later. It was the first letter I had had from her in years, and it was to be the last. She wanted to see me. Of course I knew the reason. She needed me again. It had all gone exactly as I'd planned.

"She received me in her boudoir. I was mildly astonished at this unexpected breach of etiquette, but when I saw her I realized at once why she had done so. Her eyes were swollen from weeping. Her face was ghastly, absolutely colorless. She told me that Mark had confronted her, had accused her of past infidelity and had even suggested that the child she was carrying was not his as well. He had been wild with rage, she told me further. He had cursed her, denounced her, and . . . he had hurt her. When she showed me the bruises on her throat, I wanted to kill him! It never for a moment occurred to me that I was the one who had done it, *I* was the one who had hurt her.

"She was sobbing uncontrollably. Mark had gone to Pittsburgh, and she begged me to go after him, to tell him it wasn't true, that she had never been unfaithful to him.

" 'Only you can do it, Spencer,' she said. 'You are the only one who can convince him. He will take your word above anyone else's. He loves you, he trusts you. Go after him, I beg you. Bring him back to me!'

"I couldn't believe my ears. She was asking me, *me*, to convince Mark of her fidelity. She wanted him still, despite the reprehensible thing he had done to her.

"I think that's when my sanity deserted me. I caught hold of her arms and shook her violently. 'I love you,' I told her. 'I love you and Mark doesn't! He never loved you, he never wanted you.'

" 'He does!' she insisted, struggling to free herself. 'He does love me. He is only angry because he thinks I have been unfaithful to him. Spencer, you must help me. You must tell him—'

" 'Tell him what?' I said, furious. 'What do you want me to tell him, Lenore? Shall I say I've made love to you? Shall I corroborate the rumor that is sweeping the city? Do you want me to tell him that Alan is *my* son?'

" 'What?' she cried, horrified. 'Spencer, have you gone mad?'

" 'I will do it!' I said in a rage. 'I will do anything to have you. Anything, do you hear me?'

" 'No,' she begged, 'no. Spencer, you cannot, you must not—'

"She stiffened suddenly, her hands flew to her throat as if she could not catch her breath, then she gave a low moan and collapsed in my arms. Her face had gone ashen; I was dumbstruck with fright. I got her to bed, rang for her maid, and dispatched her to fetch a physician. He came almost at once. He brought a colleague. He was worried, you see. Lenore was not strong.

"She went into labor. It was not her time, but fear, I suppose, had brought on her pains. She was in labor all day and all night. The room rang with her screams. I shall always remember the sound of her screams. She finally gave birth to a stillborn son. And then she died. I stared at her body and wished myself dead alongside her. I did not want to live, I deserved not to live. I had killed her, you see. I had murdered the woman I loved."

"Dear God," I said sickly. "Dear God in heaven, how could you have done such a detestable thing? Why did you threaten her like that?"

He gave me a strange look that silenced me. His brow furrowed into an irritated frown. "But I had to do it, don't you see? I thought if I frightened her enough, she would have no recourse but to leave him. I never had any intention of actually telling Mark."

"That's no excuse! You needn't have chosen so vile a method. You needn't have lied."

"Lied?" he said, puzzled. "Lied about what?"

"About Alan!" I cried, my voice trembling with rage. "You needn't have threatened to say he was yours."

"But he is mine," said Spencer. "I thought you understood that. Lenore *was* unfaithful; we were lovers for months. Alan Van Holden is my son, not Mark's."

XXXVI

WHEN I WAS finally able to speak, I asked him outright, "Does Mark know?"

"Does Mark know?" he echoed dully. "Are you joking?"

"Then why does he hate you?"

How clear my voice was, and how inordinately calm, but my hands were shaking and my heart beat so tempestuously that I feared at any moment I might faint.

"Mark hates me," said Spencer Halston, "because I told him I was the one who had started the rumor about Lenore."

"You told him? Then he does know?"

"No, no." He shook his head impatiently. "I convinced him that it *was* a rumor, with no basis in fact. I admitted I had loved Lenore, and I also explained what I had done to free her from him, but I made him understand that her infidelity and the question of Alan's paternity had all been a pack of lies. I don't know why I told him. Perhaps I thought he would kill me; perhaps I wanted him to kill me. At any rate, he spoke not a word for the longest time—I think he couldn't fully believe what I was saying—and then he said in a low, brutal voice, 'Do you know what you've done, Spencer? Do you know why she died? Do you know the vile and degenerate acts of which I accused her? Oh, you bastard,' he uttered fiercely. 'You contemptible bastard.'

"He went on to say more, much more, and I think if I had stayed, he would indeed have killed me. I left rather quickly. You may add cowardice to my other faults, for as much as I felt I deserved whatever Mark might do to me, I quite frankly wanted to save my skin.

"I went abroad immediately thereafter. I was terrified that Mark would seek vengeance, that at the very least he would blacken my name, expose what I'd done. My future in New York society looked bleak, so I leased a villa in Milan and reconciled myself to an expatriate life. But as time passed, my fears began to lessen. I wrote to some friends, inquired obliquely about Mark. Their replies encouraged me; obviously they knew nothing of what had happened, for they were delighted to hear from me and they urged me repeatedly to come home. That's when I knew Mark blamed himself for Lenore's death. I realized that he had kept silent those many years because he felt the guilt was his. He had believed the rumors; that was the greater crime. He was convinced he was at fault, that he had betrayed his wife even more foully than he had thought she betrayed him."

Spencer leaned against the back of his chair. His face was very white; he looked about to faint, yet at the same time, a curious peace seemed to have descended upon him, as if the simple act of confession had thoroughly cleansed all trace of his horrendous sin.

I stared at him mutely, at his haunted, remorse-filled blue eyes. Dazed, I rose from my chair. I had to get away from this man and be alone.

"Will you excuse me?" I said in my most courteous voice. "I should like to retire now. Please don't think me rude, but all at once I have the most frightful headache."

I stared numbly at his ashen face. He looked even more anguished than I, but he got to his feet, took both my hands in his, and said rapidly, "You do see why I've told you? You now know the reason?"

"Yes, of course," I said in a fog. "I understand everything now." But I understood nothing at all.

"You'll forgive Mark, then? Whatever he's done to cause your estrangement, you'll forgive him? You must do this, Joanna, you must help him. You are his second chance, his opportunity for redemption. You must absolve him of past guilt by pardoning him for present sins. He must be forgiven, don't you see? He *needs* someone to forgive him.

Because all these years he has held himself responsible for a crime which I alone committed."

"I shall do what I can," I assured him, but my reply was automatic, I hadn't any idea what I was saying. "Will you excuse me now, Mr. Halston? I really must take something for this headache. Kelsey will show you out."

I disengaged my hands from his, and I knew he was watching me as I trailed from the room, but he made no effort to detain me.

In the hall, I encountered Kelsey, whose staid, dour countenance took on the same look of puzzled alarm which I had seen but not deciphered on Mr. Halston's pale face.

"Mrs. Van Holden," said Kelsey, "is anything wrong?"

"Wrong? Why, no, nothing's wrong. Why do you ask?"

But before he could reply, I said vaguely, "Kelsey, would you please see Mr. Halston to the door? You'll find him in the drawing room. I believe he is ready to leave now."

Without waiting for an answer, I walked away, climbed the stairs, and proceeded, like a somnambulist, to my room. I tried not to think, I attempted in vain to sweep clean my mind of disorderly thoughts, but Spencer's confession resounded in my ears, and the most appalling mental images kept flashing through my brain. I felt stifled and sick; I wanted desperately to escape, to flee the vile sound of those odious words: "Lenore was unfaithful; we were lovers for months. Alan Van Holden is my son, not Mark's."

Why had he told me? Why had he reopened old wounds long healed? If Mark was unaware of Lenore's infidelity, what was Spencer's purpose in bringing it to light after all these years? "You must forgive Mark," he had told me. That was his reason for divulging the unspeakable past. But what was there to forgive in Mark when he was the one who had been wronged? And who but God could ever forgive Spencer Halston? It was a nightmare, a repulsive, repetitive nightmare, and I simply hadn't the strength to endure it a second time.

"Mrs. Van Holden!" Myrna exclaimed as I entered the bedroom. "What in the world . . . ?" And when I raised my blank gaze to hers, she took my arm and said briskly,

"Come, madam, come sit by the fire, and I'll fetch you a nice hot toddy."

I let myself be led to a chair, and when Myrna returned, I submitted apathetically to her skillful ministrations and soon found myself clad comfortably in soft nightclothes, with a cup of steaming liquid in my hands.

"Drink it all now," she bade me. "It'll warm your bones. It's a raw, cold night, it is, and Mr. Van Holden's heating system is quite as inadequate as was Mr. Sinclair's, God rest his soul. Do you remember?" she asked with a nostalgic smile. "Do you remember that house cold as ice? Many's the night we spent huddled around the fire, thanking heaven for same, and for the comfort and warmth of our woolies. How young we were then. Do you remember, madam? It all seems light years away. Dear Mr. Sinclair, what a saint of a man he was. I daresay you miss him—meaning no disrespect to Mr. Van Holden, of course. But Mr. Sinclair was a more . . . peaceful man, a *predictable* man. Do you know what I mean, Mrs. Van Holden?"

"Yes," I said dully. "I know all too well what you mean."

How much simpler life had been when I was married to Edward, simpler and sane and secure. And after he died, when I married Mark, I had mistakenly thought that security would be increased, that all I had had with Edward would continue, on a grander scale. But I soon learned that with Mark I was expected to *give* as well as receive, to return love, to fulfill needs, to heal wounds, to support and sustain. In short, Mark had expected a woman, when in fact he had married a child.

"Yes, he was good to us," Myrna was saying. "Mr. Sinclair asked little of anyone but gave much of himself. God took him too soon. . . . Oh, forgive me, Mrs. Van Holden, I don't mean to bring up sad memories, especially now, with Mr. Van Holden . . ."

"Don't apologize, Myrna. You're right about Mr. Sinclair: He gave me everything, I gave him nothing. But I didn't learn from my mistakes. Mr. Van Holden gave me everything too, and I brought him only heartache and despair."

"Madam, you're too hard on yourself. You've been the best of wives to Mr. Van Holden; you've given him a beautiful baby. And"—she paused for a moment, took the cup from my hand, then gave me a long, pensive look—"it appears you'll soon be giving him another."

I caught my breath sharply. "What are you talking about? Why did you say that?"

"Mrs. Van Holden," she sighed, "unless I miss my guess, you're carrying a child. The signs are all there, as they were with Noelle. You've been ill in the mornings, and although you've lost weight, your waist has thickened and your breasts are fuller—"

"No!" I said, panicked. "I can't be pregnant. I can't be!"

But in the same instant, I knew that I was. I had known it in my heart for weeks, but I couldn't face it, I couldn't accept it. I was carrying Mark's child, and the memory of its conception was something I had tried to erase from my thoughts. Mark had loved me and left me, like one of his whores.

"Madam," said Myrna, misinterpreting my distress, "there's no need to fret. On the contrary, this child is a godsend. Don't you see? Mr. Van Holden is sure to come back to you now."

Would he? If he knew I was having his child, would he forgive, forget, all that had come between us? Would his jealousy end? Would he make up his quarrel with his son?

But Alan was not his son, he was Spencer's son.

And knowing this, I would once again be forced to be party to a lie. The deception was reborn, only now it was real, there was no misunderstanding. Alan Van Holden was not Mark's son. And as a consequence, I would have to pretend as before, and evade and ignore and elude and . . .

Dear God, I couldn't. Not again, not again.

"Myrna," I whispered wretchedly, "I don't know if I want him to come back."

And as the honesty of my thoughts became cold, ugly words, my stomach contracted, I struggled to my feet, stumbled dizzily to the bathroom, and was violently ill.

XXXVII

I WAS PREGNANT. Dr. Shelley confirmed it.

I had not seen Dr. Shelley since the death of my first husband. Mark's friend, Morris Feldman, had delivered Noelle. But with this pregnancy, I felt the need to seek my own physician, or rather Edward's physician, in a reversion, I suppose, to old friends, old values, old securities.

The years had not changed him; he was as kind and as warm as I remembered, and his congenial manner put me at my ease.

"What a pleasure to see you!" he greeted me. "Please sit down, Mrs. Sinclair. I beg your pardon—Mrs. Van Holden."

He held out a chair, then took his own seat behind his desk and gave me an amiable smile. I returned the smile readily, and my nervousness all but disappeared.

He inquired after the Monroes; I told him Carrie had married.

"Married?" he laughed. "Good Lord, the last time I saw her she was a gauche, bashful chick of thirteen. Where has the time gone? I feel like a doddering old man!"

Which made *me* laugh; because he looked like a fresh-scrubbed young boy.

We talked at length about the old days, and especially about Edward.

"I think of him often," he told me. "He was a fine and exceptional man."

"Yes, he was," I said softly.

Before I knew it, an hour had passed most pleasantly, and finally, when we had thoroughly exhausted every last memory we shared, Dr. Shelley cleared his throat, rested his elbows on his desk, and said in his professional voice, "I trust your complaint is a minor one."

"My complaint, Dr. Shelley?"

"The reason you've come to see me, Mrs. Van Holden."

"Oh, yes, my complaint." My nerves tensed. I looked down at my hands and began to twist my wedding band round and round on my finger. "Well, you see," I explained, "I think I'm . . . expecting a child."

"Ah," he said, relieved. "I should have suspected. You're looking so radiant that I should have guessed it right off. Come along," he said, rising and ushering me toward the adjoining room. "Let's have a look at you."

Did he really think I looked radiant? I wondered irrelevantly. How strange I should hear that, now, at a time when I had never felt more unattractive.

His examination was thorough; his diagnosis did not surprise me. "Yes, you're pregnant," he told me. "About ten weeks, I'd say."

He left me to dress, and several minutes later when I joined him in his office, he was making notations in a file; then he put down his pen, looked up with a smile, and bade me return to my chair.

"This is not your first child, am I correct?"

"It is my second," I answered.

"Your first pregnancy went well? There were no complications?"

"No, none. Why do you ask?"

"Routine questions, Mrs. Van Holden, nothing more. If I had delivered your first child, I should more or less know what to expect with your second."

"Dr. Shelley," I said, embarrassed, "I very much wanted to have you attend me during my first pregnancy, but my husband—"

"Please," he stopped me, and now he too looked embarrassed. "I was not implying . . . I merely wish to acquaint myself fully with your obstetrical history in order to avoid the possibility of any difficulties which may arise."

"Difficulties?"

"Now, now," he said quickly, "don't be alarmed. My

findings are completely satisfactory; I anticipate no problems. And if you say your first pregnancy went well, there's no reason to believe that this one won't progress in a like manner."

He leaned back in his chair, and his direct, hazel eyes studied mine. "Mrs. Van Holden, why have you come to me with this pregnancy? Why haven't you gone to your own physician?"

His question was disconcerting, and rather difficult to answer. I wasn't at all sure why I had come to him. It occurred to me that I might be specifically avoiding Dr. Feldman in order that Mark should not learn of my condition. But it was more than that, I realized dimly, yet less than I understood. At length I said simply, "I don't know, Dr. Shelley. I honestly don't know why I've come here."

He watched me a moment, reflectively. "Were you dissatisfied," he suggested, "with the care you received during your confinement?"

"No," I replied. "Not at all."

"Then was it your husband's decision, perhaps, to—?"

"No," I said flatly. "The decision to see you was mine."

He fell silent again, and I regarded him tensely, with a fearful suspicion that he was deliberating a refusal to attend me.

"Mrs. Van Holden," he said, "you do realize, don't you, that there are certain ethics violated when one physician takes on the patient of another?"

"Dr. Shelley," I responded with some heat, "my husband chose Dr. Morris Feldman to care for me during my first pregnancy. They were classmates at Harvard; my husband did not think to ask my preference in the matter, and I did not at the time wish to cause dissension in my marriage. But my husband and I are now estranged. I am therefore at liberty to select whomever I choose to see me through this pregnancy. If, however, you still feel that certain ethics are being violated, by all means tell me, and I shall the endeavor to locate another, less principled, physician."

I rose abruptly, shaking with anger. My husband had left me to fend for myself, yet my every thought and action seemed dictated still by his infuriatingly ubiquitous authority.

"Please," said the doctor, "sit down."

I remained on my feet, poised for flight. He came round his desk and put a lightly restraining hand on my arm. "Please," he said again, "sit down, Mrs. Van Holden. Forgive me if I've upset you. I was not aware of . . . What I mean to say is, I should very much like to take your case. That is," he added softly, "if you still want me to."

This time when he gestured for me to sit, I complied. I was hurt and confused. I felt lost, abandoned, totally alone. It did not occur to me that these feelings had developed concurrent with Myrna's reminiscences of Edward Sinclair, my first husband. Nor did it occur to me that in seeking out Dr. Shelley, I was, in essence, reaching back for a way of life that was as irrevocably lost to me as my youth and my trust and my innocence.

"Dr. Shelley," I said carefully, "my husband is unaware of my condition, and I should like him to remain so for as long as possible. May I count on your discretion?"

"Madam," he said, stung, "I am not in the habit of discussing my cases without the express consent of the patient."

"I'm sorry," I said at once. "I am not questioning your loyalty. I am only concerned that my husband might inadvertently learn—"

"Mrs. Van Holden, he *will* eventually learn you are pregnant. It is not a condition which can be hidden indefinitely. Moreover, it might be a good idea if you were to tell him yourself, and the sooner the better. I daresay he'd want to know you're carrying his child."

"I don't want him to know yet," I maintained. "I shall tell him when . . . when I am ready."

"Very well," he conceded. "I suppose you know better than I how to handle the situation."

But the fact of the matter was I hadn't the slightest idea how or when I should tell Mark I was having his child. Nor was I completely certain I wanted to tell him at all.

* * *

A week before Christmas, I received a letter from Alan. It was the first I had heard from him since his marriage to Carrie.

My dearest Joanna,

How I love married life! And how I loved London and Paris and Rome! We're in Madrid now. What a glorious city! The sun shines all day, a great regal sun, glinting radiantly gold on colorful plazas and sprawling haciendas and splendidly hued flowers which exude the most heady aromas imaginable. I have taken innumerable photographs with the Kodak, as zealously as any novice tourist, and when you see them, I think you will agree that they have captured at least the essence, if not the grandeur, that is Europe.

Carrie is happy, as am I. Especially so since this morning when I collected the post and found, to my utter delight, a letter from my father, in which he wrote that he bears me no enmity, that he loves me and misses me, and that he greatly looks forward to my return to America.

Joanna, can you believe it! But of course you can, for I'll wager you had something—no, *everything*—to do with it. Are you reconciled, you and he? His letter was brief, he did not mention your name, but I think all the same that he has forgiven me as a direct result of your gracious and blessed intercession.

God, I love you for that! I love you for every loving thing you've ever done for me. I love you and honor you as profoundly and as reverently as ever I did my mother. You took up where she left off; you guided me unwaveringly through a choppy sea of adolescence; you recharted my route when I went off course; you were my strength when I was weak, my courage when I knew fear. You've been more than a mother, and there aren't words enough to express to you my love and my thanks and my everlasting gratitude.

He had written more, but I could not read it for the tears in my eyes.

Mark had forgiven him; *thank God, oh thank God.* And Alan had most obviously forgiven me for the havoc I had wreaked with his life. Why then did I weep at his paean of unabashed praise? Why did I grieve when what I had desired had come to pass?

I spent Christmas alone with Noelle. Adele had invited us to Pleasant Valley, but I pleaded indisposition, which had not been altogether a lie. My second pregnancy was not passing as pleasantly as my first. I was sick all the time, it seemed, and listless and weak. My appetite had dwindled to almost nothing, and I had barely enough strength to rise and dress in the mornings.

Myrna was concerned. She was extrasolicitous, exceptionally kind. Throughout the day she would bring up trays of delicacies to tempt me, and occasionally I would pick a bit to allay her anxiety, but mostly I would find myself unable even to look at food, and with a worried frown, Myrna would return the tray, untouched, to the kitchen.

She went out of her way to spend time with me. If I was in the bedroom, she would find drawers that needed straightening or a dress that needed mending. In the midst of these chores, she would talk to me constantly, as if to bring me out of myself. More times than not she would talk of Edward, of the old days, of a time when adversity and sorrow had been virtually unknown to us. Perhaps I encouraged these talks; I honestly cannot recall. I know only that I liked to hear her talk of Edward; it seemed somehow to ease my troubled mind.

Christmas Day passed quietly. Even Noelle was subdued, and the mountainous pile of gifts she received did little to raise her spirits.

"Where's Papa?" she asked me. "When is he coming?"

"Papa is away, darling," I told her. "He could not be here today, but he sends you his love."

"If he loved me, he would be here," she pouted, and her logic seemed impossible to refute.

I put her to bed at seven. The evening stretched endlessly before me. At eight I sat down to a solitary dinner which I scarcely touched, and at ten, just as I was prepar-

ing to retire, Kelsey announced that a visitor awaited me
in the drawing room.

I sighed irritably. "Kelsey, whoever it is, send him
away. Say that I have already retired."

"Madam," he murmured, "it is Mr. Van Holden."

My heart gave a sickening lurch. I attempted to speak
and could not.

"Shall I tell him," Kelsey prompted, "to return in the
morning?"

"No," I managed to say. "No, Kelsey."

"Will you receive him here then?"

I was in the family room. Uneasily, I glanced about, recalling the night Mark had made passionate love to me
here. I could not see him in this room.

"No," I told Kelsey. "I shall meet with my husband
downstairs. Please tell him I'll be with him in a moment."

I sped to my room, roused Myrna from a near doze in the
fireside chair.

"Myrna, help me! Quick, help me change! Mr. Van
Holden is here. I want to look pretty, I want to look well!"

She scrambled to assist me, pulled a half-dozen gowns
from the wardrobe. I made my choice swiftly: a cream-
colored sheath, cut simply and stylishly, with long, fitted
sleeves and a high, handsome collar of Valenciennes lace. I
was not so overtly pregnant that it showed in the dress.
Myrna brushed out my hair till it crackled with electricity,
then she arranged the shining masses in a stunning profusion of curls.

The drawing-room doors were open. When I entered I
made certain to leave them that way. Mark stood near the
fire, watching the flames. Above him, captured on canvas
in elegant perpetuity, shone the pure, perfect face of Lenore.

I did not speak, but he must have sensed my presence,
for he turned, and his dark eyes scanned my figure, then
came to rest, with a curious look of disappointment, on my
deceptively self-composed gaze.

"Good evening," he said. "Merry Christmas."

I bade him good evening, but refrained from returning
his holiday greeting.

"Won't you sit down?" I said in my most formal voice. "May I offer you some coffee, or a whiskey, perhaps?"

He frowned slightly, shook his head no, then slipped his hands into his trouser pockets and watched me as I settled stiffly on a Chippendale chair near the fire.

I felt dizzy and sick. The heat of the fire was stifling me, choking me, but I would not move; I was afraid if I moved, I would be ill.

"May I ask why you've come?" I inquired at length.

"I've come," he replied, "to leave some things for Noelle. I've put them under the tree. And I've also come to wish you a good holiday."

"You're too late," I said coldly. "The holiday is over."

I had not meant to say that, but the words, once spoken, could not be retracted.

"I'm sorry," he said. "I wanted to be here earlier. I've been in Washington for several weeks. It seems the President has decided that the Eastern Seaboard trust has become a detriment to the ideals of free enterprise. It is his wish to see the membership disbanded, and so he has asked the Justice Department to bring suit against the company, as a consequence of which I've spent the past ten days talking with federal officers in an effort to— Well, I doubt you're interested in what I've been doing. The fact is, I was only able to get away this morning, and I've been traveling all day to get here."

I looked up at him at last, really looked at him, and I saw his tension and the lines of fatigue near his weary, dark eyes. He was impeccably dressed, as always—it was hard to believe he had been traveling all day—but his hard somber face was heavily etched with exhaustion and stress.

I felt more ashamed than ever for my rudeness, but a dark, nagging fear held me silent. I kept thinking of Spencer's disclosure, of his affair with Lenore, of their child conceived in sin; and at the same time I was thinking how important it was that Mark should not learn I was pregnant. What one thing had to do with the other, I could not, at that moment, imagine.

"I've been worried about you," said my husband at length.

"Worried?" I echoed listlessly. "Why?"

"My sister wrote me. She told me you refused her invitation to spend the holiday with her. She said you seemed lonely. She said you looked ill."

He paused. I was silent.

"Are you ill, Joanna?"

"No," I said faintly. "I am perfectly well, Mark. I have never felt better."

"Are you sure?" he persisted.

"I am sure," I replied.

"Joanna," he said, "my sister also mentioned . . ." He paused. I felt him draw nearer, but I kept my eyes on the fire, afraid to look at him. "She has been trying for months to—to effect a reconciliation between us. I've been thinking . . ." He hesitated, and I heard him draw a long, weary breath. "Well, I've been thinking that perhaps you and I should consider it."

Again, as with Alan's letter, another prayer had been answered. And again, as before, I felt grieved and bereft beyond words. To reconcile was impossible, couldn't Mark see that? Didn't he know that our problems were insurmountable? Didn't he realize that the solace and comfort he sought was not to be found in me?

That Mark loved me and needed me was clear to me. That I was utterly incapable of becoming the wife he so desperately needed was painfully clear to me as well. I could not help Mark as Spencer had asked me; I could not forgive him. I hadn't the strength, and I most certainly hadn't the maturity to cope with so complex a dilemma, as much as I wanted to. I saw Mark now from a peculiarly detached perspective: he was a lonely and anguished soul, and in choosing me for a wife he had sought the serenity which he himself lacked. He had thought me to be a renewal of life, a balm to his conscience, a fortress, a haven, to which he could retreat from the torment of his memories, of his past. Yes, I knew how much Mark needed me, but I hadn't the courage to acknowledge his need. I was consumed with my own need, the need to be coddled, to be pampered and cared for, an elementary, childlike need, which had always, during my marriage to Edward, been satisfied. Mark, on the other hand, demanded too much, he demanded much more than I had in me to give. I had told him, I had warned him: "I cannot make you happy." But he had gambled that I could. And he had lost.

"Joanna," he said, "did you hear me?"

"Yes, Mark," I answered. "I heard you."

"Can you tell me what you're thinking? Can you tell me what you feel?"

Numbly I said, "I feel nothing." But the truth was, I felt much too much.

"You feel nothing?" he echoed. "For me, do you mean?"

"Yes," I lied faintly. "For you."

I sensed his deep shock, I perceived his fierce pain. I did not have to look at him to know I had hurt him.

"Then it's finished?" he said in a voice barely audible.

"Yes," I replied, my voice, too, a whisper. "It's finished. I want you to free me."

"You want a divorce?"

"Yes."

"You won't think it over?"

"I have thought it over."

"You won't try once more?"

"No," I said brokenly. "No."

"Try," he said softly. "Try, just once more."

"It's no use," I said, aching. "I have tried before. I've tried and I've failed. I warned you I would. I warned you I couldn't love you. Oh, don't you see, Mark? I can't love anyone. I haven't the capacity nor the purity of spirit which you so erroneously ascribe to me. I'm selfish, self-centered; it's my own happiness for which I strive, while glibly proclaiming to ensure that of others. I've failed in both my marriages; I never made Edward happy either. I never loved him as he deserved to be loved. I continuously took from him, as I did from you, and gave absolutely nothing in return. I'm just like my mother, you know. She was greedy, acquisitive, and a harlot at heart. And . . . and I think I proved to you the last time we were together that I too have the heart of a whore." I broke off with a choked sound, and for the second time since I had known him, I wept like a child in Mark's presence.

He stopped where he stood. His expression had changed in a strange, subtle way. His dark eyes grew darker, then brilliant with light. His face was portrait-perfect, portrait-still. He looked as he had on the night I first saw him: magnificent, beautiful, and utterly, hopelessly unattainable.

"Then it's finished," he said at last.

I nodded. I could not speak.

He watched me in silence for fully three minutes, then he slowly approached me, and stopped in front of my chair, a hair's breadth away from touching me.

"Stand up," he said quietly.

Bewildered, I stared at him, the tears drying stiff on my cheeks.

"Stand up, Joanna."

"Why?"

"I want you to kiss me good-bye."

"Why? No, I won't kiss you."

"You will kiss me. You are my wife. It is still my right. Stand up, I tell you."

"No," I said, frantic. His intention was clear. "No!" But he caught hold of my wrist and forced me to my feet, confining me with ease within the inescapable prison of his arms.

"Kiss me," he said, his hard mouth close to mine. "It will mean nothing to you who feel nothing for me. Kiss me good-bye, and then I shall give you the freedom you seek."

"I seek nothing but peace of mind. Let me go, Mark, let me go."

"When you've kissed me, I shall free you. Only then will I let you go."

His mouth moved closer, his hands pressed insistently at my spine. I could feel his warm breath on my hair, on my face. I was dizzy and faint; I hadn't the energy to resist him.

I gave him my mouth, succumbed to his will. His lips parted mine, his kiss sapped the last of my fast-waning strength. I was drowning, foundering helplessly in a vast, dark abyss of confusion and fear . . . and desire. But I could not surrender. I must not submit.

"No, don't," I gasped weakly, and tore my willing mouth

from his. "You mustn't. Don't kiss me. Please, Mark, don't do this."

"Be quiet," he murmured, and kissed me again, kissed me long, kissed me sweet, kissed me till my arms circled round him, till I pressed close against him with love and with longing, till I whispered his name in enraptured surrender, till he knew without doubt he had won. And when at last he drew away, it was I, trembling with passion, who clung to him hungrily, who again sought his mouth and the sweetness and warmth of his kiss.

"No more," he said hoarsely, and he trembled too. "No more, darling, or I shall have no recourse but to take you right here, and at once."

He still held me close, his arms crushed my ribs, but while my passions ran rampant, his were most rigidly restrained.

He led me to the sofa, then sat down beside me. He took my hand, pressed it first to his cheek, and then to his sensuous mouth. "I won't let you go," he said shakily. "I love you too much, and I need you."

"But, Mark—"

"Joanna, no protests, please. We are going to reconcile. This marriage will survive in spite of both our efforts to destroy it."

"What . . . ?"

"What I mean," he explained, "is that I've been so concerned about what's best for you, and you've been so concerned about what's best for me, that we have both lost sight of what's best for the marriage. To be more specific, darling, I love you, and I think you love me—"

"Oh, I do!" I cried softly.

"Yes. Well, if that's the case, then the problems which plague us will eventually be dealt with, and subsequently solved. But only if we're together, Joanna. We can solve nothing while the wall of estrangement separates us."

"But, Mark, there's so much—"

"Hush," he said firmly. "There is nothing the two of us can't deal with in time. Time, my darling; it heals all and solves all."

No, I thought, panicked. *Time solves nothing. It only distorts and intensifies what cannot be changed.*

"Listen to me," he said. "Don't torture yourself by dredging up the past. I, more than anyone, know it serves no purpose, that it's irrelevant to the present and to the future. You said before that you couldn't love your first husband properly, that you never made him happy. And I tell you that even though I met him but once, I never in my life saw a happier man. You also said you think you're like your mother. Dearest girl, if that's true, I should very much like to have known her. Whatever your mother's . . . inclinations, she raised a daughter as near to perfection as I've ever known."

"Mark," I said fiercely, "my mother was a slut and a hypocrite!"

"Joanna," he scolded gently, "that's unlike you. And it's unfair, darling. Your mother may not have conformed to the strictest code of social and moral behavior, but—"

"Don't defend her," I whispered. "You didn't know her."

"No," he agreed, "but I know who she was. I know how she lived. Don't forget, darling, I am more your mother's contemporary than yours, and when she lived I knew several gentlemen who were . . . well acquainted with her."

"Oh, God," I said miserably. "You've known all along? You've known what she was, and yet you've never said anything? Why? Why did you never tell me?"

"I was waiting for you to broach the subject. And when you never did, I assumed you preferred not to talk of her, and so I followed suit. But you're not like her, if that's what's been worrying you all this time. You are only like yourself. It's you I love, not your mother's daughter, not Edward Sinclair's wife. It's you. I'm willing to wager that this fear of being like your mother is what has stifled your emotions for years. You were afraid, I think, to be loving, to be ardent, associating those feelings with what you considered to be your mother's 'wicked ways.' Tell me the truth, darling, when you said that you wanted me, didn't you regret it, didn't you wish you had kept it to yourself? Wouldn't you rather have died than admit it?"

"Yes," I said wretchedly, my face hot with shame.

"But why, foolish child?" he said with a smile. "Do you realize how happy you made me when you said it? I knew then that you loved me, Joanna. I knew then, for the first time in our marriage, that you truly loved me."

"But, Mark," I said, mystified, "you left me that night."

"Yes, so I did. But it was wrong, it was stupid. I should never have left you, and especially not after—" He broke off abruptly, embraced me fiercely, kissed my cheek, then my mouth, in a violent burst of contrition and regret. "I was so ashamed," he said, "so grossly ashamed of making love to you like that. I wanted you so much. I wanted you, but at the same time I knew I should leave you because I was terrified of hurting you. I realized afterward that it was too late, that I had already hurt you in the most detestable way possible. And the irony of it is, I had promised myself years ago that I would never again hurt anyone, doubt anyone, as I had done with—"

He broke off once more with a shuddering sigh, then got to his feet and strode to the fire in great agitation.

He was thinking of Lenore. I knew he was thinking of her whom he thought he had wronged. But he hadn't wronged her. He had justly doubted her, he had justly accused her; yet for the rest of his life he would suffer a guilt that was not his to bear.

Dear God, how I longed to enlighten him! How I yearned to unburden my mind of every last, vile detail which Spencer Halston had imparted to me. But I couldn't, of course. I could not ease Mark's pain on the one hand, and on the other, inflict the greater pain of telling the truth about Alan's paternity. No, the secret and the burden were mine. Mark must never know that Spencer had fathered his son, which meant, unfortunately, that Mark would forever hold himself responsible for the death of his faithless first wife.

But could I do it? I wondered doubtfully. Was I strong enough, wise enough, to maintain a deception which would simultaneously harm and comfort my husband? In years to come, would a casual word from my careless lips expose it all and forever destroy Mark's love, his faith, and trust? No, I had to be strong. I must never let Mark know. Forever, my love must lend me strength to keep silent.

"Mark," I said, hesitant, "you told me before not to torture myself with thoughts of the past, but I think you are doing the very same thing now."

His dark eyes scanned mine; his elegant face was abstracted and grave. "Yes, you're right," he said at length. "Shall we both make a vow, then, to put the past behind us, to think only of the present, and to hope for the best in the future?"

"Yes," I agreed with a faint spark of hope. "I should like that more than anything. I want never to think of the past again. Let's bury it forever."

I crossed the room, and slipped a hand through his arm. He watched me, preoccupied, his thoughts, I imagined, still on Lenore.

"Mark," I said, in an effort to distract him, "would you like to see Noelle? Shall I wake her? She asked for you today. I know it will delight her to see you."

"It's too late," he said quietly. "I shall see her tomorrow. Was she very disappointed I wasn't here for her birthday?"

"A little," I admitted. "But it will all be forgotten once she sees you."

He sighed and said nothing.

"Mark," I then said, "there's something I want to tell you."

"Yes?"

"On the night we last saw each other . . ."

"Yes, Joanna?"

"You . . . you gave me your child on that night."

He drew a sharp breath. His dark face grew radiant with joy.

"A child? Are you sure?"

"Yes," I said, breathless, for his arms had gone firmly about my waist. "Yes, Mark, I'm sure. Are you pleased?"

"Pleased?" he exclaimed. "I'm ecstatic! A child. My God, darling, I couldn't be happier!"

He pressed me close, kissed me soundly.

"Joanna, I hope it's a boy. Let's pray it's a boy. I should very much like to have a son."

How strange, I thought as he kissed me again. How strange he should say that he wanted a son. He had a son. Alan was his son. At least, Mark thought he was his son. *Or did he?*

Was it possible, could it be he knew the truth? Had he known all those years that the boy he called son had been fathered by another man? Adele had told me of Mark's intense loyalties; she had also said that he never spoke ill of anyone, not even of those who had hurt him. Was that the case, then? Did he know his first wife had betrayed him, and was he protecting her because he had once loved her?

I was strongly tempted to ask him straight out to explain his most curious remark. I couldn't, of course; there was no safe way I could broach the subject without his learning I had talked with Spencer Halston. And so I kept silent. On later reflection, it occurred to me that he had merely meant to say he very much wanted a son from *me.* But I still never asked him. I was not all that certain I wanted to hear his answer.

THE AVON ROMANCE

RANSOMED HEART
April 1983

SPARKY ASCANI

A lovely young woman offers to sell her jewelry to pay her father's gambling debts but the buyer, a dashing jewelry designer, will accept nothing less than the most precious jewel of all—Analisa! The twosome must overcome separation and danger before Analisa's ransomed heart is free to love.   83287-9/$2.95

NOW COMES THE SPRING
May 1983

ANDREA EDWARDS

Adventurous, creative newspaper photographer Tracy Monroe agrees to pose as the fiancee of cool, tough-talking star reporter Josh Rettinger because he can't face Christmas with his family alone. But their role playing becomes more than make-believe, offering them unexpected feelings of desire...and a passion that brings the warmth of spring.   83329-8/$2.95

AVON Paperbacks

Available wherever paperbacks are sold or directly from the publisher. Include $1.00 per copy for postage and handling; allow 6-8 weeks for delivery. Avon Books, Dept BP, Box 767, Rte 2, Dresden, TN 38225.

FROM *NEW YORK TIMES* BESTSELLING AUTHOR
PATRICIA HAGAN

GOLDEN ROSES is the vivid, romantic novel, set in colorful Mexico, of a Southern belle who, torn between two passions, is forced to fight for a man's love with a woman's courage.

| An AVON Original Paperback | 84178-9/$3.95 |

Also by Patricia Hagan:

LOVE AND WAR	80044-6/$3.50
THE RAGING HEARTS	80085-3/$3.50
LOVE AND GLORY	79665-1/$3.50
PASSION'S FURY	81497-8/$3.50
SOULS AFLAME	79988-X/$3.50

Dear Reader:

If you enjoyed this book, and would like information about future books by this author and other Avon authors, we would be delighted to put you on the mailing list for our ROMANCE NEWSLETTER.

Simply *print* your name and address and send to Avon Books, Room 419, 959 Eighth Ave., N.Y., N.Y. 10019.

We hope to bring you many hours of pleasurable reading!

Sara Reynolds, Editor
Romance Newsletter